THE SCORPION'S STING

JACK RITCHIE

FIRST EDITION PUBLISHED 2016

To Alex
Best wishes
Jack

**COPYRIGHT © 2016
JACK RITCHIE,
PUBLISHED BY LONDON PRESS, ST JAMES' PARK,
WESTMINSTER, LONDON**

All Rights Reserved. No part of this publication may be reproduced, stored in a retrieval system, or transmitted, in any form, or by any means, electronic, mechanical, photocopying, recording or otherwise, without the prior permission of the author and copyright holder.

For Maya
Because you never know

with my love
AGRQC

THE SCORPION'S STING

CONTENTS

CHAPTER 1 : **MADAME PETRA'S PART I**   7
CHAPTER 2 : **STRINGFELLOWS**   13
CHAPTER 3 : **THE HOOK**   25
CHAPTER 4 : **THE BACK DOOR**   52
CHAPTER 5 : **A LESSON IN TERRORISM**   80
CHAPTER 6 : **GENERAL RANDOLF'S STRATEGY**   105
CHAPTER 7 : **DO NOT TRUST THE TAILOR**   117
CHAPTER 8 : **ENTER THE SCORPION**   124
CHAPTER 9 : **FRANCOISE DEBOUSSEY**   140
CHAPTER 10 : **DIANNE TRATTORINI**   163
CHAPTER 11 : **THE TRIAL**   194
CHAPTER 12 : **THE LIST**   222
CHAPTER 13 : **PLEASURE AND PAIN**   237
CHAPTER 14 : **TO THE DEMISE OF THE FIRST SECRETARY**   243
CHAPTER 15 : **THE TAILOR**   249
CHAPTER 16 : **PARK LANE**   278
CHAPTER 17 : **OPERATION NOVEMBER**   292
CHAPTER 18 : **THE UDBR**   311
CHAPTER 19 : **MADAM PETRA'S PART II**   334
CHAPTER 20 : **UNINVITED GUESTS**   343
CHAPTER 21 : **THE SCORPION'S STING**   365
CHAPTER 22 : **THE FLYING EYE**   375
CHAPTER 23 : **ON THE WING OF A PRAYER**   393
CHAPTER 24 : **THE POISON EXTRACTED**   406

EPILOGUE : **THE KLEPTOMANIAC**   421

CHAPTER 1
MADAME PETRA'S PART I

KRASNOVODSK, RUSSIA, 1988

Vladimyr Zachristov pointed decisively towards two of the eight girls who were sitting patiently in the lounge of Madam Petra's.

"A good choice comrade, if you don't mind me saying so. These two arrived fresh last week from the Ukraine. Both are virgo intacta of course."

Vladimyr raised one eyebrow slightly.

"Don't worry Colonel. They have been tutored, intensively, for the last six days. I handle that side myself. You will not find them uninteresting, I assure you."

"Tutored?" Vladimyr's momentary smile was the first flash of humanity Madame Petra had been able to discern in the two hours since the Colonel had arrived. She handed him the key to the twin's bedroom, smiled in her renowned, maternal manner, then bowed and glided away on a wind of Chanel No5. Vladimyr stood watching for a second. He wanted to see the reactions of the girls when they were told that they had been chosen to please a Colonel in the KGB.

At Madame Petra's approach, all eight girls fidgeted in eager anticipation. She touched the chosen ones on their shoulders and whispered to each in turn. They glanced furtively at each other and then at Vladimyr. A delightful mixture of fear and respect radiated from their innocent faces. The cream of soviet feminine pubescence was fired by the challenge of the unknown and the fear of his power.

To the twins, the KGB was the dark terrifying side of the State. Exhibiting itself, during their youth, through awkward silences between their parents.

"Why is daddy not home for dinner?" They would ask, and mother would fall silent. Days later, father would come home, tired, angry and a little less the man that he once was.

Now, they were face to face with the dread that had dulled the light in their father's eyes.

The girls wore identical uniforms - starched white shirts underneath matching grey jackets and skirts. Their legs were sheathed in coarse fishnet stockings running into shiny, knee length, leather boots.

Vladimyr turned, raised his glass to General Uri Krasilova who was standing at the bar with three other officers and went upstairs to the second floor. He walked straight into the bedroom without knocking, and closed the door. Opulence was the word he would have used to describe Madame Petra's decor, but he hardly noticed it.

Vladimyr had become used to the trappings of the State's higher echelons. He had enjoyed the induction course provided to officials who were marked for high office. At a certain point in the careers of all party members the decision was taken whether they would be capable not only of perpetuating the State organisation but also of handling the apparent hypocrisy of the Communist Party cocooning it's high party members in opulence.

For Vladimyr the privileges of position had come naturally. His father was a national political figure who had been able to provide for his children the best in state education and nepotistic advancement.

A bottle of Moet & Chandon in a silver ice bucket stood proudly on the table beside the antique, king size, four poster bed. The French windows at the far end of the room lay open and peach silk curtains swayed gently in the evening breeze. Vladimyr could see the harbour through the gap between the curtains and beyond, the dark and inviting Caspian sea. He breathed deeply and turned towards the bottle. As he thumbed off the cork the girls walked in and closed the door. He poured three glasses, handed one to each girl, toasted them and sat down in the nearest gilt edged chair.

One girl took his now empty glass and threw it into the fireplace. It smashed with the unmistakable resonance of crystal. From the high backed wicker chair he could only face the bed.

"I am Natasha. This is Maxine. Relax and enjoy your evening. We will warm you up after your long journey from Moscow, Comrade Colonel."

Maxine stretched out on the bed. She was a natural blonde, about five feet five tall with a full firm figure for her tender years. Her chest stretched her starched blouse like a stiff spring breeze on the canvas of a sail. Her long, wavy hair cascaded over the pressed grey suit with the teasing contrast born of experienced couture. Her tongue slipped out of her mouth and licked capriciously at her thin pink lips. It carried with it the expectation which Vladimyr was experiencing.

She slipped her right hand slowly inside her blouse then gently caressed her breast, at one time cupping it and then passing each outstretched linger slowly over the now erect nipple. The presence of the fabric between the girl's hand and Vladimyr's view only heightened the eroticism of her actions. His senses were beginning to warm to the atmosphere. The soft sound of her skin against the starched cotton electrified him.

Natasha was taller and thinner than her sister. She had not yet blossomed to full maturity. Her legs sprouted from her pert buttocks shouting at the world that she would make a fine model. Once again the effect of the almost punishingly taught grey fabric of her skirt, which clamped the swell of her rump, created an appearance of strict control, almost Naval in its severity. Hard on soft. Colour beneath dullness. Young vibrant life within the control of the State. Vladimyr was in no doubt as he watched the two girls that what he had heard about Madame Petra and had initially disbelieved, was altogether true. She was a woman who had perfected the art of pleasing men.

Natasha stood slightly to the left of her sister at the bottom of the bed. She lifted her left leg at right angles and placed her leather boot onto the bed covers. Her breasts did not attempt to attract the same attention as her sister's but her slim, aquiline face and warm, brown eyes combined with the little upturn of her nose, made her cheeky and boyish. Madame Petra had illuminated this by cropping her black hair. The cumulative effect of the cut of her hair and the clothes was transsexual.

Natasha slid her right hand into the top of her boot and unfastened the zip on the inside agonisingly slowly. The clicking blended harshly with the soft rustle being made by Maxine's skin against her starched shirt

Then suddenly the zip was ripped down to the heel and the boot was thrown across the room over Vladmiyr's head. It flew past his hair, high enough to be safe but low enough to cause him to take his eyes off the girls. When he looked back at the bed Natasha had removed the second boot and was turning towards Maxine. She ran her small hand slowly up Maxine's stockinged leg. It slipped under the hem of the skirt and up to the smooth white inner thigh above the harsh black line of the stocking top.

For the first time Vladimyr could see the thin white silk of Maxine's undergarment. A shot of adrenalin flooded into his veins. It wasn't that he hadn't seen a young girl before but the combination of the presence of the other girl doing his work for him and the totality of the build up to the disclosure stirred him. He was utterly transfixed. Natasha was kneeling on the bed with her rear facing Vladimyr. Maxine slipped her hand between Natasha's thighs and inched her skirt up and over her buttocks exposing a tiny pair of black lace knickers. Maxine's hand ran underneath the top of Natasha's suspenders and caressed her inner thigh.

Suddenly Natasha took her hand away from Maxine's groin and grabbed the front of Maxine's white blouse. Maxine feigned surprise as the fabric began to tear from the hip and expose the spotless white skin beneath. Natasha ripped the white blouse from Maxine's breasts and lowered her eager mouth onto the exposed nipples. She licked voraciously. Gone was the previously gentle searching naivety. It was replaced now by eagerness. Gradually the bed became a frenzy of tearing cloth and lithe, sweet scented flesh as the girls accelerated into overdrive.

Vladimyr's past sexual experiences paled beside the sight and smell of the two sixteen year old girls. As Maxine's erupting primitive guttural screams reached into Vladimyr's sexuality he could hold himself back no longer. He threw away his clothing in a frenzied haze and plunged violently into the melee.

For what seemed like an eternity, but was merely a matter of minutes, he tried to hold back and savour the eroticism of the ménage. Finally he could wait no longer. Maxine cried out and Natasha followed a few seconds later with her own frenzied release.

The three spent the next one and a half hours in the room. Neighbouring rooms heard a series of screams and groans during the period. When Vladimyr needed time to regain his strength the girls would work on his body with exquisite touches. When he thought he was finally spent they lay him naked on the bed and tied his arms and legs with leather straps to the four posts. Then Maxine lowered her steaming body onto him. Natasha took a bottle of baby oil and rubbed it soothingly over his chest then down his thighs and so it continued.

When finally he could take it no longer they instinctively knew. They untied his hands and feet and one girl under each arm they led him to the shower and washed him, head to toe, with finest Ukrainian soap.

Vladimyr Zachristov left the twin's room feeling as if he was floating on the warm Caspian sea breeze.

The girls left the room bruised, riddled with guilt and consumed by disgrace.

He could not have cared less.

He went downstairs to the lounge bar, ordered a Vodka and sat beside Uri Krasilova, in an armchair on the veranda. The night air filled his lungs. He felt at peace with the world. Dwarf palms lining the driveway swayed gently to the wind's tune and there was an audible wash brought up by the wind from the seashore. He knew it was time to talk business. The General had not brought him to the most expensive and exclusive club in the Soviet world for fun.

"You were right Uri, Madame Petra provides a handsome service."

"I see that you have a taste for her peculiar form of perversion."

For a moment the Colonel felt a twinge of embarrassment. He was acutely aware of the power and the puritanicalism of the Chairman of the Komitet Gosudarstvennoe Bezopasnosti (KGB) in his public life. But he reassured himself when he glanced apprehensively at the Chairman and found that he was laughing silently.

A waitress passed their table and they ordered more vodkas. When the drinks arrived the two men toasted the night and continued the conversation.

"You know my worries about Perestroika Vladimyr. It is changing the way of things in our great country too fast. Making fools of the wise old ways and idols of fatuous ideas like 'democracy'. I have seen the fallacy of democracy. It is an unruly horse. If it continues to trample on our present constitution we will soon no longer have an 'empire'."

"There are many who think as you do, Uri."

The conversation which these two men held in the twilight hours that night changed the course of history and the lives of a generation.

CHAPTER 2
STRINGFELLOWS

LONDON, MAY 1988

"A month's salary is what a man should spend on the ring Mr ...?" she raised an eyebrow.
He nodded, "My name is Grant and if I told you how small that sum is I don't think that you would want to continue serving me."
"Well! I wouldn't judge a good looking gentleman like you only by the money. You're a catch for any woman."
Grant smiled shyly and picked up the ring. The light from the counter bulbs shone into the rear of the diamond and diffracted into a splendid explosion of colours. He thought of putting it back but something inside him was driving him to buy the damn thing. Hard as he tried he couldn't stop his hand reaching into his shallow pocket and pulling out the plastic with which he tortured himself at the end of each month.
"It's a beautiful choice, if I may say so and she is a very lucky woman." The elderly shop assistant winked at him and took the ring to be boxed.
Grant sat down slightly shattered by the decision. It had been welling up inside of him for about two months and as a result he had not been able to think straight during his waking hours. He had stepped into the path of an oncoming car the day before. Then he had put diesel into his own car rather than petrol. That very morning he had thrown his newspaper into the washing machine and buttered his toast with mustard.
He needed to get the proposal over and done with as much for his own safety as for romantic reasons. If she said no then at least he would be able to cross the road safely, though not happily.

He resolved to take her for a night on the town and then to propose when the moment took him. Perhaps at over breakfast at a little café he knew in Wardour Street.

*

The couple walked in though the black glass entrance past the black marble clad walls and saw the hostess smiling at them.

"Good evening Mr Grant, Miss Schaeffer. May I take your coats?"

"Thanks Fifi, is our table ready?"

"Of course. It's the double on the balcony above the piano. Harry will start in about five minutes, OK?" The waitress smiled broadly showing a fine set of teeth and winked at Joanne. Stringfellows' waitresses are renowned for their figures and Fifi was no exception to the house rule but Joanne Schaeffer did not feel threatened.

It was a foul rain-swept May evening and Joanne Schaeffer had needed little prompting to leave the little flat in Old Church Street, Chelsea to drive up to the West End for a meal, some dancing and some relaxation.

"I'll have a Bacardi Bloody Mary please Fifi and a Gin and Tonic for Jo." Grant said.

"She is soooo beautiful sir!" The waitress replied as Joanne walked towards the powder room.

"Run along Fifi and put the claws away." The waitress bowed cheekily and swayed her buttocks provocatively as she walked to the cocktail bar. Grant sat down at the smoked glass dining table and put his cigarettes on the tidy pink table cloth. He was nervous and he noticed that his right hand was shaking a bit. He took a deep breath.

"Dreaming, George?" Jo asked a few minutes later as she sat down gracefully, sweeping her flowing blond hair away from her right shoulder and frowning momentarily as she looked at him.

"Yes. When you're not around to tease me, or take care of me, I seem to have become a bit accident prone lately. I was nearly run down by a bus yesterday and today I spent most of the afternoon in the park talking to a wino about an Ibsen play."

"Are things that slow at work?"

"Undoubtedly. Jack has been doing most of the routine work and since he gave up the booze he's had more energy than a six month old puppy."

"Why don't you try to pull in some larger clients then?" she asked and then taking a deep breath went on, "or close the agency and get a proper job?"

The waitress arrived just in time to prevent Grant from snarling like a caged tiger. He took a long draw on the Bacardi and looked down at the piano player who was arranging the sheet music on top of the polished black Bechstein.

"It's not that easy Jo. You know what I'm like. Within three weeks I'd be causing havoc in a desk job. Ten years in the Marines and other bits does not prepare you for getting on a commuter train every day. Anyway you don't want me to lose this lovely trim tummy, do you?"

"George, it's been six weeks since your last worthwhile client. You're not really running a business at the moment. Take that client who came to you last week. What was her name?"

"Mrs Dilworthy," he shook his head a little.

"You can't make a living checking up on cheating husbands for suspicious wives for the rest of your life can you?" Joanne squeezed his arm warmly indicating that she was not getting at him, just testing out the boundaries of his boredom.

"The agency is new Jo. Jack hasn't been all that well and it takes time for any business to get off the ground. You of all people should know that."

"True, but I didn't take on a burnt out old lush like Jack MacDougal when I started up my company. You know, last month I found him pissed out of his brain in your waiting room with one of your clients. He started to try and get her to have dinner with him. When was the last time he earned any money for the agency?"

"He has done better lately. He will do more soon Jo. In the last few weeks he has earned quite a bit. He was meant to hold the routine jobs down. The ones which involve a little less than my subtle, light touch."

Joanne Schaeffer smiled and when she did that Grant could not feel morose for long. She had helped him get over more than a little trauma when he had left Military Service at the end of the summer of 1986. Now he sat nervously waiting for the moment when he could take the box from his pocket and ask her to spend the rest of her life with him.

"Other than cracking that policeman's cranium last month I can't think of one useful thing that he has done for you since he first joined the agency." Jo chuckled at the memory.

"At the time Jo, that was an exceptionally useful bit of head cracking. Anyway he is my friend and I like the worn out old sod, as you know."

"So do I George. I love him! Perhaps not as much as you do but enough to be able to call myself one of his closest friends. Even so I can still see what his problems are. Friendship is not blind acceptance of fault. It is being able to see your friend in his true light and even so still loving him."

She had a force about her when she argued. She was right of course. He had been letting Jack freeload for too long but she was missing the point. Jack MacDougal had the kindest heart and the most courageous loyalty that Grant had ever encountered. And they had agreed to set up together.

"I'm just not quite ready to let him go yet, Jo."

The pianist slammed ten fingers onto the ivory. It was an old Errol Garner song and he played it like a sweating pauper from New Orleans. That was not surprising because Harry had arrived in London from New Orleans for a holiday five years before. He had liked London so much that he had decided to stay on. Illegally. Later he married a girl from a poor family in Brixton and gained his right to stay. Some said he left a wife and kids back home. No one really knew. But everyone knew Harry. When he finished the song Jo leant over the chrome railings pushing back the fronds of the midget palm behind Harry's head and said, "If you play that stuff all night I'll be tempted to throw caution to the wind when it comes to the last dance."

Harry ran his hand up to the last key and pressed it gently.

"You got a deal Jo, but first you got to dump the dingo you came with." She looked round and smiled at Grant.

"I care for you too Harry," he replied.

Dinner arrived and the conversation began to loosen up with the second bottle of Tattinger. Jo looked stunning and once they had cleared the air of Jack and Grant's work she slipped back into the easy humorous gear that was so much her own. Joanne's company had been working twelve hour shifts to bring out a new range of Winter wear. It had to be ready for the launch in early May. She had hired two fresh young designers to bring her own ideas up to date. The work they had done had shocked Joanne. She hadn't realised how out of touch she had become from the ideas of the students fresh out of college. It had been an impulse thing to hire them last winter. She now couldn't survive without them.

At midnight the sound of the discotheque began to reverberate upwards through the floor of the restaurant and a low blue haze of cigarette smoke hung over the dining tables. They finished desert and dawdled.

"Come on George, let's go and see what the young trendies are doing on the dance floor." Joanne slipped out of her chair, leant over and kissed Grant on the lips. There might be a 'Schaeffer' on display which I could gloat over."

"Probably will be," he replied and stood up.

Grant left a tip and followed Jo down the circular chrome banistered stairway into the bowels of the club. They weaved through the morass of jostling bodies towards the bar at the far end of the dance floor. It was practically impossible to order drinks so Grant caught a passing hostess and ordered two double gins.

Stringfellows was vibrating with the cascading beat of the latest London club music. The dance floor flashed enticingly in time to the bass guitar and the dancers threw themselves wildly about their partner's sweating bodies. Grant thought of discotheques as the modern equivalent of a tribal mating ritual. Frantic vertical exercise leading, only if successful, to more frantic horizontal exercise. He noted that they did not make wildlife programmes about the human mating dances and when they did it was called pornography.

The coming summer fashions mingled with the ever present class couture of the well off at play. On stage Fifi and her co-DJ swirled and turned in formation executing erotic jungle hip thrusts perfectly to a calypso beat.

"Let's watch for a few dances." Joanne said as the drinks arrived on the arm of a waitress so skinny that she would have won a slimming contest with an ice cream wafer.

"That sounds like business," Grant replied.

"The world's most beautiful bodies are my business, darling."

"Well at least when God was handing them out he gave you a fair share," Grant squeezed her hand and kissed her.

At one thirty after a half hour on the dance floor they were both steaming and bruised and ready to poison themselves with a little more alcohol. They squeezed away from the dance floor and ordered another round of gins. Grant was ready to leave and head for a filling breakfast at Harry's bar off Wardour Street when a splendid couple arrived at the top of the spiral stairway.

"Who are they?" Jo asked as the couple descended the stairs laughing and shouting animatedly at each other.

"That is Terry Smith, the footballer. He has spent most of the last two years providing the best copy for Fleet Street gossip writers since Cynthia Payne. And she is the eldest daughter of Solomon Goldstein. Which means she stands to inherit the second largest fortune in the western world when her father dies. She probably bathes in Mouton Rothschild."

"Sounds marvellous." Jo said lighting up a Galoise. "Just the sort of clientele I'll be milking at the Paris show."

"For a liberal you are obsessed with money in a most vulgar way." Grant responded.

"It comes second after sex, darling" she smiled and headed off towards the young couple with a wink to Grant that suggested it was time to leave.

*

Chaos erupted just as Jo reached the group of youngsters standing at the foot of the entrance stairway. The floor exploded with terrifying force and the stairway splintered into a searing blaze of burning heat. Chunks of deadly sharp glass flew across the crowded room and a battery of disco lights collapsed brutally onto the teaming dance floor. Grant's nostrils filled with the burning stench of the Sulphur from the spent explosives. Three seconds later a more massive explosion devastated the bar from the other end. Molten iron and jagged metal flew at head height across the crowded basement. It pierced flesh and tore grossly into the limbs of the dancers.

A fire began under the stairway at the root of the first explosion. Within a few seconds the whole room was filled with the unbreathable gaseous by products of the melting plastic and burning furniture. The sounds of the blasts had deafened Grant and the force of the second explosion had thrown the body of a young man halfway across the dance floor knocking Grant to the ground under the lip of a drinks table.

For at least half a minute he lay there unconscious. The room was filled with the screams and eerie wailing of scores of maimed and half dead human beings. The roof around the staircase groaned then in one terrifying down pour collapsed into the discotheque bringing a thundering pile of breeze blocks and plaster crashing onto the hell below.

Grant was shaken into consciousness by the noise and cast the lifeless body which lay prostrate across his chest to one side. He raised himself from the ground then collapsed as his right leg gave way. A foot long spear of jagged metal jutted out of his right thigh and a trail of dark red blood ran down the right leg of his trousers. He experienced surprisingly little pain considering the severity of the injury but he did not consider it. The scene around him possessed a morbid lack of reality. It didn't fit into his comprehension of what was possible that evening. He felt that he was only partly alive, floating in a terrible quagmire surrounded by death and destruction.

"Joanne!" he shouted, desperation prevalent in his scream. He breathed in, ready to shout again and then on bended knee he collapsed as the swirling black smoke engulfed him, displacing the oxygen from his lungs.

*

One week later a doctor caught a nurse by the arm as she left one of the rooms on the 4th floor overlooking the Houses of Parliament.

"How's he coming along nurse Jones?"

"Terrible, doctor," she rolled her eyes to the sky.

"How strange, he seemed much improved yesterday," the doctor replied.

"Well this morning as I was giving him his bed bath he was complaining about the food and the lack of alcohol. Then when I tried to take his temperature he wouldn't open his mouth unless I brought him a cake," she looked at the floor coyly.

"And did you Nurse Jones?"

"Oh, thanks for the support doctor! Eventually I threatened to take his temperature rectally. Then he agreed to open his mouth."

"Sounds like he is getting much better to me. If he causes you any more trouble nurse, tell sister McMekin. I'm sure she'll know of some way to keep him under control."

"Bromide is what I'd use doctor."

Nurse Jones was a fifty three year old auxiliary. She had seen casualties come and go at St Thomas' Hospital in Westminster for the best part of three centuries. But nothing that had gone before could protect her from the horror of the terrible injuries which the casualties of the Stringfellows bombing had suffered.

Doctor Ranjiban Patel, smart and clean, with a battery of gleaming pens perched purposefully in his top pocket, strutted into Grant's room. "I hear you're getting better?"

"Damn right doctor. I want to get out of here before I turn into a professional patient."

"I'll be the judge of your departure date if you don't mind. How's the leg?"

"Not so bad. Did you keep the bit of metal? My mantle piece was looking a bit bare and it was just the right size." Grant liked Dr Patel and looked forward to his visits and their little chats each morning.

"I suppose you've heard of the shortages in the national health service?" Dr Patel asked.

"Sure, what of it?"

"Perhaps we will send your scrap metal to our recycling department. It may become part of an NHS crutch by next month."

"I am glad I could be of use." Pleasantries over he asked, "How is Joanne?"

Dr Patel shook his head a little.

"She is still on the critical list I'm afraid. I'm sorry it is so slow. My personal view is that she will pull through." He hesitated searching for the right words not to offend. "She has a lot of courage".

Doctor Patel didn't look at Grant as he spoke. Grant tried to ignore the fact and pressed on.

"Has she come round yet?"

"Yes, briefly last night." Grant's heart skipped a beat.

"What did she say?"

"She asked for her father and she sent her love to you. She could hardly speak. It was all that she could do to say those words."

Grant fell silent for some seconds. It had been a hellish few days. "Tell me your honest opinion. What chance do you really think she has?" Grant raised his shoulders from the bed and the fear in his eyes thrust straight into the doctor's heart. Doctor Patel disliked emotion. It ruined good decision making and tarnished competent performance.

"She has a less than evens chance. That is more than I can say for most of the poor wretches who were caught in that slaughterhouse. We are doing our best to keep her alive. There is no more we can do."

George Grant slipped back onto the pillows. He felt sickened. He felt bereft. He had not yet developed the anger which would emerge later.

"May I leave here tomorrow please?"

"I think you will be ready." The doctor turned to leave but sensing the mood of the patient he said, "but before you get any ideas of playing rugby or jogging across the Yorkshire moors, you should know that your leg muscles will not be fully healed for another three months. The multiple lacerations to your chest and arms will need at least half that time before you can be regarded as recovered. However, we do need the bed you are occupying and the nurses certainly need a rest.

One more thing. The Police are waiting outside and an officer from the anti- terrorist squad wants to see you this afternoon. So don't commit any crimes."

"Thanks doctor. If Joanne comes around again, can you tell the nurses to inform me straight away? I want to be by her side."

"Of course," he smiled and left the room as the salmonella arrived, disguised as lunch.

*

At three o'clock Jack MacDougal came to visit. A large forthright man with a warm friendly manner and a closet full of vices, Grant loved him like a brother. The sight of Jack's huge bulk and quizzical face cheered him up immediately.

Grant sat up, greeted him and felt better.

"You are a sight for sore eyes Jack. What has been going on at the office?"

Jack looked a little defensive.

"It's all under control George. I haven't had a drink for weeks and I'm feeling great. I promise. How are you?"

"Much better." Jack sat his enormous frame down on a small metal chair and straightened his tie. He never seemed to fit the suits he bought.

"I haven't seen you wearing a tie since we were discharged. You look healthier Jack."

"Thanks," Jack replied, flushing a little. "I've been down to see the bloody quack again. He tells me that if I don't slow down, my ticker will slow me down permanently."

Grant guessed that it wasn't just the smoking and drinking that had caused the problem. But he and Jack had promised each other not to discuss their time in the services together and he was happy with that.

"Before I go and see Joanne will you just tell me what I should do with Mrs Dilworthy? She has been paying me £200 per day just to follow her husband to and from work each day and confirm that he is not having an affair with his secretary."

"Sounds like easy money to me. What is the problem?"

"Well, I have followed him for the last two weeks and he hasn't made a move on the secretary. Which is strange because she is a very attractive girl. I've told Mrs Dilworthy but she is convinced he is having an affair."

"If we keep charging at that rate Jack we will be able to pay the rent on the office soon."

"That's all well and good George, but the difficulty is that he's having an affair with someone else."

"Have you told her?"

"She is such a nice woman, I feel terrible. I don't think she could stand to know."

"Why? Is it her best friend?"

"No, his boss. A ..well... a man."

Jack really was not cut out to be a Private Detective. His set of rather Victorian morals made nearly every job difficult for him. However his 17 stones and six feet three inches of height made him rather useful when Grant needed a writ served.

"Tell her anyway Jack. Otherwise if she finds out elsewhere, she may demand all our fees back. Do you want me to tell her?"

Jack looked strangely troubled for a moment then stood up in his rather ungainly way.

"No George, you have enough troubles of your own at the moment. Want a stick of gum?"

"Is that your alcohol substitute?"

"I'm chewing 40 a day at the moment. I think these are going to be more expensive than the booze ever was." He offered Grant his hand and shook firmly.

"Get well old pal, I miss you. When you're better we will go and find the arseholes who did this to you and tear them apart."

CHAPTER 3
THE HOOK

11PM, 13TH JUNE 1988

Henry Blythe-Stafford sat, quietly sweating, in the small oak panelled study at Checkers. He had endured a terrible night. He hadn't slept. He found that before he went into difficult situations he often didn't sleep. Strangely it didn't seem to affect his performance when the time came. His wife told him that it was nature's way of burning off the excess energy that his body produced as a result of being the descendant of an ape. "When under attack, we are biologically trained to respond by running or fighting," she would say. The sedentary city life did not allow him to use his body physically so he stored up the excess energy. "That's bad for you," she had told him. According to her he was lucky that his body burnt off the excess energy in the way that it did.

At that precise moment he would rather have been running away over the lawns of Checkers than sitting in the study. Perhaps she was right.

Henry Blythe-Stafford disliked the meetings and press conferences about the wave of kidnappings and Terrorist bombings which had ravaged Britain. He didn't enjoy the attention. He was a career policeman.

He had begun work on the force as a lanky flatfooted copper on the beat in the Walworth Road, South London, in 1950. Now aged fifty four he was the Metropolitan Police Commissioner for Greater London and therefore the highest ranking policeman in the Country.

THE SCORPION'S STING

Unlike his predecessors, he was not an image-maker. He had no liking for limelight and deeply resented the press attention thrust upon him by the broadsheet and the tabloids alike. He knew the business better than any damn journalist and his duties were to the man in the street and to the letter of the Law, not to the press.

After five years on the beat, learning the rope, he graduated through station sergeant to the CID. Later, being the prime instigator behind the fast deployment arm of the Special Patrol Group, he had received swinging criticism for their harsh tactics. He had survived the difficulties, perhaps because he had always been a policeman's policeman. In the mid-seventies he was promoted to operational commander of the Anti-terrorist Squad.

In June 1982 he was appointed MPC and now maintained positions on several Government Commissions. He was widely liked by his men and respected for his unswerving past service to the State. He understood the needs of the modern police force but he was one harsh bastard when it came to criminals.

Today, Henry Blythe-Stafford had news to report to the Special Executive Committee for National Security, (the SEC), which would probably throw them into a state of civilised terror. The thought had not rested well in his breast in the still hours of the preceding night.

Miss Pickles, the secretary to the SEC, picked up the red phone from her leather topped desk. This was her moment of power. In that moment she knew something that the Metropolitan Police Commissioner wanted to know. She loved her little game. She grunted, put down the phone and looked at the Commissioner. As he started to raise himself from his chair in the inevitable expectation of being asked to go in, she looked away to the window and then at her watch. He sat down, embarrassed. She smiled to herself, raised her prim sexless backside from the chair, and said to the room in general, so as not to appear servile.

"You may go in now."

She walked over to the oak panelled doors, opened the right hand one a bit, then stuck her head round and whispered something,

"Oh let him in Pickles and stop shilly-shallying!" Said a voice from inside. Henry Blythe-Stafford went in, scuffing his heel on her ankle as he did so. She couldn't show the pain, it would look clumsy. He disliked petty discourtesy.

"Good morning, Commissioner. Please come over here and sit down," the Prime Minister waved him to a chair at the end of the oval table farthest from her.

"Thank you, madam."

"You know most of the gentlemen here, of course, but if you will permit me to introduce them anyway."

It wasn't a request. It was a command. The PM waved her hand in the direction of each man as she spoke his name.

"Field Marshal Carshalton: Commander-In-Chief of Her Majesty's Armed Forces and Joint Chief of Staff; Admiral James: First Sea Lord of the Navy; Wing Commander Harris: C in C of the RAF."

Her manner was unemotional and clean-cut. It suited Blythe Stafford and put him immediately at ease. He knew his place and respected his democratically elected superior.

"On your right hand side, I'm sure you know The Right Honourable Francis Harrow, my Secretary of State for Defence; then Sir John Epcot: the Director General of the MIG; Lord Birch: the Foreign Minister, and Lord Carver: the Director General of MI5. Finally, the Right Honourable Phillip McNaughton, the Defence Secretary."

"Good day Gentlemen," Blythe-Stafford nodded to the table at large.

The Prime Minister started the meeting brusquely. "I presume that you will all have read the copy files delivered to you by hand yesterday?"

There was a concerted nodding of heads. "Then it remains for us to hear the Commissioner's conclusions. Henry, if you please?"

The Metropolitan Police Commissioner rose to his feet and suddenly the nervousness was gone. He had a job to do and he concentrated on the subject which had taken up more of his time in the last six months than any other.

"As you know, in the last six months the country has been under siege. Not, this time, from the invading forces of a foreign power in the historic sense, but from invading forces all the same. They are now deeply rooted in the very fabric of our Society to such an extent that our conventional security organs; the Police, the Secret Services and the other forces of law and order are incapable as a matter of numbers let alone resources, of purging the country of these parasites.

"You know some of the facts. Three hundred and twenty seven separate acts of terrorism, violence, extortion and coercion have been reported within the six month period. I can assure you that the figures in front of you represent only the tip of the iceberg. Criminologists have been telling us for years that crime recording figures represent only, on average, 20 to 30% of the crimes actually committed in this country. This figure is the reported total. Of course it can be said that at the unreported crimes, more are minor acts of domestic violence or theft, but even so, the actual total is more than three times as large as the reported total.

"It is an accepted fact that for crimes such as blackmail and coercion the reported total is considerably lower. It is around 18% of the actual total!

"My first conclusion is that the reported total of the number of terrorist crimes in my initial report in front of you is only one quarter of the actual total. I believe that approximately a thousand separate acts of terrorism have occurred in this country in the last six months."

"My God!" Field Marshal Carshalton gasped. That means about five are happening every day. This is a bloody war not a terrorist wave."

"Precisely General," the Commissioner replied ignoring the blasphemy, "for this to be achieved, terrorist manpower of considerable size and resources must be present in this country. That is my second conclusion.

"The reported crimes fall into three categories:

First: those involving violence, usually murder, or some form of crude mutilation. Second: those involving coercion, usually to persuade the victim to perform or omit to perform a certain act,
Third: those involving overt action upon property either destructive or manipulative.
The categories overlap to a greater or lesser extent in each case of course.
"My third conclusion is not a conclusion at all, it is a mixture of observations and questions. The crimes involve members of our society in all walks of life: MPs, directors in industry, officers in the armed forces, trade unionists, civil servants and people from many other echelons of our civilisation.
"The questions which we need answered are: ONE, what Is the objective? TWO, who or what is the propagator? THREE, how do we stop them?"
The Commissioner sat down. The room was cloaked in silence. Field Marshal Carshalton lit up a cigar and drew deeply upon it. He was visibly shaken.
"Thank you Commissioner. As always, your report was concise and your conclusions searching and useful. The committee will retire for lunch and reconvene at 2pm. For the present we all thank you for your help and advice. I will be in contact with you once have made our decisions on the course of action to be taken."
The Prime Minister rose from her seat and pressed a button on the intercom beside her. Miss Pickles showed the Commissioner out with complete and deferential decorum.
Henry Blythe-Stafford climbed into the chauffeur driven Jaguar XJS, which stood in the sweeping gravel covered driveway.
"How did the meeting go Sir?" Asked the chauffeur. "God help this country if it gets any worse," he replied.

*

"I'm Mike Douglas, I'd like to ask you a few questions if I may?"
Douglas was a tall slim man. He wore a light grey, single breasted suit and had a direct workman-like manner, reflecting

experience at fact finding built from years of questioning both victims and aggressors. But the gold Rolex on his wrist seemed strangely flashy for an officer of the Anti-Terrorist squad. Grant suppressed his urge to judge the man by first impressions.

"Fire away! I'll help all I can, but I don't think you'll find me much use."

He sat on the small metal hospital chair and opened his note pad. As he did so he straightened his back. He had back trouble, probably due to being over six feet tall.

"You were present at Stringfellows two weeks ago when a bomb was detonated?"

"Yes," Grant responded, feeling suddenly unhelpful.

"What were you doing there?"

"Dancing."

"Who were you with?"

"Joanne Schaeffer, a fashion designer. She is presently in intensive care across the hall."

"Yes, I know. I'm sorry."

"How many bomb blasts do you remember?"

"One at the foot of the stairway into the basement and one larger explosion at the bar at the southern end of the disco."

"Which was first?"

"The blast at the foot of the stairs."

"Who was standing in that area at the time?"

Grant closed his eyes. The pain in his leg throbbed as his mind pictured the group of people just before the blast. He could see Joanne's beautiful figure walking purposefully towards the stairs, towards the blast, towards scars for life. He grimaced.

"Joanne Schaeffer, Terry Smith and Carole Goldstein. There were about five others but I didn't recognise them."

"Where exactly were they standing at the time of the first blast?"

"Smith and Goldstein were coming down the stairs. Joanne was heading across the dance floor towards the stairs. The others were standing about drinking."

"Was anyone else coming down the stairs at the time?"

"I think so, another couple."
"What time did the first blast occur?"
"Approximately half past one."
"And the second?"
"No more than ten seconds later."
"Who was at the centre of the second blast?"
"Don't know. I wasn't looking that way, but the bar was packed."

Douglas stopped for a second and lit up a cigarette. He offered. Grant took one.

"One last question. Have you been threatened lately in any way? Any phone calls, letters, personal threats? Anything at all?"

"No. Look, they weren't after me. I think they wanted to hurt as many people and achieve as much publicity as possible. Stringfellows is ideal for that. You can always expect to blow up a few pop stars and you automatically get the front page in the morning."

Douglas nodded and closed his book.

"Perhaps," he said, "but I don't think so. I am sorry I've had to trouble you whilst you are recovering. These things are best investigated whilst the memory is still fresh. However painful that may be. I hope Miss Schaeffer pulls through. Thanks for your time."

Douglas walked out of the room and Grant slumped back onto the pillows.

*

A small boy stood at the end of what appeared to him to be a corridor which went on forever. Perhaps into eternity. He was naked, and he held in his left hand, something which he could not bear to look at. He breathed in and all he could do was gasp, as once again, no air would enter his lungs. There was a terrible warm dampness creeping around the fingers of his left hand, but he just could not bring himself to look at the frightening object.

Suddenly, there was a noise at the other end of the corridor. It was black and cold down there, but he knew he had to go towards the noise. He had to because he could not stay where he was. He was bound to go. He had to hear what they had to tell him.

He stepped forwards. He tried again to breath, and though his lungs were working, the air that seemed to surround him, just would not enter. Yet he walked on. He had never felt such fear before, such loneliness. And he knew it was because he had done something wrong. He was being punished for that. Oh God, he was being punished.

It was so cold as he stepped along the corridor. The walls appeared to be frowning at him, so he lowered his head in shame.

As he approached the end a smudge appeared in front of him. It swirled and transformed into an horrific face filled with hate and anger. Yet the face was above a white coat which flowed down to the ground.

Suddenly the face screamed at him. "You killed her!" and the boy fell backwards dropping the thing onto the linoleum. Juddering with fear and scrambling to escape, his tiny naked body thrashed about in a vain attempt to stand and run away. But try as he did, he just could not make his feet move, they petulantly refused to obey his commands.

He cried out desperately, "It wasn't me," but the face would not listen. It hovered over the boy's prostrate body then picked up the thing that the boy had dropped and taunted the boy with it. Waving the severed hand in front of the boy's contorted face. And as the blood splattered out of the severed arteries onto the boy's face, he saw the ring shining on the wedding finger of the hand. Only then did he know why he could not look at the hand and only then did he realise why it was his fault.

He had taken her there.

It was a Monday morning in early June and the summer was beginning to break into its stride. London had sweltered through a week of dry and grimy sun drenched days, wholly lacking in wind. The morning sunlight spliced through the blinds in the flat. A rather over eager bee had been trying to mate with the window for the last half hour. Old Church Street was jam packed with commuters, bumper to bumper, on their way to their offices in the Square Mile. George Grant's terrible scream sliced through the tranquillity of the room. He sat bolt upright in bed and opened his eyes. His whole body was soaked in sweat. He wailed for a few seconds as his mind returned from it's terrible journey and then he breathed in and out slowly for the next two minutes with his hands over his head.

The dream had haunted him every night since Joanne had died.

He reached for a Galoise and lit up before getting out of bed. His head was thumping. A carpenter was hammering in his cerebellum. He hated smoking before breakfast but for the last few weeks he has done so automatically. He waited for a second as his head slowly drifted out of a grey alcoholic haze. Where had he been the night before? What was he doing?

"Jesus I must have been drunk," he thought to himself. The evening before didn't exist. It was a blank screen with only patches of colour. A party, a bottle of scotch, a trip down the river, someone drove home. Oh God, was it him? Had he driven home drunk again?

He looked about for a second scared to speak. Afraid of the words his mouth might say. The telephone rang. Relief! He climbed out of the double bed and staggered over to the phone.

"May I speak to George Grant please?"

"Grant speaking, who is this?"

"My name is Goldstein. I understand you undertake private investigatory work Mr Grant."

"Yes. I used to, er, I mean yes I do." Grant needed to get his mind into gear. What was he saying? "Wake up!" he shouted to himself.

"Make your mind up. Either you do or I go elsewhere."

"Whatever suits you Mr! Try phoning the Agency." Grant slammed the phone down wondering how the man had obtained his home phone number. Who gave a damn anyway?

The thought of Joanne Schaeffer had been kept out of his mind by a series of drinking bouts that was worthy of Oliver Reed. She had died after her tenth operation. Fourteen hours on the operating table. "'Internal haemorrhaging", the doctors said. Over one hundred stitches internally. She was a patchwork doll held together by stitches, desperately trying to repair what God has made and man had torn asunder.

Grant threw the telephone against the wall and walked into the bathroom. He stood under the cold water of the shower for a lifetime. It felt good, clean, cold and pure. It eased the pain of losing her and the feeling of emptiness. And the hangover.

He sat down naked on the edge of the bath and the tears came slowly from within. He just couldn't hold it any longer. Three years of love had been wasted in one dreadful night of terror. The self-pity, the pain, his loss, the stupidity of it. He couldn't hold it in.

At lunch time the phone rang again.

"Mr Grant are you capable of talking lucidly now?"

"Mr Goldstein?"

"I have work for you. Are you available?"

"I suppose so. How did you get my phone number?"

"I have contacts. I didn't receive any satisfactory answer from your agency."

"What do you want?"

"To talk. What I have to say will interest you, believe me."

"Ok," Grant replied.

"Come down to my estate on Saturday night. Eight o'clock. The address is Seven Yacht Club Drive, Itchenor, in West Sussex. Dress is formal." The man rang off.

Grant phoned Jack to obtain confirmation that Goldstein had rung there first. Jack sounded flustered.

"What is the problem?" Grant asked

"It is that Mrs Dilworthy, George. When I broke the news to her last week about her husband she went mad. I calmed her down but she's told me to uncover all the muck about his private life."

Grant noticed the tremble in Jack's voice.

"Fine Jack, charge her £500 per day and do the job."

"She wants to file for divorce George," MacDougal squealed, as if that was a rare occurrence in the 1980s.

"It happens Jack. It is not your fault."

There was silence at the other end of the phone as Jack summoned up the courage to say what was really troubling him.

"I will have to follow him to all those poofter places!"

Grant smiled at the thought of Jack being propositioned by some transvestite in a seedy backstreet in Soho.

"I am not ready to come back yet Jack. You will just have to cope on your own."

"I need you to keep me out of trouble George!"

"Go buy yourself a dress Jack. I'll see you soon."

*

3PM, 13TH JUNE 1988

"Please sit down gentlemen," the Prime Minister took her chair at the head of the oval table in the third conference room at Checkers.

"We have heard from the Commissioner, you have each submitted and read the various dossiers prepared for this meeting. It is now time to make decisions."

The Prime Minister was wearing a light blue dress with a matching jacket. Both were pressed and spotless. She looked sharp and incisive but she had an air of solemnity about her which was born from the depressing facts which she had heard throughout the past six hours.

"Field Marshal Carshalton, what is your opinion on the course of action we should not take to combat... no that's not the right word," she hesitated. It was rare. Carshalton waited patiently.

"To eradicate this parasite?"

"All of the resources of the Army, the SAS and Army Intelligence Services are at your disposal Prime Minister. But to be frank I don't think this is an Army matter. It would not be conducive to public confidence in the Government if either the Army, the Navy or the Air Force were seen to be questioning suspects, raiding houses or stopping people in the streets. Not yet

Madam. After all we're not in Northern Ireland. The best I can do is offer the SAS and the Red Berets, out of uniform and undercover, to your security services."

"Thank you," Sir John Epcot and Lord Carver both replied in unison.

"Do the Navy and the Air Force agree with Field Marshal Carshalton?" The Prime Minister asked.

Admiral James and Wing Commander Harris indicated their agreement.

"Mr Defence Secretary?"

Phillip McNaughton nodded and put down his water.

"Prime Minister. This is a primarily a matter for MI5. It is after all a matter of internal security. Our two security organisations will have to work together more closely than they have even done before. And we will need a new level of communication between them and the Committee. In view of the proposed placing of responsibilities I think we should set up a subcommittee consisting of Lord Carver, Sir John Epcot and myself. This should implement the decisions made here today and make such other purely administrative decisions as will be required. When further executive decisions are required the full committee will be convened. In this way we will be able to move fast and save time."

This was agreed unanimously. Phillip McNaughton continued in his rather judicial tone.

"Turning to the methods to be employed. I propose the following four basic decisions. We can refine them later, but from what we have discussed in the last three weeks I think you will agree these propositions are necessary:-

PROPOSITION ALPHA: In view of the far reaching and wide spread nature of the terrorist activity, a selection process must be implemented from within the security services. The filter must be so fine that the chances of the chosen agents being infiltrated is reduced to the absolute minimum.

PROPOSITION BETA: The chosen agents will work in cells. Beta Cells. Each unaware of the work of the others, so that if one cell is penetrated the whole operation is not jeopardised. Each cell will report directly to the members of the subcommittee I have already mentioned.

PROPOSITION GAMMA: The highest security classification will be given to some agents chosen under proposition Alpha. They must be able to use all available police data, information from GCHQ at Cheltenham and from Interpol and the CIA and other sources without restrictions.

PROPOSITION DELTA: We will need a failsafe security sweeper from outside the services. Someone who can report directly to the subcommittee. Someone who is aware of the operation and who is working towards the same goal independently. This person will have to be chosen with the utmost care. Stringent tests will have to be passed and we may need him to carry out the covert actions which may be too sensitive for security service operatives, and must be dispensable."

"Do you mean an amateur?" The head of MI5 interrupted with an element of disbelief in his voice.

"Not exactly. The parameters will have to be determined, but he must be someone outside the services. Most of our agents will not be aware he is working in parallel. This will achieve a checking or corroborating mechanism which will not be tainted by anyone who has been reached within MI5 or MI6."

"My God! What you're saying Phillip is that you don't even trust the chosen agents in the Beta cells," Lord Carver replied.

"That's overegging the pudding and it will cause a lot of confusion. And paperwork."

"I do not exclude the possibility that one of us around this table could be eventually reached!" McNaughton responded..

The Prime Minister rose out of her chair and walked over to the window at the end of the conference room.

"Phillip, that would mean you believe the power of the terrorist organisation, or whatever is behind this invasion may be, or may become such that it can reach into the highest echelons of Government."

"It's possible Ma'am. Five terrorist acts per day. That's five influential people reached per day. How many will give up their son, their wife or their parents to stick to their principles? I think we may assume that 20% will give in to the coercion and turn."

"More," said Sir John Epcot, the Director General of MI6, in the sea of gloom that threatened to encompass the whole room and drive them all into a spiral of foreboding.

"If your fears are correct, this enemy challenges our democracy at the most basic level," the Prime Minister whispered the words.

'That is what I fear."

Phillip McNaughton was not noted for being a great optimist. He had shown a tendency to wear brown suits at University and date the girls with spots and glasses. But if you wanted level headedness under pressure he was like an oak in the autumn gales. When all around him were bending or dropping their principles like autumn leaves, he would thrust out his chin and provide a moral shelter for the forest of scared and shivering political animals.

The decisions were made and the subcommittee was set up. The title it was given was SUBSEC.

When the members of the committee had all left, the cleaner found that there was one ashtray missing from the conference table. It had been stolen.

*

George Grant slipped the gear lever into third and decelerated as his 1974 Alfa Romeo Spider 1750 approached the wrought iron gates of number seven Yacht Club Drive, Itchenor. It was a warm, balmy summer evening in June and the trees surrounding the narrow pot-holed road which leads to Itchenor Yacht Club wore their finest summer coat of leaves.

The gates opened automatically as he approached. He drove slowly up the curved lane beneath a roof of touching branches perfectly entwined as if from one plant of many stems.

Solomon J Goldstein's summer house lay four hundred yards from the gate. It was a surprise to see classical Spanish architecture in the heart of southern England's yachting community. The villa consisted of a central body with two satellite wings joined by arched cloisters. The white washed walls shined under a red tiled roof. The ground floor windows were surrounded by beautiful purple flowering clematis.

The sound of a Strauss waltz wafted over the grounds. Grant parked beside a row of Bentleys and walked towards the front doors, throwing a Galoise stub onto the drive as he pushed the bell. The doors opened immediately.

Initially the doorman frowned at the six foot man with stubble and a tatty barber standing nonchalantly on the step.

"George Grant?" He said.

"Please come in, right this way Sir." The doorman, wearing a splendid burgundy dinner jacket, looked with austere disapproval at Grant's dishevelled suit then led him through the main hall straight onto a vast patio overlooking the lawn. The grounds stretched down to the dark waters on the south side of Chichester harbour.

The garden was crowded with guests in dinner suits and long evening dresses.

"Champagne?" Asked a waiter, instantly at his side.

"Thanks."

"Mr Goldstein will be available between midnight and 1pm Sir, in the library. If you would care to eat, there is a cold buffet on the East Wing patio by the pool." The doorman smiled professionally and walked quickly back to the hallway.

Grant looked down at his single breasted black suit and cursed.

"Four hours of banal party bullshit before Goldstein can spare the time to tell me what this is all about," he said to himself.

"My dear boy, what are you wearing?" The voice with a German accent came from behind him.

"Isn't it obvious?" He replied to a rather aristocratic old lady in a purple satin evening dress supporting the shop window of Aspreys on her hands.

"Well it just won't do will it? You come along with me now and I'll see what I can find for you."

She wrapped five lumps of flawless river diamonds and a rather withered hand through his arm and led him back into the hallway.
"What's your name?"
"George Grant."
"Oh darling, are you a relative of the Huntingdon Grants?"
"Not to my knowledge."
"I'm so glad. They are a bunch of shysters in my view. Not at all kosher, if you know what I mean." They were climbing slowly up a marble spiral stairway.
"Solomon throws such marvellous parties doesn't he? You know about the death of his poor daughter, my granddaughter, of course. Such a terrible waste. Poor Solomon has been distraught for weeks."
"So why has he thrown a party?"
She shot him a brief salutary glance, then proceeded with her task. "You don't mince words do you? It is a tradition in our family to celebrate both life and death George. Death comes to all of us at some time. Mine is all too close now. The Goldstein's mourn for one month. There is no contact with the outside world for that period. None what so ever." Grant thought about the telephone call and nodded. "When that time is up the past is discarded. The black clothes are discarded and we praise the good Lord that those who remain have life by His grace. This party celebrates the end of that period."
"Are you his mother?"
"No, my dear boy. She was murdered by the Nazis many years ago. I am Francesca Bertelson. His wife was my dear daughter Carol. Now come in here."
They entered a large bedroom. Mrs Bertelson began searching through a vast wardrobe.
'There we are now," she bellowed with glee. "That should fit you perfectly!" She handed him a sparkling new dinner jacket and trousers. "Go on now, don't be shy. Put it on and don't mind me. I've seen more men's underwear in my time than most."
In ten minutes he was back on the patio wearing the very same dinner jacket she had chosen. She had been right, it was a perfect

fit. A good Jewish eye for the correct cut, she had said, as they descended the stairway to rejoin the party.

Grant thanked her. Then he asked, "what keeps a man as rich as Goldstein motivated?"

She smiled warmly at him and stopped walking.

"Look," she said and raised her left hand. On her second finger rested a platinum ring clasping an enormous oval diamond of about three carats. "To some people this is just a diamond. To Solomon it was an adventure. It was the desire of a relative. To fulfil that desire he did not just go to a shop. He took a trip to the producing country. He negotiated a deal to buy a mine. He turned a simple request into an opportunity to reorganise an old fashioned worldwide distributing and refining operation."

"I don't understand."

"I turned eighty-two last year. I asked him for a diamond ring. He treated the request as a chance to learn. He bought the mine in South Africa and a refining and cutting shop in Amsterdam. He personally searched for the perfect rough stone to cut. And he polished the main face himself. To Solomon life is a curious challenge. He needs to own, control and change things he cares about. That is his persona."

She smiled knowingly and then vanished into the crowd.

Grant strolled quietly over towards the east wing patio where a group of guests were stripping off and diving naked into the pool. In the centre of a group of five men was a young girl aged about twenty with a mane of dark black hair. She was laughing voraciously as one of the men tried to duck her, whilst the others sang a blue rugby song.

The other guests near the pool wandered away towards the band at the end of the garden. Grant sat down and watched. He knew he was in a bad mood and wanted to cheer himself up.

One by one over the next ten minutes the men climbed out of the pool and ran into the house to dry off and retrieve their clothes. Finally, only the most eager young man was left sniffing around the girl, and making cack-handed advances. He was desperately trying to shield a growing concern in his loins.

After two rebuffs the girl swam to the pool edge and climbed gracefully out in front of Grant's chair. Her body glistened and heaved magnificently in the evening half light. She was a sparkling shimmering animal overflowing with vitality and youthful beauty.

"Do you think I'm attractive?" She said.

"You're certainly precocious and probably spoilt," Grant replied. "You should be sent to bed after a sound spanking."

She looked hurt, then her brown eyes flashed with cheek and she stepped towards him. Her damp pubic hair touched his right arm.

"Will you spank me?" She whispered. The young man in the pool drew his breath for a second.

"Where I come from we have a phrase for young women who behave like you."

"What's that handsome?" She asked, rubbing slightly against him.

"Prick teaser," he said and took a sip of his drink. She ran into the house. The young man in the pool swam over with determination and climbed out.

"That was damned rude of you. Do you know who she is?"

"I don't care if she's the Queen of Sheba. She's behaving like a fool and making you look even more foolish."

The young man advanced. His stomach muscles tensed and his fists clenched. Grant stayed seated and caught his eye.

"I weigh at least four stones more than you and I'm not drunk. If you took a swing at me you might conceivably bruise me. If you were lucky. I would then probably break your terribly straight and pretty nose and that would ruin the party for you. We would probably both be thrown out and that would ruin the party for me. So what's the point?"

The man stared at Grant venomously then, quite suddenly, his anger left him. He looked down at his naked body, shrugged and walked into the house.

At twelve o'clock precisely Grant knocked at the large oak doors of the library on the ground floor of the west wing of the villa. They held the inscription "vene vidi vici" above a coat of arms displaying a globe with a scythe through it. He turned the handles and walked in.

"Come in Mr Grant. Do come in."

Solomon J Goldstein was sitting in behind a magnificent polished redwood desk by the glorious bay window overlooking the gardens.

"Would you like a Drink?"

"A Bacardi Bloody Mary with ice please." A waiter appeared almost immediately from behind an alcove and handed Grant the glass.

"Please sit down. Are you enjoying my party?"

"Not really."

Goldstein chuckled.

"How frank. I do like a man with a sense of purpose. You strike me as just such a man."

Goldstein was a large well fed man. Even when sitting his frame exuded power and energy. His face resembled a plump aubergine. He carried a shock of silver curly hair swept back behind large ears. His unmistakably bulbous noise had clearly quaffed the odd claret in its time. This man was used to good cooking.

"I'll come straight to the point. I need your help."

He rose from his chair and walked around the large desk.

"You are a Private Investigator and I need a private matter investigated."

"I'm listening."

"There are few things in this life which I do not own. Or at least few things which I cannot buy. You may regard that statement as arrogant, but for the large part it is true. The excessive wealth which I now possess facilitates this. But I can't protect my family from terrorism. I cannot bring the dead back to life.

"My eldest daughter was murdered recently. She was taken from this life by a group of terrorists calling themselves 'INTERFERON'."

Grant sat up. The blood ran out of his face. His hands gripped the chair with such force that after only a few seconds the knuckles were as white as ice.

"Joanne," he mouthed in a whirl of emotions.

"Your girlfriend was also murdered that night at Stringfellows. I know, I am truly sorry. My proposition is simple. You have lost a loved one. I have lost a daughter who was everything to me. We should join forces. You to discover who committed this act of barbarism and I to provide you with whatever you require."

"Why do you expect me to succeed? The police have failed!"

"With this wave of terrorism sweeping the country the police are unable to cope. I don't intend to see my daughter's murderers walk away because the police do not have sufficient numbers or intelligence to catch the bastards."

"It was a bombing in central London. That type of crime is at the top of the police's list. There is no way that the anti-terrorist squad will ignore your daughter's death. I know that they are investigating the bombing at present."

"Sure. Even so, you must admit that not one of the perpetrators of the terrorists crimes committed recently has been brought to justice."

"As far as we know. But that doesn't mean the authorities haven't arrested some of them. They may be within an inch of catching them."

"Is that what you really think?"

The question hung in the air for a while and Grant let it tease him until the answer just stewed up inside him.

"Frankly no," he replied.

"Let's not play games. If you don't think you're up to the job then I will look elsewhere." Goldstein turned away and stared out of the bay windows in silence. His shoulders a little more slumped than before.

"I know a little about you. I don't think that you will let this matter rest until you have an answer." Grant realised that for the last month his sole contribution to humanity had been to support the country's distillers. He had been drowning his mind. Numbing the terrible thoughts of that horrifying night. In reality his was trying slowly to kill himself.

Now he had a reason to live. A reason to fight. He had guessed after Goldstein had phoned his flat that this would be the request. He had simply refused to consider the realities.

"I honestly don't know if I am up to it," he replied. "I have been going through a bad patch since Joanne's death."

"I too. But I know your history. I'm not a fool. You have resources within you which will be invaluable to our task. All your past bears witness to that. Your years with the Marines. Your escapades in West Africa and your recent past as a Private Investigator. I have researched your background thoroughly. I am not embarrassed to say that I know you right down to the type of tie you prefer."

"Hmmph," Grant responded.

"I am not unaware of your vanity either. I do not choose my employees lightly. I did not reach my present position by making errors of judgement about people. I know my strengths and one of them is choosing the right man for the job."

It wasn't difficult for a man in Goldstein's position to find out a lot of personal information about Grant.

Before the meeting Grant had himself carried out a little research on Solomon J Goldstein in the library of the Daily Telegraph in Fleet Street. He had access to the wealth of information there through a friend who worked on the news desk.

Goldstein had already been the subject of two unauthorised biographies and countless news stories.

It was said that he was born in Germany in 1925. His parents were of Polish-Jewish extraction. His father a tailor in Dusseldorf. In 1937, at the age of twelve, he had been sent to boarding school out of the city because of the Jewish persecution. Solomon and three other Jewish boys had volunteered for a biology trip to the German Alps late in 1939. The boys ran away on the second night and trekked for five days over to the Alps to safety. Only Solomon survived.

In 1938 his parents were arrested and tortured at the local Nazi headquarters. His mother was sent to Auschwitz in 1941.

His father died in custody that year. The authorities had said he died of a heart attack. After the war he had discovered that his father was killed by a massive electric current being applied to his groin after three days of torture.

He spent the war in Switzerland and, at the age of 20 when the Nazis were defeated, he travelled to the USA, via Rome, as a deck hand on the 'Transatlantic Star,' a passenger liner owned by The Peninsular and Oriental shipping company.

As he passed by Monte Carlo, penniless and alone in the world, he vowed to God and to himself that he would someday own the largest cruiser in that harbour.

In New York, Solomon slipped over board one cold winter night, and swam through the filthy waters of Manhattan Bay to the nearest dock.

He lived in Harlem for five years as an illegal immigrant. Then he married a local girl of Italian extraction called Donna Ellena Proberti, thereby gaining American citizenship. False papers and names were provided at the wedding. Solomon J Goldstein became Simon Gold. At twenty-five, he had seen enough of the American way of life to know that it was unbearable without money. And he wanted a lot of it.

He enrolled at the New York East college of higher education and passed his finals in a record two years. After three years in a distinguished city firm of Accountants he had made his mark.

The next part of his life was based on rumour, but he had never sued the biographers who wrote it. Simon Gold was well known within the firm for getting in early and leaving very, very late. One Thursday in early fall, he copied the draft balance sheets and profit and loss accounts for a major electronics company. Then went home and studied their performance over the past five years from copies obtained in the firm's library. In the morning he collected all his savings, the cash collected on the sale of his car and the maximum loan the local banks would advance him for the setting up of a fictitious partnership of accountants to be called S. Gold and Co. He invested it in the shares of Western European Electronics Inc. Three days later when the company's record profits were announced he sold all his shares.

The name he had used to buy the shares was one "Solomon J Goldstein," a fictitious self employed interior decorator, with an out of state address. He made $50,000 clear profit after repaying the loans.

In 1954 that made him a rich man.

Two months later he retired from the accountancy firm on grounds of ill health and changed his name back to Solomon J Goldstein. At that time he obtained a divorce from Donna Ellena Proberti Gold on grounds of adultery. His own adultery. She was delighted. He had never shown any love for her in the eight years since their marriage.

In 1959 he joined forces with David Salzburg, a man of dubious background, and founded a stock broking firm. Using bent sources from within the accountancy world he continued to prosper on the stock market and by 1964 he had made his first million dollars.

Women took no place in his life until that year, when he met and fell in love with the most beautiful woman he had ever laid eyes upon. She was a petite Jewish stockbroker called Carol Bertelson. Their first child was born six weeks after their marriage. People talked, but they didn't care. For the first time in his life, since the murder of his parents, Solomon Goldstein experienced love, safety, security and happiness.

In 1964 he founded a record distributing company and heard about a rather quirky English group called the Beatles. He obtained exclusive distributing rights for the group's records in twelve American States and the whole of Canada and by 1969 the company had grown to the largest record distributor in the United States. With serious capital now available he turned his mind to industry.

A young inventor had approached his wife's stock broking firm for a loan. The merchant banking arm had turned him down as 'too risky'. Carol asked Solomon to meet the young man. Two weeks later Solomon purchased a bankrupt electronics company at a knock down price and made the young man Managing Director of the firm: 'Goldstein Electronics' began producing a revolutionary new power supply for computers which was three times smaller, and 500% more efficient than any other on the world market at the time.

After a world patent and sufficient advertising in electronics magazines, the largest computer company in the world, IBM, signed a bulk purchase agreement with Goldstein Electronics and for the next five years the GE 21B switch-mode power supply became the only viable computer power supply. The world market exploded with demand for the GE 21B. Goldstein Electronics granted licences only to reputable manufacturers in selected countries and sat back raking in the royalties.

Solomon Goldstein was a multi millionaire by 1972.

Now, finally he was not only secure but he was a respected investor and manufacturer. He purchased property worldwide and made frequent prolonged trips to the Far East, Europe and the USSR. Trade between the Goldstein empire and the eastern bloc countries grew exponentially as the cold war became colder.

People whispered that he never lost touch with those terrifying formative years. He never lost his dark side.

He traded electronics, arms, aircraft and even oatmeal. Then he bought into the shipping world in 1972. In the first twelve months of his ownership he cleared a profit on his shipping operations of £66 million. He saw the oil price boom coming two months before it hit the market. He filled every ship that he owned with oil and had them sailing around aimlessly for four months. Others said he was mad. When the price went through the roof he eventually sold and the world was crying out for crude.

Solomon knew no trade barriers, only the ability to profit from good sales and sound products. He was an empire builder. A friend of politicians the world over and a confidant of Royalty.

In 1977 he moved unexpectedly to England and settled there. The move was brought about by the kidnapping and murder by terrorists of his beloved wife Carol. He refused to pay the ransom demanded, so they killed her.

For two years after her death he became a hermit. No one knew where he went or what he did in those missing years. But when he emerged from seclusion he had turned grey. It was said that he had personally run a vendetta against the terrorists who murdered his wife. Certainly there were some serious setbacks for the terrorists in those two years.

He had decided that their children would gain most from English higher education, so he sent the girls to Roedean at the ages of eight and thirteen.

Now the older of those precious children was dead. Murdered by a terrorists bomb blast at a London night club. Perhaps that would send the old man mad. Perhaps he was just repeating what he had done before. Grant did not know.

"How do you know the name of the terrorist group which planted the bombs?" Grant asked.

"They called me after the blast." The thought of the conversation plainly disturbed Goldstein.

"It was a woman's voice. She said I would suffer for what I am. For what I had done. She called me a two faced double-crosser. Those were her very words. Then the anti-Semitism. And finally she said INTERFERON was going to stop me. The police interviewed me after the call. I phoned them immediately. They have the full transcript of what I could remember. Blasted Nazis! Bloody terrorists! They never die you know. They re-emerge and return with new faces, new covers, but always the same blind hatred. They are vermin Mr Grant, vermin. Help me find them, please.

"They killed my wife and now they have killed my dear daughter Carol." He smashed his palms down onto the tables. They were shaking. No doubt, emotion was partly the cause but there was something beneath it, something terrifyingly steely. Grant couldn't quite touch on it.

"What does INTERFERON stand for?"

"I've no idea. M's the name of a new cancer cure is it not?"

"I think that's right. I'll start with the police."

"There is one more thing, Mr Grant. I want you to keep an eye on my other daughter at the same time. Carmine may be in danger too. Can you do that?"

"I'll do my best but I can't provide a personal bodyguard service to an eighteen year old. Why not use your own men?"

"She's nineteen. Just contact her and be there if she needs you. She's quite a fireball. Rebellious." He drifted away for a second. The thought of his daughter distracting him. My men are doing what they can but they failed with my oldest daughter. I'll introduce you. Come on my boy."

He led Grant out onto the patio. The band was still playing and the guests were dancing close as the evening mists rolled off the harbour across the lawns.

As they approached the dance floor Solomon called her name. She lifted her head from a young man's shoulder and withdrew from his embrace. When she approached, she floated like a leaf on a still pool. She was stunningly beautiful. More so now she was clothed. She recognised Grant instantly.

"Carmine I want you to meet George Grant. Mr Grant, Carmine."

"We've met Father," she said with a coy smile and raised her hand for Grant to kiss.

"Are you going to spank me Mr Grant?"

"Pardon?" Goldstein asked raising his left eyebrow with the tired look of a father who has come to expect to be shocked by his offspring.

"Carmine is referring to an earlier conversation we had about corporal punishment." Grant said not wanting to go into the topic any further.

"I see, I had not noticed Carmine showing any interest in politics recently. Perhaps you are growing up my dear. Well I am going to retire Mr Grant, please contact me as soon as you hear anything. Anything at all."

"OK."

"Good night." He kissed Carmine and walked briskly back to the villa.

"You think you're rather smart don't you Mr Grant?" Carmine smiled sarcastically and swept back to the dance floor leaving Grant with the feeling that there was very little chance he and Carmine would ever see eye to eye on anything.

Grant thought he was being followed as he drove back to London. But after an improper amount of alcohol and a long evening, he wasn't sure. If it is was a tail, the head lights behind him changed at least three times. There would be no point to it. The police had no reason to keep a track on him.

CHAPTER 4
THE BACK DOOR

Scotland Yard's offices are situated in an imposing new block of offices built on stilts situated opposite St Park tube. Grant walked in through the foyer up to the reception desks.
"Inspector Michael Douglas please."
"Hold on a tick sir." The officer called Douglas' internal number, "I'm afraid he's out at the moment."
'Then get me the Chief Inspector of the Anti-terrorist squad."
"Oh, I don't think he'll see you sir. He's been very busy recently. The terrorist wave and all..."
'Try him please! My name is Grant."
"Well I'll try sir, but be it on your head." He fiddled with his switch board. There's a Mr Grant here to see you sir." Then to Grant "Your first name sir?" The officer asked incredulously.
"George."
"George, Sir. Oh! OK, I'll show him up." He replaced the receiver. "It appears you've got an audience sir."
The security officer showed Grant up to the fifth floor. He took a deep breath and prepared himself to be restrained. It had been his experience that calm reasoning was the most effective tool for breaking down bureaucratic barriers. He had heard that Chief Inspector Duffy was a very tough customer.
"Chief Inspector. Good Morning." Grant shook his hand.
"Mr Grant you are a victim from the Stringfellows blast aren't you? What can I do for you?" He was a small red faced Scot with a shock of red greasy hair and grey flashing eyes.
"I would like to see the list of people present at Stringfellows that night. Also a rundown of the injuries, and the forensic evidence about the blast. I'd also like to know whether you have

any leads, for instance phone calls or warnings relating to the attack. Does this blast tie in with any others? Which terrorist organisation do you suspect was responsible? And I'd like you to assign an officer, perhaps Mike Douglas, to liaise with me during my investigations."

"Is that all or is there more?" The Chief Inspector asked, grinning broadly.

"Yes. Please get your tail off my arse!"

"What?" Chief Inspector Duffy's grin now stretched from ear to ear.

"Don't mess about Chief Inspector. You've had me followed for the last four weeks. It's only recently that I've been lucid enough to realise it."

After twenty nine years in the force Chief Inspector Duffy had seen enough of Private Investigators to know they fell into two categories. Annoying and very annoying! Oh, he admitted there was a need for them in minor domestic cases where the police didn't have the time or the personnel to deal with the situation. But for serious crime all his experience showed him that PI stood for pain in the arse.

"Why should I give you anything at all, Mr Grant?" He asked whilst he composed himself.

"Because you've been on this case for six weeks and come up with nothing. Because I can spend all day and all night on the case and I don't break off at 5.30 when the wife has dinner ready. Because my girlfriend was butchered by those bastards and because you know I'm not connected with the terrorists so it won't jeopardise your investigations if you do help me."

"Not totally true, but persuasive I'll give you that. You have a disarmingly direct manner."

The Chief inspector leant back in his chair and put his arms behind his head.

"Will you help?" Grant demanded.

"If it was up to me I'd say no without any hesitation. In my experience loners like you just mess things up. You jump in with both feet stamping on all the evidence leaving broken fragments for the professionals to piece together. You're more trouble than help. However, I'm instructed by a higher authority to help you. God knows why!

"So go ahead. As requested, your contact will be Michael Douglas. And let me tell you he is one of my best officers so don't get in his way. I will give you security classification to allow you access to all our evidence. But you will have to draw your own conclusions. I will not feed you with my officers conclusions. If you think you're so damned good and obviously someone higher does too, you can work out your own conclusions."

Grant hadn't expected it to be so easy. Goldstein must have pulled some strings high up in the force.

"Thank you Chief Inspector," Grant said with considerable surprise. He got up to leave.

"Oh, before you leave. You should know that this department hasn't been tailing you. Good morning." Inspector Duffy lowered his head and lifted a beige file out of his 'in' tray.

Michael Douglas arrived back on level five after lunch.

"Mr Grant! How are you? Is your leg better?"

"Considerably, Good lunch?"

"Bacon, sausages, eggs, beans, tomatoes: sheer bliss. Coronary Thrombosis on a plate, but I needed it. I had a long night last night."

"I've never liked health food either." Grant replied.

"Now. Vic had a word with Gruff Stuff."

"Who?"

"Chief Inspector Duffy. I understand you've already spoken to him."

"Well we exchanged words."

"Quite. That's what most people do with Gruff Stuff. He is usually as rude as you were to me the last time we met."

"I am sorry. But you know what was happening at the time. How quickly can you get me what I want?"

Douglas led the way into his office and threw a file about ten inches thick across his old wooden desk.

"It's all here. Names, injuries, forensic reports, interviews, expert opinions from the bomb squad. The lot."

"Thanks. Does Gruff Stuff know you've included opinions."

"No, but I won't tell him if you won't." Douglas smiled.

"Thank you. Tell me, do you know who gave Duffy the OK to give me security clearance?"

"No idea. But believe me, it came from the top. Henry Blythe-Stafford, the Commissioner was in with Gruff Stuff for a least twenty minutes this morning That rarely happens round here. They don't meet in Gruff Stuffs office. He goes to the Commissioner's office. There is something going on which humble State Servants like me are not privy to."

"OK, give me an hour or two to read through and then I'll get out of your hair."

"No problem. You can use that desk over there. I have a million bits of rolled Norwegian forest to deal with anyway."

*

Grant sat and read for five hours. Names of victims, injuries, type of explosives, method of detonation. He summarised it on a note pad:-

1. Four Hundred and Twenty nine people present.
2. Recognisable notaries -
   a) Two Arabs of undetermined wealth.
   b) Three Civil Servants in minor posts.
   c) Two Corporals from the Army on leave: based in Aldershot.
   d) Two well known pop stars.
   e) An Israeli diplomat.
   f) Terry Smith and Solomon J Goldstein's youngest offspring.

3. The bombs were made of a new type of plastic explosive called Cemtron. They were detonated by a remote control device with a range of approximately ten to twenty yards.
4. The bombs were not intended to destroy the club. They were placed at the two spots where the terrorists could be certain all guests would pass at some stage. To destroy the club they could have needed to be placed by the two main support arches. For some reason the second blast was considerably more forceful.

At 7pm Douglas leaned back in his chair, a Marlboro clinging tenaciously to his lower lip. He had spent the last half hour trying to persuade his wife over the telephone that the death of their cat was not related to his investigation of the terrorist wave. It had been run over. He also gave her his apologies for working late once again. He said he would be home after midnight.
"Are you finished?" Douglas asked.
"Yes." Grant responded and stretched his arms.
"What do you think? The whole thing eludes me. Why place the bombs at the foot of the stairs and the bar when they could destroy the whole club?"
"Because they didn't want to destroy the club."
"OK. I've been through this thought process. So they wanted to hit a specified person. And who did they kill? A bunch of teenagers, your girlfriend and the Israeli Diplomat," Grant winced.
"Do you have anything on the Diplomat?" He asked trying to ignore the thought of Joanne gliding across the crowded dance floor.
"Yes, he's low level administration. Of no international importance whatsoever. He has never made any reported statement about terrorism nor has he been involved in any parties or committees that could be connected with Terrorism. Of course there is always the PLO but if they were going to hit someone why this bloke?"
"What about Joanne?"
"You should know George."

"Sex doesn't open the door to a person's past, Mike."

He cleared his throat. "I ran a check on both of you and she was as clean as a whistle. It's more likely that you were the one they were after, than her. Take your background in the marines and the SAS and your spell in West Africa."

"It was not me they were after. That leaves Terry Smith and Goldstein's daughter doesn't it?"

"Yes." Douglas looked worried. "George I'm going to tell you something I shouldn't. But for some godforsaken reason I trust you."

He reached into his desk and pulled out a half bottle of scotch. "Want one? It's 7.30 so I am officially off duty."

"Yes."

Douglas started pouring. "Lord Carver, the head of MI5 was poking around here last week. I did not understand it then. Perhaps he was interested in the Stringfellows' file."

"Why?" Grant asked. "Perhaps they have been following me. Goddamn MI5."

"Most probably."

"Do you think they suspect me?"

"No. Who is your client on this case?"

"You know I can't tell you that."

"Don't be coy George. I have been frank with you. I've included our conclusions in the file. I have even provided you with ATS. special reserve coffee."

"Solomon J Goldstein hired me last night."

"Phew! Why? Do you know anything about him?"

"Yes. I went to a few sources in Fleet Street and pulled their files on him. He's quite a character."

"You're telling me. He has connections in places I haven't even dreamt of."

"Well he can afford to, can't he?"

"Grant, this whole thing stinks. There is something going on here. Something so big that the likes of you and I cannot even imagine. I have a sense for these things and it's telling me to stay away. I'm thirty five, George. I've been in the Anti-Terrorist Squad for four years. I'm good. Not the best but damned good. I've seen countless IRA bombs, atrocities by Libyans, Israelis, even KGB, believe it or not. But there is something strange about this one. It doesn't have the reason or the hallmark of most terrorist acts. I don't know if you can understand this but I feel there is something really dirty going on here."

"I can't say I do understand, explain it to me."

"Well most terrorist acts in the UK are 'claimed' either before or after the act. After all, what is the point of terrorising, if the victims don't know who the terrorist is and what his object is? Publicity is usually the reason for these acts. Either a political statement or a retribution for a government act which the terrorists think was unjust. This one is different No-one has claimed responsibility."

"So who is responsible?"

"I have no idea. Really. No bloody idea, except that one thing strikes me. It resembles an East End gangland killing. Bloody enough to hit the newspapers but unclaimed so only those in the know get terrorised."

"You mean the families of the victims? Terry Smith or Solomon J Goldstein?"

"Exactly." Douglas downed a large Scotch and scratched his armpit with distraction.

"Do you think it could be an internal MI5 matter?" Grant asked.

"No. The services would know immediately if one of their own men had done this. MI5 and MI6 may get away with a lot of stuff but not letting off bombs in London night clubs. It's too public. It's stupid. If they want someone killed it takes us ten years to find the body. No, I think it's something Lord Carver or Goldstein are involved in. Either personally or in their respective lines of business."

"A private matter? They or one of them has been dabbling in dirty linen?" Grant pressed Douglas.

"No. My guess would be it was part of the terrorist wave. Perhaps they are being blackmailed. Perhaps economic or social pressure wasn't enough to make them give in, so the terrorists killed a member of their family. There has been a hell of a lot of this sort of stuff going on George."

"Have you told Gruff Stuff about this theory?"

"No. He'd drop me three ranks if I even whispered it. Duffy deals in hard facts. Court evidence is all he's interested in. Now come on George let's attack this again tomorrow. Anyway I've got a date tonight." He winked at Grant and got up to leave. Grant looked blankly at Mike for a second. It was none of his business that Douglas was cheating on his wife, so he gathered up his notes and the two men walked out together into the summer evening rain.

Grant had decided not to tell Douglas about INTERFERON. He could not understand why the police interview with Goldstein was not in the Stringfellows' file. Douglas was either unaware of it, in which case he should have asked to interview Goldstein. Or he was part of the cover up.

Grant slept badly that night. He turned the facts over in his head but he couldn't begin to guess what Goldstein could be caught up in. What sort of problem would lead the terrorists to kill his daughter? He needed to pinpoint who had pressed the button. The man who had wanted to kill Goldstein's daughter was the man who had destroyed Joanne's life.

The next morning, he dressed, ate breakfast and drove to Hampstead Cemetery for Joanne's funeral. The ceremony lasted an hour. It was false, hypocritical and plastic. He hated undertakers for their feigned sympathy. They picked over the carcass of the family as do vultures a spent animal life. Pecking at the wallets of the dead.

He comforted Joanne's parents for an hour. They were too shaken with grief to gain much succour from his words. Eventually all he could do was hold her mother in his arms for a hug that lasted an eternity. He then took the engagement ring from his pocket and gave it to her. She looked at the ring and then at George.

"Oh you poor boy. We knew it would come but we didn't realise that you had finally decided."

Joanne's father shook Grant's hand and walked alongside him to the gates of the cemetery.

"What are your plans George?" He asked.

"I am not sure. I am having difficulty understanding where I go from here. I had planned to... well, to spend my life with Jo. The wedding. Settle down. Raise some kids. God, I might even have tried to find a respectable job."

"Don't punish yourself George. If you are too hard on yourself you will tear apart. Joanne would want you to get over her."

"Sure, but it is not easy to come to terms with myself when I do not understand why all my plans were shattered. How can I start to build again if I cannot be sure that any new plans will not crumble the way our old ones did?"

"You can rarely be sure of anything in life George. We do our best to make our lives safe and secure. To protect the ones we love and to provide for them. But there are no guarantees. You knew that when you returned from your days in the Services."

"I did not seek guarantees. I just wanted some happiness. I believed that I had served my time. Hell, did she deserve to die? Why the fuck wasn't it someone else?"

"There will be some reason for it George. You and I cannot see it now but it will become clear if you let the pain pass."

"I need to find out why she died. Without that I just cannot justify my own life." Grant replied.

Mr Schaeffer turned the collar of his raincoat up against the wind and offered Grant his hand. They shook firmly and he noticed Mrs Schaeffer, signalling by the car that she did not have the keys.

"I had better go," Mr Schaeffer said. "You find her killers if you must. But be careful son. Don't let hate cut you up. I recall a Colonel in my regiment in 1942, who set out on a crusade. He was driven by a burning desire for revenge. He lost forty men needlessly, one Sunday afternoon, because the brass sent the air cover to the wrong co-ordinates on the day he was meant to take a small village of some strategic importance to the Allies. They were slaughtered because a General in head office failed to take the Colonel's advice and introduce a double check with the local field officer before giving final co-ordinates to the RAF.

"This man took the village against terrible odds. Then he secured the ground and drove back to HQ. He burst into a joint Chiefs of Staff meeting and made a bloody fool of himself by accusing the general of negligence in from of all of the Joint Chiefs. Then he hit the General."

"What happened to him?" Grant asked.

"We all expected him to be court Marshalled. He was right in a way, but that did not matter, his hate had blinded him. He failed to see that the General was only human. A man like any other, with hopes and beliefs. When the Court Marshal finally convened after the investigation, he discovered that the General had in fact checked with a local Field officer. Although there was a standing order not to do so because of the likelihood of Axis picking up the transmission and decoding it. The General had listened to his recommendation. It was the field officer who gave the wrong co-ordinates. The General lost his command and the Colonel was sent home.

"After the war they became close friends."

"I must find out why she died."

"I know. Just remember the Colonel if you do ever meet the man who you believe is responsible." Colonel Schaeffer turned around and walked away towards his wife.

He left the cemetery utterly depressed and confused. The ashes had been placed in a small clay pot. He could only think of all that life, the humour, the electric sensuality of the woman reduced to a small pile of ashes. Where was her soul? Where was her mind? He loved them both more than he could have realised when she was with him. Now she was just a small pile of ash.

He ran into the back of a black Golf GTi at the traffic lights before the flyover in the Edgware Road.

"What the hell are you up to?" The driver screamed as he jumped out of his car aflame with anger and determined to avenge the serious wrong done to him. Grant sat for a second then lifted himself slowly out of the leather seats of the Alfa Romeo Spider and walked towards the man.

"Look what you've done, you moron. Can't you drive? Are you blind?"

Grant looked at the small dent in the Golf's bumper and took out his wallet.

"Will £150 cover it?"

"Well it's not cheap, a new Golf bumper you know, but I reckon that will do it."

Grant handed him three crisp new fifty pound notes and swore at the driver. He wasn't proud of himself but it made him feel better. He drove away and had to stop a few minutes later. He was shaking with fear. When he looked in the mirror, he saw a man he barely recognised. A frightened insecure man desperately trying to hold himself together.

*

BELGRAVE SQUARE, LONDON, JULY 1988

"Fifi, it's George Grant, will you let me in?"

"George. What a surprise!" She opened the wooden door and stood panting slightly in a skin tight leotard. It was red with a yellow V between the thighs. She looked hot. Sweat trickled down her forehead and welded her hair to her checks.

"Come in. How did you find my address? How are you?" She turned and that beautiful backside swung down the circular iron stairs into a large cushion covered living room. She turned off her Jane Fonda workout record and pointed to a large cushion by the trench windows.

"I am fine. I am trying to find out who planted the bombs Fi."

She turned pale at the very mention of the topic.

"George. I am so sorry about Joanne. What can I say that would ease the pain?"

"Nothing. Just tell me all you can about that night."

"Sit down. What can I get you, tea or coffee?"

"Coffee please Fi, you look like you've been working rather hard."

"Forty minutes a day George. Keeps the tummy flat. At twenty five you're nearly over the hill in modelling. If I put on an inch round my waist I'll start getting parts in glove advertisements instead of fashion displays."

She soon returned with the coffee.

"She was a fantastic girl. It must have really cut you up! Look I am sorry she was killed. I mean that more than you will ever realise."

He sipped the coffee letting the sympathy slide away into the past. He was not yet able to cope with it. Her way of expressing it was unnerving. But he was an emotional bolognese and he could not hope to rationalise other people's emotions.

Fiona Galliani lived well in a penthouse flat overlooking Belgrave Square. She had an income in the hundred thousands, but no boyfriend. She was independent in the extreme. To such an extent that she worked in Stringfellows' Discotheque at night, not because she needed the money but because she fell it kept her on her toes with people.

A woman with short cropped brown hair came out of the bathroom wrapped in a small yellow towel which barely covered her brown torso.

"I thought I heard voices, who is this Fi? The fella you dated last night?" Fifi ignored the jibe.

"George, this is Diane, isn't she divine?"

"Yes, divine!" Grant replied.

"Diane dear, go and put some clothes on will you? You'll catch your death walking around half naked."

"OK, Fi." She kissed Fiona on the cheek and walked rather determinedly towards the bedroom, giving Grant a fleeting glare as she entered.

"What do you want to know George?" Fi had turned back to him smiling.

"The bomb blast Fi, I need you to remember everything about that night." Grant tried to apply his mind to the task at hand.

"Why?"

"Because I want to find the men who planted that bomb."

"Why men?" She stood up then added quickly, "no, you're probably right. It just galls me that everyone immediately assumes all acts, good or bad, are perpetrated by men."

She walked into her kitchen. Grant's eyes passed slowly over her book shelf. Three shelves of rabid feminist literature containing everything from 'the feminine Mystique' by Betty Friedan to 'Women in Power' by the Women's League.

"Do you remember seeing anyone with any sort of remote control device, it would be a small box probably no bigger than a cigarette pack, with a radio aerial?"

"No, but I do remember seeing two men leave the club about the same time as the first blast occurred. I was in the upstairs bar ordering three double gins and these two Irish guys collected their coats from the check-in at the entrance and were joking about Rod Stewart. I remember it clearly because earlier they had both tried to manhandle me. You know the sort of thing, £10 down the top of my boob tube and a hand up the skirt."

"Did they really leave at the same time as the blast or before?"

"Well. They seemed to watch the stairs for a few seconds then they put on their raincoats and left, it was about then that the blast went off."

"The first bomb?" Grant shot the question out. His heart beat raised dramatically.

"Oh yes. They were gone by the time of the second bomb."

"Damn! They couldn't be the ones. The detonator only had a range of twenty yards maximum. That's about the distance from the basement to the door. Once outside it's unlikely that the detonator would have worked."

"But George, couldn't the second bomb have been activated by the first. Like on a time delay or something?"

For a second Grant looked at Fiona and wondered how the hell she would have known about delay detonators, then he dismissed the thought as ridiculous.

"I suppose so. That's not what the experts at the yard thought." Diane returned to the lounge in a pair of dungarees with a large CND badge pinned to the front. She might be mistaken for an astronaut, except for the badge.

"You should change out of that leotard Fi. It's sweaty and you're making the room smell." She bitched grinning at Grant.

"Thanks dear. You're all heart."

"Do you want to stay for lunch or must you go?" Diane asked. She seemed to stress the 'must you go,' so Grant climbed out of the cushion which wanted to swallow him whole and headed for the door. "Thanks Fi. Oh, one more thing, can you remember what these guys looked like?"

Fiona stopped at the bedroom door.

"Not really. One sees so many people each night you know. But they definitely had Irish accents and raincoats."

"OK thanks Fi. By the way, when is Stringfellows re-opening?"

"Don't know and don't care much. I've resigned. I'd had enough anyway and this just finished me off."

"I understand. You were a classy waitress Fi. They will be sad to lose you."

"Good-bye, George."

Grant took the lift down to Belgrave Square and walked slowly back to the car. He hadn't realised Fiona was a lesbian. It's funny how people seem so totally different at work. He had never been to her flat before. The Police file had provided her address. He regretted going now. He felt like he had invaded her privacy. Her private life was hers and he didn't want to tamper with it or pass judgment. He fired the Alfa Romeo and swung round towards Sloane Square.

Something was niggling him. Two Irishmen in raincoats. Men who Fiona wouldn't recognise again. They had left at the time of the first blast.

The IRA? If it was them why hadn't they claimed the bombing? Maybe it was the INLA? Was Mike Douglas wrong in his assumption that it was not a political bombing, or were the Irish trying to blackmail Terry Smith or Solomon Goldstein? Perhaps they wanted to kill the two British Army Soldiers.

Grant picked up the ringing phone as he walked into his flat in Old Church Street.

"Hello," Mike Douglas sounded worried. "Mike?"

"George where have you been? I've been trying to reach you all morning."

"Working."

"I need to speak to you more desperately than you could imagine." The word 'desperately' didn't seem appropriate.

"Are you alright mike?" Grant considered driving straight over to the Yard but he had other tasks to carry out that afternoon.

"I am fine. But I think I have found out something which is going to scare the shit out of us."

"You sound scared yourself Mike. Shall I come over now?" Grant asked.

"No. Look I can't speak right now. Where shall we meet?"

"At the City Pipe pub in Holborn at about six o'clock tonight. Do you know it?" Grant asked.

"No but I'm a policeman. Remember?"

Grant put the phone down and dialled Goldstein's office.

"Hello. Goldstein Enterprises Ltd." Said the very proper receptionist.

"I want to speak to Mr Goldstein."

"Who is it please?"

"My name is Grant."

"Oh yes Sir, Right away." He came to the phone quickly. "Grant, Goldstein here, what's happened?"

"Solomon I think the terrorists intended to kill either your daughter or the soccer player Terry Smith. You must have known that they were dating?"

"Yes, of course. It was common knowledge. The Gutter Press had been dissecting it for weeks. Why do you say that?"

'The bomb was intended to kill specific people, not to destroy the whole club or cause maximum damage."

"Remote control?"

"Yes. From not more than twenty yards away."

"That is dangerous for the bomber isn't it?"

"No. The Club is on two levels. The bomber was upstairs, so he was pretty safe."

"How could he tell who he was aiming for then?"

The first bomb was at the bottom of the stairs. He just needed to watch the couple going down the stairs. He estimated how long it would take to reach the bottom. That's easy."

" INTERFERON! Bastards. Find them for me George. Is there anything I can get you. Transport, money, some men, a gun?"

"No Solomon. But I need a reason. Think! What is INTERFERON? What do they want? You must have the key Solomon."

"Who knows why Nazis do what they do. Terrorists killed my wife for mere money. I have spent years chasing after the Bastards. Perhaps this is just a warning from them."

"Perhaps. I do not yet know. I'll report later."

"Thanks."

Grant rang off and headed out to the car. He needed more information about INTERFERON.

*

Grant sat in the gloomy conspiratorial atmosphere of the City Pipe's stone floors, wooden seats, oak bar and candle light. Douglas was half an hour late. He got up, walked to the door and up the stairs towards the street.

Douglas was stepping onto the Zebra crossing not ten feet away. He waved cheerily and walked across. A red and white Evening Standard van screeched round the corner and ploughed into the crossing.

"Douglas, look out!" Grant screamed, lurching forwards. The front bumper broke his legs at the knees. His head swept down and collided with the bonnet. His body was lifted into the air and his back arched over the windscreen. The small of the back impacted with the edge of the passenger side of the roof. Mike Douglas screamed in agony as his back broke and blood spurted from his lacerated neck.

The van accelerated through the crossing and the limp body flew over the side and hit the tarmacadum of the road in a vile distorted pattern. The back arched like a tuning fork, the arms stretched and legs bent forward in a horrifying, crossed pattern. Mike Douglas was dead before he hit the ground. Grant stood for a second, stunned and disgusted, then turned to the wall and vomited.

The Police kept Grant in a cell for two hours whilst they interviewed witnesses. Eventually an Officer came down and led Grant to the fifth floor of Scotland Yard by the stairs. The traffic roared along Victoria Street as they walked up the cold concrete stairway. Eventually they walked through two Formica clad swing doors, along a corridor with a patchwork covering of carpet squares and knocked on the door at the Southern end of the building.

"Come in." The Chief Inspector shouted.

"Evening, Chief Inspector." Grant sat in the same chair he had used the previous morning. His hands were shaking again. He could see the top of Westminster Abbey from the picture window behind Duffy.

"Mike was a colleague and a friend of mine," Duffy said. He was also badly shaken by his death. He resembled a cabbage patch doll wearing too much rouge.

"What happened?" he asked.

"I phoned Mike and arranged to meet him at the City Pipe. He was half an hour late. I was leaving and saw the accident."

"It wasn't an accident Grant." The Inspector Duffy blurted out angrily. "We have the registration number of the van. The Evening Standard have no record of a van with that number. They switched plates within five minutes and the van became untraceable. There are hundreds of vans working for the Standard in London at that time of the evening."

"Do you think it's mixed up with the Stringfellows' bomb?"

"Frankly, I don't want to discuss it with you Grant - as I told you yesterday. Private Investigators always mess things up for the Police. I've lost one of my best men within one day of assigning him to you. I hate that. Bloody hate it. He was my friend. A good friend and a married man. It is I who will have to tell his wife." He slammed his palm on to the desk top.

"Look Inspector, I liked Mike. I wouldn't have done anything to endanger him. I had no idea his life was being threatened. Anyway, how can you be sure it's my fault that he was murdered?"

"Only you and he knew where you were meeting."

"Maybe his phone is tapped?" Grant replied.

"That's not possible. All Scotland Yard lines are checked weekly for taps."

"So check them daily, or maybe it's an internal problem."

"Or maybe it's your phone that's being tapped Mr Grant!" It was the obvious solution. Both men knew it was probably correct.

"MI5." Grant said under his breath. He wasn't sure. He just wanted to see his reaction.

"I don't know Grant," replied Duffy. "It's possible. After all, that is where your security clearance came from".

Duffy was tapping the top of his leather bound desk with a gold plated Parker pen.

"What?" Grant replied shocked.

"Grant, I have the feeling you and I are being used in a larger game. I don't know what it is. I have read a short report which Mike prepared for me about you. He spoke highly of you. I have also read your file quite carefully. You have an impressive history."

"That did not help Mike much, did it?"

"It wasn't your fault. Or mine for that matter. Mike must have stumbled onto something. Let us hope that we find out what it was sooner rather than later."

"I will help in any way that I can Chief Inspector." Grant replied.

"I suggest that you report and liaise directly with me on this. Do not contact Goldstein or anyone else for that matter until you have spoken to me. Use public phones and don't tell me anything relevant on the phone. Just tell me where to meet you. We will then decide what you will tell Goldstein."

"Why?"

"Because by using you I can reach outside the bounds of my authority. I can investigate areas which my department is not authorised to look into. Also I can provide you with the backup you will require if you stumble across the terrorists. God help you! Lastly I can find out who killed Mike and what the hell MI5 are up to."

"You know that I cannot do that. I have a duty to the client."

"Fuck your duty Mr Grant. If I am going to be leant upon from a great height by your bloody client then I will damn well impose some of my own conditions. If you want my help then you had better get used to them."

"Since you ask so sweetly. I accept."

"This conversation never took place, understand?"

"Yes absolutely. But one last thing. There may be a leak here at the Yard. I don't want to end up like Mike Douglas," Grant responded then continued. "And what about the meeting places?"

"We will use a code. Your name will be Pain, I will be Bruce. We will write out a joint list of meeting places here and now. When you mention the first meeting place it will mean we go to the second. Next time you will name the second and we will go to the third. Only in cases of extreme emergency will we use the last place. Which will indicate the first on the list. Those will be Old Church Street indicating a meeting at the Falcon Pub in Wardour Street. OK?"

"Fine."

"That's unless you've discovered anything earth shattering already?" Grant paused for a second then decided he had to try it. " INTERFERON."

"What?" There was no visible falsity in Duffy's response. Grant was relieved.

"What does that mean to you?" Duffy looked blank.

"Absolutely nothing."

If Duffy had not seen the interview with Goldstein after the bombing then it must have been removed from the file by someone higher up.

"OK, try this. Two Irishmen in raincoats left Stringfellows at the exact time the first bomb went off."

"But it was May." Duffy replied. Grant smiled. "Yes, but it had rained all evening."

"Oh, I thought perhaps that was a lead."

"So did I. Don't you see. Raincoat pockets are ideal for hiding radio transmitters."

"Hmmm. Does your witness have any identification of these men?"

"No."

"We'll check up. Go through the interviews and see what we can come up with. Is that all?"

"For now. Oh, do you mind if I photocopy a few pages of the file on the blast?"

"I suppose not," the Inspector replied. "But destroy them once you've finished with them."

Grant copied the file at the copier in the room next door. It took him 3 hours, then he walked out through the security booths on the ground floor towards St James' Park tube.

*

Grant sat in his offices in the Kings Road the whole of the next morning, reading the copied pages. The interviews with the Arabs produced nothing. Neither did the interviews with the pop stars. The Israeli Diplomat's family had been distraught, they had returned to Israel. Only the two army corporals gave some useful facts. Times and positions. Faces noted. Good army training.

He left his office at 1.30pm for a good pub lunch with Jack and a full run down of the activities of Mr Dilworthy and the rag-bag of other clients who were misguided enough to use their Agency.

"Mrs Dilworthy's husband has been doing some rather unusual things," Jack said as he tucked into a pasty at a corner table in the pub.

"Like what Jack?" Grant asked as he finished his pint of Young's bitter. "He and his boss make regular trips to a massage parlour in Charing Cross."

"So?" Grant replied, starting to smile.

"Well, I summoned up the courage to go in there yesterday." Jack began to turn a little pale.

"Did you enjoy yourself Jack?"

"Give me a break George, it was for poofs! I nearly died."

"Good work MacDougal. If only your old company commander could have seen you there." Grant started to laugh. "What have you told Mrs Dilworthy?"

"I thought that it would turn her green, but she listened without emotion. I do not understand her at all. She said 'very well done' and handed me a bonus cheque. She is an exceptionally odd woman George. I really wish that you would take this case over for me."

"I don't think so Jack. The client is used to you. She is clearly pleased with your service. Anyway I have become involved in a new case."

Jack looked surprised and put his pasty down.

"Who is the client?" he asked.

"Oh, no one special," Grant feigned disinterest.

"Come on you fly bugger who is it?" MacDougal demanded grabbing Grant's arm.

"Solomon J. Goldstein," Grant paused and let the effect sink in.

"Of Goldstein Enterprises! The multimillionaire?" Jack's jaw dropped onto the carpet.

"Sure," Grant said and slid off his seat. "Keep out of trouble Jack." Grant winked at MacDougal and walked out of the pub.

*

Grant drove to Trafalgar Square, headed North and parked at the back of Leicester Square. He walked to Stringfellows in the warm afternoon sunlight. The refurbishment had nearly been completed. It looked practically the same as before the bomb blast. He walked down the stairway and timed himself. Fifteen seconds at most. then he paced from the top of the stairs to the coat stand at the front door, twenty five yards! Over the maximum range. He walked it again. No mistake, then he walked outside through the metal glass doors. Forty yards to the pavement. There was no way it could have been detonated from outside the club.

"George, what are you doing here?" Peter Stringfellow fits his name perfectly. A cross between Peter Pan and a very thin trapeze artist.

"Just checking a few things out Peter. I see the club is nearly ready to open up again?"

"Yes, we're having a celebrity evening, two hundred pounds per ticket. Champagne and Caviar. All in aid of the victims' families. Should rake in about £80,000 just at the door!"

"I'm glad Peter. Joanne's parents could do with the cash. That's good of you!"

"I know."

"Look I need to talk to Jean and Sam about the bombing, are they here yet?"

"Yes, downstairs cleaning up. I'll call them." He went downstairs. Grant lit a Galoise and sat down by the piano.

"Peter said you wanted to talk to me?" Jean was six foot nothing tall, with long red hair which touched her buttocks. She had an intelligent, thin smooth face and perfect legs.

"I'd like to talk about the night of the bomb blast. Do you mind?"

"Suppose not." She said chewing gum and picking her nose at the same time.

"You were serving at the coat checkout that night, as I remember."

"Yer."

"Can you describe the five minutes before the first blast?"

"Yes. No-one came in until about ten seconds before the blast. Two army boys came in. A bit straight faced they were. Gave me their Great coats then ran towards the stairs. Didn't even take a drink. They said they were desperate for some 'fluff.' Then two other blokes collected their coats and left."

"Do you remember anything about them?"

"Irish, I think."

Grant felt a shot of adrenalin enter his arteries. "Did you feel anything, in their coat pockets as you handed them over?"

"No, I don't do that Mr. Grant. If I did Peter would fire me before I got my hand out of the coat." She replied, feigning hurt.

"I didn't mean it that way." Grant replied, stroking her ego.

"I know. But I make a point of not putting my hands near the pockets. Makes the customers feel better."

"Did these guys leave before the first blast?"

"Yeah. Definitely."

"Bugger." Grant reached into his pocket for another Galoise.

"Is that all? I've got to go and finish up." Jean asked, ever keen to avoid doing anything to tax her intelligence.

"Yes, thanks. Tell Sam to come up will you?"

Sam Lord was a large black bouncer. He had spent most of the evening of the bombing on the door. He walked slowly up the stairs and straight towards Grant. His eyes were quiet and friendly. You couldn't meet a nicer guy. Lord knows why Sam Lord was a Bouncer.

"George, how you doin' man?"

"Fine thanks, Sam. I need to borrow your memory."

"Dat been rotted by alcohol many years back man."

"Smoke?"

"Yer thanks."

"Were you on the door at the time of the blast?"

"George. I know you. You know the answer to dat. You got de Police records."

"Uh hu."

"You know I answered dat to the Police."

"Sam, you've got to help me. I'm nowhere near finding out who killed Joanne."

"She was a foxy lady, dat woman. I liked her George." The thought of Joanne seemed to spur Sam into action.

"OK. I was at de door till about one. Den I went down to the back door. We'd had trouble de previous night, people trying to break in. I was there for about half an hour when de blast 'appened." Grant drew a deep breath of the cigarette and exhaled.

"Sam, why didn't you tell the police about the back door?"

"Best not to. It's a hidden door in de wall. No join like. It's for some guests dat don't like to be caught by de press entering de disco. Royalty uses it."

"Who was at the door just before the blast?"

"Oh, no one. Jus' me and Fi."

"Your girlfriend?" Grant asked.

"No man. Fifi. You know her, de waitress."

"Oh God!" Grant couldn't quite believe the reply.

"What's wrong man?"

"Fifi lied to me. She said she was upstairs at the time."

"No man, she was rubbing up some other dyke at de back door. A small bird with no hair. Far as I could see."

"Was she wearing dungarees?"

"Yeh, how d'you know?"

"Just a guess, Sam. Just a guess. Look, I've got to run, thanks a million. Believe it or not you've helped a lot."

Grant ran down the stairs and headed for the wall behind the stairs. He stood there for a minute then inched along it. He came to an arch and went through. Beyond was a passage to the toilets and another small arch leading to a black wall about two feet indented into the main wall. He ran his hand along it. The sharp edge of a join ran up the wall. He turned and could just see the foot of the stairs from where he stood. He paced over to the stairs - 15 feet That was where the murderer had stood when the button was pressed. Fifi must have seen the murderer. Perhaps she was too afraid to tell the police about what she was doing when the blast went off.

*

George Grant parked the Alfa Romeo in Belgrave Square and raced up the flight of stairs into the building. The lift was open. Up to the seventh floor and out into the hall. He pressed the bell. Ten seconds later the door inched open.

"Yes what?" A small woman in a hair net peered out from behind a chain lock.

"May I speak to Fiona please?"

"Who?"

"Fiona, Fifi, she lives here."

"Not anymore mate. This is my flat now, I moved in yesterday evening."

"What! Where's she gone?"

"None of my business mate. Now piss off." The door slammed shut.

The landlord lived in the basement flat. Grant simply raced downstairs. He was a small flabby man wearing an ill fitting toupee. He needed a Wellington to persuade him to recall what had happened.

"Fiona Galliani left here yesterday. She paid her rent in full and I returned her deposit."

"Did she tell you where she was going? Leave a forwarding address or anything?"

"No."

"Damn."

"She your girlfriend old man?"

"Not exactly."

"Good, because she was gay you know. Into women and all that, if you know what I mean. I'm not prejudiced or anything but I don't like it at all myself. She used to hold all women parties up there. I don't mind telling you I'm glad she's gone." Grant left and stopped at a pay phone in Belgrave Square.

*

"Bruce?"
"Yes what?"
"Pain here, meet me at 'The George' in the Strand. 7 o'clock."
"OK."

*

Chief Inspector Duffy arrived at the Cheshire Cheese Pub in Fleet Street at 7 o'clock precisely.
"The wife will kill me. I said I'd be back by 6.30. What have you got?" Inspector Duffy asked as he sat down beside Grant with a double scotch in his hand.
"Fiona Galliani has disappeared."
"One of the waitresses from Stringfellows! Not a good sign. Do you know why?"
"I don't yet," Grant lied, "but she's just quit her job at the club. She's left her flat in Belgrave Square. There's something odd about it. I talked to her two days ago. She seemed fine then. She did mention she was leaving the club but not leaving town."
"OK. Do you want to know whether she's left the country too?"
"Definitely. Also see if you can get me a run down on her past. Political affiliations et cetera."
"You're not telling me something Grant. If I'm going to play straight with you, you'll have to play the game with me to. What is it?"
Grant lit a cigarette and looked across the crowded pub.
"Inspector she may have pressed the button." He said with a conviction based entirely upon speculation.
"The waitress?" Duffy laughed. "No Grant. Firstly, she had been working there at least three months. Secondly, she wore a skin-tight outfit that just couldn't conceal a radio transmitter and thirdly, she's not a terrorist. Well, I don't think she is anyway. I've seen her file or at least part of it. We seem to have lost part of it."

"She lied to you about where she was in the club. I know who she was with." Grant was becoming frustrated. He had done all the work and all the anti-terrorist squad was doing was sitting on its backside and making pooh pooh noises when he suggested anything constructive.

"She lied did she? Where was she then?"

"She was at the rear entrance, not at the front door."

"But .... there isn't one. Is there?" Chief Inspector Duffy was becoming embarrassed.

"The staff didn't want the police to know about it. They were worried it would get into the press. Then he'd lose some of the distinguished "rear entrance" customers. Excuse the phraseology."

"Who was she with?"

"A lesbian called Diane, five foot eight, short cropped brown hair, about eight and a half stone. She has a great figure. Usually wears faded blue dungarees. Pro CND and probably countless extreme feminist movements too."

"You could hide a radio transmitter in loose fitting dungarees."

"Exactly," Grant replied and downed his bloody Mary.

"And she could slip out of the rear before the police arrived."

"That is what she did."

"Whilst Fiona Galliani stayed around to help clear up the mess and throw us off the trail."

"That's the way I see it."

"How did you find this out?"

"I talked to the door-man, Sam Lord."

"We interviewed him. He didn't mention this."

"So maybe I am more use than you might at first have thought?"

"Shit." Duffy got up. "By the way, I checked up on Mike's movements on the evening before he died. I have had to be discreet. He told his wife that he was working late and he didn't get home until 2am. But he clocked out of the Yard at 8.30pm with you. I understand that he was cheating on her?"

"He was Inspector. The question remains. Where did he get that latest information which so worried him?"

"I'll get back to you as soon as I have anything." Duffy turned away then looked back. "Grant, thanks." His grey eyes flashed with the only warmth Grant had noticed since meeting him. It was a genuine compliment.

"We're not done yet Gruff Stuff," Grant replied not really intending the Chief Inspector to hear him.

"So you know about that nickname, do you?"

"Mike was a trusting man."

"Too trusting." The Chief Inspector turned and left the pub. His small muscular frame pushing determinedly through the crowds of half-pissed journalists.

Grant phoned Goldstein and summarised events then went home to bed.

CHAPTER 5
A LESSON IN TERRORISM

When Grant got back to Old Church Street, it was 9pm. The phone rang almost immediately. As if someone knew he had just got in.

"Mr Grant?"

"Speaking."

"We need to talk."

"Who is this?"

"A friend." Someone did know he had just got in.

"Oh marvellous, I immediately trust you with my life."

"Meet me in Old Church Street." Grant heard the words but knew it wasn't Duffy.

"Old Church Street! Bruce is that you?"

"Who?"

"Oh, shit." Grant slammed down the receiver. They must have Duffy! Who the hell were they? INTERFERON? The word suddenly sounded terrifying. Did they kill Mike Douglas? Did they kill Joanne? What did they have against him? Against Solomon Goldstein? How did they find out about Duffy's code? Had they taken Duffy? Oh Lord, was Duffy one of them? Maybe Mike had told Duffy of their meeting at the City Pipe and of his revelations and Duffy ordered his death! But it wasn't Duffy on the phone. And they didn't know the code name, Bruce. So maybe they didn't have Duffy. The phone rang again.

"Meet me at the cinema in Old Church Street at 7am sharp tomorrow. Don't be late Grant."

The phone went dead. Maybe it was coincidence. Old Church Street was after all where he lived.

Grant drank two Hennessey XO cognacs and went to bed and slept until 6.30 in the morning. He suffered no nightmares that night. When he climbed out of bed he felt calm and only the last vestiges of the depression seemed to remain within him.

He looked at the photo of Joanne that he had taken in the Piazza Basilica in Venice which sat on the sideboard. It made him smile. "Don't worry Jo," he said to the photo. "I am going to find those bastards."

*

Grant ate breakfast and read the Times cover to cover. The front page carried this lead story:-

'*July 31st, 1988*: **Terrorist wave continues. Horror Killings**. *Two Generals murdered in bed: Generals Alex Wolf and Peter Cuthbertson were murdered in their beds last night by masked gunmen who also callously shot and killed the Generals' wives and children."*

The article described the carnage. Grant turned to the obituaries:

"*General Alex Wolf was a family man. He had served in the army for thirty eight years. He fought at Dunkirk and was present at the liberation of Paris. He distinguished himself countless times during the intervening years at Suez and in the Middle East. He was the leading protagonist for a strong nuclear deterrent in the UK and was instrumental in the deployment of cruise missiles in the UK. He leaves a son."*

After breakfast Grant searched the flat for surveillance devices. There were none. Telephone tapping had come a long way since bugs were put in the phone mouthpiece. The line could be bled at the box in the street. A fake British Telecom repair operation or perhaps a real one if it was MI5 could be set up. Ten minutes is all it would take.

Grant left the flat at 6.58am for the meeting. A man stood outside the cinema on the corner of Old Church Street and the Kings Road.

"Good morning, my name is Judas, Daniel Judas!"

"The betrayer?" Grant retorted.

"Yes the name was unfortunate wasn't it. Won't you come this way please?" He signalled to a brown Austin Princess which was parked at the curb side. It started up. They both got into the rear seats.

"Who are you?"

"MI5."

"Bingo!" Grant whispered and looked out of the window as the car moved slowly away. "So you boys finally decided to talk to me after following me around for over a month."

"Are you always so aggressive?"

"It keeps me alive." Grant replied.

Judas was a tall, thin man with thinning black hair. He resembled a rather world weary accountant but he had no ink stains on his hands. He wore a blue pinstriped, single breasted suit and fingered his umbrella with a nervous circular movement.

"Where are we going?"

"To see Lord Carver, Mr. Grant, The Director General of MI5. By the way, who is Bruce?"

"Just a friend of mine."

The Domestic Security Services Head Quarters are situated in Lambeth, South London. Not quite as scenic as we are led to believe by the James Bond image portrayed in the movies. The car pulled up outside a nondescript concrete building in a one way street.

Grant was given a yellow name card at the desk which he stuck to his lapel and led up to the tenth floor.

"The Director will see you in a minute," Judas said and left Grant in a rather pokey cream painted waiting room. The Director's Secretary, an old lady with grey hair and a cigarette hanging lazily out of the side of her mouth, ignored Grant completely. A light flashed on her intercom and she pressed a button on the steel casing.

"Send him in Miss Porter."

"Lord Carver will see you now," she said without even looking up. The ash from her cigarette fell onto her arm and she cursed as he crossed the room. Grant went through the large oak door and closed it firmly behind him.

"Mr Grant, good morning, please sit down."

"Thanks."

He sat in a deep burgundy leather chair. Lord Carver said nothing. He just sat calmly behind a magnificent carved mahogany desk and puffed on a cigar. The smell indicated a fine Cuban Havana. The room was furnished with a mixture of classic English furniture and hi-tech appliances, wood panelling and leather chairs.

Grant moved to speak but Lord Carver held up his head. Grant relaxed again into his chair. The man had an undeniable authority about him, bred from years of command Grant supposed. They sat for at least two minutes in complete silence. Then the door opened and a tall, well built man entered. He slammed the door behind him, moved fluidly towards the desk with his hand out stretched and said, "Carver old man. How are you?"

"Fine thanks, Disney."

"This is Mr Grant."

Disney turned to Grant and offered his hand.

"Grant, delighted to meet you. I am Sir John Epcot, the Director of MI6, the foreign arm of the British Secret Service."

"Yes." Grant turned the name over in his head. Disney? Walt Disney. Disney Florida. Disneyworld. Epcot! The new Disney Centre. A nickname! How childish. How very English.

Epcot sat down opposite Grant in a matching burgundy leather chair.

Lord Carver looked at Grant, put down his cigar and spoke.

"As you know we have been following your movements for precisely five and a half weeks." Lord Carver raised himself from his chair and paced slowly around the plush square office. "We had a reason to do so of course and I will explain that to you presently."

He switched off for a second. "Would you like some tea or coffee gentlemen? This may take some time."
"Coffee please," Grant replied.
"Tea, the usual," Epcot replied blankly.
Lord Carver arranged it with Miss Porter and continued.
"You are acutely aware of the terrorist wave which has been ravaging this country in the past six months Mr Grant. You have felt the sharp edge of the terrorist blade. The British Government will not tolerate such occurrences and has therefore set up an organisation designed to combat this wave and for that matter, any future ones.
"The constitution of the committee directing the organisation is not your concern but suffice to say that the Government, the security forces, the military and the police are represented.
"The committee has set up a subcommittee which we will refer to as SUBSEC to manage the day to day running of the organisation. Are you with me so far Mr. Grant?"
"Yes."
Grant had no idea where the conversation was leading or why he was being informed of high level state organisations, but he had no wish to ask questions until the heads of the British Secret Services had completed their tasks at hand. He was sweating lightly. His stomach was tense. His usual reaction occurred. He lit up a Galoise.
"If you were an employee in my organisation Mr Grant I'd ensure that you gave that filthy habit up." Sir John interjected. Lord Carver smiled, lit another cigar and blew a plume of smoke at Sir John. Then he continued.
"You are requested, Mr Grant, to fulfil a function in this present operation. A function which is of the utmost national importance and will, if successful, be of invaluable assistance to our fight against terrorism."
He paused and puffed on his cigar as Miss Porter entered and distributed drinks. When she had left he continued.
"The organisation we have decided to establish will consist of selected officers from the security forces, police, SAS and anti-

terrorist squad. These men have already been picked and are commencing operations next week. If you accept our offer Grant, you will undoubtedly come into contact with some of these men during the course of your field work. You will be informed how we wish you to interact with these agents."

Lord Carver glanced at Epcot and Epcot nodded slightly.

"Your function, if you accept the offer, will be to act as a field catalyst. A field barometer and a double-check." He walked back to his chair and sat down. No-one spoke for a moment. Grant was intrigued.

"Why me, why not one of your own agents?"

"Because you're a virgin. You've never been reached by the opposition. You're clean. You're qualified and you're capable. Most of all, we have investigated you as thoroughly as any man in the history of the security services and we feel you are one of the few men in this country who can achieve this function.

There are, of course, countless agents from within the forces or our services who could do the same job as well. But we needed an outsider. Only a virgin can act as a true double-check. Others can be or have been tainted, or reached. Too many contacts, too many favours owed, you know how it works.

You see, Mr. Grant, life in the services dealing with security, espionage, foreign operatives etcetera inevitably taints even our best operatives. For this task we need a fresh unsullied operative. For your information I will tell you that, on average, an operative can be expected to survive three assignments of this nature. If he survives more than five, he is suspect, a double-agent, a paid informer or merely a coward avoiding the flash points. We retire field operatives after the fourth operation as a matter of course. Desk jobs or diplomatic jobs follow."

"Then why not choose a fresh operative in MI5 or MI6?"

"Because we already have done so for the main thrust of the operations. We need you as a back-up. A sweeper. Think of yourself as the Franz Beckenbauer of the operation."

"What about the army or the navy or the SAS for God's sake?"

"There were forty candidates chosen from the forces. A short list was drawn up. The special qualities we are looking for: independence, resilience, intelligence, experience, a clean record, motivation and courage, existed in all of these men, but the circumstances were not right.

Ten were in hospital already as a result of a recent covert operation in West Africa. A country which I believe you are quite familiar with.

Thirteen are on present assignments which we will not terminate without endangering them. One turned it down flat, he was getting married the next day. Five on closer inspection, i.e. positive vetting turned out to be suspect on various fronts.

Another three were already recruited to the organisation and eight were killed in the last two months by the terrorists."

"Eight?"

"Yes, Mr Grant. We too noticed that a leak may have occurred for there to be that number of deaths in two months."

"Congratulations. You fill me with a deep sense of security. But I still do not see why I am qualified for the job."

"In two words Mr Grant, because of the 'Critical Test,' " replied Sir John Epcot.

"That was a fluke and you know it." Grant felt himself blushing.

"Perhaps. But you are still the only man who has survived the test with a 100% clean pass."

"That was a long time ago."

"When the marines set up the Critical Test, George. May I call you that?"

"Sure."

"They designed it to be impassable. It was there to teach the men the cost of war. No war can be fought without cost and it was vital that the best men understood that there would be situations in which some losses had to be suffered. Normal training so often fails to train men to accept the death of their colleagues.

"Before you took the test, the best mark that any man had achieved was 53%. You alone achieved the magic figure. Not even the inventor of the game could achieve that. We know because he underwent the test three months before you did and only achieved 52%!"

"He probably played with a straight bat. Did not break the rules." Grant replied.

"Undoubtedly, but in certain circumstances rules have to be broken and your decision to reprogram the computer before the critical decision had to be taken, effectively saved 150,000 imaginary lives and so avoided the loss of 47 percentage points."

"I cheated Sir John."

"You were the only man who before the critical moment arrived, felt it's approach and had the wherewithal to think laterally and redefine the perimeters of your situation. That quality may make a critical difference in our present predicament."

"How can I agree, when I don't know what the predicament is?"

"We can't tell you that until we have your agreement to take the task on." Lord Carver said politely, with a slightly impatient air.

"Chicken and egg, is that it?"

"Exactly," Sir John Epcot interjected. His large blue eyes flashing impatiently. He seemed less pleased with the task of recruiting Grant than Lord Carver.

Lord Carver thought back to an earlier conversation with John Mason, an old personal friend and psychology consultant. "Build his ego. Build his interest. Build on his patriotism. Get him excited, then most of all, play on his guilt. If he is allowed to think too long he will, as would all reasonable men, refuse this suicidal offer. Don't give him the time. Plunge him in so deep that his curiosity won't let him surface. That's why it's vital that you and Epcot see him first. To impress upon him the national need and his importance. He has an in-built natural dislike for authority. Contact by a lower agent would never be able to overcome that. Only the combined effort of Sir John Epcot and you can avoid that hurdle."

Lord Carver continued. "Mr Grant, you've lost the woman you loved. You have a chance here to set the record straight to help bring the perpetrators to justice. How can you turn away from that?

It's not in your nature to shrink away from the chance to avenge her."

"Really?" Grant replied.

"Or would you rather go back to your Bacardi bottle and your cocaine?" Sir John Epcot added, almost whispering the words.

Grant sat back astonished. "You bastard."

"Quite possibly Grant. Maybe we all are in our own ways. But if we are going to beat these people we need to play down to their level. We can't just ride around on our white chargers, waving the Union Jack and preaching from the Bible."

"Poetic bull shit! You haven't given me one good reason why I shouldn't just go on as I am. After all, I have found out far more in one week that you experts have in seven weeks."

Sir John Epcot put down his Home Office china tea cup and answered in an off hand way. "Oh, the lesbians? Well yes, you might say that. But you see we knew who planted the Stringfellows bombs before you went to see Solomon Goldstein."

"What?"

"Yes, INTERFERON. A group of fanatical terrorists funded by Colonel Gaddafi. Theirs was an act of retribution against Goldstein for various activities he carried out in Libya over two months ago. Solomon came to me a few years ago seeking retribution for the death of his wife at the hands of those men.

I'm afraid the girls were just used as paid dummies. They didn't know there was a bomb in the discotheque. They had been shown a picture of Carole Goldstein and told to press a button on a radio transmitter to inform the Libyan group when she was at the bottom of the steps, so that a couple of hoods could steal his Ferrari which was parked outside the club. The keys had been lifted by the waitress Galliani as she handed her coat over to the girl at the coat room."

"And in fact it let off the bomb?" Grant responded.

"Yes. She has fled the country now. We let her go because we had obtained all the information we needed from her before she left and because she may lead us higher up at a later date."

"Then why didn't you tell Goldstein?" Grant asked.

"Well we wanted him to hire you. I suggested he should do so after he was interviewed by the Police." Sir John Epcot stated unemotionally.

"Why?"

"Let's call it a test, shall we? An exam which you passed with flying colours Grant. We were very pleased," said Sir John. His patronising manner made Grant feel rather silly. Like a schoolboy at sports day who after running his fastest ever one hundred metres, is told he was three seconds slower than the school record.

"That is why you kept the interview with Goldstein out of Scotland Yard's file. You wanted me to make the connection." Grant said.

He looked first at Lord Carver, then at Sir John Epcot. These two men held more power in their hands than the Prime Minister of Great Britain. They could legally order the taking of life, loss of employment, imprisonment, interrogation, torture. The funds at their disposal were not open to public inspection and their manpower was awesome.

Yet they had chosen Grant for their task. Grant had no reason to doubt that they were telling him the truth. What he disliked was the lack of choice.

"You've cornered me haven't you? You knew that I had to find the bombers. So you laid a trap for me. Solomon was the hook, the bait was the chance of finding the bombers backed up by Goldstein's finances. But you knew that if I was able to discover that Fiona Galliani detonated the bomb, I would be truly impaled on the hook. Once I had reached that stage you facilitated her escape leaving me with a dead end. Frustration. Partial success, but ultimate failure. No way I could discover who gave the orders without Fiona. So you've hidden her and closed that door.

"Now you're opening another door. But this one leads into a different world. A world where you want me to be. You want me to work for you, to risk my life, because you say that is necessary! God I hate that word when it's used by people like you."

"But it is necessary Grant - you know it and we know it". Lord Carver's silkily persuasive tones washed over him, cooling him down like a shot of morphine.

"And if I refuse, what would I do?"

"You tell us." Sir John replied.

"I would go home. You would withdraw the help of Scotland Yard. I would have lost my lead on Fiona Galliani and I would be at a dead end. Finished investigation. No success, no revenge for Joanne, no employment. The terrorists win. You know I couldn't live with that. You've used me, my loss, my bereavement. You've used it for your own purposes. And I don't know whether your purposes are equivalent to mine, do I?"

"You're perceptive but you're also getting things a little out of proportion. Look at it this way. We are giving you something which no other victim's relative in this country has. The complete support of the British Security Services to help find and destroy the perpetrators. Is that so terribly devious old chap?"

Word twisting. Situation management. Abuse of life. He was entering a new world. He had been involved with MI6 once before in an SAS operation in West Africa two years earlier. It had ended well for MI6 but badly for Jack MacDougal. He had spent three months in a stinking West African prison as a result. Grant had returned alone to free him. It cost him £25,000 in bribes and hired hoodlums to get Jack out.

MI6 refused to sanction a second mission in the country to rescue just one man when the primary objective had already been achieved and the lights of the international press were already beginning to shine into the murky waters of the politics of that troubled state.

Despite that George Grant knew he couldn't turn back.

"I'll do it. I'll need background information and I'll need support from personnel and hardware."

"We are not amateurs. That has been catered for." Lord Carver raised himself from his chair and offered Grant his hand.

"I'm glad you've joined us old man. Your code name will be Delta." His smile was warm and reassuring. As Grant got up to leave he remembered one thing.

"What about Goldstein, will you tell him?"

"I asked him to hire you, Mr. Grant. I'll ask him to terminate your employment when the time arises. For the moment he will provide you with a rationale for being involved. If you are captured you can use his name as the reason for your investigations. It may save you a lot of questions about us," Sir John Epcot said and waved Grant out.

*

One hour and twenty minutes later Grant was on the seventh floor in room 718 awaiting his briefing. Daniel Judas walked in.

"Hello again. I understand you're hired?"

"Yes, they've had me signing the Official Secrets Act and some other bureaucratic paperwork for the last hour."

"Happens to the best of us. Well, I'm here to brief you!"

"On what? Methods of espionage for the beginner?"

"Not quite George." Daniel Judas turned off the lights.

"Oh I see, sex education?"

"A slide show, actually." Judas pressed a button in the panel beside his chair and a screen lowered from the ceiling on the far wall. The projector in the rear wall switched on and a word appeared on the screen.

"TERRORISM."

Grant sat up straight in his chair.

"We will be here for about a week George. I've arranged for your car to be picked up. You have quarters arranged downstairs in the guest's section. The briefing should take three days. The rest of the time we will leave to you to study the files on terrorist activities over the last five years in the UK. Is that OK?"

"I suppose so."

"Good, then let's begin. The first part of the course will be a general appraisal of terrorism from the 1940s all the way up to 1988. Then its background. The main groups. The finance of terrorism. The training of terrorists and the weapons of terror. Their strategy, who's who and finally how terrorism is combated and hopefully defeated."

"Looks like I'll need a steady supply of nicotine for this. Do you have a ciggy shop in the building?"

"Sure. First floor at reception. Duty Free. The operatives bring them in regularly!" Judas busied himself with the projector.

"One advantage of signing up I suppose." Grant sat back and awaited the lecture.

"There are others," Judas continued.

"I'm all ears."

The screen illuminated and Daniel Judas began to speak in slow measured tones.

"Firstly, the reasons for terrorism. The urban terrorist is a chameleon. The terrorist organisations are comprised of many types of human beings, idealists, jihad junkies, criminals, psychopaths and political thinkers and religious leaders who preach violence as the method of improving the world for *their people.*

The historical basis for terrorism arises out of a difference in wealth between countries. The third world countries' poverty when compared with the wealth of the West creates an atmosphere ideal for intellectuals to write volumes upon inequality, unfairness, injustice and methods of changing the systems established in capitalist countries.

Terrorism per se doesn't exist in the Soviet Union. The state organs having the power to imprison without trial can nip it in the bud. Religious leaders, intellectuals, ideological deviants, malcontents and dissidents merely disappear to prison or rehabilitation centres. There is no police accountability so there is no comeback. Terrorism cannot flourish in that habitat although if Gorbachev's Perestroika completes its course, terrorism may begin there too. You can already see the unrest on the streets of Soviet Armenia.

The problem occurs mainly in the West and in developing countries. The terminology is interesting. In the West a guerrilla is a terrorist. In the Latin American bush a guerrilla is a guerrilla. All are so called freedom fighters but all use methods appropriate to their environment.

The inspiration for terrorism in Latin America was the triumph of Castro's small terrorist group against the vast army of the Fascist Dictator in Cuba. This proved guerrillas could win, could change systems and quote, *'liberate the poor people from the yoke of a violent Dictatorship.'*

Students throughout the Western World soon had reams of literature to absorb on revolution and liberation. Violence as a means of social liberation in developing and colonial countries was advocated by philosophers such as Frantz Fanon, the head of the psychiatric Department of Bilda Hospital in Algeria.

In the 1952 war between Algeria and the French violence was not only preached as an acceptable method of change but the only one to combat the robbery of the Third World by capitalism and colonialism.

The whole idea was and is used to play upon the guilt of the Western Student. Guilt about his wealth built from the poverty of the colonies which his forefathers conquered.

Young terrorists grew in this fertile soil of guilt for the sins of the fathers and soon reacted against their wealth. They tried to free the poor and abused in the West from the yoke either of what they saw as capitalist repression or from colonialist invasion."

Judas stopped for a while and paced slowly down to the screen. He lit a cigarette and looked back up the room at Grant seated in the middle of three rows of cinema seats.

"I realise you have been through some of this already, George. Your Marine training is as thorough as our own. But it was thought best to give you the complete course, not just cut in with an update. Do you mind?"

"Dan, if an hour of this will give me a one second edge in the field, I'll sit through weeks of background information."

"I'm glad you see it that way. To continue... we must consider the inspiration of terrorism. Historically many of the major terrorist methods used today were developed in Latin America.

A famous Brazilian guerrilla leader 'Marighella' wrote, *'Bank raids are the guerrilla's entrance exam. An apprentice shop for revolutionary war.'* But there is a philosophy to be maintained in such raids. The guerrilla regards himself as a friend of the people, so he will not indulge in gratuitous violence against the customers and will not rob them either, the bank alone, the system alone, must be hurt, not the people. The Baader-Meinhof terrorists indulged in this naive form of robbery and even went so far as to hand out chocolate cakes to customers and employees during bank raids.

Marighella was extremely successful for a period of time. Those who failed their entrance exam and were caught by the police were retrieved by blackmail or kidnapping. Marighella kidnapped various ambassadors and forced their governments to release prisoners. The Brazilian government for instance released a great many prisoners. In one case he obtained the release of seventy prisoners for the Swiss Ambassador. God knows why!

Hostage taking was therefore proven to be effective and profitable. It was the key used to unlock the gates of capitalist prisons. Marighella's book *'Handbook of Urban Guerrilla Warfare'* still influences the acts of terrorists today even though he was actually killed in 1967. Marighella's greatest innovation was to transpose the principles of rural terrorism to the Urban environment.

Lets move to Che Guevara who practised in a 'foco' or 'focus'. A place for the peasants in the field to collect and learn. In contrast Marighella worked on the intellectuals and students, not just the peasants in the field.

Che Guevara's cult and writings also influenced Western thinking to an extent. He taught the young to, *'fight first, the political statement will become clear later.'* When he was captured and killed in Santa Cruz in 1967 by the Bolivian fifth division, his face became a symbol for everyone under thirty. The sign of rebellion. It also made T-shirt manufacturers a lot of money.

Merber Marcuse, the professor of political thought at the university of California summed up the West's problem in the mid 60s thus: *'The scientific and technological revolution had so advanced the conditions of the working classes that the poor people had televisions and a second car. They had lost the desire to overthrow the system. So the only true revolutionaries were the people with a conscience, a sense of guilt at the poverty in the developing states. These free thinkers were cast out of society by their own beliefs and so fought against it. Student aggression was thereby justified.'*

"This theory fuelled the student unrest of the late sixties but not the political freedom fighters like the IRA. This group are a world apart from the naive idealism of the Latin American terrorists, it is a force in its own right.

The IRA believe they are patriots fighting for their country. Their discipline is strict and their soldiers are not students. For instance the IRA inflict knee cappings on deviant members. Eighty-two were inflicted in 1977 alone!

Their political objectives are well known. The withdrawal of UK control from Northern Ireland. Between 1969 and 1978 the IRA, murdered 490 members of the security forces and 1,400 civilians. This was done with a small membership, no more than 1,000 and the active support of a tiny proportion of the natives of Northern Ireland. The IRA is suspicious of outsiders and does not welcome student revolutionaries. Irish-Americans are their support line and the only foreigners with whom they associate.

In the past the majority of the IRA funding came from the Irish-Americans in Boston and New York, who gave US$600,000 in 1972 alone. This has fallen, as far as we know in recent years mainly due to the publicity given to the IRA's atrocities on the USA television networks. But the funding still comes across the Atlantic and recently large arms caches have been discovered heading for Ireland from the US on American vessels."

Daniel Judas had spoken for five hours. There had been breaks for food and drink. It was getting late.

"That's probably enough for today George. I'll move on to the main groups tomorrow."

Grant raised himself from the sweaty cinema seat and cringed as Daniel Judas turned on the lights. "Fancy a beer?" he asked.

"A beer?" Judas was taken by surprise.

"Come on. Let's go and have a quick pint before last orders."

"OK." Judas was not a man used to social drinking. Grant had guessed that from his demeanour. He had asked on purpose. He wanted to put Judas in an unfamiliar environment and see how he reacted.

*

They went to a local pub and sat by the bar with a pint of warm beer.

"How did you get drawn into the service Daniel?"

"It was a logical step for me." Judas replied.

"Why?"

"I was in the Foreign Office at the time. I gained a strong interest in anti- terrorist methods."

He didn't explain the reason but his look startled Grant as he said the words. He was suddenly distant and as cold as frost.

"I had an introduction through a minor operative who needed a favour. I suppose I was in the right place at the right time."

"What about your family?"

"I'm not married. No kids either."

"Is there someone waiting for you at home now?"

He smiled. "Yes, Jasper my dog and of course my constituents in the local council. I have been chairman of the Chiswick local Council for 3 years."

"A Tory, I suppose?"

"Of course!" he replied. "What about you George?" As soon as Daniel said the words he regretted them. "Oh I am sorry. I didn't mean to remind you of Joanne Schaeffer."

Grant let the small jolt of pain subside, then he swallowed and it was gone. Time was slowly healing the wound and he was beginning to cope with her loss.

"I'll survive Dan, but I need revenge."

"I know George. Believe me I know exactly how you feel."

Grant looked at Judas for a second, holding back a desire to tell him to go and screw himself because he could not have any idea how Grant felt but he saw the glazed look on Judas's face and restrained himself. There was something in the tone of the comment that indicated that it was entirely sincere.

At twelve midnight Grant's head hit the pillow in the guest room at the London H.Q. of the British Security forces. He lay awake for a while, his head spinning with pictures of Che Guevara, Carlos Marighella and Fidel Castro. He slept fitfully that night. Waking twice in a hot sweat with the sheets rumpled at the bottom of the bed and Joanne's face covered in blood staring blankly at him from the bottom of a deep grave.

*

The next morning Grant rose early and went to the records department. He withdrew Daniel Judas's file.

Daniel Judas was the son of an affluent Harley Street surgeon with a large private practice. He was raised in Hampstead, North London and at the age of ten he went to Eton. His parents wanted a little stout English discipline beaten into their rather spoilt child. They had signed his name on to the school's books when he was born.

He was a skinny, rather effeminate child with a brain as sharp as a razor and a mop of dark hair covering his skinny face. His house master once described him as *'brilliant at annoying teachers, not by his behaviour, but rather by his immense capacity to show up their incompetence or their unacceptably authoritarian commands.*' He obtained ten A's at 'O' level and straight A's at 'A' level. His favourite subject, history, soon became too small for him and he obtained a place at Trinity College, Cambridge to study Philosophy, Politics and Economics in the Tripos.

He was a quiet teenager. His tutor in politics at Cambridge soon recognised his brilliance but felt a slight sense of pity at his inability to socialise and relax. *'He was a rather intense young man,'* were the words of his tutor in Philosophy, *'lacking in social graces'*, which was surprising considering his school background. At the age of twenty two he entered the Foreign Office after a little nepotistic wining and dining by his parents with the head of the FO recruitment sector and a free hernia operation.

When Grant read the next part of the file he understood more about the conversation they had held in the Pub the night before.

Daniel Judas's parents were killed by the Baader-Meinhof group in 1971 in a bombing raid carried out on a US army base in Frankfurt where his father was working as a forces medical officer. Within six months Daniel Judas had learnt every fact, figure, personality and act ever connected to the group.

He joined MI6 in October 1973 and had only one aim. To achieve such status within the service that he could command anti-terrorist operations within and outside of Europe. He would then destroy the men and women who had murdered his parents. He never made that position of command because of his basic personality defects and his inability to communicate with others, and therefore to lead men.

He was, however, the foremost authority historically and factually on terrorism and terrorists in Western Europe. At thirty seven he had reached his zenith and plateaued. He was and would always be invaluable in any anti-terrorist organisation. His field activities were however restricted to advisory only. The outside of the file was marked 'Field Controlled'.

George Grant put down Judas' personal file and stretched his arms out above his head.

"Is that all Sir?" the filing clerk on level two inquired.
"Yes, I've seen enough."
"I'll replace the file then, Sir."
Grant left the room and headed for the seventh floor. As he climbed the stairs a figure came hurtling round the corner and bumped into his shoulder. He stumbled. The figure tripped and regained balance immediately.
"Watch where you're going, you clot," she yelled. Grant saw a flash of angry blue eyes and then she was gone. He picked up a pearl earring set in a gold leaf and put it into his pocket.
His security clearance was high enough for him to be able to pull the file on everyone in the service up to his own scale. Judas was a scale four. So was Grant. Scale three was for overseas Directors. Scale two for undercover and double agents. Scale one for the Director General and the heads of department worldwide. The day before Judas had proudly boasted that he, of course, had been given special clearance to inspect all files as a part of the Beta cell operation.
Grant entered room 718.
"Good morning, George. You're early."
"Hello Daniel. Let's start shall we?"
"Keen to get on?"
"No Dan, keen to get it over with and get out in the field." Grant could see this hurt Judas but it was the truth.

*

"Terrorist organisations Past and Present." The lights dimmed. The screen lit up with the words of terror. A list of human beings with inhuman aims. Grant shivered for the hundredth time and concentrated.
The Baader-Meinhof gang, (Red Army Faction) Germany; the Red Army (Sekigun) Japan; Black September in Palestine; PFLP (the popular front for the liberation of Palestine); Black June, (the

corrective movement for Al Fatah) Palestine. The Provisional Irish Republican Army (Provos); The Armee Revolutionaire Bretonne and the Action pur La Renaissance de la Course in France. Republic Malakau Selatan in Holland. Euzkadi Ta Askatasna, (ETA) Spain. The Croatian Revolutionary brotherhood in Yugoslavia. The Turkish Peoples Liberation Army in Turkey. The Red Brigadein, Italy. The International Federation of Freedom Fighters (IFFC) in the Middle East and so many more."

The list of terror was never ending. The destruction horrifying. The pain and mutilation caused in each case stultified Grant. Every country seemed to have the cancer. Every state was infected. Nowhere seemed safe. And still Judas continued.

"In 1978 the following major terrorists acts were perpetrated:

London: Jan 4th, Black June believed behind killing of the PLO's representative in London.
Nicosia: Feb 18th, PFLP murder Egyptian Editor Yusef Sebai then hijack.
Cyprus Airways Jet. Egyptian Commando raid misfires. 15 die.
Turin: March 9th, 47 Red Brigade members tried in court.
Rome: March 10th, Red Brigade murder Judge Rosario Berardi and a prison official.
Rome: March 16th, Red Brigade kidnap Aldo More and kill 5 guards. **Rome:** May 10th, Aldo Moro found dead.
Kuwait: June 15th, PLO representative found assassinated by Black June. **Brussels:** June 24th, Iraqi Embassy bombed by PLO.
London: July 9th, General Al-Naif former Iraqi Prime Minister killed by Iraqi Secret Service.
London: Jury 26th, Britain expels 11 Iraqi diplomats for involvement in terrorist acts.
London Beirut and Paris: PLO gunmen bomb, machine gun and invade embassies of Iraq in each town.
Karachi: August 2nd, Gunmen attack Iraqi Consulate. One dead, one wounded.

Paris: August 3rd, PLO representative assassinated by Black June. **London:** August 20th, El Al air crew bus attacked by Black June. One dead, one wounded. **Dusseldorf:** September 6th. Police kill Peter Stoll of Baader-Meinhof. **Milan:** September 13th, Police arrest Red Brigade suspect with apartment full of guns and explosives. **London:** September 15th, Astrid Proll of Baader-Meinhof, arrested in Finchley where she has worked for 10 months. **Dortmund:** September 24th. Angelika Speitel and Michael Knoll of Baader-Meinhof, arrested after shoot out."

Judas switched on the lights.
"That's just one of the quieter years, George."
"My God. Is no-one safe?"
"Don't worry old man. It affects everyone that way. I've lectured to a hall with forty hardened anti-terrorist officers in it at the start of the lecture. At the end there were twenty one. The rest had either been sick or had taken 'some air', at some stage. Admittedly the slides I show are not pretty but they are factual."
They broke for lunch and started again at two o'clock that afternoon.

Judas outlined the training and indoctrination of terrorists throughout the world. Grant quietly took notes using the reading light beside his cinema seat.

*

That evening, lying on his bed in the guest room, he read them through.

Carlos Marighella, 'the guru', summarised the training: *'you can only become a good fighter by learning the art of fighting.'*

The training is a combination of political or religious indoctrination and military procedure. The wide skills should include physical training; driving all sorts of mechanised transport on land, sea and air; knowledge of mechanical communication,

electronics, geography, topography, chemistry, forgery, first aid, and most important the handling of weaponry, submachine guns, revolvers, automatics and larger weapons. The best instructors in the world today are the Arabs and the Palestinians. There are numerous training camps in the Middle East set up to train men and women for guerrilla activities. Baalbek in Lebanon was the most widely known camp in the early seventies.
Although most were keen pupils, Andreas Baader was described by an instructor as akin to a tourist. *'He was more interested in smoking dope and making love than training.'*

Jusad had said "The training does not compare with that of our British SAS, your own training, George, or the German GSG9, but it is supplemented by the cruelty and viciousness of the recruits.

Disguise is also a major training area. Prague, the centre of the world for plastic surgery, has played host to many re-vamped terrorist faces. In the early seventies, Egypt had a large hand in training terrorists but since the Yom Kippur war this had fizzled out and Libya, Iraq, Algeria and the USSR have taken over.

The camps at Hit, Habbanga and Baghdad in Iraq and at Nahar-al-Barad near Tripoli have all been strong bases for terrorist training. The camp at Tocra in Libya was at one time capable of training 5,000 men!

Finally, the major force in terrorism today is the KGB. Carlos Marighella himself was trained in Cuba by General Vitito Simenov of the Soviet KGB. Lumumba University in Moscow is a sieve for KGB agents collected from the third world students who are offered free education there. From these a very small percentage are trained by Department V, the KGB assassination and sabotage squad. The 'Dirty Tricks department'. On the surface, the Soviet Union condemns terrorism, but underneath they are a major supplier, trainer and manipulator in the international terrorism field. The head of the department is currently Colonel Vladimyr Zachristov.

The United States have a similar setup to train and supply guerrillas for their Latin American neighbours. Take Nicaragua for instance. Their network is, however, less developed."

Grant closed his notebook and tried to sleep, and so the second day of training had finished.

*

At 9.30pm after the third day of training George Grant raised himself from the rather hard bed and walked over to the window of his room in the MI5 building. Old Church Street seemed a thousand miles away. Reality seemed a lifetime ago. Peace, safety and happiness seemed merely a transient stage interspersed between periods of anarchy. Where was the reason? The reasonableness? The religion? The charity? He suddenly felt very alone, very small and frightened.

Grant dressed, picked out a coat and went down to the foyer. The security guard waved and the plate glass window opened, releasing him into the outside world. It was raining. He was just turning the corner into the car park when he heard a small smash. He walked towards the Alfa. A pair of car headlights shone directly into his eyes. For a moment he was blinded. He ducked and dodged to the side of the glare, then the lights went off.

There was someone leaning over the windscreen of the Alfa Romeo. He walked over quietly.

"What are you doing? stealing my windscreen wipers?" She turned round suddenly and glared at him.

"Is this your idea of parking? You selfish oaf, you've left me approximately 4½ inches of space to get out of."

"Well, it's my car but..."

"So move it. I've been trying to get out for 20 goddamn minutes. I'm due at an armaments and tech meeting at this very moment and this bloody penis substitute is blocking me in."

He reversed the Alfa out and stopped. She moved her car and drew up beside him. In the glow of her car's inside lights Grant noticed the blue eyes again.

"Do you want to jon me for dinner?" He asked.

"Are you kidding? It's 9.30. You've just caused me half an hour of hassle. I'm tired and I want to go to bed and I've got another meeting to go to right now!"

"OK, let's have breakfast then?"

She smiled for a split second then returned to her charge.

"You must be a new boy."

"Perhaps, what about dinner then?"

"Are you always so persistent?"

"No, I tell you what, I see you've lost an earring whilst you were reversing into my car. If I find it, will you have dinner with me?"

She thought for a moment. It was clear that she knew the earring had been lost earlier in the day. She smiled knowing he could not possibly find it.

"You have one minute. It's raining. If you really want to scrabble around in the puddles, the least I can do is have dinner with you after the meeting."

"Is it a deal? Dinner for the earring?"

"OK!"

Grant parked his car and got out and locked it. The heavens were open and the rain was coming down in buckets. She started her engine. He walked over and got into her passenger seat.

"It's not out there," he said.

"You didn't even look!" He reached into his pocket and produced the pearl earring set in the gold leaf.

"The Dorchester. OK with you?"

Marianne Marchant didn't get to bed till 6 o'clock that morning, but she had laughed more in those few hours than she had for ten years.

CHAPTER 6
GENERAL RANDOLF'S STRATEGY

On Sunday morning, at eight o'clock sharp, Grant awoke with a cracker of a headache and drooped out of his aged pine double bed in Old Church Street. He washed and shaved, then dawdled through to the kitchen for breakfast.

'Why do all kitchen floors seem so goddamn cold in the morning?' He wondered as he switched on the coffee percolator. Over a steaming hot plate of lean bacon and poached eggs he opened the Sunday Times. The front page contained only one feature. It stretched the full width of the page. There wasn't even room for the advertisement for 'Harrods' which usually occupied the bottom right-hand corner. The headline read:

'ARMY GENERAL HITS OUT AT GOVERNMENT'S INABILITY TO TACKLE TERRORIST ONSLAUGHT.'

Half the article was taken up with the public statement by General Randolf condemning the government's handling of the terrorist wave. The other half was a list of the top Armed Forces, Police and Government men and women murdered in the last eight months by terrorists. The total was three hundred and eighty four.

Grant read the cover word by word then turned to the full text of the public statement inside. He left his breakfast to go cold. The statement contained three main points. Firstly, it suggested the passing of a new Emergency Powers Against Terrorism Act, allowing the police vastly increased powers of questioning, arrest, detainment and interrogation. Secondly, it suggested that the Army be deployed nationwide to keep the peace and aid the police in their inquiries. Thirdly, it suggested that a vote of no confidence in the Government and its present policies should be raised. Grant sat stunned.

*

The Prime Minister made a number of telephone calls between 8 and 9am that Sunday morning. One to Sir John Epcot, one to Lord Carver, calls to the Secretary of State for Defence and the Defence Secretary. Finally, to the Metropolitan Police Commissioner and to the Commanders in Chief of the Army, Navy and Air Force. The Special Executive Committee for National Security would convene at 12 midday at 10 Downing Street.

*

A small wooden fire was lit in the second conference room on the ground floor at number 10, Downing Street. The walls were painted light blue and cream, the curtains were dark blue velvet and the Georgian furniture highly stained combined to give the room an ominous and serious feel.

At 12.05pm on 5th August 1988 the Special Executive Committee for National Security sat expectantly awaiting the arrival of its chairman. The Prime Minister of Great Britain.

The double oak doors opened.

"Gentlemen," Margaret Thatcher said as she walked crisply in and sat down without ceremony. The atmosphere was set by the tone of her entry. Businesslike, efficient and serious. "I have a problem. No, we all have a problem, but mine is the ultimate responsibility for solving the problem. This terrorist war is undermining business confidence in Great Britain. Investment funds are being channelled abroad. This is a disastrous state of affairs for industry in this country. But much more importantly, people are dying out there in our streets. Over one thousand so far this year and we have four and a half months of the year still to go.

We do not want this to continue. The country wants it to stop. We gentlemen all want it to be stopped. So why has it not been stopped?"

"Madam, if I may?"

Lord Carver was interrupted by the Prime Minister.

"Not you Sam. Mr Defence Secretary, let's start with you shall we?"

"Well, I've been in touch with the Metropolitan Police Commissioner and the head of the Anti-Terrorist Squad. They didn't have time to prepare a full report but I have a summary of the situation from them in front of me now, Prime Minister."

"Read it, Mr McNaughton".

"I'll paraphrase it, if I may?"

"Fine."

"As far as we have been able to ascertain from our normal sources it is not one single group of terrorists who are responsible. At least ten, maybe more groups have been active in the country. The targets have been so diverse that we cannot conclude any one section of the population is the target. There seems to be no one sole aim or strategy. It is more of a free for all, an orgy of violence unleashed on our system."

"As if to test the system?" It was Field Marshal Carshalton, Commander in Chief of the British Army who spoke.

"Yes, you could say that." McNaughton continued. "Many of the terrorist campaigns in the country and abroad end due to lack of funds. That has been the case with all except the IRA campaigns. What we find hard to fathom in this case is the diversity of the targets and the lack of publicity. It is difficult to pinpoint the aggressors or their aims. And the funds don't seem to be running out which is very odd."

"What suggestions do you have Mr. McNaughton?" The Prime Minister was becoming agitated by his negative approach.

"Well, the Special Branch Forensic Department have been examining three recent bombings. The Stringfellows' bomb, the Harrods' bomb and the Israeli Embassy bomb. All three were differently made, detonated differently and used different explosives. No one group would bother to create three different types of bomb for similar size jobs. It's a waste of time and money. We therefore assume these were perpetrated by three different groups."

"Which groups, Mr. McNaughton?" The direct question.

"Well, the Harrods bomb smacks of the IRA. Although as you know no-one has claimed it. But the resemblances to last Christmas' Harrods' car bomb are substantial Prime Minister."

"And the others?"

"The Israeli Embassy bomb is a Palestinian job but we do not know which group. Black September are the most likely but we're not sure. Again it's unclaimed. Very strange indeed."

"I see. What about Stringfellows?" Mrs Thatcher pressed on.

"Well, that's the strangest of the lot. Without doubt, it was neither the IRA nor any of usual groups."

"How do you know that?" Field Marshal Carshalton interjected.

"Well, the detonation was the same as the Israeli Embassy bomb but the reports which our men have submitted, together with the forensic evidence and the report from Delta, show that it doesn't exhibit the characteristics of any known terrorist group. Furthermore, this one has been claimed!"

"By whom?" The Prime Minister interjected.

"A group, or person, called INTERFERON."

"Who?" Field Marshal Carshalton asked.

"I.N.T.E.R.F.E.R.O.N." McNaughton spelt it out.

"What do we know about them?" The Prime Minister demanded.

"Next to nothing I'm afraid! They have never operated in the UK before and we do not know what nationality their operatives are. In fact we don't know a single person even vaguely connected with the group".

"Lord Carver, is MI5 in the same situation?" The Prime Minister fired the question like a bullet.

"I'm afraid so Prime Minister. I understand the name was used by an unidentified caller to the father of one of the victims of the Stringfellows' bombing".

"Do you have a transcript of the conversation?"

"No Ma'am, but we have a transcript of the subject's recollection of the conversation."

"Mr McNaughton, has the phone now been tapped and traced?"

"Yes Ma'am, since the call we have installed all the usual surveillance equipment. But let's not get too bound up in detail."

"What's your view, Lord Carver?" The P.M. asked.

"We think that it was a personal attack against Mr Goldstein connected to his and our operations in Libya a few months ago." Lord Carver replied.

"I see. I am sorry Sam. We all have to bear the constant threat to our families that go hand in hand with our positions. Now, Sir John, what do you have for me?"

"Well, it's strange Prime Minister, ever since SUBSEC was set up, MI6 has had practically nothing to contribute. From our information foreign involvement in this situation appears to be zero. I for my part cannot believe that is the case. Our agents in the USSR have heard nothing of any Russian involvement, above the normal money channelling to the IRA which has been going on for years. There is no information that we can ascertain from within the KGB which suggests any connection with our present problem. In fact they have repeatedly condemned it at the highest level.

Likewise, the CIA have confirmed, as we would expect, that US involvement remains at zero level except, once again, for the channelling of funds from the American Irish to the IRA. There has been no noticeable increase in the flow of those funds as far as they can detect. In fact, it has dropped a little since the start of our problem. Presumably due to the effect which these acts have on the contributors when they see them on American TV.

General Gaddafi is a different kettle of fish altogether. There has been some activity diplomatically going on between him and the Eastern Block for years, as we all know but once again no visible increase over the past year. Unfortunately our sources in Libya have not turned up with anything positive."

"You don't sound convinced, Sir John. Why?" The Prime Minister pressed.

"Well I have an old contact out there who I personally admire a great deal. He is a personal friend and I have relied upon him on frequent occasions for advice and counsel. He has sniffed something in the air that he doesn't like."

"How sound is he, Sir John?"

"Well, the depends Prime Minister. We are in contact in a purely personal capacity. He is not connected with MI6 and never has been, but he's been helpful to me on frequent occasions on various jobs."

"Do I take it that you cannot reveal your source's name?"

"Yes, Ma'am."

"Why, for God's sake?" Field Marshall Carshalton interjected, astonished.

"Because he's known to more than one of us around this table. He has now retired from his work and lives in the Middle East. He has given enough to his country already. I wouldn't put him through any further battles, even if it meant losing my job here and now!"

"Admirable sentiments Sir John, but bloody useless to us don't you think?" Field Marshall Carshalton retorted.

"Easy Jack," the Prime Minister cut in. Field Marshall Jack Carshalton sat back in his chair and turned away from Sir John Epcot. The tension in the room steadied.

Lord Carver cut in: "What does this man, whom you will not name, have to say?"

"Well he has only just sent his first impression. But he says there is an unhealthy silence which has descended on his contacts in the Middle East. A calm before the storm so to speak. Someone has imposed a curfew, a blanket on talk and for the first time in many many years it is being observed. No-one is saying anything. He feels fear is the key."

"So who does he feel is behind the black out?" Lord Carver asked.

"That I can't tell you yet. But I consider that it must be a country not merely a single terrorist group. The fear is too widespread for one group to have been responsible and the funds involved are too great."

There was a short pause in the conversation as they all considered this news.

"Thank you, Sir John." The Prime Minister said. "Now I must turn to a rather distasteful topic which is related to this matter." The Prime Minister turned to Field Marshall Carshalton.

"You have read the statement made by General Randolf, I take it?"

"Yes, Prime Minister." Field Marshall Carshalton was looking distinctly uncomfortable.

"What do you have to say about it and what can be done? You must understand Jack that we cannot have members of the armed forces making political statements to the Sunday Press which not only criticise the Government's present policies but also suggest new laws and actions to be taken. Via Her Majesty The Queen, I am the Commander-in-Chief of the forces and I do not like the tone or the content of General Randolf's public Statement."

"Here here," said Phillip McNaughton and the Defence Secretary in unison.

"Well Prime Minister I'm deeply sorry for the embarrassment caused. As you know General Randolf doesn't hold the same views as the army in general. But we live in a free country and I don't see that there is much I can do about him expressing his views to the Press."

"With respect Jack that is rubbish. You damn well can. If he perks up again, even a single word to the press, any syllable of his views on any new legislation required in this country to combat terrorism, I'll have his job away from him so fast he won't know what day it is. Then he can put himself forward for election to Parliament and he can then talk to the press all he wants, as a civilian. That is his right. But not as a General in my armed forces!"

"I understand, Prime Minister. I'll warn General Randolf."

"You do that Carshalton." The Field Marshall had received a clear order. He knew how to obey.

"Now what's to be done gentlemen? I need a decision from the committee. Is SUBSEC sufficient to combat this problem? Do you have enough men and funds? Mr McNaughton, Lord Carver, Sir John, what do you say? If you need legislation to back you up, Parliament will be returning in a month, I will need to get the Civil Service to draft it out as soon as possible."

The Defence Secretary answered first.

"Ma'am, the Police and the Anti-Terrorist squad are not content but let me at least say they are doing their best and they do not request any further powers at present.

"SUBSEC has only been operational for one month. I move that we give it more time to come together."

"We are a little short of time Mr McNaughton but I appreciate your caution. Lord Carver?" The Prime Minister barked.

"I agree with Phillip. SUBSEC is operational. Delta has been primed and is at work. We need more time, that's all."

"Sir John?"

"I'll agree with my colleagues but I must state that I have a very bad feeling about this Prime Minister. I would like your permission to reactivate D section as a safety measure."

"We will discuss that, Sir John, after the meeting. OK gentlemen it appears we agree to wait and see. Although God knows how many will die whilst we do so. Thank you for coming. Good day."

They all left except for Sir John Epcot. When the door finally shut he got out of his seat and went over to the drinks cabinet at the far end of the room under a tall oil painting of Earl Mountbatten of Burma.

"May I pour myself one?"

"Go ahead Disney. What's the problem?" The Prime Minister's mood had changed. The formal meeting was over. She was now talking to a friend and trusted adviser.

"I can't quite put my finger on it but I'll try to explain it to you by an analogy. When you have a river running through your land and its water level drops there are two possible reasons. Either because there hasn't been enough rain or someone upstream has been diverting the water. Now I know that there is a lowering of the level of my river of information about this terrorist wave. And I don't think it's because there hasn't been enough rain. God knows we've had a down pour in the last year."

"I see. Who is it Disney? Where is the blockage or the leak?"

"I don't know but I'm damn well going to find out."

"Do you need section D for that purpose?"

"Yes. But I also have overseas operations which may require D Section if we find that INTERFERON or whoever else is behind this is based abroad."

"Can you survive without Section D?"

"Frankly, yes Ma'am. But I would prefer to have their power now. It strengthens my hand. Our hand."

"You have my permission Disney. But you know I'm not happy about D section. You also know the label the Press gave them before they were disbanded, *'The death squad'*. That caused previous Governments acute embarrassment. Be subtle Disney, for all our sakes."

"I will. Thank you Ma'am."

*

At three o'clock that same day Grant answered the front door of his flat in Chelsea.

"Hello George, may I come in?"

"Judas! Of course. Can I offer you a coffee?"

"No thanks. I've got your brief here. It's hot off the press. The Director General has just returned from Downing Street. You are to be activated tomorrow. Your code name is Delta."

"How classical," Grant sat down in a deep lounge armchair and lit a Galoise.

"Now let's start at the bottom and work up. What do you make of the files I gave you yesterday?" Judas asked.

"We have a big problem."

"Obviously George. Be more specific."

"Well frankly the whole thing stinks."

"Come on George. I want your views then I'll colour them with my experience. Finally we will look at your brief and decide on your first moves."

"OK, Daniel. I see it like this. We seem to have a wide range of terrorist groups operating in the UK contemporaneously. That's unusual for a start. Previously we have been hit separately, spasmodically and for a reason. The IRA for instance wage a campaign then take a breather. The Palestinians commit an act of violence for a reason then melt away. No pattern, but at least we can see the reason because they always tell us afterwards. Presently with the density and frequency of the attacks the old pattern has been broken. We have to ask why? And how? For instance the money! Where is it coming from?" Grant continued. "There doesn't seem to be any single source. But we must not assume it is coincidental that so many terrorist groups are all operating here at the same time."

"Agreed." Said Judas.

"We must, however, assume that unless we are lucky and catch some of the terrorists soon, their funds should run out in the near future. This after all is by far the longest campaign we have ever suffered."

"Perhaps, but if they are all working separately what would then tell us about the ringmasters?"

"If we could cut off the funds we would accelerate the end of the campaign."

"We've tried that before. It's practically impossible. Diplomacy requires a certain freedom of movement of diplomatic luggage."

"So that leaves us with why?" Grant stubbed his cigarette out and continued. "The reasons for the IRA actions, the Palestinian actions and the German groups' actions are obvious. But the lack of publicity now is confusing. Also the dark horse seems to be INTERFERON."

"Once again we agree. Except I would add that INTERFERON is now believed by the Director to be a hoax."

"I've considered that view and I do not agree with it."

"OK, so what do you think we should do?"

"Show me the brief Judas. Then let's take it from there."

Judas opened his brief and pulled out one of the standard issue beige folders issued to all Government departments.

"Firstly in relation to Goldstein you may as well continue to operate under the cover of being hired by him. In that way you are given a raison d'être. If any of the Beta cells operating under SUBSEC comes into contact with you, use that as your excuse for investigation."

"Fine by me. It will, at least, pay the gas bill whilst I'm out in the field."

"Report to him anything relevant to the Stringfellows bombs but don't let him loose on the perpetrators' financiers if you do uncover them. We can't have him wading in and screwing up our operations just because we wants to avenge the murder of his daughter. Sir John has spoken to him to make that clear. Does he know about SUBSEC and my involvement with you?"

"Are you kidding? No way. He asked Sir John Epcot who he should hire to find his daughter's murderers. The DG then asked Goldstein to test you out. You passed. So here you are. As Delta! Next, this woman Galliani. Forget her, she's a dead end. We'll deal with her if and when the time comes."

"OK. If you say so." Grant replied. He was lying.

"Next your relationship with the Anti-Terrorist squad. Stay in touch, but don't let on that you're with us."

"Why? They already suspect it."

"Because it's irrelevant to them and the fewer people who know the safer it is for you and us."

"Makes sense. OK."

"Right. Your next move. We'd like you to start with the Palestinian bombing at the Israeli Embassy."

"Any reason?"

"Yes, because the Palestinians are the smallest group to have hit the country so far and so may be the easiest to trip. Their operations have accounted for only approximately 5% of the problem so far. Let's start small and work up."

"What will the rest of SUBSEC be up to whilst I am on the Palestinian group?"

They are working in Beta cells across the whole range here and abroad. Anything they discover will be reported to MI5 and MI6 and then by me to you. You will be used to double check and to fill in the gaps. You may find it all a little piece meal at the start but you'll pick it up."

"Judas. I'll need a gun."

"Sorry George. No chance of that. If you get near to trouble, I'll know. Well give you back up before you can say "bingo"! You'll contact me at this number. 6000600. It's a scrambled line. Never call from here, always use a phone box. If I want you I'll find you."

"Is it really that easy?"

"You'd better believe it." Judas got up and walked to the door. He turned round in the hall way and looked straight faced at Grant.

"Frankly, George I don't think you'll find you're involved to a very large extent. But I may be wrong." He left quickly. Grant sat quietly for a few minutes than grabbed his jacket and left.

CHAPTER 7
DO NOT TRUST THE TAILOR

Scotland Yard's Forensic department is situated in a squat new building near St Thomas' Hospital on the Southbank of the Thames. Grant flashed his security card and walked through the lobby then turned to the left. Professor Jacobs was to be found in the basement lab 4, the Pyrotechnics and Incendiary Devices Department.

"Good evening Professor, you're working late and on a Sunday too. Do they pay you overtime?"

"No way old chap. I'm Jacobs, who are you?"

"George Grant. I'm...."

Jacobs interrupted impatiently. "I know, I know. Inspector Duffy, told me you'd be around sooner or later. He said I should co-operate with you in every way possible. What can I do for you? As you can see, I'm very busy."

"Well, I've read your report on the Israeli Embassy bombing. I wanted a personal view from you on it. Your conclusions were purely technical."

"That's the way the anti-terrorist squad ask for them."

"So can you humour me please?"

Professor Sam Jacobs was a small chubby man with a greying beard and small rounded spectacles. His eyes had been poor since his early twenties when he'd spent too much time pouring over text books and too little time socialising. His first love, in his youth was gambling. His second love was the bomb. He was now 49 and had devoted the last ten years of his life to forensic research on and the analysis of bombs. His wife had threatened constantly to divorce him. He hardly knew his two sons but he loved them dearly. As a father when he was at home he was a brick, solid and dependable. As a scientist he was a skilled technician and an enlightened expert.

"My view, Mr. Grant, is one with which you will not agree."

"How do you know that professor?"

"Because it's the view of a Jew on a Palestinian terrorist bomb and you will think I'm biased."

"Maybe but tell me anyway."

"We are in for big trouble." The professor took off his glasses and walked over to an electron microscope. "Look here," Grant didn't move.

"Come on, don't be shy, look here!" He pointed to the Electron Microscope screen. He switched a knob and the screen lit up with an eerie green light. Grant lowered his head to the lenses and saw small strands of shiny material against a network of other fabric.

"Gold," the Professor said quietly.

"So what?" Grant asked politely.

The Palestinians always use plastic explosives in their bombs for embassies. They get it from two common sources. They steal it or they buy it on the black market. Either way it's traceable to one source or another."

"So which did this come from?"

"Neither!" the Professor turned off the screen.

"You mean you don't think it was a Palestinian bomb at all?"

"No, now don't jump two stairs when you haven't yet grasped the banister." The professor sat down on a tall stool and brushed nonexistent dirt from his white lab coat.

"The bomb was definitely a Palestinian one. All their normal methods of planting, detonating and positioning were used. But, and this is my point, it wasn't their normal explosive.

This was Cemtron. The most advanced and expensive plastic explosive on the market. It's British and it has only just been tested in the UK let alone the Middle East. I don't see how it could have gotten onto the black market so soon. The army only took delivery of it two months ago."

"Are you saying the army may have been involved?"

"Maybe, but I am saying it must have taken very big money to get this and most Palestinian terrorist groups don't have money to waste. Why use expensive stuff when their normal stuff would have been quite sufficient for the purpose. It's crazy. Unless they have money to waste."

"Or have a contact within the army or the firm which supplies it."

"Maybe so, may be so." Jacobs looked at Grant with respect and the creases at the side of his mouth showed for a second, indicating a flash of a smile.

*

George Grant slipped into the Alfa Romeo Spider and turned on the ignition. As he drove over Westminster Bridge and round Parliament Square the frown on his face deepened. Before he continued his investigation he had a personal call to make for Goldstein. He was beginning to feel distinctly uneasy about things. At each new turn he was encountering an unknown element. Something unusual about the terrorist wave. Something sinister. No publicity. High funds, no pattern, or was there a pattern? Was he just too entangled in the jigsaw to be able to see the whole picture. He parked on a double yellow line in Park Lane and walked up a flight of curved marble steps towards two large blue Georgian doors adorned with a massive brass knocker. Grant straightened his tie and knocked three times firmly. Two minutes went by and he knocked again. Without the warning of approaching footsteps the door swung open quickly.

"Oh bugger." Carmine Goldstein was wearing a silk kimono and nothing else at all.

"Good evening Carmine. May I come in?"

"What do you want Grant?" She spat the words into his right shoulder as Grant walked straight in.

"You're such a nice, hospitable young lady. So well mannered."

"Look." She held the door open and pointed outside into the evening darkness. "I don't want visitors thanks. And I certainly don't want you in my house."

"Come now Carmine, it's not yours."

She slammed the door and ran over to the lounge door at the far end of the carpeted hallway.

"You are my business Carmine. Your father wants me to keep an eye on you."

"What? He wants what?" Her brown eyes flashed with rage and indignation. "What for?"

"Can we sit down or is that too much to ask?" Grant smiled sweetly and stood still in front of her.

"OK, go in there. I'll be with you in a minute."

She headed for the stairway as Grant entered the lounge and sat down on a semi-circular couch in front of a large screen projector TV set. The room was plush to say the least. Opulence oozed from every inch of it. The gold plated fire place. The gold plated curtain rails. The gold plated poker and the deep pile carpets.

Carmine returned in a pair of leather trousers and a white cotton top and sat down in a cream armchair by the fireplace. Her black hair straight as an arrow was brushed back over her head. She wore no makeup and she looked flushed. Grant heard the front door slam.

"Boyfriend gone?"

"None of your business you nosey bastard. Now what has dad hired you for?"

"He thinks you may be in danger. He thinks the people who killed your sister may try to reach you."

"Jesus, really?" Suddenly the resentment evaporated.

"Well it's possible."

"Jesus," she turned her head and looked out of the bay window over the park. She was trembling. "Why?"

"I don't know Carmine. He's a rich man. He must have stepped on a lot of toes on his way up. I'm sure he has enemies out there."

"You bet. But why me?"

"Why your sister?"

"I see what you mean." She moved her arms across her torso and clasped herself as if cold. "That's terrifying. I don't know what to say."

The sound was barely perceptible. A rush of air, a thud, a small tinkle of glass onto the thick pile carpet. Carmine didn't really notice it at all. Grant looked up at the window and frowned. The whole bay window shattered into a thousand pieces and glass cascaded about the room. Cold air flooded in and those quiet rushes of air sounded four or five times around the lounge. A china vase exploded and a line of small holes appeared on the far wall facing the bay window.

"Get down!" Grant yelled and threw himself onto Carmine as the back of the sofa juddered with the impact of a bullet. Carmine Goldstein rolled under him on the floor. Her scream was a loud shrill guttural yell. The rushes of air stopped. Ten seconds later a car engine fired outside the bay window in Park Lane.

"Stay here. Stay down and don't move," Grant yelled as he climbed to his feet and ran across to the velvet curtains on one side of the bay window, flicking out the light switch on the way.

A silver Audi Quattro was pulling away southwards down Park Lane. The four wheel drive caused all the tyres to screech as they burnt the tarmacadum.

"Call the police immediately," he shouted, then smashed the remaining glass with his hand in the curtain and jumped out through the large frame onto the circular terrace at the front of the house. He ran to his car.

The Alfa Romeo Spider fired first time and he accelerated to 6000 revs in first gear. The 1750cc engine yelped with the strain then quietened as he rammed the car into second gear and accelerated past a Rolls Royce in the middle lane of the three lane highway past the Dorchester Hotel.

The Quattro was at least four hundred yards ahead with five cars between them. But Hyde Park Corner would slow it down. As the Quattro approached the lights they turned green and the two cars in front began to pull away slowly. The Quattro swerved between them and bounced off the door of a Ford in the outside lane. It screeched to the left up Piccadilly. Grant swerved into the slow lane and turned left past the Hotel Intercontinental coming up behind the Quattro on Piccadilly. Now the gunman braked for a second to allow the car on his inside to come up near to his back bumper then he swerved violently to his left in front of the car. The Quattro disappeared down a side road and the car in the slow lane jammed on his brakes and swerved 90 degrees to the left blocking the entrance to the street down which the Quattro had just disappeared.

Grant braked hard and yanked the Alfa to the left. The rubber of the front wheels hit the kerb at forty miles per hour, the wheel rims connected with concrete and the bonnet of the Alfa jumped into the air and then crashed down onto the pavement and back onto the road heading North off Piccadilly. The Quattro had disappeared.

There was a junction at the end of the side street. Grant glanced both ways then cursed and accelerated away to his right. Tyre tracks on the tarmac indicated someone had skidded in that direction. The tracks could be someone else's. The road bent sharp left and then right as it ran between the tight restaurants of Shepherds Market. Grant reached the T junction of Hertford Street and Curzon Street and saw the Quattro accelerating away to the East.

He turned, narrowly avoiding an oncoming black cab and slammed his foot flat on the floor with his left hand tearing at the gear lever. A Police car on the opposite side of the road saw the Quattro coming and U turned into Grant's path. The Alfa swerved into the wrong lane and weaved between an oncoming truck and the police car, then raced away after the Quattro. They drove practically bumper to bumper around the West side of Berkley Square, then the Quattro braked hard and the Alfa collided bonnet first into the Quattro's boot. The radiator grills smashed and steam billowed out of the radiator. The temperature gauge on the dashboard moved into the red.

"Shit!" Grant shouted. He knew he had about one mile left in the car before the engine overheated and the pistons blew. The Quattro accelerated up Davies Street and came up behind a delivery van at the junction with Oxford Street. It swerved to overtake the van and went through red lights into Oxford Street.

THE SCORPION'S STING

The driver's door impacted as the radiator of a London cab cut straight into the driver's arm. The Quattro lurched sideways and spun across Oxford Street balancing precariously on two wheels. The roof collided with a lamp post which became embedded three feet into the metal roof. Finally, crumpled and exhausted of momentum the car collapsed back onto the road. The driver's head rebounded off the steering wheel and out through the driver's side window and smashed down onto the bonnet of the black cab.

Grant braked hard and screeched to a halt slamming the bumper of the Alfa into the side of the cab. His body jerked forwards and his head thumped into the steering wheel then bounced back onto the headrest. He sat dazed for a second then struggled out and ran to the point of the collision.

Grant leant over the bonnet of the black cab and saw the face of the driver of the Quattro.

"You!" he gasped.

Her fair hair was splayed across the bonnet of the cab, blood dripping slowly onto the dark paintwork. Grant lifted her head gently and looked down upon the pretty but catastrophically fractured face of Fiona Galliani. Her eyes opened and flickered. Through her pain she recognised Grant and her lips parted. Blood trickled down her bottom lip. She tried desperately to speak, to whisper. Grant bent over, his ear touching her nose.

"George," the word came out as quietly as a falling pin on a deep pile carpet. "Help INTERFERON. They are good. Beware the Tailor..." she gasped in pain. "He is the ....Grim .... Reaper." Her blue eyes closed and her breath subsided. The blood stopped dripping. Fiona Galliani had died.

The Police sirens grew closer and louder. Grant turned and ran. He ran fast and hard down Oxford Street and turned north into James Street, then up into Wigmore Street. He was suddenly afraid, confused and dazed. His natural instincts took over. Get away. Get free. You need time to think.

CHAPTER 8
ENTER THE SCORPION

At 7am on a Monday morning in August 1988 a long black Mercedes drew up in front of a large stately building on the outskirts of Guildford, Surrey. The security guards at the door, both dressed in plain clothes to avoid attracting attention, walked down the three steps across the small semi-circular courtyard and out through the gateway onto the road. The chauffeur pressed the appropriate button and the opaque reflective glass descended.

"Candlestick 452," he said.

"OK, Sir, I'll open the gate," the guard responded.

The Mercedes drifted quietly in behind the large stone wall which kept the courtyard out of sight from the road. The nearest house was two miles away and very little traffic used the road. Privacy was all important. A tall figure in a dark mackintosh stepped out of the Mercedes and was up the steps into the Georgian building within seconds.

"Good morning Sir, the meeting is in the conference room as usual," the doorman bowed courteously.

"Good, get me a strong coffee, no milk."

He left his coat at the door and walked with speed to the conference room. As he reached the door he squared his shoulders and breathed in deeply. He walked in.

"Ah, good, you've arrived Candlestick. Please take your seat."

"Butcher, Baker, Tailor, Security," Candlestick said the words in his usual monotone. No feeling, no recognition or friendship, just business.

The man known as Tailor, at the end of the table began. "Gentlemen, NATUS is now in session. If you will all report your progress as usual, beginning with the Baker."

THE SCORPION'S STING

"Colleagues, we have thirteen more targets to hit before I can be sure that the current atmosphere and balance within the armed forces will be ready to begin conditioning the uninitiated for the new beginning. At present, my NATUS staff have been arranging holiday leave for those we will want abroad. The plan for the transfer of groups and equipment into position has all but been completed. I will present it at the end of this meeting for you to peruse and we will then consider it in detail at the next meeting. Suffice to say that General Randolf's public statement achieved the desired effect and the ball should now be set finally rolling towards our goal."

"Good Baker. May I ask you next Butcher?"

"The security services are inching closer to the terrorists, as we expected they would. I have slipped as many NATUS men into Beta Cells as I could possibly manage but not as many as I would have liked. As we all know the unsympathetic targets in industry and commerce have all but been silenced. We have 700 key men and women under our control, either directly or via kidnap and blackmail pressure. That is 180 more than at our last meeting. NATUS operatives are continuing through the list which we drew up in February. I estimate we will reach safety level by mid September. We are well on target gentlemen."

"Thank you Butcher. Candlestick maker?"

"Tailor, gentlemen. My plan is now complete. I typed it myself this morning and have brought a copy for each of you.

"Destroy them in the burner at the end of the room before you leave. If one of these falls into the wrong hands we will have to disband.

"You will see that I will require three men. A pilot, a cleaner and a missile expert. Execution of the plan will be simple if the expert does his job well. It would be best for him to be a NATUS man. The cleaner need not be NATUS but must be under our control. The pilot must be totally dependable."

The board all sat quietly and read the plan. Five minutes later Tailor spoke. "Quite superb Candlestick. Quite brilliant. It's so simple I'm surprised no-one has thought of it before. I'm impressed."

"Thank you, Chairman Tailor."

"I agree. It's fool proof, simple and totally undetectable. Worthy of a mind such as yours Candlestick."

"Thank you, Baker."

"Butcher, what do you think?" Tailor asked.

"I like it. It will work. But, as you all know it is only the first step. The army must be ready."

"It will be Butcher, don't fret." Baker replied with a hint of arrogance in his voice.

"Good, now two further points. Firstly, the publicity. Are we ready to bring it into operation?"

The Chairman left the question open to the whole Board.

"As soon as possible, so we can make use of the effect of General Randolf's statement." Baker replied. All agreed. Tailor continued.

"Next the Galliani affair. I understand Delta was there when she died. Is that correct?"

"Yes, Chairman Tailor." Butcher replied.

"Did she talk?"

"We don't know."

"Shit!" Tailor smashed his palm down onto the table. "I want Trattorini and her friends. I want ALL of them. Every one. Do you hear me? Butcher, Candlestick get them. Use Delta if need be. Make him lead us to them. Then destroy them. Give it first priority. Understand?"

"Yes, Sir." Butcher and Candlestick agreed in unison.

"Once Delta has achieved that, kill him. He's too dangerous to have around once that job is done. Also I want to know if she told him what she knew."

"Quite." Butcher replied.

"Right, that is all. Baker you'll find the pilot - yes?"

"Fine. I have one in mind." Baker replied.

"Good. Butcher, you'll deal with the missile expert and the cleaner. Don't forget to burn the files on the way out. I will deal with the publicity. Good day Gentlemen."

Tailor rose from his seat, picked up a copy of Candlestick's report and walked quickly to the door. He left three minutes later in a white Rolls Royce. No-one had seen him enter. No-one saw him leave. The meeting had been satisfactory. He would contact base that evening to report.

*

George Grant had stopped running later that evening and entered a call box.
"Inspector Duffy, please."
"He's not in the office now. Will you leave a message?"
"Tell him *Pain* will cull him first thing tomorrow morning."
Grant caught a cab home. When he reached Old Church Street he paid the fare and walked down towards the Thames. Halfway down he turned in to number 21 and let himself in through the side entrance. There was a note on the mat. He opened the envelope and pulled out a small white piece of Basildon bond writing paper.

"Do not trust the Tailor.
INTERFERON."

"INTERFERON are good," is what Fiona Galliani had said. The words of a dying terrorist. Maybe the concept of good in her mind was different from good in his mind. He poured himself a Bacardi Bloody Mary from the fridge and picked up the phone. His hand was shaking as he dialled.
"Hello, who is it?" she answered sleepily.
"George. Did I wake you?" He asked.
"No, I'm still asleep," she replied.
"Fancy an ice cream?"
"Where can you get one at three thirty in the morning?"
"Your fridge freezer."
"Come round, I'll unlatch the door," Marianne replied.
"I'll be there in two minutes."
He walked the short distance to Marianne's flat, which by coincidence was East by 1 mile along the King's Road. It was a 3rd floor new build with a small balcony overlooking an underwear

shop on the opposite pavement. He shut the door behind him and climbed the stairs, breathing deeply as he did so. Not because he was tired. More because he was excited

She was lying probably naked under a silk sheet on a king size double bed mattress on the floor of the bedroom. The Chinese blinds were pulled fully down but the orange glow of a street lamp lit the room with a dull warm incandescence. The sheet lay covering the her body. The smooth swell of her buttocks was accentuated by the paleness of the silk. Her dark hair lay over her shoulder blades. Even in sleep it seemed to maintain order. Grant stood looking at her for two minutes. She was so peaceful that he thought about letting her sleep on. But the thought faded as his libido fought it. He stripped and bent down over her running his tongue along the line of her back bone.

"Is that you George?"

"No, it's the milkman. I'm early this morning."

She slowly turned herself over and her hands wandered with almost sloth-like inactivity up his forearms and around the curve of his shoulders. She didn't open her eyes. Her lips parted. He kissed her so gently that she hardly felt his lips. Then his mouth glided tenderly down her chest. She raised her back into an arch as his tongue flicked gently across her left breast. The swell of her body heaved beneath him and her breath quickened slightly as his left hand slipped down her belly.

She adored making love with this man. It wasn't because he was attractive, she didn't find him particularly so. Rather animalistic in appearance. No, the pleasure came from the unknown limits and testing, the talking and caressing. They had no sexual barriers, no inhibited sexual secrets that evening. They both tore at each other like ravenous terriers at times and made love like tender butterflies at others. He seemed driven by a fire of passion as if trying to escape from the real world into their own erotic one. That night went on forever. And neither of them wanted the cold light of morning to come. But eventually it did.

At 6.30am Grant crawled off the mattress and walked naked through to Marianne's study. Her desk was littered with the tools of her trade. She was one of the three MI5 experts on armaments. Her bookcase was littered with tomes on airborne fighters, submarines built in thirty countries and explosives manuals. What a job! He sat there for a half hour thinking, then went into the breakfast room and filtered some fresh coffee. Marianne slipped up behind him and slid her slim arms around his stomach. He felt the softness of her groin on the back of his thigh and the warmth of her chest on his back. He sighed with the realisation that her body soothed his pain, even if it made him feel guilty.

"Can't you sleep, George?"

"No, I've got a problem running around my mind."

"Do you want to talk about it?" She asked.

Marianne was a level 5 operative in MI5 working in the Admin. She had been Beta cell filtered and was involved in a cell allotted to investigate the materials and armaments used by the terrorists.

The evening before had been a strange mixture of searching and discovery. She had built up plenty of psychological barriers in her 32 years. Scarred not by pain, but just by experience. She didn't drop her emotional defences easily.

Her parents had lived in North Yorkshire in the small mining village of Corby. When the coal had run out her father was made redundant and he had just wilted away. He had given his life to the mining industry and he couldn't understand how they could throw him away without so much as a thank you. The redundancy money was not enough. He died of liver sclerosis three years later.

Marianne Marchant told him that she had left her local secondary school at 16 and travelled the world with a rucksack and a boyfriend. By the age of 23 she had worked in fifteen different countries and spoke three languages fluently.

She returned to England in 1979 and took a degree in languages at Oxford, as a mature student. In 1981 she had landed a Diplomatic post in the British Consulate in Cuba and by 1985 she had been involved in the running of a considerable number of MI6 operations in the Caribbean Section headed by Mr St.George Cumberbache. She then went on to liaise with the CIA's armaments special arm and co-chaired UK/US arms procurement negotiations for 6 months.

She returned to the UK in 1987 to work for MI5 in her chosen area of interest, armaments.

"Want some coffee?" He asked.

"Yes, I'll make it. You sit down and pour out the problem. I'm a good listener." She replied.

"It'll sound odd."

"Most of your life probably is George."

"Where do I start?"

"Try Joanne's death."

"You know I'm looking for her killers?"

"It's the only thing that was capable of pulling you together George. I've seen your file."

Grant looked at Marianne and suddenly lost the guilt he had felt about reading her personal file.

"I'm afraid it's more complicated than that Mari."

"Tell me," she said casually as she tipped coffee into the filter.

"The basic facts are these. Firstly, there is the terrorist wave. Top men and women throughout the country being killed from industry, the army, navy, trade unions, the lot." He summarised the occurrences of the past months in detail. He left nothing out. Even the briefing by Daniel Judas at MI5 headquarters. It helped him to sort things out in his mind. He knew her security classification didn't warrant it, but he didn't care. Explanations often help the explainer more than the explainee.

They drank the coffee and she was silent for a minute after he had finished.

"Do you think this woman Galliani did detonate the Stringfellows' bomb herself or do you accept the MI5 view that she was tricked by the Libyans?"

"Before last night I accepted Lord Carver's view. But Galliani said herself she was bound up with INTERFERON when she died. Why should she lie then? I believe she was part of INTERFERON. In which case she must have detonated the Stringfellows' bomb. Either her, or her girlfriend, Diane what's her name."

"So the Service was wrong about her."

"Yes, or they lied. Lord Epcot told me that Galliani had left the country."

"Why would they lie?"

"Because they are using me as a sweeper. A double check. If it serves their purpose to feed me with the odd piece of false information they won't hesitate to do so. I'm only a tool being used for an end."

"I'm prepared to accept that George, but where does that leave you? Do you play it straight with them or do you hold back and perhaps protect yourself?"

"I don't know. I'm in the middle, you see. I have been given high level security clearance. The services of the police and the resources of the Anti-Terrorist Squad are behind me and yet I'm on my own. On paper I'm working privately for Solomon Goldstein."

"What will you tell him?"

"What do you suggest?"

"That depends upon whether you trust Goldstein."

"Well, he's already been hit. I suppose I must trust him. He also has some connection with the security services because they put him onto me, as a disguised route of hiring me. INTERFERON still want to murder his other daughter. He may well be next. I have to believe he is trustworthy.

The problem, as I see it is that I'm not just dealing with a straight investigation into who killed his daughter and Joanne. There are wider political, and I suppose, national interests at stake. I can't tell him everything because he may go and do something silly. After all, he has the money, God knows and lots of it. He also has the manpower to run a private army and probably does."

"But do you trust him?"

"Yes Mari, if I need finance or a bolt hole if this thing really blows up, I would turn to him."

Marianne finished her coffee and went into the bedroom. She returned in a small white cotton shirt.

"A thought has occurred to me George. One which I don't think you've considered."

"What?"

"Maybe this Galliani woman was trying to kill you, not Goldstein's daughter. It is a bit of a coincidence you being there when the shots were fired. Why didn't she wait until you had left?"

"I don't know. I don't think so. If she did wanted to kill me why did INTERFERON leave that note at my flat. They must want to contact me in some way."

"Perhaps." Marianne responded.

*

Grant phoned Inspector Duffy at 8am sharp. He was at his desk in Scotland Yard.

"What the hell happened to you? Where the hell have you been? I've had an all points out on you since the Galliani woman was identified," Duffy growled.

"I needed time to think, Inspector."

"Well get your arse over here now!" The Inspector slammed the phone into its cradle and cursed.

Grant arrived at New Scotland Yard at eight-forty am. He went straight to the Duffy's office.

"Ah, Grant at last, come with me," before Grant could answer, Chief Inspector Duffy had moved his large red frame towards a side door and then had paced quickly into the adjoining room.

"This is Professor Sam Jacobs from Ballistics. Have you met?"

"We have, hello Professor." Grant nodded.

"Pleased to meet you again," he replied. "I've got news for you about the shooting in Park Lane last night."

Grant sat down and lit a Galoise whilst Chief Inspector Duffy paced about the room, too agitated to sit.

"You're a very lucky man. Lucky to be alive. Do you know what saved your life Mr Grant?"

"Poor aim?"

"No. Parallax error. The terrorist fired the gun through the windows. They were double glazed. The first two shots went through two panes of glass and the bending of the light from the lounge through the glass made her aim inaccurate by about four inches at that range."

"After the first two shots we were moving and avoided the rest," Grant replied.

"Thank God for physics eh? Anything else?" Duffy asked.

"Only one further point. The bullets were fired from a MAKAROV PISTOL. It is a Russian 9 millimetre pistol with a maximum range of 54 yards. It can fire 36 rounds per minute. It's in standard use throughout the Russian supplied armies of Eastern Europe. Most good killers use rifles not pistols.

Terrorists usually get their hands on these through Arab Intermediary groups who source from Soviet arsenals. It is solid and reliable and a widely used terrorist weapon.".

"OK, OK, enough," Inspector Duffy bellowed. "Off you go Professor and play with some more guns. Come with me Grant." The Inspector was already through the adjoining door into his office.

"Now, what happened last night?" he demanded as Grant sat down.

Grant explained the events of the evening in detail.

"Did she say anything before she died?" Inspector Duffy finally asked.

"Yes. She said she was in INTERFERON."

"The same group which threatened Solomon J Goldstein before the Stringfellows' bomb?"

"Yes, why did it take so long for the Anti-Terrorist Squad to connect that call with the Stringfellows' file?"

"It didn't. I was asked to lift that part of the file by MI5 before I handed it down to Mike Douglas and you."

"Devious sods. There is something more." Grant reached into his pocket and put the death threat note onto Duffy's desk.

'Do not trust the tailor.
INTERFERON'

"What does it mean?"

"I've got no idea, Inspector. Perhaps it's because they know I'm working for Goldstein, or for Scotland Yard, or for MI5 or 6?"

"You'd better be careful Grant, this bunch obviously don't make false threats. I want you to dictate a full report on last night then you are free to go. Do you know what you're going to do next?"

"Yes, I want all the information you've got on Fiona Galliani and her friend Diana, what's her name?"

"Diane Trattorini. We got that from the neighbours at Belgrave Square. Go down to records and tell them."

"Thanks. I've got a few other loose ends to follow up."

"What do you mean by that?" Inspector Duffy disliked vagueness and was beginning to understand that Grant made few moves without a considerable amount of forethought. Grant did not want to tell him he would be investigating the Israeli Embassy bombing for MI5, so he stood up.

"Just a personal matter for Mr. Goldstein."

"Keep me informed Grant. Oh, by the way. I found out that Mike was away from work all morning on the day he died. The night before, he had been out nightclubbing with a tall blond bird."

"If that is true, he did not have time to get any hot news."

"Unless..." Chief Inspector Duffy shot a quick glance at Grant to see if he had reached the same conclusion.

"The silly bugger wasn't knocking off a witness was he?"

"A witness who was a waitress?" the Chief Inspector responded.

"Oh Lord."

In the Records Department, Grant sat in a government chair and opened the large green cardboard file.

"Fiona Galliani"
Age: Twenty five.
Educated at Winchester School for Girls and the Dragon School, Oxford. She graduated in Politics, Philosophy and Economics from Cardiff University, then was employed in local government for six months before leaving her job. Reason unknown. Parents: wealthy land owners in Surrey, Italian second generation immigrants. Foreign journeys: Palestine twice for protracted periods. Suspected

further trips to: Syria and Italy. Not confirmed. The rest of the file had been removed. The corners of the removed pages were still threaded through the treasury tag in the file. Someone had doctored the file in a hurry. He closed it and turned to the other file on the desk.

"Diane Trattorini"
Age: Twenty nine.
Italian born and educated. Upper middle class girl. Degree in Biology from Milan University. No employment since leaving University. Came to the UK in 1987. Odd jobs taken in restaurants and bars. Recorded personality disorders. Drug use convictions. History of severe Schizophrenia in her early teenage years.

The rest of her file was missing.

Grant sat looking at the two doctored files and felt an uneasy mood of frustration well up inside. MI5 must have something on these women.

Later that same day, Grant rang Daniel Judas. "Dan. I need the files of Fiona Galliani and Diane Trattorini."

"Galliani, we have. I don't know the other one, but you may find one. I'll request them and leave them in room 118. Ask Security for the key. OK?"

"Good. Thanks."

Grant took a taxi to Lambeth and went straight to room 118 at the Security Services HQ.

When he opened the files, what he saw shook him for a second. The papers missing from Scotland Yard's files were there. They had been removed by MI5 without Scotland Yard's knowledge.

Was that the product of higher rank, more power or perhaps mistrust?

Fiona Galliani was of Italian extraction. Her parents were second generation English land owners. Her grandparents had emigrated to the UK in the early 20th century and purchased land in Surrey. The family came from Milan. Fiona had spent a year after leaving the UK in Italy. Her whereabouts were unknown but someone had put a footnote to the travel section.

"Note photograph of customer at Red Brigade bank raid in Turin in 1984. Striking resemblance to F.G.?"

The photo was unclear. Two gunmen were holding up a bank in Milan. In the background were several customers. One had short straight hair and a hat.

He couldn't be sure it was Fiona, but there was a resemblance. The summary at the end of the file read as follows:

"An intelligent well off woman, she holds down a model's job and various other menial ones for short periods of time and travels widely. Exhibits lesbian tendencies, but dates men."

There was a footnote to the file which read as follows:

"Suspected involvement with terrorist organisations. Coincidences of time and place with terrorist acts are too strong to disregard. Turin, October 1984. London, November 1985. Cairo, April 1983. Politics: feminist, communist, anti-Capitalist. Involved in political marches in the UK. No hard evidence yet."

The evidence was hard now.

Next, Grant turned to Diane Trattorini's file. Grant read it slowly and carefully. Diane was quite a girl.

Diane Trattorini had been at a convent near Milan until the age of 18. The Convent specialised in teaching teenagers with severe psychological disorders. After failing her politics course at Milan University she had travelled to Lebanon and been trained in the Baalbek Terrorist camp for 6 months. She was a fully trained terrorist, but she had not been involved overtly in any terrorist act so far as the International Authorities could ascertain. She was allowed the freedom to come and go throughout Europe without more than the normal customs checks of her baggage. Her funds appeared to come from a Swiss bank account which kept her well supplied. She lodged with friends, always women, in London, Rome and Beirut. She was in Milan for a period of three months in mid 1984 and stayed with one Fiona Galliani.

Present whereabouts: London. Living with Fiona Galliani in Belgrave Square.

"That information is out of date now," Grant said aloud. The summary said much the same as the footnote about Fiona and stressed the lack of overt connection with any known terrorist act to date.

Grant dialled Judas on the internal line. "Hello Daniel, it's Grant."

"Oh, hello. Are you finished George?"

"Dan, I need a quick word. Can you come down?"

"Sure."

Judas arrived five minutes later in a pressed, blue pinstripe suit. "That's a snappy little tie you're wearing Daniel."

"It's my one rebellion in this job George. Suits are fine, black shoes, desk etc but I like to keep a flash of colour alive as a sign of independence and free will."

"Good for you, but pink and yellow?"

"What do you need George?" Judas said irritably.

"The truth, Daniel. Why did the Director lie to me about Fiona Galliani and Diane Trattorini?"

"I don't like having to dig other people out of their holes."

"Do it Daniel. I need to know and you've been instructed to cooperate fully with me."

"Well, George, I see it like this. The Director needs you for a particular function. He doesn't want that function to be ignored. If you narrow mindedly chase the killers of your girlfriend, you'll be wasting time. The greater need is the overriding factor, all minor interests must be given second place. I think he felt you needed to be steered away from the Stringfellows' bomb in order to concentrate on the whole of the terrorist war."

The explanation was sensible and Grant felt embarrassed at his own obsession with the Stringfellows' bomb when so many other crimes had been committed, so many other people killed or maimed.

"Look, I'm sorry, Daniel. I was out of line. But I'd like to think you'll help me find Dianne Trattorini, as well as help with the other areas."

"You have my word on it, George." Judas smiled in a comforting manner and turned for the door.

"I think I've got something upstairs which will interest you. Why don't you come up?"

They took the lift to the third floor. Judas led the way along the corridor to a secretarial bay.

"Sally, have you finished typing that report yet?"

"Yes, Mr Judas, it's in your tray." Judas's secretary replied.

"Thank you." They both entered Judas' office and sat down.

"Coffee?" Judas asked.

"Yes. White no sugar please."

"Sally," Judas pressed his intercom, "two coffee's please."

"What have you got Daniel?"

"It's a report from a Beta cell in Southampton. We have been watching the Port and guest houses there for the past two months. The agent is reliable. It came in an hour ago. Look at this photo which came in with the report."

Grant took the black and white photo. It had been blown up about 20 times and was indistinct. But the face on it was of a Mediterranean man with a dark moustache which featured prominently. He had dark eyes and thick, dark black hair. He wore a pair of plastic rimmed "Rayban" sunglasses and was holding a cigarette in his left hand.

"Who is he?" Grant asked.

"Well. We're not sure. But it's 60/40 that he is 'The Scorpion'."

"Who?" Grant responded.

"If it's him, he is a very dangerous man. His name is Farhad Fee."

"Am I supposed to know who he is?"

"Unlikely. I did not cover him in our in house training for you did I? He is a contract killer, a terrorist and a Muslim fundamentalist fanatic and a man who wishes to overthrow Western civilisation and return the Middle East to a strict Muslim Caliphate. He runs a dirty little group called the IFFC."

Grant raised his eyebrows.

"What the hell would he be here for?"

"If you think about it, it's not all that strange that he would turn up here considering the terrorist orgy we are experiencing at present. You know we had another five killings last night. We're keeping as many quiet as we can but even so the press are rampant at the moment. Especially after that dumb blow off by General Randolf last week. The public are getting close to hysteria about all this killing. All we need now is someone as troublesome as Fee in the UK and the whole thing could blow up. Literally and Politically. Do you know that last week the Police had to disband five vigilante squads in London alone. Private citizens are getting very nervous about this terrorist wave."

"Do you know if any of the rest of his group are in the UK?"

"We are checking now. But we haven't turned up anything so far today. The International Freedom Fighters Council (IFFC) don't exactly announce their arrivals. They are the most unpleasant group operating in the Middle East and Europe at present. We know for sure that this man, Farhad Fee, has been responsible for the deaths of thirty six diplomats in the last five years alone. That is ignoring the industrialists, the politicians and incidental victims he has murdered."

"Why don't you pick him up?"

"It's not that easy. He's not a sitter. He has already disappeared. He is a very experienced traveller. Disguise is his way of life and his contacts, even in the UK are extremely diverse. I would be surprised if we hear another reported sighting until he makes his first hit."

"We have got trouble."

"So we have, George. You're involved too, up to your neck. Who knows. He may even be here to kill your client Goldstein!"

Grant looked quizzically at Judas but said nothing. For some reason that comment seemed out of place.

CHAPTER 9
FRANCOISE DEBOUSSEY

CLAPHAM JUNCTION, AUGUST 7TH, 1988

"The train at platform 10 is for Vauxhall and Waterloo," the tannoy blurted out in a humourless Pakistani voice.

Three passengers disembarked. Farhad Fee glanced at his watch, noted it was 9.35am and walked down the concourse towards the ticket barriers. He wore a pair of tight faded jeans, dirty white pumps on his feet, a green check lumberjack shirt and a brown leather jacket with both sleeves rolled back to the elbow. He was carrying an Adidas sports bag.

He passed through the ticket barrier and walked lazily towards St John's Hill. He wore his hair long and filthy dirty. His dark round sunglasses made him resemble the late John Lennon. As he strolled away from the ticket barrier, the British Rail inspector glanced at him and grinned patronisingly. "What a mess! He's a bit late. Flower Power died over 15 years ago!"

"Well he certainly looks like he's past his prime," replied the other ticket inspector.

"I was a mod myself."

"No surprise to me, mate."

"What do ya mean?"

"That old Vespa you come into work on. Gives ya away easy." The conversation faded behind Fee.

"Got a light, kid?" A taxi driver parked 20 yards from the station asked as Farhad stopped at the rank.

"Only smoke dope and I've lost my matchbox" Fee replied.

"Oh. Here's my lighter, how silly of me?"

"A Calibri. You must be rich!" Farhad Fee responded.

THE SCORPION'S STING

"No Cabbie is rich, kid, only struggling. Get in kid."

The black cab swung out onto Lavender Hill and Farhad Fee reclined into the black leather seats.

"You got the fourth word wrong it was 'boy' not 'kid'."

"Shit. I'm sorry Sir. I was only told ten minutes ago."

"How long do you need to learn 18 words? A week? Now shut up. I want some peace." Fee slammed the dividing glass shut and opened the Adidas bag.

He lifted out the cold steel barrel of an Armalite AR-18. Screwed the specially designed barrel onto the black breach, then lifted out the body of the rifle. It clipped into place and was screwed into the shoulder rest. 36.38 inches in length. The magazine carried two hundred rounds. He counted them. 5.56mm cartridge. Muzzle velocity 3250 feet per second. Capable of firing eighty rounds a minute. Maximum range, five hundred yards. Farhad Fee always chose his weapon with precision. It was American built. It had been supplied by 'the Tailor'. Ironic really. The taxi stopped outside Chelsea Barracks.

Twenty minutes later, a tall middle aged officer walked with purpose out of the six storey building to his Jaguar. He got in and the chauffeur started the engine and steered the car slowly out of the gate. He indicated right and died instantly. Lead penetrated his left orbital cavity and splintered his skull and obliterated substantial part of his brain. He slumped forwards onto the steering wheel and his foot slipped off the accelerator. General Bruce Morgan ducked instantly. Twenty rounds of ferocious fire tore into the armour plated Jaguar smashing the windows and ricocheting around the inside of the vehicle. The General's body stopped eight rounds. He died in a pool of blood two seconds after his chauffeur. The Jaguar slid quietly to a halt across the road outside the barracks and hit a lamp post.

The taxi moved slowly away towards Battersea Bridge. It crossed the bridge then turned into Battersea Park. It stopped at a lay-by in the woods overlooking the River Thames and the driver changed the plates and stuck two different advertising plates on the doors. He also changed his cab number.

Seven minutes later the cab containing Farhad Fee was driving slowly towards the Hotel Intercontinental at Hyde Park corner. Fee carefully dismantled the Armalite and placed it into the bag.

*

Henry Klein Jnr kissed Lady Helen Windsor's hand.
"Lady Helen, it's been a charming evening. I do thank you."
"The pleasure was all mine, Henry. Mrs Klein, thank you for coming. The Save The Children Fund appreciates your support and values your verbal and financial help, most highly."
"You know, the Government of the United States' view of the fund. We will help in any way we can. This is, after all, an investment in the future of all of our children."
"You are most kind," Lady Helen replied.
The American Ambassador and his wife walked out of the revolving door and waved at their limousine. It swung round the drive way beneath the awning outside the hotel and the couple climbed gracefully inside the shining black American car and wound down the windows. A taxi-cab drew up beside the limousine and a green RGD-5 anti-personnel hand grenade containing a hundred and ten grams of TNT flew in through the driver's side window of the limo. Three point two seconds later the limousine exploded with a sickening violence that shattered all glass within thirty yards of the blast. The Ambassador and his wife became unidentifiable. The taxi had already accelerated away and executed a screeching turn into Piccadilly, then climbed an island and U- turned back to Hyde Park Comer. It raced under the underpass and disappeared into Knightsbridge. The plates were changed once again in a small backstreet behind Harrods.

*

George Grant left the Israeli Embassy at five in the afternoon and breathed in deeply. The warm evening air filled his lungs. It

had been stuffy inside and builders dust filled the air inside the building.
One of the advantages of working for a client like Goldstein was that money was no object. That morning, he had walked into 'Len Street Motors' of Chelsea and purchased a brand new 2 litre red Alfa Romeo Spider. It was no match for his old 1974, 1750cc model, but that would be in the garage being repaired for at least another month. He drove South and turned into the Fulham Road. As he pulled up at the lights, a paper boy slung him a copy of the Evening Standard and he reciprocated by throwing a 20 pence coin to the boy.
'Terrorists murder American Ambassador and General Morgan amongst others.'
Terrorists finally speak - 'Great Britain under siege'.

Both headlines rattled him. He pulled over to the kerb and read on.

Evening Standard - August 7th 1988. *'At two thirty pm the editor of 'The Times' was rung at his office by an anonymous caller who informed him that a package awaited him in the foyer of 'The Times' offices at 200 Grays Inn Road.*
The package contained a list of people who have been murdered since January 1st this year in the terrorist wave. It also contained this chilling message to the Government of Great Britain:

"The International Freedom Fighters Council declare the United Kingdom a war zone. In 1985 the IFFC convened and decided to liberate the Proletariat of the United Kingdom from the oppression of the capitalist land owning ruling classes.
Our targets have been exclusively and remain, the men and women who by their acts have collaborated to oppress and enslave the working classes in the war zone.
By the Autumn of this year with the aid of the IFFC there will be a radical upheaval in the governing structure of the war zone. A new constitution will be demanded by the people. The

IFFC have been requested to aid in the reconstruction of a nation destroyed by centuries of cannibalism by the ruling classes. To the honest and hardworking people of the war zone we say - "have no fear, freedom is near" - to the ruling classes we warn - "your time is short, repent or be destroyed." '

Grant sat quietly and read the details of the killing of Henry Klein Jnr and General Morgan.

When he had finished, he rang Duffy.

"It's Grant. What has the Professor got to say about the killings?"

"Grant. I can't talk now I've got the MPC on the other line and the press are besieging reception. Come over and talk to him yourself." Grant arrived at the laboratories at 6.30pm. Sam Jacobs was in his private lab. His spectacles were sitting on a desk top. His eyes were glued to the twin tubes of a high powered microscope.

*

"Evening Professor, how are you?"

"Uh? call me Sam please and I'm fine. I'm a bit busy at the moment. Perhaps you could come back later." He didn't even look up.

"You needn't worry. This will only take a minute. I've got just one question."

"OK then, ask away," he raised his head and grappled for his spectacles.

"What gun was used to kill General Morgan this afternoon?"

"An Armalite AR-18 with 5.56mm cartridges. Weighs about 7.75lbs when loaded. Fires 80 rounds per minute on automatic. The cartridge holds two hundred rounds. Is that all?"

"Yes. Bye." Grant ran to the end of the concrete corridor and phoned 6000600, Judas' number.

"Delta here."

"What do you want, I'm besieged by superiors," Judas responded.

"The file on Fee."

"Are you kidding? It's like a red hot potato at the moment and only the Director has the oven gloves."

"Then answer me one question," Grant pressed on determinedly.

"Make it quick and I'll try," Judas replied.

"What gun does Fee usually use for close range assassinations?"

"Either the berretta 12-sub machine or the Armalite AR-18."

"Thanks. Bye."

He slammed down the receiver and ran back to Professor Jacobs' lab. "Professor?" Grant requested urgently.

"You said just one question."

"That was then, this is now, investigations are not an exact science, the American Ambassador, what type of bomb was it?"

"A grenade, old boy. No doubt about it. Probably a three to four second delay fuse. I haven't done the work myself, but my colleagues conclude it was an RGD-5 anti personnel or something similar!"

"How do you know?" Grant asked.

"They know. They will have seen it before in Israel. Bloody nasty."

"Thanks Prof. Good night."

"Take care, and remember, if you can get some sleep, you'll work better."

"OK Prof." Grant ran back down the corridor and dialled 6000600 again. "Judas here."

"It's Delta again. One more question."

"Delta, for God's sake, this line is for emergencies," Judas bleated desperately.

"I need a copy of Fee's file. The part relating specifically to hand grenades he has used."

"Why?"

"I'll explain tomorrow. Just get Sally to leave it at reception OK? No, on second thoughts, get her to stand at the rear entrance to the building. I'll be there in ten minutes."

"Anything else? Can I get you a Boeing 747 or something?"
"Not yet Daniel, later maybe." Grant replied and put down the phone.

Grant picked the copy up from MI5 headquarters at 7.25pm and walked back to his car. He opened the brown envelope and read the two pages carefully. '...And in Hamburg in 1983. Fee was believed to be responsible for the murder of the eminent German politician, Hanz Bernbekker. The victim was killed in his car by a grenade (RGD-5-anti personnel, a modern Russian built grenade, deadly in confined spaces with a coated liner which bursts into a pattern of killing fragments).

"So," Grant whispered, The Scorpion is here."

*

At 8am on Wednesday the 8th August 1988, Grant was pacing around his flat in Old Church Street.

At 8.10am the SEC met at Number 10, Downing Street. Everyone was present except Admiral James and Wing Commander Harris. Field Marshall Carlshalton looked tired. He had been up all night. He sat at the oval table quietly stroking his handlebar moustache. Sir John Epcot, in contrast, looked as crisp as a morning snowfall.

The PM entered wearing a grey two piece dress suit with a light blue handkerchief in her top pocket. She sat down, opened the file in front of her, and sighed.

"Mr Defence Secretary. Who the hell are the International Freedom Fighters Council?"

"Ma'am. I could answer your question, but it would be better explained by Sir John!"

"OK. Disney. Let's have it."

Sir John Epcot opened the file in front of him. He started to read in his slightly high pitched voice. His fingers turning over the pages slowly and with military precision.

"The IFFC were formed in 1975." He cleared his throat. "Excuse the rather dull factual presentation of this information Prime Minister, but that is the way that our information boys like to prepare these files.

They took, as their primary objective, the liberation of the proletariat from their inferiority complex and from their despair and suppression. They desired to make the native fearless and free and restore his or her self respect.

That objective dates back to the theories of a black doctor named Frantz Fanon. Fanon was born in Martinique and took over as the head of the Psychiatric Department of Bilda Hospital, in Algeria, when the war between the French and the Arabs began in 1952. He died of Leukaemia before independence in 1962, but the anti-colonialist theories expounded in one of his books, *The Wretched of the Earth,* were adopted by the IFFC at their formation.

In summary the IFFC believe that only violence committed by the people, educated by their revolutionary leaders makes it possible for the oppressive, colonialist masters to understand social truths and gives the poor people the key to freedom."

Margaret Thatcher shrugged.

"Sounds like a lot of communist bullshit to me but others will find it chilling. Sir John, but what does it mean?"

"Well, Ma'am, the really horrific side to the present problem is that the IFFC seem to have developed Fanon's theory to its logical conclusion. Let me explain. Fanon believed that European affluence was scandalous in itself because it derived from the robbery of the third world. Theft of their minerals and the press-ganging of their inhabitants' into black slavery. This 'debt' built up by Europe, owed to the third world, has to be repaid.

It would appear from the IFFC press release yesterday that they have taken upon themselves the task of collecting the debt. And that Great Britain is to be the first ex-colonial country to repay."

"Do you mean that they want money?" Field Marshall Carshalton looked quite mystified.

Sir John replied, "it's possible. But I think it is unlikely. From the tenor of the statement it looks more likely that they want revolution. They want the working classes in Great Britain to rise up against the system and overthrow it."

"You mean that they *are* a bunch of commies as the PM just suggested?" the Field Marshall was beginning to find his feet.

"Yes Jack," replied Sir John patronisingly. "They are a bunch of commies."

"That, of course, involves overthrowing Parliament, I suppose?" The Prime Minister asked.

"Yes, Prime Minister, that is a logical conclusion," Sir John Epcot replied. "And it would seem that this revolution is set to occur in the Autumn."

The Prime Minister was fiddling nervously with her wedding ring.

"That is what I believe is planned, Ma'am." Sir John Epcot stated quietly, acutely aware of the Prime Minister's discomfort.

"And who are the people behind the IFFC?"

"Prime Minister. Our expert on terrorism, Daniel Judas, informs me that they comprise a new generation of terrorists who have learnt from the mistakes of their predecessors. They cannot be categorised as ex-members of one group or another, although undoubtedly some of the major Iranian and Palestinian groups certainly have influence in the IFFC. But it is a new entity."

"You haven't answered my question," the Prime Minister stated sharply.

"The total membership is believed to be approximately five thousand persons worldwide. The IFFC have a contact in every terrorist group known to Interpol. Their ruling council consists of only five people. Four men and one woman. We do not know who these people are, except that we are fairly sure that one 'Farhad Fee' is the Chairman."

Thatcher nodded.

"OK, Defence Secretary, what is the background of this man Farhad Fee?"

Phillip McNaughton opened a file which had been lying in front of him.

"He's a Libyan. Born in a small valley north of Tripoli. His father was an immigrant Iranian farmer, a Sunni Muslim and his mother a local...er..." Phillip McNaughton was struggling for words. "Lady of easy virtue, if you know what I mean?"

"I'm sure we all do, Phillip. Go on." The Prime Minister urged.

"Well, Ma'am. He was not educated at all until the age of eleven. He worked on the farm with his father, whom he adored, being rather neglected by his mother. At the age of eleven, he suffered a blow that appears to have changed his life. His father was murdered by the village Wali, Baron in our terms, after a furious row about the tribal dues payable for Fee senior's farm. The Wali was Shi'ite Muslim. He was apparently run through with a medieval sabre. He was unarmed at the time. Farhad Fee saw his father die. The Wali then took Fee's land, his wife as his whore and left Farhad to fend for himself on the streets of Tripoli."

McNaughton stopped for breath and poured himself a glass of water.

"There is no definite information available on the boy between the ages of twelve and fourteen. He seems to have disappeared, perhaps he lived rough. We just don't know.

He later enrolled as a Member of the Colonel's revolutionary Young Guards under an assumed name. Anyway, he gained a taste for killing when he was given the same terrible powers that other children of the revolution were endowed with by the Mad Colonel. He rose quickly due to his blind allegiance to the new strict Muslim code imposed in Libya.

Then he disappeared. He deserted after a Sunni massacre in a small village outside Tripoli. Thirty women were raped and shot by members of Fees' squad of young revolutionary guards.

Interpol first noticed the teenage Farhad Fee, at a terrorist training camp in Lebanon, that was 1968.

He became a member of the Italian Red Brigade and was instrumental in as many as thirty of their hits. Then in 1972 he went solo. Hiring himself out to the highest bidder as a professional assassin and torturer.

Between 1972 and 1975 he is believed to have assassinated twenty-four people, including two heads of state. He is undoubtedly a millionaire. He has many Swiss Bank accounts with, it is believed, upwards of thirty million US dollars in them.

He lives well, in the South of France. The French Police have tried desperately to convict him, but failed. The evidence from his activities is all too circumstantial to pin him down for good. Of course he has been in custody frequently, but he has some very sharp international lawyers and he never stays inside for long. So far the only convictions he has collected are for driving offences. He drives a Ferrari Dino.

Finally, his nickname is *'The Scorpion'*. They say that one chance is all he needs and his victim is dead. The latest information we have on the Scorpion is that he is in London. We believe he killed General Morgan and the American Ambassador."

The Right Honourable Phillip McNaughton closed the file and looked around the table slowly.

"He's a bloody madman!" Field Marshall Carlshalton growled.

"Are the IFFC orchestrating the terrorist wave, Mr Defence Secretary?" The Foreign Minister asked brusquely.

"So they claim," Phillip McNaughton replied. "That is the tentative view of my men in the Beta cells and that is my view too."

"Where does their money come from?" The Prime Minister aimed the question at Lord Carver and Sir John Epcot.

"We don't know, Ma'am," Lord Carver replied.

"Well, I have an idea Prime Minister, but it's no more than that!" Sir John Epcot stated quietly.

"Sir John, if that is all it is, I don't want to hear it. I want answers gentlemen, hard facts:

    1. Where is the money coming from?
    2. Who are the members of the IFFC ruling Council?
    3. Where are they?
    4. What exactly do the IFFC plan to do?

5. What proposals do you have to stop them?

Time is running out, the Autumn is only a matter of weeks away. By the end of August we must have a strategy. Otherwise, not only may we not survive to the next General Election but our very democracy is threatened gentlemen. If we cannot fight this enemy from within, how can we hope to convince our enemies abroad that we can defend ourselves against them?

This country needs your best efforts, gentlemen. Needless to say, she will receive 100% commitment from everyone of you. Do not let the people down."

The PM rose and the members of Special Executive Committee for National Security left. All except for Sir John Epcot. He closed the doors quietly behind the exeunts.

"Disney. What is it?" The P.M. asked.

"My contact in the Middle East has some information. I need to send someone out there, but he won't talk to anyone from the Services because he doesn't trust our security. He thinks there are many leaks."

"Even with our Alpha filtering?"

"He is very careful."

"What about someone from Section D?"

"They are trained killers not information handlers."

"Cautious fellow, this contact of yours, Disney."

"He's survived to the age of 87!"

"I suggest you use Delta. That's what he's there for," the Prime Minister stated.

"My thoughts entirely. Lord Carver won't approve."

"Disney. Bugger what MI5 think, if you'll excuse my French. If it's a lead, we have to follow it up. Overseas operations are your domain."

"I'll send him this evening." Disney replied.

*

Grant was at Scotland Yard Headquarters reading the full report of the Fee murders when he received the call from MI6. Daniel Judas told him he was to fly to Egypt that evening.

Grant returned to his own agency office at 3 that afternoon to find Jack interviewing a new client. Once the man had left, he told Jack about the trip and asked if Jack could handle the office for a few more days whilst he was away.

"George, I've handled it for the last six weeks. I'll be fine. I'm more concerned about you. What is this thing all about?"

"It's about Joanne," Grant said. He wanted to keep Jack out of the investigations for two solid reasons. He knew that it was dangerous and he needed Jack to keep the agency on its feet whilst he was away.

"Look George, I loved her too, you know, I would really like to help."

"I know, but at the moment there is nothing you can do. Believe me, if I need your help, I will ask."

By 7.30pm, he was boarding a plane at Heathrow bound for Cairo. He had been briefed to meet Fred Smith (also know as Francoise Deboussey), the expert on Middle Eastern affairs and the only man who had ever escaped from detention at Baalbek's deadly terrorist training camp in the Lebanon.

*

At 8pm that night, when the cleaners were clearing away the ashtrays at number 10 Downing Street, Emily Jones noticed something odd.

"Harry come ere a minute."

"What's up, Emm?" Harry, the housekeeper replied.

"I reckon we're one ashtray short 'ere again."

"Not another one!" Harry responded amazed.

"Yes. There's only three 'ere and I'm dead sure there were four in the morning before that Conference."

"Anyone else been in today to see the PM?"

"Sure Harry. About ten people, but none in the Conference Room. I locked it at 11.30 this mornin' when that lot left."

"Well, it must be one of them then," Harry Jones walked over to his wife and squeezed her arm.

"You know what I think Emm?"

"What Harry?"

"I reckon one of them highfalutin' generals is a tea leaf."

"Gor blimey. You can't trust anyone can yer?" Emily went on about her business muttering about honesty and thinking of her own son who had spent two years in prison.

*

Grant landed at Cairo Airport that night. He was worn out. The City was dusty, baking and noisy. He took a taxi to the Cairo Mariott on Mohamed Abd El-Wahab Street overlooking the Nile and ordered spaghetti bolognese from Room Service. The food was terrible but the Egyptian coffee was magnificent. It was 90 degrees Fahrenheit that evening, but the hotel rooms were air conditioned. He stripped and fell into bed.

His alarm call woke him at 7.30am local time. He showered, dressed and left the hotel in 20 minutes flat.

The streets were filled with the smells of the city, a wondrous melange of coffee, herbs and animal excreta. He walked past the Islamic Ceramics Museum and through the Embassy zone with its lush green trees and orderliness. Then he doubled back and ran over the El Tahir bridge towards the Tentmakers Souk. Looking back over his shoulder from time to time and zig zagging through markets and shops he knew by the time he had walked for 2 hours that he was no longer being tailed. He ended up on Ahmed Maher Street opposite the Al Shrakia Mosque in the 'Cafe American'.

It took thirty minutes to find the place. It was by then 10 in the morning and the streets were packed with people. The street vendors were flourishing their wares and shouting out prices at anyone looking remotely European. Grant looked unmistakably European.

He sat down on the patio outside the 'Cafe American' and ordered a strong coffee and a sweet pastry.

Half an hour later a shadow of a man appeared opposite the cafe carrying a black walking stick with a silver handle. He wore a white cloak and light grey flannels. His face was barely visible under a large panama hat. He lit a cigarette, took one puff, then stubbed it out with his foot. He walked off slowly, whistling 'Auld Langsyne'. Grant followed. They walked 100 yards apart for 20 minutes in the searing heat of the early morning. When the old man was sure no-one was following Grant, he dropped a piece of paper into a pot at a small market stall and walked off. Grant bought the pot after five minutes of haggling and returned to the hotel. The note contained the name of a vessel and a time of sailing. Grant opened his copy of The Bible and translated the name of the vessel from a direct cross reference with Samuel Book 1. It was a simple code, but one which would take experts at least three days to crack. And the meeting was timed for tomorrow.

Then he translated the numbers, adding one to the first number and subtracting 2 from the next and so on.

8.30am became 9.11pm

Grant spent the day in his hotel room reading about Deboussey's past until 8.30pm, then he checked out of the hotel with his hand luggage and walked to a pontoon on El Gazira Street which jutted out into the Nile. The SPHINX was an old wooden ketch. A single sail clinker built boat about forty feet long. It was moored beside the El Morocco Houseboat Restaurant, an upmarket clip joint which was serving morning coffee and had two old customers sitting outside playing dominoes.

Grant stepped on board over the rope rail and the captain, a French man, looked up from his chart table.

"Bonsoir Monsieur. Do you wish a short trip up the Nile Delta?" the man said as Grant Stood on the well scrubbed wooden deck.

"Yes, I've never seen the Nile Delta before." Grant replied.

"Come below quickly, Monsieur. He awaits you below." The wizened old Captain scurried below and Grant stepped over a crate of cotton which was resting on the wooden decks of the ketch. Within seconds the crew had cast off and the vessel motored away from the quayside down the Nile past the Marriott and towards the delta.

"Come this way. Quickly." The Captain bowed and scurried down the stairs. They descended a flight of worn wooden stairs into the centre of the Ketch.

"Voila, Monsieur," the Captain opened an oak door and Grant stepped inside.

Deboussey was standing up next to his desk. He was tall and thin and wore a white wrinkled Egyptian gallibaya.

"Bon soir."

"Monsieur Deboussey. I'm pleased to meet you."

"Good. May I offer you a drink?"

"What do you have?" Grant asked.

"Scotch, Gin, Brandy, whatever."

"Straight Scotch will do fine."

"Bien!" Francoise Deboussey walked carefully over to the oak side board and poured two stiff Scotches.

"Now, friend, tell me. How is Disney?"

"Healthy, as far as I can tell. But I don't know him all that well."

"I understand. You are, of course not employed by either Disney or 'The Knife'?"

"Who?" Grant asked.

"Lord Carver. He was called 'The Knife' in my day. It's a long story, friend." Deboussey smiled and refilled the glasses.

"No, I'm a free Agent. As far as anyone can be these days."

"Tres Bien, because what I have to tell you is pure conjecture. A story so obscure as to defy belief. A story that a trained service minion would in all probability discount as the lunatic ravings of a senile old man. Do I look senile to you, Mr. Grant?"

"Undoubtedly."

"Ah bon. Ce'st la vie!" Grant sat down on a wooden bench and accepted the refill gratefully.

"Where do I start?" Francoise Deboussey was six feet tall and skinny as a rake. His hands were just skin and bones with protruding blue veins criss-crossed between the metacarpals. He spoke quickly and quietly in a voice tinged with caution and yet with confidence. He look world weary, his eyes carried double bags which had a slightly yellowy tinge.

"I have lived in the Middle East for forty years, Mr. Grant. For much of that time I worked directly, or indirectly, with the British Government. I myself was highly placed in the French Security Services for most of that time. I have been a military advisor to various transient Governments, a coordinator of French Policy in Greece, Morocco and North Africa. My field activities have always been minimal. The Services have always thought I was of more use behind the scenes than in the firing line.

In that time, I have, of course, built up a network of trusted friends and contacts on both sides of the iron curtain and I am kept informed by these men for two reasons. Firstly, to protect me and secondly, to protect them. We meet and exchange titbits of information so that we are all kept in touch with current affairs. But also we know that we are used to channel sensitive information backwards and forwards between the Governments, who do not want to use the normal channels, for reasons best known to themselves."

"An enviable position in many ways," Grant interjected.

"Yes, usually. But in the past year it has been an uncomfortable situation."

"Why?"

"The IFFC have been troubling many Governments."

"Don't I know it." Grant replied.

"Yes, there is not much time for your Government to realise the gravity of the threat against them."

Grant had felt an empathy and a respect for the old man as soon as he had met him. There was something timeless about this rock, who had lived through countless wars and revolutions.

"Two months ago I was rung by a friend of mine who settled in Libya. He wanted to speak to me urgently. We met at a safe place near the border and talked for only an hour. What he told me then I didn't understand. Now I think I do."

Deboussey was frowning slightly. He raised himself from his couch with difficulty and paced around the cabin. The oil-fired lights cast a flickering yellow glow on the room and the burnt residue hung like a low cloud in the air.

"He told me that 100 million of US dollars were missing from the Government accounts in Libya. Gaddafi was greatly concerned. Someone or some group had persuaded a senior Treasury official to cook the books. The money disappeared in December 1987. But what was more worrying was the subsequent event in February this year. After the Treasury official was caught, charged and jailed for life, the 100 million US dollars were 'recovered'.

This may seem a triumph for Libyan Police work. In fact my friend was informed that the KGB provided the replacement money."

"So where did the money go?" as the obvious question and Grant asked it.

"Great Britain apparently. 100 million US dollars went into terrorist organisations in Great Britain in December last year. Channelled through the Libyan diplomatic bag without the knowledge of the Libyan Government."

"How do you know? And if it did get in, how did they spread it around when it reaches England?"

"I know, because my source is the father of one of the carriers. The carriers are not supposed to look in the bags unless they are of a certain seniority, but this particular young man was over curious and got a locksmith friend to open it up before he left Libya. He filched some of the dollars. He is now dead, of course. As for distribution in the UK, they simply hand it over at arranged meets and the dollars are used either to buy arms or changed at High Street Bureaux de Change for petty cash, which the terrorists use to live on."

"I assume that you cannot tell me where this information came from, Francoise?"

Deboussey smiled and nodded.

"You are the right man to talk to about this."

Grant downed his Scotch and lit a Galoise, carefully waiting for Deboussey to gather his thoughts.

Deboussey reached for one of Grant's cigarettes and continued.

"You smoke French cigarettes. In many things you have good taste. This last piece of information will help you personally. I know where Diane Trattorini is hiding."

Grant was flabbergasted.

"How did you know I was looking for her?"

"Disney and I are old friends." Grant couldn't help a feeling of sudden elation at the thought of getting his hands on Trattorini.

"I saw her here, in Cairo, last week. She was here to take advice from me about a problem. She is a member of the ruling Council of International Freedom Fighters you know."

Grant could feel the picture coming into focus.

"What was troubling her?"

"Her confidence in me prevents me from telling you. But I can say that her decision and that of her superiors in the International Federation, will undoubtedly affect the situation in Britain. It might halt it altogether."

He smiled warmly. Grant could sense the satisfaction he gained from being potentially instrumental in the ending of the killing. An old man still relevant in the politics of the new world.

"Fiona Galliani must have been IFFC as well?"

"I don't know the name," Deboussey responded.

"She's dead now, but she lived with Trattorini in London."

"I have rarely found that to be conclusive of anything."

"There is more. Fiona Galliani tried to kill me last week. Well, I think that it was me she was after. In the process she was involved in a fatal car accident. But before she died she told me that ' INTERFERON' were good. Do you know anything about INTERFERON?"

"Yes." Deboussey responded, his dark brown eyes narrowing slightly.

Grant continued. "She was a member. I also received a note after Galliani died. It read 'Do not trust the Tailor'."

Deboussey froze. His narrow face went taut. The wrinkled weather beaten skin tensing across his cavernous check bones. He put down his glass and stubbed out his cigarette.

A slight muffled bumping sound came from the rear of the vessel and Deboussey stopped for a minute, alert, listening. Then he shook his head and he took Grant by the shoulders and said two words.

"My God! Be careful."

He walked over to the window just as the sound of running feet clattered over the decks above. Grant looked up and Deboussey frowned and the urgency in his voice increased.

"You must get to Trattorini immediately. She is the key. She is in Barbados. My God! The Tailor."

"Where did you say?"

"Barbados."

"Why there?"

"Because she was not safe in London. She has friends there. She will be well hidden. She can wait and meet with the people who matter."

The old man was trembling. He looked nervously at Grant and said in a whisper. "It's worse than I thought. His reputation is well known throughout the Middle East. Here, he is known by a different name. He is 'The Grim Reaper'. The controller of terrorism. Diane was too scared to tell me what she knew, but I worried it would be this. I prayed it was not. She came to me with a problem. She explained it in outline. She would not name the persons involved. But the Grim Reaper. He is death incarnate. Oh my God!"

The door of the cabin opened and a small round object rolled in, making a metallic clunk as it bumped into the leg of the couch. Grant looked at it with disbelief then shouted, "get down!"

Grant threw himself to one side behind the oak cabinet against the cabin wall, screaming at Deboussey as he did so.

*

The explosions ripped the vessel apart. The main mast split and fell into the murky waters of the Nile. The wooden hull of the vessel was shattered down its centre and warm dirty water flooded into the hull and then the cabin. Deboussey died at the instant the grenade exploded. His frail old frame took the full force of the blast.

The oak cabinet shielded Grant from the worst of the blast. It was torn apart. The floor of the cabin was rapidly disappearing under a torrent of mud filled river water. The furniture began to float and the air was pushed out of the doorway up to the deck and into the night above.

Grant struggled to pull Deboussey above the water, then realised the futility of it. He waited for a minute to allow the smoke to settle, then dived for the doorway. As he reached the centre of the room, the old ketch reached the point where its ability to float was outweighed by the water in the hull and she lurched downward. The deck disappeared below the surface of the water and about three seconds later a torrent of water rushed down through the doorway of the cabin. It caught Grant in the face and thrust him almost sadistically back against the remains of the oak cabinet. The water level was at chest height and rising at a terrifying rate.

Grant screamed and then abruptly stopped his cry. If he was going to get out, he didn't want anyone else to know he had done so. Suddenly the dismembered scalp of Francoise Deboussey surfaced from the water and glared bloodstained and lifeless at him. The nose and half the flesh torn back away behind the left ear. Grant reached out and pushed it to one side then dived below the surface of the water and searched desperately for the silver handled cane which Deboussey held in his hand.

He surfaced seconds later with the cane but the force of the water entering through the hole in the side of the hull was such that Grant could not swim into it. He was simply thrown backwards into the cabin again.

He drew a deep breath and waited for the cabin to fill up.

Five seconds later his nose was squashed up against the ceiling of the cabin. Then the air was gone and still the water rushed in through the cabin wall. Now it swirled for a second then flowed out of the doorway and down into the lower deck of the ketch. Grant had no choice but to follow the flow. He knew he couldn't stay below the surface for more than two or three minutes at the most. There was nothing else he could do, he had to swim with the flow of the water.

He released his grip on the roof beam of the cabin and was swept head over heels out of the doorway. The torrent of water that slewed out of the destroyed cabin met with a colder flow from below decks, which picked Grant up and threw him against the ceiling. A rafter's edge thundered into his forehead and he swirled in a dizzy haze for a second. He saw light, then the subconscious took over and he breathed in water. It entered his lungs and he coughed violently under water. Immediately after the cough, his lungs automatically drew in again.

As Grant breathed in he saw a distant white screen. A candle at the end of a tunnel. He wrestled for self control. He closed his mouth and swam desperately for the candle, like a moth to a light. His shoulders burned with cramp. His lungs screamed with pain, his legs were aflame with acidosis due to lack of oxygen, all muscles shouting for oxygen. Then the darkness was underneath him, the water broke away, he saw the moon, he breathed the warm fresh air and he exhaled and then breathed in and it was so good to be above water.

Grant swam slowly for the shore. In the gloomy Egyptian twilight his eyes could just make out the darkness of the dark muddy bosh covered river bank. His chest was bleeding profusely. Wood splinters had splayed all over his body.

When he reached the bank he collapsed on the damp mud spluttering wretchedly. Deboussey's cane lay clasped in his hand.

It took half an hour for Grant to compose himself and to struggle out of the mud on the East side of the Nile. Before him lay a wide stretch of green field laid to pasture and a small row of flat roofed peasant houses running alongside a dirt track. Grant calculated the vessel had travelled about 10 miles North of Cairo towards the delta and walked along the path towards the nearby tarmac road. When he reached the highway he could see he was on the outskirts of Cairo and thumbed a lift back into town on the back of a rice truck.

CHAPTER 10
DIANNE TRATTORINI

Grant rang Goldstein from a public payphone near Cairo Airport.

"George, is that you?" Solomon J. Goldstein was holding his phone sat at his desk in Fleet Street. He waved at his rather beautiful secretary to leave the room and close the door. He was wearing a pair of gold rimmed square glasses and his silver grey hair was combed back in a wave over his ears. His steel grey eyes hard as the hull of an oil tanker. He leant back in his swivel high back chair and spoke.

"What news do you have for me?"

"I have located the second woman involved in the murder of your daughter."

"Where are you and where is she?"

"I am in Egypt. I can't tell you how I came across the information, but must tell you that there is no doubt in my mind that INTERFERON are trying to kill me."

Goldstein pressed the 'tape con' switch on the telephone base. He did not want to miss one word. He was nothing, if not an exact man.

"What happened?"

"I was tipped off about a contact in Egypt. I flew out and just as I was about to be told about Diane Trattorini, the contact was murdered."

"Are you injured?"

"Nothing serious."

"What about Trattorini?"

"She's in Barbados apparently."

"Why there?"

"I didn't have time to find out, Mr Goldstein, but I believe that she is the key to your daughter's death."

"What can I do to help you?" Goldstein moved round in his chair and glanced out over the Law Courts in the Strand. It was 2 in the afternoon. Learned counsel were crossing the road in their dark grey suits ready to do battle in the High Court. They always looked so serious, so purposeful. It gave him a wonderful sense of superiority to see some of England's greatest minds struggling for a day's pay whilst he sat on the 4th floor of his glass fronted offices and made money hand over fist at the press of a button. Capitalism produces money makers and professionals. And rarely the twain meet in one human frame.

"I need a blank cheque. Barbados may lead elsewhere. I need firearms and I need one of your best men as support."

Goldstein was not phased by the request. "The money will be available in ten minutes from now. I will open an account at Barclays in Barbados for you. The support will take longer."

"How long?"

"24 hours."

"Tell him to meet me at the Crane Beach Hotel in Barbados at midday on Tuesday the 11th."

"No problem."

"Good. I'll report back on Wednesday."

"Wait. One more thing Grant. I want Trattorini alive. I want to know why she did what she did."

"If it's possible, I'll do it."

"thank you, goodbye Grant."

The phone went dead. Solomon J. Goldstein picked up the phone on the other side of his desk and told his secretary to take the afternoon off. He made three phone calls, then left the office. He took the lift to the basement, walked to the white Bentley Turbo convertible and operated the automatic garage door onto the street. Goldstein International Ltd could take care of itself for the afternoon. Personal business came first.

*

George Grant made two more calls that afternoon. One to Marianne and the other to Sir John Epcot.

"Sir John?"

"Speaking."

"Who else knew I was in Egypt?"

"The Prime Minister. Myself. Two operatives in the Service. That's all."

"Someone leaked."

"Oh bugger!"

"Believe me. Francoise Deboussey is dead because someone knew I was here."

"Oh no..."

For seconds the man at the other end of the international phone line was silent. Then Sir John Epcot finally spoke. "How did he die?"

"A hand grenade. INTERFERON are more dangerous than we could ever have believed. Deboussey told me that someone transferred 100 million US dollars via a Libyan account to terrorist organisations in the UK last December. That is the fund fuelling the terrorist wave in the UK."

"Good grief. I suppose that *would* be enough."

"Especially if the wave stops in the autumn, as that last press statement from the IFFC suggested."

"It might be enough for about eight months on the present scale. I don't know. Daniel Judas could tell us that. If anyone knows about terrorist funding he would."

"Look, I've also got a lead on Trattorini."

"You're wasting our time there. We've told you. She is nothing, ignore her. The root of the problem lies elsewhere. Believe me!"

"You're wrong, Sir John. Deboussey said she was the key."

"Francoise said that! But ...."

"I won't know if it's true until I follow it up."

"Where is she?"

Grant thought for a second then knew that Goldstein's backup would be enough. He did not want any more leaks. Any more assassination attempts.

"I'm not going to tell you."

"What?" He was quite plainly furious.

"It's not that I don't trust you Sir John. It's just that I only have one life and it's been hanging on a silken thread for the last few days. Someone in the service is feeding information on me to either the IFFC or INTERFERON and I won't risk giving them a second chance."

"If you can't trust me then contact Lord Carver. Don't operate in the field alone, Grant. No one can for long. It's not possible."

"How do I know that MI5 are watertight?"

"I suppose you don't" Epcot replied frankly.

"Then I'll have to rely on myself."

"No! Wait! Please ..."

Grant replaced the receiver at Cairo International Airport and glanced at the Departure board. The next flight to Hamburg was leaving in 10 minutes. He had checked in with hand luggage only. The interconnecting flight to Barbados allowed him one hour to transfer. He walked quickly to customs and produced his passport.

*

LONDON, AUGUST 1988

Sir John Epcot phoned Lard Carver at 3pm on the same Monday.

The meeting of SUBSEC was arranged for 9pm at the Defence Ministry in Whitehall.

The Right Honourable Phillip McNaughton was a tall man with fine English features. He had been Head of School at Eton and had taken two blues in rowing and rugby at Oxford. He had passed the bar exams in London at twenty-two and practised at the Bar in a commercial set in Brick Court for five years. Many had tipped him to become the youngest commercial Silk in England. Then he announced his desire to enter politics. A senior Partner at Herbert Smith, one of the top ten commercial Solicitors firms in the City at that time said of him leaving the Bar:

"We will need to employ three counsel to take each case Phillip McNaughton would have handled alone. We will have to pay more and will get a worse service and a less predictable result."

A senior commercial judge had said, in private, that the pleasure of hearing other counsel's submissions paled into insignificance when Phillip McNaughton addressed the court. He had, on at least two occasions, written his judgements using 90% of McNaughton's final submissions. Such was the quality of the mind possessed by the now Defence Secretary.

McNaughton cleared an area on the conference table in front of him in room 98 on the third floor at the Defence Ministry and put a pad of paper and a pencil at three points around the table.

Lord Carver arrived first. He looked tired. His habitual Habana cigar was held tautly between the first and second fingers on his right hand. Phillip nodded and thought warmly about his friend.

Lord Carver was a small but authoritative man. He hadn't been to Eton or any public school. He was born in Romford in Essex and schooled at the local comprehensive. He entered the army at seventeen and had worked his way up to the rank of Colonel whilst at the same time making contacts with the Security Services, first in the army intelligence corps and then latterly at MI5. He had a natural basic ability to cut a man dead with his tongue or his muscle. He pulled no punches, at home or at work.

He had cracked more spy rings in the UK than any former Director General and, as a non Oxbridge man, he was ideally suited to do so. He had no old school contacts and yet everyone spoke to him. He had no breeding and yet all men respected him. He had no money and yet he would never want for cash. He was a barrow boy at heart with the street sense of a common criminal and the brain of a mathematics scholar. 'I have never passed an exam in my life,' was his catch phrase. Many in the Service knew that was a lie, but in many ways it summed him up.

"How are you Phillip?"

"Oh, hassled as usual, Knife. You look tired."

"Yes, well I was up all night. We thought we had a lead on Fee. He vanished. We'll find him Phillip. But God knows how many he will have killed by then." At that second, Sir John Epcot arrived.

"Hello Disney." Carver's welcome was as warm as ever.

"Evening knife, Mr Defence Secretary."

McNaughton nodded. They all sat down. McNaughton started. "You called the meeting Disney. What's on the agenda for SUBSEC to consider?"

"Delta my friends. As we know Proposition Alfa is now complete. The Services have been filtered and Beta cells are operating throughout the country co-ordinating county by county, the events relevant to the terrorist wave. However, Delta may have turned bad."

"Already?" Lord Carver was apparently not surprised by the occurrence. Merely that the time element was unexpectedly short.

"I sent him to Egypt. To see a contact of mine out there who, to say the least, has been invaluable over the past three centuries. The contact was killed and Grant survived. That fact alone would normally be enough for me to recommend his withdrawal, if not..." he left the inference clear by his silence.

"But there is more, isn't there?" Lord Carver interjected.

"Oh yes. He has found out something about the IFFC and he won't come in to debrief. He says he doesn't trust the Services. He thinks either I, or the operatives I briefed on the trip, leaked."

"Amateurs! Who were the operatives?" McNaughton interjected. The barrister's brain cut straight through to the core. He knew Disney was above suspicion.

"One in Cairo, one in the UK. Names are not relevant. Suffice to say they were Alfa filtered and are long term Service members. I would place my utmost faith in them."

Sir John Epcot let the words sink in for a second then continued. "This means that Grant himself gave the game away. My contact in Egypt was the most scrupulously careful man. He had survived in the Middle East for forty years virtually unscathed. He wouldn't have made himself a target. It is inconceivable."

The Defence Secretary tapped his pencil on the table and spoke quietly. "Was he a friend of yours?"

"Is that relevant, Defence Secretary?"

"It might alter your judgement. I mean no disrespect."

"He was a *very* close friend." Sir John replied.

"Can we follow Grant now that he is operating alone?" Lord Carver interjected.

"Should be no problem. I have had him trailed since he rang me this afternoon. We will soon know where he is heading."

"But why does the death of your contact necessarily mean that Delta has turned bad. We know Grant has already suffered the loss of his lover, was her name Schaeffer? He has worked hard and I believe successfully to try to uncover her murderers. What's more, he has been Alfa filtered. Where is your evidence other than the events in Egypt?"

"I don't have enough to have him convicted in a court of law if that is what you are asking Phillip." Sir John stated sarcastically.

"Well what else do you have?" Phillip McNaughton replied.

Sir John felt a little uncomfortable. The room was not air conditioned and a rather stagnant smell lay in the air. He had a gut reaction about Grant. The fact that he was non-service was part of it. But he realised that the death of Deboussey was the main reason. Sir John could still remember Deboussey standing at the top of the craggy cliffs, 120 feet above sea level on that day in May of 1946 at Ricks Bar in Negril, Jamaica. Then Deboussey jumped off with three West Indian boys. He thought his friend had drowned in the turquoise water below. But he had surfaced. He recalled the relief and the laughter. He sighed and pulled his thoughts back to the meeting.

"If we cannot rely on him to report back after crucial meetings, he is unsafe. If he is unsafe we cannot continue to use him. If we cannot continue to use him his operations should be ended. What he may now know should not fall into the hands of the opposition."

"So what do you propose?" Phillip McNaughton asked.

"A vote." Sir John Epcot replied and wrote the propositions on the top sheet of the pad of paper in front of him:

1. Terminate.
2. Bring him in and debrief then decommission.
3. If he won't debrief, cold store until terrorist wave is resolved."

He passed the paper round to Lord Carver who initialled 2. McNaughton signed 2. Epcot received the paper and signed 1.

The Defence Secretary collected up the ballot paper and pondered the result for a second. He rose from the table wearily and looked at Sir John quickly for a reaction. Naked anger and stubbornness covered his face as completely as any mask could.

"The PM will be informed. The majority vote will he followed. Disney, you'll watch until the situation warrants re-examination. If there are any problems please report to SUBSEC again immediately. OK?"

"Sure."

"And Disney. If it was Deboussey who you were talking about and I don't expect you to tell me whether it was or not, I can quite understand your feelings. I have heard a lot about him. He was quite a man but this is business, old friend. You must ignore your feelings." Sir John smiled and said nothing.

The meeting ended with a round of gin and tonics and talk of the England Cricket team's appalling performance in the recent Test.

*

George Grant had ten minutes before boarding. He went to a public phone box and dialled the Agency in London.

"Hello Jack. How are you?"

"Fine George, where are you?"

"In Egypt still, but I am leaving soon. I am sorry I cannot tell you where I am going on this line."

"Are you in trouble?" Jack inquired.

"Not yet, but there may be some coming."

"I suppose that means I'll will have to continue dealing with Mrs Dilworthy then?"

"Yes Jack. Listen I want you to go down to Johnny's in Wardour Street and ask him for a bugfinder. He'll know what you mean. Put it on my account then search the office, especially the phones. Next, do the same with my flat and yours for that matter."

"Alright George. What the hell have you gotten into?"

"I'm close to finding the people who planted the Stringfellows' bomb Jack."

"Oh," Jack went quiet.

George knew how much she had meant to Jack. He was an old sap but he understood people better than most. Joanne having lost her grandparents in the year before she met Grant had soon come to treat jack like her grandfather. Many a day had been spent at Kempton or Sandown with Jack studying the form of the runners in minute detail from his voluminous notes and guides. He nearly always lost, but Joanne had an uncanny knack for picking winners. She left Jack MacDougal in awe on many occasions. But he loved her for it. And they loved each other in a warm and gentle way.

Grant shook himself out of his reminiscences and boarded flight BA 772 to Barbados Via Hamburg on Monday, 10th August, leaving at 5.30pm. As he boarded, a British Man wrote his description in his notebook and walked slowly to a phone.

*

A telephone rang near Guildford in Surrey.
"This is the Butcher. Who is there?".
"Tailor."
"What news?" Butcher asked.
"Delta has traced Trattorini."
"What action do you recommend?"
"Send Fee." Tailor replied.
"SUBSEC met tonight." Butcher stated.
"What decision?"
"Watch and immobilise," replied Butcher.

"I see. I'll send Fee with the same brief, but upgrade it to termination once Trattorini is in our hands." Tailor said.

"Agreed. I'll report back later." They both put the phone down together.

*

BARBADOS AUGUST 1988

Cuthbert St.George Cumberbache had experienced his most unpleasant morning for many years. He had been dragged out of bed despite his own vociferous protest at 9.30am, only to find that the whole of Station CSW was in turmoil. His normally quiet brown eyed Private Secretary was careering round the office in Broad Street, Bridgetown like a chicken with its head cut off.

London had sent a four page telex in code double Z. No-one could see the code ZZ book except Cuthbert. The book was used so seldom that Cuthbert had deposited it in a safe deposit box at Barclays Bank in the high street. He grabbed his Panama and raced as fast as his plump little frame could go, down the stairs, out of the air conditioned offices into the humid Caribbean morning air. His sweat glands pumped immediately. Cuthbert was not built for speed. He was, in his own words, built for 'deep lounge chairs and large double beds'.

He breathed a sigh of relief when he shoved his heaving frame through the large oak double doors of the bank into the air conditioned interior.

"Morning, Mr Cumberbache," the girl at the counter smiled sweetly, her quiet bajan charm cooling him down.

"I need to go downstairs my dear. Call the security guard, will you please?"

They went down two floors through two massive sets of wrought iron doors and into the vaults hewn 180 years ago out of the limestone and coral on which the whole of the island of Barbados is formed.

Cuthbert St.George Cumberbache spent two hours in the vaults translating and decodifying the telex. He was, to say the least, a bit rusty on his codes. Double Z was the toughest ever invented by GCHQ in Cheltenham, back in old England. It had stood unchanged for eight months. It was estimated that it would take the KGB another nine months before they would crack it. It was due to be changed in two months' time. No code had survived so long. It was widely accepted as the best in the western hemisphere.

The telex read as follows: To - Director of Caribbean Station West, Cuthbert St.George Cumberbache. From - The Director, London.

"Tuesday, 11th August 1984, 7.30am.
Dear Cuthbert,
I am sending Daniel Judas out this morning to liaise with you on a matter of the utmost importance. As you know, the terrorist wave in the UK necessitated the setting up of an executive committee to analyse, formulate policy and react to the terrorist wave.

The cells are all up and running. The sweeper system has been used in this operation and an agent named George Grant was employed on a temporary basis. Delta is his code name. He has failed to come in and debrief after a field fiasco and has indicated bad faith. He is presently in Barbados:

Address probably - Crane Beach Hotel, St Phillip.
Estimated time of arrival was 7pm local time, Monday 10th August.
He is following a known terrorist: Diane Trattorini. Her file has been sent with Daniel Judas, it is confidential. Your orders come direct from the SEC. The PM has concurred. The order is:
"Bring him in and attempt to debrief. If unsuccessful then immobilise."

The discretion for termination lies solely with us via Judas. In emergency, you are asked to provide every assistance to Judas on the island and to liaise with the authorities in situ in the normal way to ensure Delta is immobilised in a manner acceptable to local politics. Imprisonment as a first step appears useful. Your discretion appreciated.
Regards
SJE. London 11.8.88"

Cuthbert sat back in his chair and breathed deeply. It had been four years since he had been sent a code ZZ message from Sir John. The last time involved a termination which very nearly lost him his life. The KGB had been operating a drug smuggling operation from Columbia through a deserted shack on the northern point of the island. He had gone with four local thugs up to Crab Hill in St Lucy. Only one person returned. The operation had been smashed, but in the process an international incident had been created. It was only defused by the US embassy agreeing to cut grain prices to the Soviet Union for two massive cargoes by 45%. Cuthbert did not like all this guns and bullets stuff.

Cuthbert returned to his office and arranged for a cab to meet Judas' flight. Then he phoned his wife. "Hello Darling?" she answered.
"Yvonne, we'll be having guests to dinner tonight. Can you get the cook to serve up lobster for eight with all her normal trimmings?"
"This is rather short notice darling, what's come up?"
"Some big wig is flying in from London today. I'll tell you about it when I get home."
"9pm?"
"Fine. See you later pumpkin."
Cuthbert St.George Cumberbache was born in Barbados. He was brought up on his father's 500 acre sugar plantation. When sugar took a turn for the worse in the mid seventies, his father had

already catered for his family by starting a huge hardware store in the centre of Bridgetown.

The Cumberbaches were one of the most affluent families on the island. Cuthbert had joined the British Army at 17. He had trained at Sandhurst and with his dual nationality was an ideal candidate for the foreign diplomatic corps when he left the army at 30.

He held down diplomatic jobs with passable success in five Caribbean states. All of the time he had been involved closely with the Security side. His appointment as head of CSW was, to say the least, a surprise to many in the Caribbean British embassies, because he was not regarded as a high flyer or much of an action man, but his father had made it known that unless his son got the post, Cumberbache Import Export Ltd. would not provide the huge financial backing and local cover which had been a feature of the Bajan arm of MI6 for three decades.

Cuthbert knew that he had done a reasonable job as Station Head until the last code ZZ. He also knew that Whitehall couldn't afford another cock-up this time round. Cuthbert thought that was why Daniel Judas had been sent out to take over the running of the operation. That made Cuthbert a bit cross.

*

BA772 from Hamburg had landed at Grantley Adams International Airport on time, the day before. As George Grant had stepped off the plane the blanket of heat had enshrouded him. He had never visited the Caribbean before. He had looked at the huge arched roof of the airport and wondered why, on this small island, they had built such a gargantuan structure.

Immigration had taken five minutes. He had only carried hand luggage. He had left the airport and taken a taxi from the rank waiting outside the check-in lounge.

"Where to, friend?" The Bajan driver had a warm Caribbean lilt and a hearty light brown complexion.

"Crane Beach Hotel please."

"You staying on the island long?" The driver asked as he rammed the old Morris Marina into second gear and screeched round the tight corner out of the airport.

"A week, maybe two. I'm not sure."

"You on holiday or business?"

"Business," Grant proffered, clutching the door handle as the suspension of the British Leyland car took a series of thundering pot holes.

"What do you do? No, let me guess." The cab driver was enjoying himself. He lit a cigarette with one hand on the wheel and at the same time wrenched the car round an impossibly blind corner. "You're in agricultural machinery, yes?"

"No." Grant answered blankly as he searched desperately with his left hand behind the passenger seat for a seat belt.

"Import, export then?"

"Yes, of sorts."

"OK, I give up."

"I'm here to determine the demand on the island for engines for fishing boats. I own a small manufacturing company in the UK."

"Well, I wish you luck." The driver took a sharp right turn into an avenue lined with tall windswept palms. He negotiated two sleeping policemen with nonchalant disregard for his suspension and drew to a halt outside the doorway to a magnificent series of low, white stone arches. Grant stepped out of the car, paid the cab driver and went carefully into reception enjoying the safety of terra firma.

He checked in at the reception desk.

"Mr. Grant, your room is ready. Just follow the porter." The receptionist said.

They went through the lobby into an oval courtyard open to the sky with its western edge on a steep cliff falling directly down to the ocean. The view was breathtaking. To the left lay Crane beach, 200 feet below and the dark blue of the Atlantic Ocean met with the light blue of the Caribbean Sea. The sea mixed in a vast expanse of warm frothy turquoise. The hotel lay on two layers and its western terrace jutted out over the ocean surrounded by a row of proud Grecian pillars.

"It's beautiful, isn't it, Sir?" the porter stated as he led Grant to his room past a shimmering swimming pool.

"Yes, sure is." Grant replied, distracted by his plans.

He showered and shaved, then took a dip in the pool and ended up in the bar with a tall golden rum punch, overlooking the white sand of the beach. He took a pen out of his cream jacket and wrote the words, *'Diane Trattorini,'* and continued to plan for what he needed to do on the island. Grant retired early after a splendid dinner of flying fish and local fruits. As he wallowed in the shallow waters of forthcoming sleep, his right hand gripped the silver handle of Deboussey's cane. It seemed to comfort him.

At noon the next day, Grant left a message at reception. At two minutes past twelve a tall, well built man with short dark hair and a healthy tan walked into the bar, ordered a straight rum from the bartender and came over to Grant's table. His skin appeared plastic and unhealthy.

"George Grant?" He asked in an American accent.

"Yes."

He offered his hand and shook firmly. "My name is John Reagan. S.J. sent me."

"Solomon Joshua, I suppose?"

"Sorry that's what we call him out in the States. I imagine you all in England call him Sir or something like that, eh?" He sat down in the forthright way that his type always do.

"No, I call him Solomon. Do sit down though." Grant added sharply as Reagan accepted the drink from the bartender. He downed it in one, put it back on the tray and asked for another double.

"So what's the play, George?"

"The play?"

"Jesus, you are stiff brit aren't you. SJ said you were uptight about your girl getting topped, but I never thought you'd be so plummy."

Grant put down his rum punch. Got up from the table and left the bar. When he returned to his room he phoned Goldstein. The time difference meant it was the evening in the UK, so he rang the Itchenor number.

"Hello, Mr. Goldstein's residence."

"Goldstein, please."

He came five minutes later.

"What is it George?"

"Who is this Schmuck you sent down here Solomon?"

"John Reagan! He is abrasive, I give you that. I imagine you are referring to his lack of table manners?"

"You're damn right."

"Don't judge the book by its cover, George. He fought in Vietnam. He has been in active service for me for over fourteen years. He is brilliant with all types of weapon, from laser to machete and he is without parallel, the most loyal man I have ever had the pleasure to employ. Just put up with the personality defect will you please?"

"OK, Solomon, I'll take your word on it." Grant put the receiver down and returned to the bar. He sat down opposite Reagan and smiled laconically.

"Let's start again."

"Look, I'm sorry if I rubbed you up the wrong way. I got a big mouth, that's no lie. But that's the way I was made. Back in Texas we don't put a brake between our brains and our mouths, we put a beer instead." He smiled broadly and Grant let it go.

"OK, let's walk along the beach and talk this through." Grant and Reagan left the bar and walked down the hotel's wrought iron spiral staircase which descended directly from the sun terrace down the cliff face to the bleached sand below.

They walked and discussed Trattorini and all that they knew about her. Reagan had been well briefed. At the end, Grant felt more secure. The plan was quite simple. Check the immigration forms for the last week. Every person entering the island has to fill one in. Trattorini would have used either her own name or one of her known pseudonyms. It wouldn't take long to find her and her accommodation. The police kept the register of visitors at the station by Garrison, just to the south of Bridgetown. Of course Grant had to get access to them and that was the first challenge.

At 4pm that evening, Grant received a call from Cuthbert St.George Cumberbache.

"I guess it wasn't that difficult to find me then?"

"That's what we do, you know" St George replied.

Grant accepted dinner gracefully. He had a pretty good idea who Cuthbert was. After their plans were made John Reagan left the hotel to contact the police and Grant dressed for dinner after a long swim in the pool. The taxi arrived at eight. The same Leyland car drew up and Grant grunted.

"Are you the only cab driver on the island?" Grant asked.

"'No way man. Just the fastest." He replied. The driver took Grant up the West coast, through Bridgetown and over Spring Garden Highway and past the Cunard Paradise Hotel. The cab pulled up half an hour later at a large gateway, guarded by two huge coral pillars. The gates opened automatically as if they were living things, and the cab drove up the semi circular driveway through lush, green vegetation to the steps of a low slung, white washed villa standing in its own flamboyant garden next to the shore. Grant got out and thanked the cabby, hoping he'd never see him again. He walked to the large wooden front door and rang the bell.

"Mr Grant, I am so pleased to meet you." Cuthbert St George said as he opened the door. He was looking very diplomatic, wearing a white dinner suit, black bow tie and holding a gleaming gold cigarette holder. He looked like a red hot coal in a baby's nappy and he was sweating.

"Local MI6?" Grant said, shook him by the hand and followed him into the lobby.

"Indeed, I will explain it all in a minute. But please come through to the terrace."

Two minutes later Grant was sat, rum in hand, on a marble terrace ten yards from the shimmering Caribbean sea. The terrace was surrounded on both sides by dwarf palms laden with ripe green coconuts.

"I do indeed represent the British Government's Security Services on the island. Sir John asked me to make your stay here is a pleasant one and to provide you with every support possible." Cuthbert, lounge lizard extraordinaire, was oozing pleasantry. It made Grant feel pretty uneasy.

"That's kind of you and Sir John. But there is nothing much you can do for me. The hotel is fine, the food is a little poor, but one expects that in the Caribbean. I think my holiday will be a pleasant one." Grant was waiting for the stick. He had just refused the carrot.

"And the fishing boat engines, Mr. Grant? What happened to your business trip?"

"So, the cabby was one of your men?"

"My wife's cousin, you know. Twice removed. It's a small island, Mr. Grant. News travels fast. Already, I have heard of four fishermen who would like to talk business with you. I hope you won't disappoint them?"

Games are games, thought Grant and played the bouncer over to square leg.

"Would 8am tomorrow be a good time to start? We will use the conference room at the Crane. It's really most kind of you to arrange the prospective purchasers for me, Cuthbert."

Grant waved at the servant who nodded and poured another punch.

Cuthbert's smile hardened a little. He looked slightly pained but he continued bravely.

"Diane Trattorini is not on the island, you know. We have checked with Immigration and there is no sign of her."

"Have you tried the pseudonyms?" Grant stopped suddenly and was momentarily shocked as Daniel Judas walked onto the terrace in a bright Hawaiian shirt and ridiculous shorts with huge pockets.

"Daniel," he said blankly.

"George, what a pleasant surprise. Well to tell the truth, it's no surprise at all, is it?"

"How many of you are there down here? Is Epcot here too? and a whole bunch of his little spies?" Grant ground the words out with all the anger that had built up since Egypt. Judas ignored him.

"Cuthbert, good evening, sorry I am so late but I didn't get back until a few minutes ago."

"Please don't apologise. How is your room?" Cuthbert indicated to the houseman to get a drinks table together and ushered Judas to a chair.

"Fine Cuthbert," Judas replied then continued the onslaught at Grant.

"You're a stubborn man, Grant. I do admire that, I really do. But don't you think it's just a little bit rash to drop us just because of a little heat in Egypt?"

"This is going to be a tiresome evening," Grant said under his breath and lit a Gauloise.

Dinner arrived as did Cuthbert's wife and four other local embassy staff.

After dinner Judas suggested a short walk on the beach and the other guests tactfully declined. Grant took a glass of brandy and a Galoise, and walked down to the waterfront.

"You know that Sir John is livid?"

"It's what I expected."

"The PM herself approved your appointment as Delta in this operation. How on earth can you justify failing to debrief now?"

"It's simple Daniel. You have a bloody massive leak in your Services. Alpha screening or not, you are leaking like a sieve. INTERFERON, or the IFFC, or whoever is behind this are picking off the people I speak to as fast as I am finding them."

"You mean, Mike Douglas and then Deboussey. We all see your point George, but you knew this wasn't going to be a trip to a monastery when you took the job."

"Daniel, I'm no use to you if I'm dead!" Grant picked up a pebble and threw it into the sea. There was a slight cool breeze. The beach was empty and glowing pink in the moonlight.

"We think it could have been you that tripped up in Egypt".

"It's possible. I have thought of that or course. But it doesn't make sense. The IFFC have no need to kill me. They have never even heard of me. I'm not a Government agent. Until one month ago I was just a dumb ex-Marine trying to survive self-employed in London following errant husbands. The IFFCs targets are politicians, church leaders, generals, managers and directors, not me."

"So?" Judas stopped walking and tried to understand.

Grant continued, "but you see as soon as the SEC hired me I was marked. Mike Douglas was killed. Then Deboussey."

"Douglas was killed before MI5 ever contacted you."

"Not before you started following me."

"Oh God. You're right." Judas' mouth dropped open for a split second then he closed it

"And the Deboussey trip was arranged at short notice. Only Sir John, you and two others in the Service knew about it supposedly. I know I wasn't followed out to Egypt. There are ways of telling. I booked to Frankfurt and then changed planes. No-one changed with me. I watched the airport for a long time after my arrival. No-one from London was tailing me. I was picked up in Egypt. That means that INTERFERON or the IFFC knew I was going there. Someone in MI6 must have told them."

They walked slowly back to the villa. Judas was silent for a while deep in thought. Eventually he asked "Will you liaise directly with me please George?"

"No Daniel, I won't take the chance. No disrespect, but you would report back. Someone back there is waiting to take Trattorini and slit her throat. I have to find her first. I have to know why she is so scared. Why did Galliani try to kill Goldstein's older daughter? And why did she try to kill his younger daughter?"

"You know I can't let you roam around this island shooting people, George."

"Who said I would be shooting people?"

"You'll not catch Trattorini with a smile and a rum punch."

"We'll see... "

THE SCORPION'S STING

The dinner party ended at midnight and Grant caught a cab back to the Hotel. He fell into bed, half drunk, at 2am. He left a message at Reception for Reagan to call in at 7am.

*

John Reagan walked into Grant's suite at 7am sharp. Grant was already washed, shaved and ready to go.

"Morning, George. You been on the hooch? Look like a rodeo cowboy after a night in a police cell in Waco."

"Yes, what did you find out?"

"A Diane Gunther, one of Trattorini's pseudonyms, passed through Immigration last Wednesday. The local information is that she is staying at a small plantation house just off the West coast near the Sandy Lane Hotel. She is staying with some other girl. Police say she's a well known local Dyke prostitute. Services all the rich white women who are into that sort of thing. Never been any trouble. You wanna go off there now?"

"How on earth did you find that out John?" Grant asked astonished.

"I went down to Bridgetown yesterday evening. Got no joy from the police so I broke into the Italian embassy and stole all of their files. Italian security is so country they think a seven-course meal is a possum and a six-pack."

Grant had raised an eyebrow.

"What about the local information?"

"I took a hooker. She's got some snap in her garters. She asked some of her mates, it's always the best way to pick up local knowledge, man!"

*

Grant and Regan spent the whole day finding a shack to hire in the lowlands near the airport in which to question Trattorini. Grant purchased some provisions and Reagan paid for a week's rent in advance, which pleased the owner no end.

The house where Trattorini was staying was a small wooden two storey villa in its own grounds overlooking the plush greens of Sandy Lane Golf Course. It was a cute wooden house under a central triangular roof and it nestled beside a dilapidated garage. Grant and Reagan settled down in a hired Toyota outside the entrance.

It was two hours later that Diane Trattorini and another woman left the house and put two bulging sports bags in the back seat of a mini moke. Grant experienced a terrible foreboding sweep through him as he looked at Trattorini.

The car drove out of the entrance and turned left past the parked Toyota. A woman's hand appeared at the passenger side window. Grant and Reagan raised their bodies from their slouches, gunned the engine and turned the car round. As they did so, the road in front of them exploded. Hot tarmacadam splattered all over the windscreen of the Toyota. The bonnet flew up and the front wheels collapsed outwards so that the chassis thumped down into the five foot wide chasm left by the bomb. Two palm trees which caught the brunt of the blast toppled onto the road and a yellow and blue bus coming in the opposite direction screeched, brakes locking, into the trunk of one of the trees. A cloud of acrid blue smoke hung low over the road as Grant kicked at the gnarled door of the Toyota and spluttered for breath.

*

Diane Trattorini put the second bomb back into her sports bag.
"Who was he Diane?" her female driver asked.
"MI6 I think. I saw him in London. He killed Fiona Galliani." Trattorini replied. "Now put your fucking foot down."

Grant ran round the road block and waved down a motorcyclist. He handed over $BD3000, then took the bike and the helmet. Reagan jumped on the back and they accelerated away along the open road. The Moke had disappeared. Reagan was bleeding from a large wound in his right cheek but he did not complain.

Ahead and out of sight of Grant the Moke pulled into the drive of a large house. Trattorini thrust open the passenger door and threw a grenade through the open doorway. The explosion destroyed the lobby and the bottom quarter of a magnificent stairway.

*

At that same moment in Bridgetown Cuthbert St.George Cumberbache awoke with a start as the telephone rang in his office. It took twenty seconds for the police officer to explain there had been an unusual road block near his house, out at Sandy Lane.

Diane Trattorini flicked off the safety catch on the Russian made sub-machine gun and sprayed the veranda of Cuthbert St.George Cumberbache's house with a hail of red hot lead. Two men servants danced like marionettes to the rat-tat-tat of the bullets, then fell like clay to the floor. Trattorini ran over to the bodies and glanced at the remains of their faces without emotion.

"Shit. Where the fuck is he?" She swivelled at the sound of a scream behind her and fired a volley of bullets into Yvonne St.George Cumberbache's neck and head. Her jaw was torn out of its socket and thrown across the hallway against the far wall. He lifeless body slumped to the ground. Trattorini raced upstairs, jumping the first four which were now partly covered in rubble.

She kicked down each upstairs door systematically and sprayed each room with a hail of bullets, then dropped a timer activated grenade into each just to make sure.

Trattorini left the mansion 4.5 minutes after she had arrived. Her driver screeched out of the gates and swerved as Grant and Reagan swept past them into the driveway. Trattorini lobbed a short fuse grenade out of the window and ordered the driver to veer left up Risk road. The grenade exploded behind the bike and Grant slammed his foot on the brake, the back wheel skidded round on the ground and at that second the whole of the top floor of Cuthbert St.George Cumberbache's house ruptured in a series of fearsome thunders which tore the guts out of it. In a rain of wood and glass,

Grant accelerated out of the driveway past a local policeman and turned sharp right, then left up Risk road after the Moke.

Cuthbert St George received the second call ten minutes after the first. It destroyed him. His secretary then phoned the Chief of Police. The Chief of Police phoned the National Guard and a train of fourteen jeeps left Garrison, South of Bridgetown, eight minutes later. They had instructions to find and detain two men on a motor bike, suspected of murdering the senior British Embassy Official's wife and housemen.

A young police cadet who had seen the bike leaving Cuthbert's mansion at the moment it went up in flames had not seen the Moke leave just seconds before.

Trattorini rummaged in the sports bag for her sunglasses. The driver threw the Moke round a hairpin and slammed her foot down onto the accelerator. The motor cried in agony as its pistons pumped furiously, driving the vehicle deep into the sugar cane fields in the centre of the island. But the bike was faster, better at negotiating the light bends and driven by an experienced rider. Grant soon reduced the gap between himself and the Moke to twenty feet. Reagan reached into his shoulder holster and drew out a hand gun. He raised his arm over Grant's shoulder and rested the barrel on the shoulder bone. The red dot of the laser sight jumped around the rear of the Moke like a butterfly in a cornfield. He squeezed the trigger three times. Two shots flew into the boot of the Moke, the third hit the rear offside tyre and it exploded. The Moke lurched left, then right and suddenly disappeared into a cane field skidding as the dirt track leading into the field ate the rim of the rear wheel.

Grant could not turn that fast. He braked, revved and swivelled the motorbike round, then accelerated up the dirt track. The Mini moke thundered round a bend between the high green canes and turned sharply off the track, splicing violently into the canes and disappearing from view. Grant dropped a gear and turned the bike into the tight alleyway of broken cane left by the stricken motorcar. As he entered, he gasped, the car had stopped. Both doors were open and Trattorini was crouched behind the passenger door pointing a machine gun straight at him. He screamed to Reagan and threw the bike to his right, hoping that the tail of the car would come between them and Trattorini's sight. The bike hit a boulder and flew up into the air landing in the cane to the right of the car. Canes thwacked repeatedly into Grant's face as he parted company from the bike and landed head over heels onto the soil cushioned to some extent by the upright canes.

Reagan was already on his feet. The right hand side of his face coated in dried blood.

A burst of machine gun fire cut through the canes above their heads. Trattorini released the trigger from her grip and shouted. "Throw down your arms or I'll throw a napalm grenade into the field. You won't have a chance."

Both Grant and Reagan had already started running in opposite directions attempting to encircle the Moke. Grant ran, head down, shoulders taking the crunching force of the breaking canes as he thrust through the thicket. Then he heard the moke's engine start. The car reversed quickly out of the path it had made through the field, turned and accelerated up the path back to the main road. As it skidded round the corner the Adidas bag fell out of the rear onto the path. Reagan was already running back towards the motorbike which was lying on its side, ten feet into the canes. His muscular frame downing massive canes like blades of grass.

Grant headed for the gravel road. Within a minute, Reagan had started the motorbike. Then he noticed the bullet hole in the petrol tank.

"Stay there," he shouted and accelerated towards Grant.

"Get on!" he screamed. "They can't get far with a flat tyre and the rim will skid on the tarmac when they take a corner. We'll find them."

Grant swung his left leg over the rear of the seat and hooked an arm round Reagan's waist. Then he noticed the Adidas bag lying on the path.

"Wait" he shouted, jumped off and picked it up. When he was safely on again, Reagan turned left onto the highway and took it slowly so that they could follow the track left in the warm tarmac by the wheel rim. After a couple of wrong turns and a confusingly angry exchange with a local person who appeared to be accusing them of being criminals, they picked up the trail of the Moke. It led up to a peak in the Scottish area of the island and then down to the East coast. Reagan was taking the bike down the steep hill overlooking the Atlantic coast when the Moke came into view turning into a beach house overlooking a long sweeping beach. Tall sea rollers washed onto the island direct from across the Atlantic and Western Africa, discharging their energy into the sand, as if exhausted by their long journey.

Two green jeeps were passing the entrance as the Moke turned in. Reagan took the rest of the hill at 110 miles per hour and flew past the jeeps. He pulled the bike to a halt 20 yards down the road and Grant climbed off. He put the Adidas bag behind a dustbin in the neighbouring garden, then returned to Reagan.

"Go round the back, John. Give me two minutes then fire a volley through the rear windows."

Reagan nodded and headed into the front garden of the beach house neighbouring the target. Grant crouched by an old wooden gatepost outside the small drive where the Moke was parked. Exactly two minutes later Grant heard a volley of shots thud into the rear of the beach house. He raised himself ready to run and stopped suddenly.

"Don't move, Mr. Grant." The Bajan voice came from behind him. It was a controlled male voice. An army voice. He froze.

"Drop your hand gun, slowly."

He obeyed.

An explosion occurred at the rear of the beach house and a plume of black smoke rose above the roof. Reagan was taking the beach house alone. Grant turned round and saw five soldiers in full battle dress coming up the road. Each aiming a rifle at him.

"You have murdered enough people for one day don't you think?" The Bajan sergeant said the words calmly and then spat chewing tobacco onto the hot tarmac and indicated to a soldier to disarm Grant.

*

THE SCORPION'S STING

Reagan couldn't understand why Grant had not responded. He swore and stood stock still with his back to the wooden wall of the beach house directly below the raised veranda which jutted out on stilts towards the ocean. He breathed deeply. Trattorini had to be caught. He slotted another cartridge into the laser sighted hand gun and looked up above. There was no movement on the balcony. He slid quietly sideways towards the corner of the house and came up against the cold steel barrel of a bajan rifle. The man was as startled as Reagan was.

Reagan fired his pistol into the man's belly and dropped to one knee. He fired a salvo round the corner of the house hitting another soldier in the leg then realised that these men were not Trattorini.

"Shit! What the fuck is going on?" A green figure moved stealthily along the dry grass behind a flowering bush at the end of the garden.

"It's the fucking army! Grant, where the hell are you?" He shouted and stood back against the wall and tried to cool down.

"Reagan!" Grant shouted from his position of confinement. "It's the Bajan army. Put down your gun. That's an order!" Grant sat down and the sergeant said. "thank you."

Reagan watched five figures position themselves in the shrubs around the beach house. He knew what to do. He put his gun on the ground and showed that was the end of his fight. But he pointed upwards to the beach house, then indicated by drawing a straight palm across his neck that there was still danger above.

*

Two hours later Grant and Reagan sat in the cool darkness of a basement cell in Garrison in cuffs. The old red fortress had housed the traditional base of the Bajan army since the days of English colonisation. The door bolts clanked, top and bottom and the door opened. They were led out of the cell up a dark corridor to a flight of tight circular stairs. At the top they were pushed roughly through a set of security doors and out onto a parade ground. Three sides of the square were bordered by the barracks buildings. The fourth side supported the central offices of the island's Defence forces.

Reagan and Grant were marched across the yard by two young guards. At the other side, they climbed a set of white wooden steps onto the veranda of the central offices. The guards shoved them through the main door and they turned left into a large reception room housing a long antique dining table. The walls were covered with pictures of past regimental figure heads hung in golden frames. At the far end they went into a small room with bare cream walls and a large ceiling fan.

"Sit down both of you. My name is General Alleyne." He pointed to two iron chairs in the centre of room. He was a tall, well built man with a tanned rough face, short dark curly hair and a small black beard. He was really pissed off.

"You bloody lunatics. What the hell were you doing? Four murder charges will be put against you in the High Court in Bridgetown tomorrow and countless subsidiary charges of criminal damage, trespass, assault, damaging public property. You name it, you are going to be charged with it. Where shall we start?"

"Where is Diane Trattorini?" Grant asked.

General Alleyne stood up slowly, walked round his desk and stood square in front of Grant. He bent down and put his nose within two centimetres of Grant's. He frowned and said very, very quietly,

"I ask the questions, you lump of shit."

Reagan grinned wryly. "I suppose you do the gardening round here too? Busy as a one-eyed dog in a smokehouse."

The General spun round and lashed Reagan's face with the back of his hand. He bellowed so that saliva flew thickly out of his mouth over Reagan's face. "You stupid Texas punk, we don't murder people in cold blood here."

He straightened his back and walked quietly back to his desk. He was regaining his lost composure. He lit a cigarette and sat down.

"You should realise in this country we have a system of Justice second to none in the Caribbean." He drew smoke into his lungs then looked directly at Grant and asked. "So why did you do it?"

Grant sat bemused.

"Why kill her?" General Alleyne asked again.

"Who?"

"Mrs St.George Cumberbache! The wife of an official of your own embassy?"

"We didn't," Grant suddenly felt a tinge of panic. "Oh God, John. They are going to frame us!" Reagan looked at Grant and seemed quite unmoved. His weather beaten face just calm and sanguine.

"This is no frame up, Gentlemen. You were seen riding out of the drive when the mansion went up. You were seen careering off up the road in your desperate attempt to get away from the horrific murders you had committed. You were caught, firearms in hand on the other side of the island. What more is there to say?"

Grant shook his head. "You can't be serious. Check the ballistics. Do the bullets match up? You haven't even thought of that, have you?"

Then Grant started putting it together. The message that London must have sent to Barbados was becoming clearer. They intended to tidy him up by imprisoning him for the rest of his life. Very convenient for London. No danger for Subsec and no loose ends.

"It was Trattorini and you know it was. You didn't even arrest her did you?" Grant looked at Regan and rolled his eyes. "Fuck you, Disney," he whispered inaudibly.

"Ballistics will be a matter for your defence lawyer, Mr. Grant. You will of course have every chance to prove your innocence to a jury. As for this imaginary woman Trattorini, we have no idea what you are talking about."

*

The General waved to the guard and the door opened. Diane Trattorini walked in. She was dressed in a light summer dress with a floral pattern and had a couple of leather wristlets. She wore no rings or jewellery. She had a smug look and a rounded pleasant faces but her mouth was thin lipped and taught. Of medium height she did not make it into the category of elegant nor was she particularly hard looking. But she was certainly edgy. Trattorini had a sort of electric quality which made he seem dangerous.

"Sit down, Miss Gunther," the General said.

"Grazie," she replied staring wildly at Reagan.

"This is the chief prosecution witness, Mr. Grant. She is herself to be extradited to England at the request of the British Government after the trial is over to stand trial on two charges of murder there, but whilst she is here she will give evidence at your trial. I hold witnesses such as her no esteem. But the evidence against you both is overwhelming."

"Oh, brilliant Disney," Grant said.

"What do you mean?" the General asked.

"What a perfect exchange. MI6 give you two murderers and a showcase trial in exchange for what they really want. Her!" But Grant could not figure out her thinking. He turned to Trattorini and asked. "Why are *you* helping *them*?"

She shrugged and said "I don't work for the IFFC now Grant. Ask the bloody Tailor!"

The General was becoming bored and he had finished his announcement so he indicated to the guards to take 'Miss Gunther' out. As she left, she shouted over her shoulder, "Arrivederci Scorpion," and her voice trailed away.

Grant sat confused. He realised he was completely destroyed. He realised that MI6 had stitched him up. But he cold not see why MI6 would let Trattorini get away with murdering St George, unless they were content to use that as a simple excuse for looking him up for good. They would get Trattorini back to London after the trial anyway and Judas could interview her in the Island in the next few days so they would get whatever information they wanted, either with drugs or more old fashioned persuasion. But what had she meant by the words "Scorpion". Then looked at Reagan. He was calm as a cucumber. Swarthy, sun tanned, Texan through and through. The phrases were text book Texas. Absolutely text book. But then Grant figured it out.

"You're not Regan are you?"

"You are so slow," Regan responded.
"Scorpion? Oh, God. You are Farhad Fee." Grant's spine tingled with a wave of fear. Sweat broke out on his brow. Reagan turned to him and smiled.
"Welcome to Hell, Mr. Grant."

*

"Enough!" General Alleyne shouted ignoring their words. "Get back to your cells and contemplate your trial. I will send your lawyer to you tomorrow morning. You'll be in court by 10 am."
"Oh, that's fine General. That'll give us two hours to prepare our case." Grant said over his shoulder.
"If you are innocent, that will be enough. If not, no amount of time will save you." The General retorted.
They were taken to separate cells. Grant tossed and turned on the mattress on the floor all night, thinking it through. Francoise Deboussey's words rang in his ears:
"I have never met the Tailor, but here in Egypt he is known by a different name. The Grim Reaper. He is death incarnate."
He thought of Diane Trattorini and of the words: "I don't work for the IFFC," and of the notes he had received in London: " INTERFERON are good." "Don't trust the Tailor."
Who was the Tailor? The Grim Reaper? Trattorini had said: "Ask the Tailor."
Was it Sir John Epcot? Was he the Mastermind behind the Terrorist wave? Had the Spymaster really become a Master of Terror?
"Oh Christ!" Grant thought. He needed a drink and a smoke. "Where are you, Jo?" He whispered to himself as he lay sweating in the humid dampness of the cell.

CHAPTER 11
THE TRIAL

AUGUST 13TH, 1988

"Court is convened." The usher spoke the words he had said so many times before:

"Oh yea, oh yea, draw near and assemble all those persons who are concerned in the trial on this thirteenth day of August, year of our Lord nineteen hundred and eighty eight of George Grant, Englishman and John Reagan, American, jointly indicted this day on charges of murder."

The charges were read, all fourteen pages of them. There were four counts of murder. The main ones were those of Mrs St.George Cumberbache and the two man servants which were laid against both Defendants. The further charge was laid against Reagan for the soldier. Countless criminal damage charges and other minor charges were also laid.

The public gallery in the old stone building in the centre of Bridgetown was packed full. The State had flown in a top Silk from London to handle the prosecution. Grant and Reagan had both been given local lawyers for their defence. Grant had not been allowed to phone Goldstein. He didn't know if it would do any good anyway.

The local jurors were empanelled.

The first prosecution witness was the young police cadet who had seen Grant come out of the driveway of St.George Cumberbache's house on the bike. He gave his evidence well. There was little he could be cross examined upon. Grant and Reagan had admitted leaving the grounds as the house had exploded. They had to. They had been there.

The first nails were entered into their coffins in the minds of the Bajan jury. There were four white and eight black jurors. Each man and woman started the trial with the same look of utter contempt for the prisoners in the dock. They had read their morning papers. Had seen the pictures on the front pages. 'The Nation' had cried:

'Murder Most Foul'.

It had ran a series of horrific photographs of the house, the man servants prostrate on the veranda floor and worst of all of Mrs Cumberbache's head split top from bottom. That sort of picture didn't usually get to Press but the authorities had let these photos through this time. 'Local pressure' was the excuse.

London was taking a hand in every stage of the trial.

Cuthbert St.George Cumberbache gave evidence next. He was a shell, a shadow of his former self. His life force had gone. He told of the dinner party in a dead pan way. No emotion. No fretting. He just answered questions, staring incomprehensively at Grant. The jury took the evidence as a further sign of Grant's callousness. He ad eaten dinner with his victims then, like a praying mantis, he had slaughtered them.

"He is a monster." Cuthbert had shouted, pointing at Grant, "and a murderer!" When he stepped down from the witness box the only question troubling the Jury was the motive. Why did Grant and Regan do it?

Diane Gunther was called next. She gave her evidence in chief firmly by covering all her lies with fine believable details and delivered her evidence with practised skill.

"I came to the island last week for a holiday." She appeared clean, and she wore no makeup. She fitted the part perfectly. Just a pretty girl looking for a good time in paradise. She said that she was unfortunate enough to be passing the house when Grant and Reagan were in the act of killing Mrs St.George Cumberbache. She saw the two men go in and they saw her as they came out. She thought that they must have decided she was a witness so she drove off and they chased her. Grant felt sick.

*

Joey Jones, Grant's Attorney, had come to Garrison that morning in his best pin stripe suit.

I've got to be square with you Mr. Grant. This is only my third criminal case. I've only done pleas in mitigation for petty criminals before now. Shoplifting and driving offences, you know. God only knows why they gave you me."

Grant's heart sank further.

"So I would be convicted of course, why do you think?" Grant felt tired and hungry and despondent. They hadn't allowed him to eat or change his clothes since his arrest.

"If you don't want me, I will leave of course. You can conduct your own Defence." Joey had his pride. Grant looked across the table and saw the calm eyes of an honest man and he decided to take the only help he had been offered. He drew breath and asked Joey to sit down again.

"Joey, what I'm going to tell you, will probably be unbelievable. It may endanger your life. Do you want to take that risk? We are all expendable. The Government of the UK don't give a shit for your practising certificate, your career, or your life for that matter. Are you sure you want to take the case?"

"So long as you tell me you're innocent. I'll fight with all the guile and strength I can muster."

"Where were you trained Joey?"

"At the London University and at Bar School in Chancery Lane. I am a member of the Inner Temple, fully qualified at the English Bar." Joey answered with evident pride.

"OK, boy. Here goes."

In the following hour Grant ran through the events of the last two months. Details he ignored. Facts he stated calmly and succinctly.

After sixty-five minutes, Joey stopped him.

"This is no good man. I don't understand half of it. The Jury won't understand any of it, and none of it is relevant to the trial. You have until 10.30 this morning to come up with a defence. A hard, real defence, like insanity, or diminished responsibility, or an alibi. But not all this terrorism stuff."

"Don't you understand Joey. This is my alibi. I worked for MI6. I was tracking Diane Trattorini, a suspected terrorist. I had no reason or desire to kill Cuthbert St.George Cumberbache's wife. What good would it do? I wanted, I want Trattorini. She killed my girlfriend you see."

That is when the young lawyer became animated.

"Wait!" Joey cut in. "Can you prove that?"

"I don't know. There is a Professor in England who might be able to prove it. He took the Disco apart after the explosion. He found the bomb segments. He knows how the bomb was detonated. Then there was a doorman at the club who saw Trattorini that night. It's all so vague. Anyway, they wouldn't come over here for me. The Security Services would stop them. We have to fight this alone."

"Then we have to attack Trattorini." Joey was beginning to think like a lawyer. Grant smiled for the first time in 48 hours.

*

"What did you do that morning, Miss Gunther?" Counsel for the prosecution, Sir David Nutley QC asked matter of factly, twirling the sides of his silk gown in his left hand.

"I got up. I had breakfast and then went for a drive to the beach with my friend Carey Nicholson."

"What happened next?" The eminent Queen's Counsel asked.

"Well, we got into my car and just as we left the house, the road behind us exploded. I was so shocked. I looked back and saw a man. That man (pointing at Grant) get on a motorbike and race past us into the mansion house. I suppose the explosion was a decoy..."

"I object your honour," Joey Jones was on his feet, his new wig perfectly in place.

"The witness is not here to suppose, only to give evidence of what she saw and heard. Her opinions are not relevant or admissible."

"I agree Mr Jones," said the Judge. Sir David smiled patronisingly at Jones and turned to the Jury.

"Members of the Jury, I'm sure you will ignore what the witness just said about a decoy." The point was re-emphasised. The jury would never forget it. Trattorini and Nutley were working hand in hand like a pair of ice dancers. Perfectly in time.

"Go on Miss Gunther." He purred.

"Well, when they drove into the big villa I decided to take a look, so I parked the car and watched from the gate. That man (pointing at Reagan) got off the bike with that other man (pointing at Grant) and they took some huge guns out of their rucksacks and ran into the house. Then there was this terrible shooting and screams. Oh, they were awful."

Most of the jury grimaced. The pictures from the morning papers racing through their minds.

"Then they came out. One was covered in blood. I suppose Mrs St.George Cumberbache put up a fight."

"Your honour.. I object strongly. This witness knows she is not here to suppose..."

"Yes, thank you Mr. Jones," the Judge nodded impatiently, waiting to hear the rest of the story.

"Miss Gunther, please restrain your imagination and just tell us what you saw. Now continue," Sir David coaxed.

"Well, your honour, it was then that they saw me and Carey. God, I was so scared. He (pointing at Grant) looked straight at me and shouted 'kill her!' I ran. Carey got in the car and drove like a maniac up Risk Road. They caught up with us and shot one of our tyres but we escaped. We got to Carey's mother's house at Bathsheba and they started shooting at the house. Then, thank the Lord, the Army came. We prayed they would and they did. I was so relieved. They would have killed us I am sure, God help us both."

She played on the devoutly religious Bajan heart so beautifully, Grant would have stood up and applauded if it hadn't been his own trial.

The Court adjourned for lunch.

*

Joey ordered sandwiches and they were provided with a room, close to the Court, to discuss the case. Four armed guards stood outside.

"She has tied it all up nicely hasn't she?" Grant was exasperated.

"We have to go all out to attack her credibility, George. The fact that she is a terrorist, a lesbian, the whole works. We have to destroy her character completely. Once her credibility goes all the Prosecution have is the policeman who saw you come out. That is not enough to convict you of murder," Joey said convincingly.

"There is one thing which may help us, Joey. It is a bag which I hid behind a dustbin at a house in Bathsheba." Joey smiled.

The Court reconvened at 2pm. His Honour, Judge Curtis Alleyne presiding. Brother of the Commander-in-Chief of the Army, General Alleyne. Grant tried to ignore the point.

"Your witness," Sir David said, smugly to Joey.

Joey Jones stood up to conduct his first ever cross examination in a big case and his wig tipped onto the floor as he did so. The crowd in the public gallery tittered disdainfully. Grant just buried his head in his hands.

"You, Miss Gunther are a lesbian, yes?" He said as he put his wig back on. The Jury gasped. His Honour Judge Curtis Alleyne interjected.

"Mr Jones. I understand that you are inexperienced in the ways of Court procedure, but even you should know that cross examination should be confined to what is relevant. It is not seemly or proper to cast aspersions on a witnesses sexuality purely for the sake of tactical gain in Court. Do you understand me?"

Joey appeared shocked by the reaction the question had provoked.

"Err... Yes your honour." He sat down.

George Grant stood up and stated quietly.

"Your Honour, with your leave I would like to conduct my own cross-examination of this witness. I have confidence in my counsel, but I fear that his inexperience, this is only his third criminal case, may prejudice my fair trial, especially when pitted against so great a legal brain as Sir David Nutley QC, OBE, the distinguished Queens Counsel from London."

The Jury had never heard Grant speak before. They suddenly saw him as a man, not just a murderer. They looked at Joey and they looked at Sir David and they understood for the first time the problem which Grant was facing. John Reagan and his counsel shook their heads in disapproval.

"That is your right Mr Grant. Carry on," the Judge said.

Grant took the notes Joey and he had prepared together and winked at Joey. He had played his part perfectly. They together, had got a point across which Joey alone could never have done. Grant and Joey had the Jury's sympathy.

That was a large leap forward. Sir David noted it and wrote a note to his two juniors:

"I want you both to de robe tomorrow and sit behind me."

He was nothing if not a wise old fighter

"Miss Gunther," Grant stated. "What is your real name?"

"Diane Gunther, of course." she replied.

"May I see your Passport?"

"Yes, of course." She indicated that it was over by her chair. A member of the public handed her bag to the usher. She searched for it then coughed nervously.

"I do not seem to have it with me."

Joey reached under the table at which he was seated and lifted Trattorini's Adidas bag up into view. When she saw it she gasped. Joey took out two passports and handed one to Grant. He opened it up and held it in full view of the Jury, it stated Diane Gunther.

"Is this your passport?" He asked.

"Yes, how did you get it?"

"Is this relevant, Mr. Grant?" Judge Alleyne interjected.

"Your Honour, it goes to credibility." Joey was on his feet. "It is the defence case that this witness's name is Miss Trattorini and that she entered this country under an assumed name, that of 'Gunther'."

The Judge turned to the witness surprised.

"Is this true?" He asked.

"Well your Honour," she hesitated, looking at the two passports on defence Counsel's table. Then she looked at Sir David. The Jury took the point in, during the silence.

"Yes, your Honour, it's true." She lowered her head in shame. A few of the Jurors gasped.

"Carry on Mr Grant," the Judge said frowning.

"Why did you use a false name, Miss Trattorini, that is your real name isn't it?"

"Yes," she replied quietly.

"Well, I'm so glad you are now telling the truth about that at least." Grant added softly. He knew that the Prosecution had not had enough time to prepare their case properly. "Shall we look at your other passport with the name Miss Gunther?"

"Err." She looked distinctly uneasy.

"Is this the other one?" Grant held the second one up so that the Jury could see it.

He opened it and examined it. He passed it up to Miss Trattorini opened at page three.

"Well, Miss Trattorini. Why did you come to Barbados under a false name with a fake passport? Why have you lied to the Court under solemn oath to God?"

She started to cry. "I am sorry. They were after me."

Grant turned to Joey and smiled. The breakthrough was about to happen. Joey was beaming all over his face. "Who are they?" he asked.

"The tax authorities. I haven't paid any tax for three years. I am only qualified as a secretary." The tears came. "I inherited a great deal of shares when my father died. I was impoverished at the time. I could not tell him but I think he guessed. I took advice and invested them. I made a lot of profit from them. I did not want to lose the profits, so I did not declare them to the Inland Revenue. Then I suppose the inevitable happened. They found out. I was scared I would be put in prison. I fled the Country. I needed time to think."

The court was totally silent when she ceased speaking. The Jury were confused. Some frowned but others looked sympathetic.

Perhaps she had persuaded some of them. They suddenly saw Grant as the pursuer, not the pursued. Trattorini possessed the senses of a fox. She had lasted for five years as an undercover international terrorist. Now Grant could see why.

"That's not true," Grant shouted.

"That's enough, Mr. Grant. Please restrict yourself to questions, not outbursts," the Judge admonished him. He sat down shattered.

Joey took over. He covered the ground carefully and well. He put Grant's case. That she was a terrorist. That she had left her friend's house with a sports bag full of bombs. That she had thrown the grenade onto the road and killed all those people in Cuthbert St.George Cumberbache's house, but it all seemed so ridiculous. This little girl was no terrorist. She is just a frightened girl who has fiddled her tax returns. Grant could almost hear the Jury thinking: So what! We all fiddle the tax man a little.

The case was slipping away. Joey clutched desperately at straws. "What were you wearing on the day Miss Trattorini?" He asked.

"A yellow T-shirt and white shorts," she replied.

"Do you have those clothes nearby?"

"They are in the wash."

"Would you let our ballistic experts examine them for evidence of your having handled a gun or explosives?"

"Yes, of course," she replied readily.

"Your Honour," Joey continued, "I would ask for an adjournment for the clothes to be seized and examined overnight."

"Well, it is 4.30. Sir David, do you object?" the Judge asked.

"Not one bit. It will clear this witness from the vile suspicion thrown on her by the Defendants." He sat down.

The court was adjourned.

*

An hour later, when the bureaucratic channels had been cleared, Joey went with the Chief of Police and seized the items of clothing. Grant and Reagan were taken back to their cells in Army staff cars.

When they arrived at Garrison, Grant was taken into the central offices and left in an interview room. Five minutes later Daniel Judas walked in.

His tall slim frame appeared well at ease in the Army Central Office but he looked nervous. Grant recalled that field always did make Judas nervous. He was a planner not an operative.

"Good evening George," he stuttered.

"What do you want, Judas?" Grant sensed something unpleasant was about to happen.

"I'm sorry. I wanted to tell you that this is not my idea. I am only following orders. It's not the way I would want it."

Grant felt like striking Judas down. He closed his eyes and forced himself to stay seated.

"So why is Disney doing this Daniel?" he asked.

"The SEC can't risk you and Trattorini joining forces. They have to have complete faith in any operative so close to government. You are one of the few people who knows how the whole Beta cell operation works. You let Sir John down. You refused to debrief. You allowed the IFFC to murder Deboussey in front of your very eyes and you escaped unhurt. It stinks George. You stink. The SEC can't accept that you are blameless. Not without a full debriefing. You backed yourself into this. I gave you a chance at the dinner party. I tried but ….."

Grant interrupted, "what about the leak?"

"Alfa filtering has been redoubled. Every operative is being checked and rechecked. We have never been so thorough. We even know what type of condom most of our guys use. There is no leak, George. Not with Beta Cells."

"Then it's higher up," Grant replied.

"You're only saying that because it suits your present predicament George. Face it. You blew it in Egypt. Now you're being immobilised."

Judas fiddled nervously with the change in his pocket. There was always an undercurrent of nervousness when talking to Judas. You could never quite tell if he meant what he said or just said what he thought you wanted to hear.

"Why don't you just kill me Daniel? Why go to all the trouble of a trial?"

"We are not criminals, Grant! For Christ's sake. This is a delicate deal with Trattorini. If she squeals on you, we have offered immunity for the Stringfellows' bomb and required her to tell us all she knows about IFFC and Farhad Fee."

"And she's going along with that?" the proposition seemed unlikely and it sickened Grant. But for the moment he wanted to keep it to himself that Farhad Fee was in fact John Regan and was sitting in that very prison. He did not quite know how but he felt that the information would help him in the twists and turns to come.

"She is scared George. I don't know what of, but she is really scared. I have talked to her. She keeps saying ' INTERFERON are good!' And then there was a time when I asked her about the Scorpion and she just laughed and said 'You are blind, he sits in wait for us under a rock'. Do you know what that means?"

"No, Daniel, that's what I'm here to find out." Grant lied.

"She also mentioned a Tailor. Who's he?"

Judas slipped the question in almost casually. He really was not very good at dealing with people. Grant felt distinctly uneasy.

"Look, Daniel. If I agreed to a full debriefing and I gave you accurate information on the whereabouts of the Scorpion, would you be able to stop the trial?"

"Do you know where he is?" Judas asked shaken.

"Will you stop the trial Daniel?"

"I don't think we can now, George. Sir John would be put in a very difficult position. How would he explain it to the SEC and to the Bajan Authorities? How would he deal with the murder of Mrs St.George Cumberbache? It would really shake the morale of the services if this got out George." Judas couldn't look Grant in the eye as he made this statement.

"You shit," Grant said. "Look, I've got a defence to conduct, have you finished?"

"Oh, yes, of course. I will do my best to see that arrangements are made to make your stay more bearable. I am really sorry."

"I'm not convicted yet, you smug Bastard," Grant retorted.

Then Judas turned round as he reached the door and frowned in his rather annoying and slightly put on sort of way.

"But you will be, believe me George, you will be."

Judas slithered out and Grant was taken to the cells for the night.

*

When Grant saw Joey at 9am the next morning, Joey looked down hearted. "No help, I'm afraid George. They had nothing on them."

"Nothing at all?" Grant couldn't believe it.

At 9.30 that morning they were taken through to the exhibits room outside the court room in Bridgetown. Sure enough a Government scientist was there. He confirmed that there was no trace of powder or chemicals on the clothes worn by Trattorini. They had not been worn by anyone who had fired a gun yesterday. Yet they appeared to be the same clothes she had worn until Grant saw a small plastic T sticking out of the label on the T-shirt. The type which a price tag is attached to. The sort of thing one takes off the clothes before one wears them.

Joey made a series of phone calls before Court convened.

The Court convened at 10.30am.

"Miss Trattorini," Joey was on his feet. "Have you enjoyed your holiday so far?"

"Is this a joke," she responded.

"Please just answer the question" the judge replied.

"The first half was OK. The last part has been terrible." She replied.

"You have quite a tan, do you tan easily?"

The Judge interrupted, "Mr Jones, is this really relevant?"

"Yes, your Honour, I'll come to the point." Joey was growing in stature every day.

"Do you use sun tan oil, Miss Trattorini?"

"Yes of course!" The reply was tinged with contempt.

"Have you worn these clothes to the beach?" Joey held up the yellow T-shirt.

"Yes, twice, as a matter of fact," she had missed the point completely.

"And am I right in thinking you wore the shorts back from the beach too?"

"Well, I don't walk around topless, if that's what you mean" she replied. The Jury laughed.

"That's strange," Joey said slowly. The Jury looked at him puzzled.

"You see, Miss Trattorini, there is no trace of sun tan oil on this T-shirt. A Government scientist has examined it thoroughly."

"Oh..." She suddenly saw the point. Joey pressed home his advantage.

"This is a new T-shirt isn't it, Miss Trattorini? Bought from Cane Sheppard in town last night. Am I right?"

"No. It's the one I wore that day they killed Mrs Cumberbache!" She screamed foolishly.

Joey turned round to a small black woman sitting hidden behind Grant. She stood up and Trattorini let out a little gasp. The woman passed Joey a slip of paper.

"This is a clothes receipt from Cave Sheppard Store, Miss Trattorini. It says '1 T-shirt 33$BDs' and bears yesterday's date and a time: 5.30pm."

"That could be anyone's receipt." Trattorini cried turning on the waterworks again. This time, the Jury were less impressed.

"We will be calling evidence from this lady behind me to say that Carrie Nicholson purchased this shirt yesterday. Do you admit that she did?"

"No, it's a lie. All lies. Why are you trying to make me tell lies?"

Joey turned to Grant for a second, then picked up their prepared questions. "Carrie Nicholson is your friend, is that right?"

"Yes, yes." Trattorini snivelled. She dried her eyes realising the Jury had lost sympathy with her and straightened her back.

"Are you aware of her profession?" Joey had learnt his lesson.

"Yes, she is a hairdresser." Trattorini replied quietly.
"And in the evenings?" Joey asked.
"She stays home or goes dancing."
"She's a prostitute, isn't she?" Joey put it straight.
"No. How dare you say that!" Trattorini put it across with the correct level of indignant disgust. The Judge interrupted.
"Mr Jones. I have warned you before. If you can substantiate your allegations you can do so during the defence case. Otherwise you must accept the witness's answer."
Grant knew that no prostitute would come forward to help defend him because of Reagan. Ten had already lined up to give evidence against him. He had killed one of their colleagues. Joey had done his best. That was a dead end. They could flaunt her previous convictions, but no more.
Sir David's re-examination was masterly. He made Trattorini look like a fair public spirited citizen who had been caught doing what many do; avoiding tax as best they can. He dismissed the T-shirt as mere trivial speculation. The heart of the case was what Trattorini had seen. Two men running into Cuthbert St George Cumberbache's house firing machine guns.
The local police chief was the next witness. Chief Dalgliesh was a small thin man with tanned skin and a matted thicket of dark brown hair which he had tried desperately to comb, but failed.
Sir David Nutley QC conducted the examination in chief, in his normal confident manner. He had a style so self assured, so calm and so controlled that one felt immediately that he could be trusted. He was a guide through the maze of facts brought out in the case. Foremost, he was an overtly honest guide. At one moment asking a seemingly irrelevant question and at the next nudging and cajoling the members of the Jury towards the conclusions he appeared already to know. The correct conclusion. That was the benefit of experience, the power of his learning, the quality of his intellect.
Chief Dalgliesh appeared concerned in the witness box.
"I arrived at the villa at 11.30 in the morning. It was still burning. The fire brigade had been dousing it for at least twenty

minutes before I got there, but it was still burning. A tangled horrific mess of charred wood and scorched concrete. When the fire was finally controlled I went in through what had once been the door. The first thing I saw was the late Mrs St.George Cumberbache. She was..." He was visibly searching for the right words. The effort straining his usually tempered official vocabulary, "horribly mutilated. Half of her head had been literally blown away across the hall way. I stood there for a second and then I vomited. It was the smell of the place. The smell of death."

"I know it's unpleasant," Sir David crooned, "but try to describe the scene dispassionately Chief Inspector."

"She was lying at the entrance to the lounge. She had taken three or four shots to the head. They had torn her jaw away. I went out onto the veranda. There I saw two men. Equally lifeless, but there was no doubt in my mind that they did not die in the fire. They had a terrifying look on their faces - fear mixed with pain. Both had been shot."

"What type of weapon Chief Inspector?"

"A machine gun possibly. There were bullet holes all over the veranda. Too many for a single repeater."

"What was done with the bodies?" Sir David asked quietly. Indicating substantially his own dislike for the question and communicating the dislike subtly to the Jury.

"They were taken to the Path lab."

"That's the Pathology Laboratory?" Sir David asked.

"Yes. Doctor Bradford examined them."

The cross examination of the Police Chief was short. The evidence wasn't disputed. He couldn't say who had pressed the trigger.

Doctor Bradford gave his evidence next. Gory was the word which sprung to mind as he walked away from the Box. Once again Joey made little progress in cross examination, save to clarify that bullets from the bodies had been removed and retained.

Next in the witness box was the army sergeant who had arrested Grant. He gave his evidence and Joey Jones stood up to cross examine.

"When you arrested Grant, did he have any firearms on him?"
"Yes, a hand gun." The Sergeant replied.
"Not a machine gun?"
"No."
"And Reagan?"
"The same. A handgun."
"Did you find a machine gun anywhere near the beach house?"
"No Sir," the sergeant responded mechanically.
"What exactly were they doing when you arrested them?"
"Clearly they were getting ready to attack the beach house and kill the occupants," the sergeant responded.
"Well, you wouldn't know whether they wanted to kill or merely to capture them would you?"
"If the occupants, Miss Trattorini and Miss Nicholson, were unarmed. Why were they using weapons at all?" The Sergeant answered.
"Exactly. When you arrested Miss Trattorini she was unarmed, but did you search the house for arms Sergeant?" Joey asked.
"No, there was no point. They were clearly the victims." The Sergeant was telling the truth as he perceived it.
"But there could have been a gun concealed in the beach house. You wouldn't be able to tell the Jury for sure that there wasn't, is that right Sergeant?"
"Well, we didn't look for one. But then there was no reason to. Two men with arms were ready to attack two unarmed women, what would you do? Search the place for tanks?" The Jury tittered but Joey hammered his point home.
"If I told you there were two machine guns in a chest of drawers in the bedroom, would you be able to say, 'No, I checked and there were none'?"
"No Sir. I wouldn't"
"Sergeant, you knew that Mrs St.George Cumberbache had been murdered with a machine gun, didn't you?"
"Yes, Sir."
"Well. Grant and Reagan obviously didn't have machine guns, did they?"

"No Sir."

"So why didn't you search the beach house?" The Sergeant's brow became furrowed. He failed to answer the question. "Perhaps we should do so now Sergeant. What do you think?"

"Yes, Sir. Perhaps we should."

Joey applied to the Judge for a search to be carried out and sat down.

Sir David's re-examination of the Sergeant merely highlighted the improbability of the two girls taking machine guns round the island for no apparent reason.

The next witness was the Government ballistics expert.

"The bullets came from a high velocity rapid fire machine gun. Probably Israeli made." The expert said at the end of the Prosecution examination.

When Joey Jones stood up he looked at the Jury quietly, calmly, and his face was a picture. A message. 'This is an important question', his expression was saying.

"You examined the guns taken from the defendants didn't you?"

"Yes." The expert replied.

"Did the bullets which killed the occupants of the Cumberbache villa come from those weapons?"

"No. Definitely not."

Grant breathed in. It was the most important answer that had been given all day. It provided the proof that the Prosecution was not all corrupt. Some were merely doing their jobs as best they could. If they had wanted to nail Reagan and Grant by incontrovertible evidence, they would have needed a 'yes' man on ballistics. He suddenly felt there was a chance.

"Have you examined a weapon which could have fired those shots?" Joey asked.

"No, Sir. I would know if I had. I haven't examined any machine gun at all. If I had, I could have said for certain whether it was the murder weapon. They all leave a finger print on their projectiles. Find me the weapon and I'll tell you whether it was the one." The Ballistics expert had produced the evidence which Joey and Grant had planned for. The suggestion now had to be implanted in the Jury's minds.

"So the weapon used to kill the victims is still at large?"

"I don't know where it is."

"It could be anywhere?"

"I've answered your question. I don't know where it is!" His answer betrayed a suspicion that he was being asked to speculate.

"Did you examine the bullets in the motor bike which was driven by the defendants?" Joey Jones asked.

"No, what bike?"

The relief swept over Grant. The expert was clean as a whistle. No one had thought to check the bullet holes in the bike. If there was a bullet still in the bike's structure it would undoubtedly match the ones in the Villa Cumberbache. Joey pressed on.

"The bike is in the army base at Garrison. You wouldn't object to checking the vehicle to determine whether there were any bullet holes in it would you? Perhaps you would remove any bullets you find in that vehicle and bring them tomorrow?" Joey asked.

"Of course. If it will help the Court. I did not know that anyone had shot at the Defendants."

Joey stood stock still for a full thirty seconds and said nothing. He wanted to let the force of that last comment sink into the Jury's minds before Sir David started his re-examination. When Joey sat down, Grant patted his arm. The man was beginning to learn his trade.

The Court was adjourned for the afternoon. Daniel Judas got up from his seat at the rear of the Courtroom and walked quickly out into the humid late afternoon sun. He drove to the British Embassy a little faster than was safe. The phone call to London was made on the secure line. It took just five minutes to reach the Director General of MI6, Sir John Epcot.

"They have a chance of getting off the major charge. The bike they were riding was shot to hell by Trattorini. Ballistics may provide the springboard for them to build a Defence. They are also going to search the beach house."

"I thought that you had cleared the house, Daniel."

"We did, Sir John. It is now clean. We disposed of the weapon."

"What about the bike then? Can you lose it?" Sir John asked hundreds of miles away.

"Too obvious. The Jury would suspect."

"Can you Bribe the expert?"

"No. He's a true blue. We have nothing to suggest he wouldn't turn against us if we tried." Judas replied.

"Is he gay, can we blackmail him?"

Judas was really uncomfortable now.

"Well, is that really proper?"

"Am I hearing you right Judas? We have a fucking terrorism epidemic here, now in England, Trattorini is up to her neck in it, Grant is not co-operating and may not be sound and you are worried that we may being doing something which is not *proper*!"

"He's clean Sir John!" Judas said with resentment.

"Recommendation?" the Director General of MI6 demanded.

"Can we wait and see. If he gets off, we'll have to bring him in by force. Or …… terminate him I suppose." Judas winced to himself.

"That's a possibility. But not yet. Not 'till we've exhausted all other avenues."

Judas swore with his hand over the phone.

"Daniel," Sir John continued, "the PM ordered it that way. She won't let the terminate order go out until she is sure. For a start she does not like the fact that we are spending all this money stitching up the wrong man for killing the wife of our own Section head. If this got out it would be a catastrophe for our service's morale let alone the Government."

"What about the operatives? If it does come to that, who do we use? The locals are not good enough."

"That will be catered for, if the need arises."

"Fine, I'll report later Sir John. Don't worry, I have an idea." Daniel Judas knew what 'catered for' meant. It meant that the Section D would be notified. The most violent section of the British Secret Service. They had operated successfully at Suez, in the Israel civil war, in the middle East, in Russia and in central America. Section D was born during the Second World War. No operative was over thirty-two years of age. None were sane really. All were handpicked killers. Programmed to survive for long periods under cover. To track and to kill. Section D didn't officially exist. Judas knew that the Secret Intelligence Service were reforming it, not reforming it. The terrorist wave necessitated it.

*

That night, Grant sat in his cell sweating. It was a combination of fear, expectation and confusion. They had offered Trattorini immunity to turn State's evidence. A committed terrorist, trained in the world's most anti-capitalist terrorist camps. Why would she give evidence for the Government? For MI6? What deal had been struck? But he was more concerned about the killings. There was no overt sense in killing Cumberbache's wife. She had no place in the mosaic.

Did Trattorini expect to find Grant there? Or was it Judas she was after? She couldn't have known he was on the island. He had only flown in the night before. He had only come to keep an eye on Grant. Trattorini couldn't have known Grant or Judas were coming. No-one else did. Except MI6.

Was that where the leak had sprung? But she wasn't connected to MI6. It didn't fit. There was something missing Someone missing. Someone Grant couldn't see. Someone had planned this. What could Trattorini possibly have wanted in Barbados?

Grant had watched Reagan throughout the trial. He wasn't troubled. His lawyer was letting Joey Jones make the running in cross-examination. It didn't make sense unless he knew that a conviction would be inevitable. If that was correct then why was he was so unafraid? Maybe he had links. Precious contacts. If he was "the Scorpion" he could have links to the Caribbean underground, to drugs dealers.

Grant pondered the man called the Scorpion. Had Goldstein really hired him? Was he Solomon's man or had he himself murdered the real John Reagan and taken his place? If so, how did he know that Reagan was coming to Barbados to help Grant? And why would one member of the IFFC ruling Council want to follow another member around the world? Perhaps they were not happy sleeping in the same bed.

One thing was certain. Goldstein had been their victim. He could not be bound up with the terrorists. The bombing at Stringfellows evidenced that loud and clear.

The more he thought about it the more it made sense. In the warm damp darkness of the cell. How did he know that Reagan was Reagan. Farhad Fee could have intercepted Reagan, taken his place. Grant had never met Reagan or Fee. The telephone call to Goldstein was the only confirmation Grant had that Reagan was who he said he was. Goldstein only said, 'he's abrasive. No table manners', that's not difficult to fake.

But Grant could not see the plan. Why did they kill Mike Douglas? Who steered Grant towards the Services? He concluded that someone was involved from within the Services. The events in Egypt backed that theory up. Someone in MI6 was in league with the IFFC, with Libya, with the KGB. Grant saw the path, but couldn't find the signs to the end of it. And the greatest question of all: was not who, not why, but rather where? where was it all leading to? What was the object of the 1000 million US$? To stir up trouble was not enough. The KGB must have planned more than that. They always operated for a reason. Deboussey had sensed that.

And the Grim Reaper was the paymaster. Perhaps the man behind it all. The Tailor was running the show. A show that could be very well run if he were the head of MI6 at the same time.

' INTERFERON are good.'

'Don't trust the Tailor.'

Diane Trattorini was the key nearest to Grant. He had to get to her. To reach her alone. He had to be free to do it. Joanne's death required it.

*

Grant couldn't sleep through that sweaty Caribbean night. He lay awake sweating and churning the theories round in his mind.

Daniel Judas left Garrison at 7pm that night with a wry smile on his thin weary face. The Guard at the gate of the vehicle compound was better off than he'd ever been in his 24 years of life. US$4,000 would buy him and his Bajan wife a new car and a new wardrobe. And it was all for the good of the country. Those bastards in cells 6 and 7 were meant to hang. What harm was there in letting a British Embassy official examine the bike before the ballistics expert? He was an impartial observer. The General had let him have the freedom to roam the Garrison and check security and report back to London. He wouldn't mind Mr Judas checking the vehicle compound too.

Judas walked along the golden sandy beach at Carlisle Bay and watched the Caribbean clouds forming on the horizon. He picked up a handful of sand and weighed it pensively, then threw the sand into the sea. The two lumps of crumpled lead twisted into the air surrounded by the thousands of grains of white Caribbean sand. There were two barely perceptible plops as they hit the surface of the cool turbulent water.

'Prison is better than Section D, George,' Judas told the ocean through his clenched teeth as the bullets from the bike sank to the sea bed.

*

Sir David Nutley rose slowly to his feet.

"Dr. Frederickson. What report do you have for the court relating to the motorbike ridden by the Defendants that afternoon two days ago?"

"Your honour," said the ballistics expert. "I have examined the motorbike in question. There were two bullet holes in the petrol tank in front of the saddle. I could find no trace of the bullets in the tank itself. I am afraid that is all I can tell the court."

Sir David sat down. He was stony faced. He knew there was a problem, but it was for the Defence to expose the meaning of it. He had done his task. He had presented the facts fairly and openly.

Joey Jones had endured a terrible night. The strain of the trial was tearing him apart. Stress was something he had hoped he would learn to deal with piece by piece over the years as the caseload he took on became more serious. This case was ten years of experience concentrated into one week. He had not eaten, he had vomited in the morning. He felt really scared. But he stood up.

"Which side were the holes, Doctor?"

"The nearside of the vehicle, Sir," the Doctor replied.

"Both holes?" Joey asked pointing his question at the Jury.

"Yes."

"What, as an expert..." Joey spat the words into the court's warm atmosphere, "...is your opinion on the whereabouts of the bullets?" The Doctor of Ballistics moved uneasily in the witness box.

"Well, it's rather odd, your Honour. I would have expected the bullets to have come to rest in the tank itself. There were no corresponding holes for their exit. They went in, but they didn't come out."

"And you didn't find them in the tank, Doctor?"

"No, I didn't."

"Doesn't that surprise you just a little Doctor?" Joey asked the question beautifully. The Jury were hanging on his words like fresh linen on a washing line.

"Well, it does. Yes."

"What is your explanation?" One question too much, it is a fault any court advocate must learn to avoid. Joey Jones learnt that lesson with this question.

"Well, there are a number of reasons..." Joey's face dropped.

"It would depend on the type of bullet used. If it was a standard lead type then I would have expected it to have come to rest in the tank. However, there are other, more sophisticated bullets. Some fragment on impact. Some are mere shells. Projectiles carrying a drug or an explosive. If it was one of those, it is possible that the casing could have penetrated the metal and released its contents. Then the surrounds would have stuck to the outside of the tank. The rider could then have brushed it off with his leg or perhaps the pick-up truck which took the bike into Garrison could have knocked the cartridge free."

"Can you tell whether these holes were made by a machine gun?"

"No, not with any certainty." Joey didn't know where else he could take the point.

"But obviously someone had fired at the Defendant's bike." That question was his second mistake.

"I don't know. All I can say is that there are bullet holes in the tank. There may have been ricochets."

Grant kicked Joey to tell him to sit down. He looked round at Grant and whispered "I'm sorry George."

Daniel Judas was the last man to give evidence for the Prosecution about the dinner party. Then the Prosecution case closed.

Joey Jones called George Grant to the stand. Before he gave his evidence the court was cleared. The rest of this case was to be heard 'in camera'. Sir David had demanded it. If aspersions were to be thrown on the United Kingdom Government and on the Security Services, national interest required that only Judge and Jury would hear them. If the Defence had any substance, then the National interest had to be involved.

George Grant gave his evidence as well as he could. The truth wasn't hard to tell. But the complexity of the plot, the plethora of characters and the web of violence, death and terror was too much for any normal juror to believe. It all seemed like one big fantasy.

Sir David cross examined in the firm and suave way for which he was justly famous. There was no doubt that the prosecution case was far and away the easiest to understand. Motive was their only problem. And that had been provided by Daniel Judas. He told the Court that Grant had been a minor MI6 employee. His last assignment in Egypt had gone badly wrong. He had failed to report in. He had changed sides. Something in him had snapped. No one knew what had caused it. Perhaps it was a bribe.

He had fled to Barbados and the British Government had tried to bring him back but he had refused to return. Judas had followed him. The dinner party at Cumberbache's house was the final attempt to bring him in. He had not responded. MI6 were about to arrest him but he had tried to murder Judas instead. Probably so that he could flee to South American outside UK extradition reach. An insane man under stress he couldn't handle. Violence was his unbalanced answer. Judas fortunately hadn't been on the premises. He was taking a swim. When Judas had finished, Grant had no doubt where the orders to have him prosecuted had originated. London had decided to put Grant away where he couldn't talk.

Sir David Nutley QC delivered the prosecution closing speech at 2.30pm on Thursday, the 17th of August.

"Members of the Jury. The burden of proof lies on me. I have to show, beyond doubt that the Defendants murdered Mrs Cuthbert St.George Cumberbache and others, in cold blood. If I fail, then it will be your pleasure, no, your duty, to find them not guilty. But you are fortunate to have heard evidence from many eminent men and women. Daniel Judas of the British Foreign Office, the Bridgetown Chief of Police, Members of the Army and Scientists and from Miss Diane Trattorini. It is not for me to tell you whether to believe one witness or another. That is your province. I will simply summarise the evidence you have heard and will lay before you one or two small points which may or may not help you to decide."

Sympathy, friendliness, honesty, sincerity. He was smoother than Irish Whiskey.

"Here is a man called Grant, who used to work for the British Foreign Office. A man, given a tough job. We are not concerned with the details. That is a matter of State for the Government of the United Kingdom. But he failed to report home after a terrible fiasco in Egypt. Instead, he fled to Barbados. A representative of the Government flew out to bring him home. To seal the leak in Foreign Office dealings. Daniel Judas tried at a dinner party at

Cuthbert St.George Cumberbache's house. Unfortunately for Mrs Cumberbache, he failed."

"Grant went over the edge. We may never know why. He panicked. Maybe he felt trapped. He hired a hit man called Reagan and created a diversion outside the house owned by the Senior British Foreign Office Official. Mr Judas was staying there. Grant went in armed to the teeth and shot everyone in sight, then blew the house to kingdom come. Fortunately, Mr Judas was out swimming. But as Grant and Reagan came out, they saw two curious tourists at the gate of the drive. They fired a round at the girls and perhaps, and I only speculate here, the shots ricocheted into the bike which they had used to enter the villa."

"The girls ran like scared rabbits. But Grant and Reagan couldn't afford to let any witnesses live. They followed the girls and at Bathsheba tried to kill them. Fortunately the army arrived and arrested them both before they could carry out their common design."

"Members of the Jury, you have heard evidence of a forged passport aimed at attacking the credibility of Miss Trattorini. She explained her tax problems. You have heard of a T-shirt with no sun tan oil on it. You may say, 'Well, so what? Perhaps the washing machine she used to clean the shirt removed it all'.

"Perhaps the oil she used at the beach was not detected by the forensic scientist; you've heard from a shop assistant that Carey Nicholson bought a new shirt yesterday and that was the one examined. Well, it could be. The Defence asks you to believe it was. You may feel that is grasping desperately at straws."

"Miss Trattorini says she was scared. She may have bought a shirt that afternoon. It may be that the wrong shirt was seized by the police. Is that her fault? Does that make her a terrorist? A killer? A murderer?" Sir David fell silent for ten seconds.

"You must make your own minds up. Look at the woman, look at her friend. Do they strike you as terrorists? And if they are, why on earth did they want to kill Mrs Cumberbache? Why not rob a bank? You may think that they are what they appear to be and that

Grant and Reagan are what they are accused of being: cold blooded murderers who deserve to hang."

Sir David sat down. Grant buried his head in his hands. His river of hope had run dry.

Joey Jones did his best. His speech was fiery but convoluted. It had to be, the facts were convoluted. He attacked Trattorini for the shirt, the passport, the lies. He pointed out that the two bullets in the petrol tank of the motor bike meant that someone was shooting at Grant and Reagan. Someone called Trattorini. International terrorist. Killer. But even Joey and Grant couldn't explain why Trattorini would have wanted to blow up the house and murder the occupants. Why did she kill those people? Only Daniel Judas or Disney or Whitehall knew that, or perhaps INTERFERON! The Jury retired after the Judge's summing up.

*

Grant sat for four hours, sometimes smoking and in between mostly pacing. He must have walked ten miles. He aged years in those hours.

At 4.30pm, the Jury returned. Would they see through the lies? The cover up. The inconsistencies? The foreman, a stout black man stood up. The Court usher spoke first.

"Have you reached a verdict?"

"We have." Grant's stomach tensed into a knot.

"Is it the verdict of you all?"

"It is."

He looked at Reagan. No emotion. No response. "What is that verdict?"

"Count 1. Murder of Mrs Cumberbache.......Guilty!"

Grant stood stock still. His heart beat like a bass drum in his chest.

"Judas you bastard!" He cried out suddenly like a caged animal throwing itself at the bars in despair.

"Count 2. Guilty." And so it went on.

Reagan and Grant were found guilty on all counts.

Joey was in tears as Grant sat down after the verdicts. "Don't take it so hard Joey." Grant said. "You did your best. I truly don't think anyone could have done more."

"You're too kind George. But I believe that you are innocent. You must appeal."

"No Joey. Get on with your life." He saw the officers coming towards the Defendant's bench which he and Joey had shared for the duration of the trial. Their safe haven in the storm. He could nearly touch Joey's despair, yet strangely he felt numb. As he was grasped from behind he touched Joey's shoulder.

"I want to thank you. I believe that you are a fine lawyer, Joey. Don't buck the system this early in your career." Two officers man handled Grant to the door of the Court.

They were led out of the sparse but austere Supreme Court room built in 1724 which had seen far worse before and would see more tales death the very next day. Grant was placed into a police car, handcuffed and driven to Garrison. That awesome coral stone fortress was to be his home for the next thirty years. He had avoided the death sentence. The Judge had passed three life sentences on Grant and five on Reagan. Each minimum sentence was thirty years.

CHAPTER 12
THE LIST

Judas got into the police car beside Grant. Reagan was taken back to Garrison in a different car. Trattorini was in a third.

There was a rough breeze whipping the litter around the streets as they drove through Bridgetown.

"There is a storm coming," Judas said suddenly, breaking the silence as they passed the harbour.

"Why did you do it?" Grant asked.

"I'm only following orders."

"So were the Nazis you bastard."

"It's not the same George. We are trying to protect a nation from a nightmare."

"How does sending me to jail for thirty years help?"

"You'll get out in five, George. The Foreign Office will probably do a deal with the Government here. You'll come home quietly through the back door. New passport and all the usual extras." Judas said the words in a mechanical monotone.

"More likely you'll forget me completely. What will you do with Trattorini?"

"She'll be extradited to the UK and we'll find out all we can about The International Freedom Fighters Council from her. If she won't tell us voluntarily we'll use our modern derivative of sodium Pentathol. Frankly, I think she is a red herring. Always have. It's Farhad Fee we want."

Grant smiled at the irony of the situation. Farhad Fee was in the very next car. He held tight as the police car entered Garrison a bit too fast. Trattorini stepped out of an army jeep in front of the officers' building. She walked calmly over to General Alleyne who was standing on the veranda and spoke softly to him, pointing at Grant.

THE SCORPION'S STING

Two thuds happened under Grant's feet and the police car fell a foot towards the ground. Then the windscreen smashed into a billion tiny square fragments. Grant elbowed Judas in the stomach, snapped his cuffed hands onto the door catch and rolled head over heels out of the car as it swerved to a halt. Reagan was already out of his car. The alarm siren at Garrison screeched into action. As the iron gates of the fortress swung closed, a lorry accelerated to 40 miles per hour and snapped the iron bars like so many match sticks. Grant raised himself to a crouch and glanced back at the other car. Reagan had freed himself from a second policeman and was struggling into the driver's seat.

Trattorini head butted the General in the face and as he fell, wrenched his army pistol from its leather holster.

The officers mess door swung open and four soldiers in various states of undress scrambled out onto the veranda. Trattorini fired into the group and two men fell stone dead.

"The lorry!" Trattorini screamed to Grant as he raced towards the veranda.

He turned his head round, the driver was executing a 180 degree turn. In thirty seconds Grant knew their chance to escape would be gone. The officers mess was in pandemonium and the other two sides of the Garrison square were swarming with frantic activity.

Grant took the next four steps to the veranda at break neck speed and ducked violently as an army officer thrust a rifle through a glass window and fired a wild volley of shots at him.

He rolled twice to below the window ledge, reached up and snatched the rifle, and then raked the butt upwards over his head and back through the broken window. It smashed the officer's nose and he took two steps backwards. Grant fired a cartridge full of bullets into the inside of the building carefully avoiding all occupants then turned and ran down the steps to the lorry which had completed its turn and was heading at walking pace for the gates.

Trattorini was four yards ahead. The General walking as slowly as he could ahead of her at gunpoint.

"Leave him Trattorini. Get into the lorry!" Grant shouted. Hostages would do no good. They were on a small island. Their only chance of escape was to get off the island before the army could complete a thorough search.

"We need him," she replied.

Grant caught up with her. "There is no time. In ten seconds all of the goddamn place will be swarming with soldiers. Leave him!" She glared at Grant. Clearly she didn't like taking orders from him. But the she did not want to be held up by the General either. Then suddenly she shot the General once in the knee and raced for the lorry.

"Fucking hell, stop shooting people" Grant said.

A couple of soldiers had emerged from the Barracks. They knelt on the first floor balcony of the west side of the Garrison and fired at the tyres of the lorry. Grant reached the rear of the vehicle and heaved himself inside the metal box. A friendly face greeted him and threw two grenades into his hands. Grant pulled the rings, counted to six and then threw them onto the officers' veranda.

Reagan was driving the police car as fast as its two good tyres would go, up to the gates of Garrison and swerved round to block the exit just after the lorry cleared the gates. The officers' mess exploded with a sickening double thud. Reagan stopped the car, got out and climbed into the rear of the lorry which then accelerated away past the perimeter wall.

The clouds broke and a tropical rain storm of fearsome intensity laid siege to the island. As the lorry took an interior road past shanty houses on the outskirts of Bridgetown Grant took a cigarette from Jack MacDougal in the rear of the lorry and lit it. He took a deep drag and as he felt himself relaxing he looked at Jack and smiled broadly.

"You are a sight for sore eyes, Jack MacDougal, let me tell you."

"I can see why George. You seem to have fallen into some real shit here."

*

Twenty minutes later the van was abandoned in an old wooden garage. Trattorini, Grant, Reagan and MacDougal were heading East across the island in a soft drinks van. They reached Concept Bay at 6.30pm. The storm was worse on the Atlantic side of the island. The van was parked up behind a wooden shack and the group slipped down the hills surrounding the bay and boarded a large rubber sided, fibreglass bottomed inflatable, which took them out to a tatty light brown fishing vessel about a quarter of a mile off shore. They were soaked to the skin as they climbed on board.

The owner of the vessel deflated the dinghy and put the outboard back onto the rear gunnels of the fishing boat as the four fugitives stumbled below.

Grant and Reagan hadn't spoken since the break out. They accepted a warm cup of coffee and sat in the hull of the fishing boat in silence.

MacDougal spoke to the captain and then came below. "Are you all OK?" he asked smiling broadly. "Sure," said Reagan.

The Captain says we'll be here for another hour. When the fishing boats head into shore, we'll split off and head out to sea. There is a ship waiting for us about ten miles offshore due east."

"Why wait?" Reagan responded.

"They will have aircraft looking for us by now," MacDougal interjected, "anybody leaving the island would be stopped immediately. This boat is just another fishing vessel. When it falls dark, they won't notice us slip away. It's well thought out, believe me."

Grant raised his coffee cup in the air, "thank you Jack."

"You are welcome George, but this pair of shits can stuff their thanks in their …"

"Ok Jack…… they get the message," Grant interrupted.

*

In the two hours that followed the Bajan airforce flew over seven times. The navy passed by twice. They weren't boarded. They were asked if they had seen any boats leaving the island through a tannoy from the Navy frigate. The Captain dealt with the inquiries calmly and dishonestly.

At 8.30pm, as it turned dark and the other fishing boats headed for home, they sailed away and met up with the Ship 20 miles out.

"Some ship," said Grant as they boarded the ninety-five foot cabin cruiser. Captain Jolly welcomed them aboard.

"Well, if it's not young Farhad Fee! Ahlan wa sahlan brother."

" Mesah al-Khair Osama," Reagan replied looking distinctly at ease in the man's presence.

The Captain continued, "I am Just back from Afghanistan. The Muja are growing strong. They miss your presence brother."

The he looked at Grant.

"You are Grant?"

"Yes," Grant said staring at Reagan.

"Pleased to make your acquaintance through Allah."

He welcomed them all in a warm friendly fashion, then showed them to their quarters.

"Dinner will be at ten sharp. Dress will be informal." He said as he closed Grant's cabin Door.

Ten minutes later, Jack knocked at the door and came in. "So how are you old friend?" He asked.

"Tired Jack. Very tired. But much better now that you are here."

Jack MacDougal sat his large frame down on a small couch and explained to Grant what had happened, as Grant changed into a fresh set of his own clothes which were laid out on the bed.

"How on earth did these get here Jack?" He asked.

"I picked them up from the Hotel when I paid your bill a few days ago George. Your suitcase is in the cupboard over there."

"You seem to have covered all the angles you old sap." Grant said with enormous relief.

"Perhaps. But do you know how I got into this mess?"

"Not really."

"Your friend Goldstein contacted me at the Agency after you had been arrested George. He told me that you were being made a fall guy by the Government. I agreed to meet him and we set this up in outline."

"You mean that this is his Yacht?"

"Sure. He keeps it in the Caribbean all year round."

"And the lorry?"

"It was a local hire job. The tough part was getting my hands on the grenades, but Goldstein has an enormous network of contacts out here."

Grant finished brushing his hair and sat down opposite Jack.

"Thank god for that. You are a silly bastard MacDougal. You could have been killed back there."

"Well we are equal now George. You did the same for me in West Africa. Now I don't owe you a thing."

"You never did." Grant said and he meant it. They had been close for too long for either of them to hold debts for each other. "It feels so good to be free, let me tell you."

"OK," Jack replied in a manner of fact way. "Now tell me what this is all about."

Grant shook his head and opened a bottle of water which was on the varnished teach sideboard.

"Diane Trattorini." Grant replied. "I don't know much about her, other than the fact that she has some crucial role in the whole terrorist wave in England. She has spent the last week doing her best to put Reagan and I away for life. Then on top of that there is a hell of a story behind John Reagan."

"Solomon Goldstein told me he was a man upon whom I could rely." Jack replied.

"Well in some ways you can if you want someone knocked off. But he is not what he seems at all."

"I don't understand," Jack said raising his eyebrows.

"Apparently his real name is Farhad Fee!"

"So what George?"

"He runs that bunch of murderers and rapists who are apparently one of the groups operating the bombs back home at the moment. He may be the Chairman of the IFFC."

Jack MacDougal's jaw dropped open slowly.

"And Goldstein employs him?" He asked astonished.

"That is what we may have to discover at dinner. Come on."

As they passed Trattorini's cabin they both stopped. Trattorini and Reagan were having a blazing row. Grant could clearly hear the raised voices, but he couldn't quite catch enough words to understand what they were saying.

*

Dinner was served on the upper deck at a beautiful carved mahogany dining table. The meal was middle Eastern with a cous cous and fig starter, boiled lamb and dried tomatoes for the main and honey sprinkled Baklava for desert. It was certainly the best Grant had enjoyed since leaving the Crane Hotel and immeasurably better than that provided during his days at Garrison. The conversation was dull and formal and no one got to the point.

They retired to the bar after dinner. Diane Trattorini looked relaxed, warm and most unusually attractive. The Captain, Osama, was a good host, albeit rather intense. He told some war stories from Afghanistan and Pakistan and listened quite well despite his own sense of self importance.

The barman served drinks and Grant sat down on a couch beside Trattorini and Jack.

"Where are we going Jack?"

"Florida."

"Do we have friends there?"

"Goldstein does." Jack replied.

Diane Trattorini grunted, stood up and walked quickly out onto the rear deck. Grant looked at Jack, raised an eyebrow and followed her out.

*

George Grant paused for a second. She stood gripping the chrome rail at the rear of the Yacht with her hair blowing in the wind. He knew nothing about this woman. But he hated her with all his being.

"What is going on?" he asked.

She turned around and shook her head.

"There are elephants and they are supposed to know all of the goings on in the Jungle. Then one hears of the tiger who is famed to be the greatest hunter of them all. I have felt, from time to time, like each of those players in our great venture. But you, Mr Grant. You are a loner. A courageous animal, sure, built one who has no understanding of the ways of the jungle. Yet you seem always to survive, to grow and most of all, to make people care about you. You are Kipling's Mowgli."

Grant stood dumbfounded for a few seconds then decided to go for the throat.

"If you know why INTERFERON exists why are you complimenting me?" Trattorini looked out at the swelling sea's turbulence, thrashing beneath a piebald sky and continued.

"You want to know why I tried to put you away, don't you Mr Grant?"

"The question had occurred to me, amongst many others."

Her tight curly brown hair was tied up in a ribbon above her head. She wore a clinging black boiler suit with a shocking red sash round the waist. Her rounded face gave Grant an unreal feeling of comfort, but beneath her calm, sane exterior, he could just sense her imbalance, her madness. For she was quite mad. At one moment seemingly quite normal and then next, quite rabid. He had yet to see her wild side socially, but he already feared it more than any other on that ship.

"The trial was bad for you. Uncomfortable, for sure?"

"Of course, but why put me on the spot?"

"I thought at first that all they were after was Farhad but I soon realised that they did not know that Reagan was Fee. When they convicted you I realised they wanted you silenced, not Reagan. That means you must know something which they are scared of."

"The Foreign Office have betrayed me Diane. They want me silenced, but are you sure Reagan is Farhad Fee?"

She looked into the bar at Reagan and raised her voice.

"Farhad."

"Yes?" Reagan turned round and without a trace of alarm on his face, waited for her reply.

"Grant is not convinced that you are you! Can you believe that?" Reagan left the room smiling walked over to Grant, flicked his cigarette ash onto Grants suit and walked away down the decks.

"Disguise was a four week course at Baalbeck. Farhad was my teacher. He was younger then, but by Allah he was mean to me!"

"So that's when you two met?" Grant asked.

'Yes, They worshipped him there. He had vast experience in the field. That camp was full of bright eyed revolutionaries from the streets of Beirut, Damascus, Jerusalem and countless PLO camps all over Lebanon. They all came to learn. They all wanted to fight. To kill for their country. The right to live in your own land is denied too many people on this earth. Farhad taught them. Gun handling. Guerrilla tactics. Explosives. Disguise. He's the best. He has been caught so many times, but he always gets free."

"And why did he come here?" Grant asked.

"To find me." Trattorini smiled poignantly and sat down.

*

"Let's talk." Osama said as he stepped out onto the rear deck.

Trattorini looked out over at the ocean and the frothy white water in the wake of the ship. The rain had stopped but the wind was still high. Farhad Fee suddenly appeared from the deck on the port side. The deck light showed what Grant had never suspected. The hair had been dyed light brown. It was now back to its natural dark black. The eyebrows had been reshaped. The nose was thinner. Back to its original size. The eyes back to their original brown colour. It would take a while for the moustache to grow back, but Fee looked passably like the photo Grant had seen in Judas' office. He said nothing, turned and went inside.

"You see. He's quite something, isn't he?" Trattorini whispered through the wind.

"He has one of those faces which can look different with every hat he wears." Grant replied.

Osama added, "that's experience. The way you stand, walk, talk. You can change it all. It just takes practice. Don't blame yourself Grant. He has had more practice than you and Trattorini put together and he used a latex half mask, which is very effective."

Grant sat down on a cushioned wooden bench.

"Did he kill Reagan?"

"Who is Reagan?" Trattorini asked.

"One of Solomon Goldstein's men. He sent Reagan out to Barbados to help me find you."

"Then Farhad probably did."

"So he knew I was in Barbados and he took Reagan's place. He wanted me to lead him to you."

"No, he knew where I was." She stood at the handrail letting the force of the westerly wind blow her red waist tie frantically behind her.

"I don't understand."

"I asked him to come here. I know now, I knew then, something vital about Goldstein. It will tear the IFFC apart. I was unsafe in England so I fled here. I have a plethora of old friends and contacts out here."

"So how did Fee know Reagan was coming?" Grant asked.

"He spoke to Goldstein before he came out. He wanted to gauge the lay of the land before he spoke to me. Goldstein intended for Reagan to kill you, and once I had been found, me as well. So Farhad intercepted Reagan at Grantley Adams Airport and finished him off?"

Trattorini seemed to be telling the truth but Grant found it hard to decide.

"What did you want to tell Fee? Was it about INTERFERON?" She looked hard at Grant, "I can't tell you that."

"Then why did you escape with Jack and I?"

"Because I did not want to be extradited back to the United Kingdom. Once I had been arrested and they found out who I was, they offered me a simple choice. Either I was taken back to Britain and put on trial for the bombing at Stringfellows' nightclub or I gave them evidence against you and Reagan. They wanted you put away for a very long time to keep you quiet. They offered me immunity from prosecution, if I agreed to perjure myself at your trial and spill the beans about the IFFC."

"So you agreed. Stitched me up and broke your end of the deal with the Foreign Office when Jack came and saved me. Neat but rather untrustworthy."

"Trust?" Osama interjected. "What right do any Western Government have to speak of trust?"

Grant looked at the tall skinny figure of Captain Osama and stored away his dislike for later.

"It delayed things for a while." Trattorini responded. "It gave me time to think. It gave my friends time to arrange a breakout. It was just chance that your Jack arranged the breakout before my people did." Grant shook his head in disbelief.

"The Government were prepared to give you immunity from prosecution for murdering my fiancée Joanne?" Grant could feel an urge to break her neck welling up inside him.

"Calm down my friend," Osama said and put his hand on Grant's shoulder. "We are all fugitives here. Let us not fall into violence." Grant flicked off the hand with his arm and looked deep into the Captain's face. Who the hell are you anyway Osama?"

"Just a man who trained Farhad Fee. Just a man who seeks justice in Palestine. Just a man who loves Allah." He said these things which a disquieting air of confidence and intensity.

The Trattorini interposed.

"Oh, but don't be deceived. I did not believe the Government's promise to give me immunity. They would have taken the information from me by their normal methods if I had not agreed. I knew that they would not keep their end of the bargain when they got me back to the UK."

Grant thought of Joanne Schaeffer and of his long journey to find this woman. He fought back once again his desire to take her slim neck and wring it with his bare hands. But he couldn't satisfy his urge for revenge without understanding why Joanne had been murdered. Until that time revenge would be hollow; Joanne's death remained the unexplained mystery.

"I have hated you for as long as I have known of your existence," He suddenly found himself saying. Suddenly she looked a little shocked. Perhaps personal hate had not been that close to her recently. Perhaps all those years of terrorism were just years of business. Perhaps she did have a heart. But then the fear was gone.

"I don't give a damn about your personal feelings Grant. I need to know why they are so scared of you," Trattorini responded.

"They are not the only ones." Grant suddenly felt the anger that he had suppressed for too long over Joanne's death building again. It built up in his stomach. His head began to throb and he felt himself reaching out to grab Trattorini.

She pulled back shocked and shouted. "Stop it! The IFFC are being tricked. It is not I that you should blame for your dumb western girl's death."

Through this scene Osama sat as if unmoved.

Farhad Fee stepped out onto the deck and said, "everything all right, Diane?"

Grant struggled to regain his composure. He lowered his arms and slumped back into the seat.

"He is feeling sorry for himself and is unable to control his temper," Osama said with scorn.

"Imperialist liberal fool!" Fee added.

"What do you mean, the IFFC are being tricked?" he said eventually.

"I can't tell you until I'm sure of where you stand Grant." Trattorini responded.

"Look Diane. I stand slap bang in the middle of a hurricane. I was hired by Goldstein, then MI6. They used me then they threw me away. They fixed a bogus trial for me and imprisoned me. I don't know where I stand. And what's more, even if I did, I'm not sure I'd tell you until you tell me why you killed Joanne."

"And what about Moscow, Grant?" Fee put down his cigarette in a silver tray and kept his expression blank.

"Bluff, George. Bluff." Grant thought. What had Deboussey said? 'The KGB provided the money to fund the Libyan loss of US$1000 million'.

"I know about the KGB money," he said. "They are no friends of mine." It was vague, but it might be enough.

"When did MI6 find out about the KGB?" Trattorini asked tightly interested now.

"I'm not sure that they have," Grant responded, trying to appear to know what she was talking about.

"So why did they have you framed?" Fee asked.

"You were involved in that? Don't you know?" Grant replied to Fee.

"No, of course not," Trattorini replied as if working in unison with Fee. "I agreed to help them to get myself more time."

"But you started the whole bloody mess when you killed Mrs St.George Cumberbache. What possible reason did you have for that?" Grant fired the question at her.

"Don't you know?" Trattorini responded smiling and shaking her head.

"I have no idea." Grant replied.

"We did not want to kill her! It was her guest."

For a second, Grant sat stunned, as the consequences of the last statement filtered through him.

"You wanted Judas?" He gasped.

"Yes. I wanted that deceiving little shit." Trattorini replied.

"But why?"

"If you don't know then you are not..."

Farhad Fee stood up and stepped in between them. His waterproof glistened in the moonlight.

"Diane. We pass Mustique. I get off here if Allah permits."

"Must you go so soon?" they embraced briefly.

"I'll be back in London by tomorrow night. Thanks for the information. I'll sort it out, don't worry. Wada'an."

"Be careful, Scorpion. Use it wisely."

She smiled and for a moment looked like a little child. Then she waved as he clambered down the side steps into the inflatable and started the outboard engine. Mustique's coast line was just seven or eight miles away to the West. He pushed the inflatable away from the cruiser and started the outboard motor. Then he slid away towards the dark silhouette on the horizon. The cruiser continued north east towards Cuba and Florida.

*

Grant slept fitfully for a few hours that night. He woke a hundred times, with thoughts of such confusion that he felt his mind was aflame. He did not want to leave the cabin until he could be sure that he had pulled some of the strands together.

At 3am he walked to Diane's cabin. He knocked twice first.

"Come in," she said.

He stepped inside. She was lying on the bed with a white silk kimono wrapped around her. The curtains were closed. There was a small table lamp by the bed.

"We need to talk."

"Don't..." she said and she raised her hand to her mouth. He shut the door and took one step back against it.

She was sweating slightly, as if she had just finished a short workout, yet her perfume suggested less strenuous pursuits. For the first time since he had met her she oozed warmth and sensuality. There was a smell of eroticism in the room. Her smell. He turned to leave, repulsed at his own arousal.

As he did so she made a small sound. A rasping squeak that froze him to the floor. He looked back over his shoulder. She swung her legs over the side of the bed and the kimono fell open. Her thighs were slim and a smooth golden brown in colour. Her waist tapered to an hourglass middle, then swelled out plumply to her hips. She raised her body slowly from the bed leaving the kimono on the mattress as she did so.

All too soon she was two inches away from him. Her nipples brushed like feathers against his ribs through his shirt. She dropped her hand from her mouth and ran it as gently as a drop of rain down the front of his shirt, flicking the buttons undone as she did so.

He closed his eyes and fought back the hatred. He wanted to hit her. He desperately desired to tear her away from him. She repulsed him. Everything that she had done he abhorred. Everything that she stood for. Her very soul was the devil to him. Yet she held the key to his worst nightmares. The whole problem stemmed from her. And he knew only too well that he walked that uncertain path between oblivion and understanding. He just could not reject her, for fear of failing.

Now that she was so close and he was so desperate to find the answer, he could do no less than take the chance.

She tore his shirt off his back in one violent wrench. It fell into pieces to the ground by her side. She breathed in the smell of his skin and ran both palms slowly up his forearms and shoulders. Then she leant forward a little and circled his right nipple with her mouth and bit sharply. Grant breathed in.

"Tonight I need a man and you are that man." She said pulling him towards the bed.

CHAPTER 13
PLEASURE AND PAIN

Pleasure and pain were a terrifying and exciting cocktail. Repulsion and disgust, twin devils that spurred his fervour to new heights.

Diane Trattorini was a wild animal. She sucked and scratched, licked and screamed until Grant's whole body ached with pleasure and pain.

At four o'clock that afternoon, he got out of the bed and lit a Galoise. He couldn't reconcile whether he had enjoyed having sex with her or whether he hated her more, and yet there was something more. His guts were telling him that she was not all bad.

He was conflicted. He was scared. But he was also in a position of some power. Trattorini would never leave Goldstein's ship alive unless he got the information which Goldstein required. And she knew that.

"I'm going to level with you Diane," he said.

"You mean you're going to tell me as much as you can without feeling unsafe?" She answered.

"That depends perhaps. You see, together we both know that we have some information. Some knowledge which is vital. You want to use it for whatever INTERFERON require. I don't know what that is. I want to know why you killed Joanne and then I want to use the information so that the Foreign Office regret leaving me to rot in a Caribbean prison."

"So what do I get out of this?" She asked.

"Let's put our heads together and see if our aims can be reconciled."

Grant drew breath and gambled. "Francoise Deboussey told me that Moscow sent £1,000 MILLION via the Libyan diplomatic bag to the IFFC to fund your terrorist campaign in the UK this year. Now it is getting near the climax and you have personally started mucking about. What do INTERFERON want?"

Trattorini sat bolt upright with the sheet pulled up around her breasts. She threw a piercing stare at him and whispered the words. "You know Francoise?"

"Sure. He directed me to you last weekend. He even gave me his cane as a sort of pass to show you that you have nothing to fear from me." Grant climbed out of bed, went to his cabin and retrieved the cane from his suitcase. When he showed it to Trattorini she grasped it lovingly and held it to her chest.

"Francoise did that?" she asked astonished.

"Believe me," he lied.

"He must trust you." She fondled the cane and teats welled in her eyes. "Then I will tell you a little piece. The Tailor is a traitor."

Grant didn't know what to say.

"Go on?" he asked.

"He has plotted the perfect counter coup. Moscow are going to step in just as the Scorpion stings."

"What does that mean?"

"Perhaps we can stop Moscow. Perhaps the SEC will ensure Moscow don't win. I'm taking a great risk. If I'm wrong, if you are Moscow, then the whole raison d'etre for INTERFERON is destroyed. But you can't be. What happened in Barbados proved that to me. I hope I'm right." She whispered looking vulnerable and worried.

Grant thought of the note, 'Don't trust the Tailor'.

"Why shouldn't I trust Tailor, Diane?"

"Oh don't worry about that note. It was a probe. We wanted to see what Goldstein would do if you showed it to him." She replied.

"Goldstein?"

Grant's mind was caught in a tornado. "Is he the Grim Reaper?"

"You've lost me with that name George." Trattorini lay down again. Grant was searching for the light. Then his mind hit the switch.

"Goldstein could be the Grim Reaper. He could be a KGB sympathiser. He could be the Tailor. He may be the one distributing the £1,000 million in the UK."

"Of course he is," Trattorini said standing up fully naked and reached for her kimono.

"Look Diane, I don't think you and I really understand each other. I'm not a terrorist. I'm not a double agent. I'm a pawn. I have been used by MI6 to probe and double check. They played me till they needed me no longer. They used my grief at the death of Joanne to hook me in."

"What do you expect of the capitalist bastards who run the system you live in. That is what Capitalism is all about. The strong using the weak. The rich using the poor. Look, I'm sorry. We only wanted to kill Goldstein's daughter. I, and I mean I, never wanted to kill anyone else. Joanne was collateral damage, as the Americans say."

"Then why did you plant two bombs at the club?" Grant asked.

"We wanted to make it look like the IRA, to the public. But Goldstein knew it was aimed at him. We phoned him to hammer the point home."

"If you are a terrorist, what has Goldstein done to make you turn against him?"

Trattorini smiled at Grant. It was an oddly warm smile. Perhaps even sympathetic. "He wants Moscow to take over the Sting."

"Riddles. More riddles. Talk sense to me please!"

"I can't George. I don't want you going straight back to the SEC and reporting. I'm not yet certain what Farhad is going to do," she replied. "And if I was certain I would not tell you."

"Do you think, even if I managed to get into the country, that MI6 or 5 for that matter would listen to me now?"

"Maybe George. Some would. The true Nationalists would. Your problem is you don't know who in the SEC is part of the Sting!"

That made Grant draw breath. "Who in the SEC? You mean someone in the SEC is mixed up in the terrorist wave?"

"I'm not saying anything. Look..." Trattorini went to the porthole and opened it.

"I'm probably mad George, but I like you. I am terribly sorry that we killed Joanne Schaeffer. You'll never know why and I can't tell you, but my cause is, or perhaps was, worth more than one life. I think you're dangerous to me. To the IFFC, to INTERFERON. I know that Farhad wants you killed. He told me before he left. But there is no need unless Fee's decision in the next few days keeps the operation alive. So until then, I'm going to let you live. I know you can get to Goldstein and to Judas. You can expose them. I will hopefully kill them. But you must promise me one thing."

"What do you mean let me live? Jack and I rescued you! You are imprisoned on Goldstein's ship. It is we who may let you live." But as Grant said the words he knew that he did not really believe them. She was completely unafraid.

"When we meet again and we will, you'll remember what I've done for you and if I don't kill Goldstein and Judas, make sure you do George."

"Do you hate them that much?"

"Yes and I hate what they stand for. They are users, manipulators and ultimately power hungry capitalists who don't give a shit about the Middle East, Palestine, communism or any poor people. Goldstein was the man who killed your woman, in reality, not me."

"The Tailor seems to be an appropriate name for him then, and the Grim Reaper perhaps even more appropriate."

"Who called him that?" Trattorini asked almost off hand.

"Francoise Deboussey," Grant replied.

*

They dressed and went up on deck. Grant sat at the stern and watched the clear spray spume from the propellers into the sparkling waters. Jack came and sat beside him.

"I have a nasty feeling about this yacht George. And that so called Captain has no idea how to handle a ship. He is a fucking Saudi. Let's get out of here and soon."

"We will Jack. But I am too close to finding the answer to go just yet."

Diane emerged from below decks with a crumpled price of paper in her hand. She sat down beside them. She looked at Jack and smiled strangely. Then she thrust the paper into Grant's hand.

"Osama was telling me last night about his new terrorist group which he has called Al-Qaeda." She said as poured herself a strong black coffee from a silver pot.

"More freedom fighters? Or terrorists? Murders in any event." Grant replied.

"He has only just recruited the first 50 in Pakistan. There is a lot to do. The Russians must be dislodged from Afghanistan. Then the USA has to be cut out of Saudi and Israel must be destroyed. Osama is utterly determined."

"What the hell is he doing here then? Jack McDougal asked.

"He is fundraising and Goldstein pays a lot."

Grant looked at the note in his hand which Trattorini had given him. She pointed at it. "This is the reason INTERFERON was formed. This is why we killed Goldstein's daughter and I suppose, why he hired you to find me."

"What is it?" Grant asked.

"A list of fictitious names:
Butcher.
Baker.
Candlestick Maker.
Tailor.
Security.

Fiona stole it from Goldstein's study at his Itchenor estate. I can't tell you any more for two reasons. As yet I am not certain what Farhad is going to do as a response to what I told him last night. He might end the Sting or he may cut Moscow out of the process. Until I know the answer, I can't bring you any closer to the truth."

"But what does the list mean?"

"These are the pseudonyms George. One of these people is a traitor at the highest level within the British Government. The others are traitors positioned strategically in the security services and armed forces. One, the Tailor, you already know."

"Christ almighty. What do they want?" Grant asked.

"Power George. It is always power. At first the IFFC thought that they could change the world. Now we know that the people on this list deceived us. They want to take the power not to change the world. We were naïve fools."

"The same old, same old with young terrorists then Dianne" Grant said slightly shaking his head. "Look it's time that we got off this Yacht. I would rather not jump out of the Government's frying pan into Goldstein's fire."

"I agree." She replied. "He wants to kill me as much as he wants to use you George. Now we both know about his deception." She then broke into a broad smile, "you have had sex with me, you know some of my secrets and now I suppose you are part of INTERFERON!"

"Well I'm bloody well not," Jack interjected and as he did so Osama looked back over his shoulder from the glassed off cabin where the helmsman was powering the ship into the dark Caribbean night. He frowned and turned his face away.

CHAPTER 14
THE DEFENCE SECRETARY

LONDON. FRIDAY, 19TH AUGUST 1988

The Defence Secretary, the Right Honourable Phillip McNaughton MP, OBE sat pensively fiddling with a Berol marking pen at his desk in Whitehall, London, SW1.

The crowds outside No.10 were enormous. Things had been the same for three days. The Prime Minister's residence was under siege. She had bravely refused to have them cleared forcibly by the police. She had said to the Defence Secretary: "it will look bad sending the police in to control members of the public who are rightly afraid. But then we are all afraid, aren't we Phillip?"

So the Defence Secretary sat quietly worrying, cocooned in his first floor office in Whitehall. Two MPs had been murdered in as many days. The IFFC had issued another three press statements. The public were becoming hysterical. He lifted his hand from the Metropolitan Police Commissioner's latest report:

'19th August, 1988 - Recommendations for London and its suburbs to control terrorist activities.'

Henry Blyth-Stafford had done his usual level-headed best. Yet his conclusion was in itself, alarming.

> "I recommend a curfew on London streets from 10.30pm to 7.30am for the next two weeks. This will enable the police and army to conduct the huge backlog of investigations required to counteract the increasing number of terrorist attacks in the last four weeks. I should state that it is with the greatest regret that I make this recommendation.
>
> Yours, Henry Blyth-Stafford"

Phillip phoned his wife. "Sally, it's Phillip. I'll be home late tonight. Don't wait up."

"Phillip. Don't hang up, something has happened."

"What dear? I'm very busy."

"The children haven't come home!" She cried.

"What!" Phillip's heart stopped.

"They left school at 4.30 and didn't come home."

"Oh Jesus! Have you phoned Granny?"

"Of course!"

"And their friends. You know, Johnny what's his name and that other little twerp?"

"Yes Phillip."

McNaughton paused. Breathed in and said, "the police?"

"I phoned them a few minutes ago."

"What did they say?"

"Difficult if..." she broke down. "I'm so scared. What's going to happen to them?"

At 11.30 that evening the phone rang at the Defence Secretary's house in Surrey. Chief Inspector Duffy indicated to the Defence Secretary to answer it. "Phillip McNaughton here."

"Mr. Defence Secretary, we have your children." the male voice said. Phillip covered the phone with his hand and waved to Chief Inspector Duffy to start the tape and commence tracing the call. He had gone white in the face and his hands were shaking.

"Who are you?" he said.

"The International Freedom Fighters Council."

"What do you want?"

"You will make a press announcement tomorrow, Mr Defence Secretary."

"Will I?"

"If you want to see your children again, you will." The voice demanded.

McNaughton choked on his saliva and closed his eyes. "What do you want me to say?"

"Take this down...

> *The Defence Secretary does not consider that the present situation warrants a curfew or the intervention suggested by senior members of the opposition, the armed forces, and the Metropolitan Police Commissioner."*

"How did you know?" The Defence Secretary blurted into the phone.

"If the statement is published in the afternoon paper, your children will be released by 4pm. If not, we will sever their left legs and send them to you in the post. Goodnight."

Chief Inspector Duffy phoned the central exchange. Within twenty seconds he had an answer.

"Kilburn High Street Chief, a phone box."

"Get the police there a.s.a.p, we won't find anything, but do it anyway."

Sally McNaughton was sobbing uncontrollably.

*

At 8.30am the next morning Phillip McNaughton met the Prime Minister at 10 Downing Street.

"I'm sorry to hear of this Phillip. It is disgusting, truly appalling. What can I do?"

"I need your guidance Prime Minister. Do I give in or not?"

Margaret Thatcher walked over to Phillip McNaughton. She took his hand and in a gesture he had never before seen, she put it between both of her hands.

"Phillip. Save your children. The press statement won't change our decision and the public aren't going to be put under curfew. Not yet anyway."

"Thank you, Prime Minister." He looked as though the weight of the world had been lifted form his shoulders.

"Before you leave Phillip, let me just say that I can see why they want the curfew stopped. They obviously think it would defuse the situation. I'm not sure they are right about that. But what about the army Phillip?"

"The Police Commissioner is now ready to call them in. Have you seen his latest report?"

"Yes, and of course I am deeply worried by it."

"The SEC meet this afternoon, Prime Minister. I would like time to consider the next steps."

"All right, Phillip. But I must tell you, time is running out." The Prime Minister looked ten years older that morning. She waved him out and Phillip McNaughton left the cabinet room and made a phone call to the Editor of the Evening Standard. The article appeared on the front page of the 1pm edition.

At 4.30pm he was hugging his young son and his daughter was by his side in tears. He closed his eyes and thanked God that he himself had not been asked to choose between his beliefs and his family. At that moment he realised that 'traitor' was not always a term of abuse. It might be a term of pity.

2ND SEPTEMBER 1988

Colonel Vladimyr Zachkristov had warded off the Head of Department's worried interference for two weeks. Today he had to face facts. The Commander in Chief of the Red Army had called him to the Kremlin. The Politburo was not in session. It was a KGB matter. Even the second in command in the KGB had not been informed about 'Operation November'. The secrecy which had surrounded the operation was tighter than any operation ever staged by the KGB. But that had to be. The stakes were higher than any in history.

The colonel walked slowly down the marble floored corridor towards two huge oak doors. The Secretary, who sat at a Louis quatorze desk, nodded and opened the door before the colonel had to break step. The warmth of the room inside enveloped him like a mink glove.

"Come in, Comrade Zachkristov!" The general said with his arms outstretched and his face a little flushed.

"Good evening, General Putz."

"Sit down, sit down," the General said.

Vladimyr sat at the end of the table. He put his cap at his right hand, and his file at his left. He looked briefly round the large rectangular table, taking in the normal faces, then returned to the General.

"Operation November is nearing completion. I believe your penultimate report is now complete. We look forward to hearing it colonel." The General sat back in his favourite burgundy leather chair and lit a Turkish cigarette. He was 72, overweight, dressed in his quasi military uniform and sweating slightly. Zachristov settled himself and started to read.

"Operation November is on target and progressing as planned. The political climate is approximately right for the final strike, our coordinator in Britain is now poised to put the operation into effect."

"Who has been chosen to carry out the operation?"

"The man called The Scorpion."

"Of course, good choice Colonel. I know his credentials well, but for those around this table who do not, please explain why he is trustworthy?" the General asked.

"We have used him many times before," Vladimyr replied. General Uri Krasilova interjected. "We all know, he's the best in the world Comrades. Trained by Osama Bin Laden at Baalbec no less. Missions in Pakistan, Afghanistan, Saudi, Israel, Iran, Chile, all successful." The head of the KGB did not give compliments lightly.

"Was he not recently imprisoned for murder in the British Caribbean island of Barbados?" Interjected another General called Stoichwaltz whom Zachristov did not know well.

"It is independent now, General. Has been since 1966." Putz responded.

"Humph. Independent!" the General Stoichwaltz responded.

"We arranged for a breakout a few days after the trial, but in the event he and two other prisoners escaped on their own before we could get to them."

"Oh bravo!" General Putz liked the idea immensely. "Anyway are we agreed he is the right man for the job?" The vote was taken. There was no dissent.

"And the nuclear weapons? They are now ready for transportation?"

"Yes, General," retorted the commander in charge of the East German Army. "They can be in Britain within twenty-four hours."

"Ah, yes. Very good." General Putz eased back into his chair and took a long drag on his cigar.

"Only now do we learn the full effectiveness of covert action. You have done exceedingly well General Krasilova. Soon the Perestroika that has brought our great country to its knees will be over and a glorious new dawn of Soviet supremacy will envelope the world." General Putz walked away from the desk and poured six glasses of vodka. The assembled dignitaries took their glasses.

"To the demise of First Secretary Gorbachev, gentlemen." They drank together and threw the glasses into the marble fire place as the Western world stepped closer to the abyss.

CHAPTER 15
THE TAILOR

On 7th September, 1988, the Daily Telegraph, The Times and The Guardian, all contained editorials which said approximately the same thing. It was, perhaps not surprisingly, the first time in publishing history that this had occurred.

The Defence Secretary read the Telegraph over his breakfast table in Epsom.

> 'In our opinion there is only one course still open to the Government of this country. The Army must be called in. We can no longer suffer the terrible onslaught which has shaken the very roots of our society, protected only by the thin blue line of the police. When, in 1939, we were attacked from abroad, the armed forces saved us. Now in 1988, when we are once again under the most vicious and barbaric attack, this time from forces which have managed to penetrate the very fabric of our Society, we must call upon them again.
>
> The streets must be secured by force. A soldier is needed on every street corner. When a terrorist outrage occurs, the area should be closed down completely. Only substantial numbers of soldiers could effect this. The police just do not have the resources or the manpower to cope with the weight of the terrorist wave. They exist to prevent civilian crime, not urban civil war.'

Phillip McNaughton looked at his wife over the top of his paper. He thought, as he had thought a thousand times before, what a lucky man he was. Perhaps now a little bit wide in the hip, but boy was she an English Rose. He was after all not a particularly handsome man himself. He loved her more than any person he had ever known. Twenty three years of marriage hadn't dented that love. They had met in Margate Magistrates Court. She was a young counsel prosecuting a flasher. He defending the man.

"Sally."

"Yes Mac." She looked up and gave him that little half smile.

"Do you feel safe?" He asked. The smile left her face. She could sense the doubt in his question. After all those years of living with him, she knew Phillip's mood instinctively.

"No. Since they took the children, Phillip. I can't feel secure."

"Is the army the answer, Sally?"

"If it stops one death, Phillip, I would say bring them onto the streets." She started clearing the breakfast table.

He arranged for the family to travel to Oban in Scotland that afternoon to stay with his Great Aunt, indefinitely and then left for work.

The Special Executive Committee for National Security met in Whitehall on the afternoon of the 7th September.

It was a cold damp day in London. The black cabs were doing a roaring trade as people decided to pay, rather than get soaked on their way to work.

*

At 3pm, Lord Carver opened the meeting. The PM was tied up elsewhere.

"Good afternoon gentlemen. You will have seen from the short reports in front of you that some considerable progress has been made in the last two weeks.

"The anti-terrorist squad, working closely with MI5, have captured five terrorists and they have all been questioned at length. The picture that they paint is a queer one. They have pieced together the stories. There are a considerable number of independent groups working in the UK. The PLO, the IRA, the Red Brigade, Lebanese and Palestinian splinter groups, a new group called Al-Qaeda, Grecian and French groups, two Cuban groups and others we don't know about."

"They appear to have entered the country last year and have received large sums of money from the Libyan Embassy and other unspecified sources. As a condition of receipt, they have all had to agree to carry out a series of terrorist acts in the UK, on orders from a central body. Although none of our captives will name the body, the IFFC is the main contender for general coordinator."

"Once they have carried out their quota they take their money and run back to their own countries. Many have done so. What each group and their operatives don't know is the reason for the big hand out. However, they all concur on one other matter. Withdrawal date is one month from now. The wave ends soon. What we need to discover is why?"

Phillip McNaughton interjected.

"Let's start with the money first shall we? There can be little doubt that whoever is holding the purse strings is the controller. What information have we got on that, Sir John?"

The Director General of the Foreign Office SIS opened his folder. "All of our sources in Libya are in agreement. The government is quite capable of masterminding this sort of action. It's been done before on a smaller scale. They think the sums involved are rather too large, but it's all possible. Anti-British feeling is running high there. It's nearly equal to the Anti-American sentiment. Undoubtedly many of the terrorists now in the UK were trained at Lebanese or Libyan camps."

"I suppose that the source may well be a collection of Arab countries?" Lord Carver pointed out.

"Quite possible," Sir John replied. The Foreign Secretary shook his head.

Lord Birch raised his fingers a little to speak. "No gentlemen, that is unlikely. My embassy staff have been scurrying to and fro from Casablanca to Baghdad and I am all but certain that no other Arab state is involved in the funding. They have too much to lose. Destabilising the British economy loses them trade and influence in their world affairs. Some would love to see the USA go under, but the UK is not their prime target." Lord Birch finished his sentence and shook his head.

"What have the CIA got for us Sir John?" Phillip McNaughton asked.

"They blame it on the Russians, of course. But I must say their suggestions have not exactly been of much help." Sir John Epcot replied.

"What evidence do they have?" The Defence Secretary asked.

"Rumour, speculation. All the usual clap trap." Sir John Epcot stopped for a second. "There was one thing. One snippet. But it came from an unreliable source. *Delta* said that my old contact in Egypt had a hunch that the KGB supplied £1,000 million to cover up a huge theft by a Libyan Government official."

"So what?" Lord Carver asked.

"Well, he thought that it was to say the least, a bit odd. His idea was that Moscow had used Libya as a channel to get funds to the UK."

"Has that been hinted of or confirmed in Russia?" Phillip McNaughton asked.

"No. Not a whisper. None of my moles have any idea about this £1,000 million. That's why I say that it's pretty shaky information. And we all know what happened to Delta after that." Heads nodded,

"Has he been located yet?" Field Marshall Carshalton asked in a disinterested manner.

"No. He is believed to have headed to Florida by ship, but we don't know. The codes have all been changed since he turned. He cannot cause any trouble now. If he sets foot in the UK he'll be picked up. For all intents and purposes he's not worth worrying about. We have so many far worse problems." Sir John stated.

The conversation turned to the terrorist wave. No explanation could be found for the sudden end predicted by the captured terrorists. Phillip McNaughton closed the meeting.

"Well, Gentlemen, we are agreed that there must be something planned for the end of the terrorist campaign. Prudence suggests that we put the Army on full home alert. I want them ready to move into London within one hour of the PM saying so. Until next week, that's it. This meeting is closed." The room cleared. As McNaughton closed the door, the Foreign Secretary turned back.

"Are you going to be at the Pre-Party conference drinks party in Brighton tomorrow, Phillip?"

"I wouldn't miss it for the world. You know as well as I do that that's the only time that we will get a chance to relax all week. The rest of it will be the usual round of press conferences and boring speeches."

"What did you think of Kinnock's speech at the Labour Party Conference?"

"Impressive. I'm afraid to say. Far too impressive. But he cannot walk along beaches and stay upright can he?" They laughed and they walked slowly down the corridor towards the Bar at the far end. As they did so Phillip McNaughton slipped a crystal ashtray into his pocket from a side table. Sir John Epcot left via the Security entrance. His driver took a right turn onto Horse guards Parade and headed towards Fleet Street.

*

On Friday, 9th September, George Grant phoned Marianne from a call box in Chichester.

"George, where are you?"

"The Caribbean, Marianne. Don't speak, just do me a favour will you?"

"Are you kidding? You've been convicted of murder George. I read it in the papers. What the hell were you doing?"

"I cannot explain it now. I'm in trouble and I need your help."

"Sure. Most escaped convicts would love my help. But that is not my line of business."

"Marianne, I am not a murderer. They conducted a very effective smear campaign. I need you help to clear my name."

"Do you presume that just because we slept together a few times I will drop my career and come running? Are you mad?"

Grant put his hand over the phone and coughed. He composed himself then answered.

"Marianne! Please trust me. Your phone will be tapped. Just go to our favourite station at 8am on your birthday. And wear your red duffle coat and that bright red felt hat, a plaid red skirt and red shoes. At least let me explain. Then if you are not satisfied you can turn me in."

There was silence for 3-4 seconds, then she said "Ok."

He rang off. He knew that if the phone was tapped they would also probably know her birthday but not their favourite station. MI5 would have to follow her there. He would just have to deal with that when it happened. Next he phoned Marie Claire's modelling agency.

What he didn't know was whether her love for him would be stronger than her allegiance to the Security Service.

*

Marianne turned twenty-nine the next day. She had worked hard to become a Deputy Section Head in the Foreign Office Armaments Department at MI6. It was a desk job, but it was fairly well paid. The holidays were good and she found it quite exciting. There were times when the evenings and weekends were not her own but that was part and parcel of any job worth its salt. She considered that she was carrying out a useful function for her country and was proud of the steps she'd made since leaving Liverpool University eight years before.

What pleased her most of all was that her parents who had long since retired, were very proud of her. They were simple working class people with humble origins and strict religious and moral values. They had brought her up to believe in the Protestant work ethic. And she did so believe.

George Grant was asking her, after a few nights of passion, to throw away her job, her respectability and perhaps her life. It was not only crazy and dangerous but probably illegal. Everything in her head told her not to go. But at 29, her heart was not totally unconnected to her decision making process. And like any human being with a sense of trust in herself she maintained a healthy respect for her own ability to judge people. So she followed her heart.

Marianne Merchant left her flat off the Kings Road at 7.30am. As she got into her car, two men switched on the engine of a brown Austin Princess twenty yards away. 'Goodbye Security,' she whispered as she drove to Sloane Square and noticed the two men following her. Suddenly she was scared. It hadn't worried her last night. It was a game then. Now it hit her. This was real. It was life. Her life. She fumbled in her coat pocket for a cigarette as she drove down Sloane Street. As she approached Battersea Bridge Road she took a sharp left and accelerated away, then turned at a dangerous speed into Ebury Street, then up a one way street and left into the Coach Station beside Victoria Railway Terminal. The Princess careered around the corner behind her. The one way street was left in chaos.

One of the men in the Princess spoke into a handset. "It's Victoria."

Marianne Marchant was already out of her car and running through the coach station. As she pushed through the swing doors at the exit she bumped into a policeman.

"What's the hurry young lady?" he asked.

"Oh officer. Thank God. Two men are following me. Please help me."

"Following you?" said the officer without looking.

"Look. Over there." Marianne pointed back into the bus station. The two men were walking slowly towards the doors talking to each other.

"Those are the men. Arrest them!" She yelped.

"But they do not appear to be chasing you madam," the officer responded.

"Oh shit. They have seen me with you. They won't run while you're here. Look, I'm going to run off that way. If they run after me will you stop them please?"

"Well, I don't know madam. What offence have they committed?"

"Oh God!" She ran towards the train station. As she crossed the road to the centre aisle, she looked back. The two men had just passed the officer. They showed him something. A card. He was nodding. She turned and raced away. They were in the Service too.

As she entered the station, the two men stopped and used a hand held radio. Marianne frantically pushed through the early morning crowds and raced to the ticket office. Where would George be? She thought. She arrived and stood motionless for a second. She looked left then right. She could see no-one like him. Just commuters all going to work. Then she saw the two men one hundred yards away. Just entering the station.

She muttered "George, where are you? Don't come now! Why did you ask me to meet you here?" She tensed. Breathed deeply twice and tried to control herself. She walked away slowly. They wanted George, not her. She decided she would tell him to run like hell. He might get away.

She walked towards platforms one to seven. As she pushed through the narrow gap in the centre of the station concourse, someone knocked into her from behind.

"Don't react Marianne. It's me." Grant was beside her. She broke into a sweat.

"Oh God. They are following me George, run!"

"I can't," he replied. She made to look round.

"Don't," he said. "I know they are there."

They reached platform six. George had two tickets. They pushed through the barrier. Marianne tensed, waiting for the hand on her shoulder. The police whistle. But it never came. As they entered the train, she took a sideways glance. There were at least ten women in view wearing her clothes. Red hat, red coat, red shoes. Grant pushed her into the train. They sat down in a first class compartment. She looked at him and laughed.

"A punk George! Orange hair?" she said nervously.

"Take off your clothes," he said.

"But George!"

"Do it quickly."

She frowned and started to undress. There was a pleading desperation in his eyes that frightened her. He took the skirt and coat and shoes and put them into the space under the seats, then he pushed a bag in front of them. He opened a small holdall and gave her a black sweater and cords with a pair of flat heeled boots.

"You've even bought the right waist size. Well done!" She joked feebly. He wasn't listening. He had sat down looking out of the window back towards the ticket barrier. There was trouble coming.

"Come on," he said.

She pulled the boots onto her feet, rolled the sweater down over her chest and followed him. They slipped out of the door on the wrong side of the train and into the adjacent train on Platform five. As they closed the door, the two men who had followed Marianne came parallel to the carriage. Marianne ducked. They turned, looked into the compartment where she had changed and suddenly that train moved off. The men ran along the platform and boarded it. Twenty seconds later platform six was empty. Grant and Marianne waited for their train on platform five to leave and then sat up in their seats.

"How did you set that up?" She asked.

"A model agency. Twenty girls at twenty pounds per hour."

"The clothes were perfect."

"As close as I could get to yours."

They kissed. She shrugged him off and then asked. "Where are we going?"

"At a stop further down the line we'll get off," he answered.

"Then where?"

"Anywhere. We need to talk. I need help. A fresh mind."

"I doubt that I will help you," She stated with conviction.

"You came. We'll see," he smiled.

They got out at Oxshott and found a small hotel. After breakfast she had a shower and came into the suite to dry off. He sat watching her for a few minutes, then she sat down on the bed and asked him what had happened in Barbados.

He tried to explain. When he had finished, she shook her head in disbelief.

"But why did Trattorini go there in the first place?" She asked.

"She said she wanted to meet Farhad Fee there. But she could have done that in England. There is some other reason."

"And why did she want to kill Daniel Judas?"

"Because, and I'm only guessing this, she thinks Judas is bound up with the Tailor, my employer, Solomon J Goldstein."

"So is he working for the KGB?" Marianne asked.

"I don't know, only he can answer that." Grant replied.

"And her meeting with Fee was to tell him that Goldstein was going to ruin the Scorpion's Sting. What does she mean?"

"Fee has a nickname. He is "the Scorpion"." Grant replied.

"So Goldstein is going to ruin one of Fee's jobs?" Marianne said.

"Fee is a professional contract killer," Grant responded. "He is also the Chairman of the IFFC. It won't just be one of Fee's jobs, it will be *the* IFFC job."

"So that's how it all ties in. One last big attack?" Marianne said. "George, whilst you have been away, the IFFC have been making regular announcements in the papers. The Government are reported to be considering bringing in the army and enforcing a curfew to control the terrorist attacks."

He got up and paced around the room for a few seconds.

"Where will it be Marianne? We will have to find out. I think that Trattorini is still the key." He said.

"She or the Tailor," she responded.

"I'll be able to find Goldstein more easily than I could find her. Let's start at Itchenor, shall we?" He asked hopefully.

"We? Not bloody likely. Anyway what are you looking for?" She replied dashing his hopes.

"Someone in the SEC is a traitor. Someone is part of the Scorpion's Sting and I believe that Goldstein is controlling them."

"What are you going to do when you find him anyway? Ask him nicely?" Marianne had a point. Finding and getting at Goldstein was going to be hard. Getting him to talk, impossible.

"There are many ways of catching a rat Marianne."

"You're going to need more help." She finally whispered enticing a smile from him.

"Jack, you and I will work something out," he teased.

LONDON, SEPTEMBER 9TH, 1988

Sir John Epcot listened quietly to Daniel Judas' oral report. When Judas had finished, Sir John said. "You can be damn sure I know what to do with this Grant fellow. Call in D Section. I want him wiped out. I can't think of anyone more dangerous."

"Yes Sir." Judas replied.

Daniel Judas phoned his operatives after leaving the office of the Director and thanked them for their report of the Victoria Station fiasco. He then phoned Sir John Epcot's assistant and arranged a meeting to discuss a D Section assignment to terminate George Grant.

*

On the way to work, on the morning of the 9th of September, Admiral James was shot dead. The news hit the Services pretty hard. If the Commander in Chief of the Navy wasn't safe, then the country wasn't safe. And the Western world slid one step closer to chaos.

*

Farhad Fee reported back to the Committee of the IFFC within twenty minutes of the kill. He knew another US$200,000 would be transferred to his private Swiss bank account that afternoon.

On Saturday the 20th of September, George Grant woke up with a pleasant surprise from Marianne. For the last ten days they had carefully planned their moves and watched their victims. Now they were ready to move.

*

At 8.30am on the same morning, the SEC met at 10 Downing Street. The assembled party was far from happy. Admiral James' chair stood empty, as a mark of respect. His Second in Command, Admiral Cecil White VC took a chair at the far end of the table.

The Prime Minister clanked her spoon onto the side of her bone china teacup. Silence descended on the table.

"Gentlemen. The Conservative Party Conference has just finished, as you all know. My Cabinet and I are extremely worried about the security of this Government and the general public in the light of the terrorist wave. I intend holding a full Parliamentary debate on the subject as the first matter on the agenda for the new Parliamentary term. Before I can do so, I need to know the SEC's view on the curfew, and I need an update on our position. Mr. Defence Secretary."

The Right Honourable Phillip McNaughton had experienced a foul morning. Sally had rung from Scotland. She was in bed with flu. The children were both going down with it. The Commissioner for the Metropolitan Police force had given him a half hour lecture on lack of funds to combat the crime wave and now this.

"Prime Minister, I have little option but to vote for the curfew. I think the situation is now so serious that greater control is required, even if only for a few weeks to cool things down."

"What about the investigations of the Libyan involvement Sir John?"

"Prime Minister, we have made full enquiries. I wouldn't call them discreet, because we have been coming down hard on all of our contacts in the Middle East. We have learnt where in Libya the money came from, the account number and the name of the official who authorised it. But he has been dead for nine months now. My own view of the situation is that whatever leads were available on the financial side, have been destroyed in the year since the money was transferred. I believe we will get quicker results from this end with the terrorists we catch.

"The Libyan Embassy is under heavy surveillance. Nothing gets in or out of there without us knowing, but it is just not involved any more. Someone else in the UK is pulling the strings now. The problem is that every time we get a good lead we seem to find that the terrorists are one step ahead of us."

"Don't be defeatist, Disney. What can you suggest that is constructive? Lord Carver?" The PM scolded.

"What we need, is to break the link between the controller and the terrorists. We have caught some terrorists. They get their orders from couriers. It is only a matter of time before we find out how the IFFC are choosing their targets. We know for instance from the IRA man we caught in early July, that twice in May they received their orders in Oxford Street from a woman with curly brown hair about 5ft 5 tall, wearing dark sunglasses and dungarees. They were paid £50,000 in cash and were ordered to bomb a large merchant bank in the City. Luckily we caught them first. When we get that woman, we will be a step closer to this IFFC lot."

"What is the chain of command in the IFFC?" the Foreign Secretary requested.

"The IFFC has Farhad Fee as its chairman. There are about five or six council members. Once they decide on a target, I assume they give the orders to a number of couriers who are not aware either of the contents of the orders, but are trustworthy with large sums of money."

"Why haven't we caught one of these couriers yet?" The PM asked.

"We are close to it Prime Minister. We already know the name of the girl." Lord Carver responded.

"Who?"

"Trattorini. Diane Trattorini. The one who slipped through our fingers in Barbados."

"Find her Gentlemen. Time is short."

*

On the 20th of September, 1988, George Grant dialled Chief Inspector Duffy's number from a public phone box in Wardour Street in Soho.

"Chief Inspector Duffy speaking."

"Bruce, it's Pain."

There was silence for an eternity. Grant didn't know whether Gruff Stuff would take the chance to meet him or not.

"What is it?" The reply was unsure. Gruff Stuff was questioning himself.

"Meet me at Old Church Street." Grant put the phone down. If Gruff Stuff's line was tapped, the IFFC or Goldstein, or Moscow would not know what it meant. Chief Inspector Duffy got hundreds of phone calls per day. It would not lead them to Grant, unless the Chief Inspector told MI5, or was involved with the IFFC. Either was possible. Grant stood outside the Falcon Pub in Wardour Street and calculated where best to watch the entrance from. The agreement had been only to use that meeting place if things were desperate. They were. The usual agreement terms applied, use the last address meaning meet at the next address on the list.

Thirty minutes later. Chief Inspector Duffy's small frame waddled up Wardour Street from the Swiss Centre. His orange hair in a terrible mess. Grant waited for ten minutes after the Chief Inspector had entered the pub, until he was sure that Gruff Stuff had not brought back up or been followed. He went in at 12.10pm.

Gruff Stuff was alone. Perhaps Grant had found someone he could trust.

"Hello, George," the Chief Inspector was sitting on a wooden stool on the first floor overlooking the street. "I saw you waiting across the street, you have grown careful."

"I'm a man in a lot of trouble, and I need to tell you what's going on."

"You are wanted for murder."

"I didn't do it." Grant replied. Gruff Stuff's grey eyes narrowed a little into Grant's.

"Tell me what you can George and I'll see if I can suppress my desire to arrest you."

"The Tailor has told me everything about the Scorpion's Sting!"
"What's that, a limerick?" Duffy grunted.
"Judas has cleared me with the IFFC!"
"You're not talking sense, George."

There was no furtiveness in his face. In the split seconds before the conscious reaction is controlled, Grant thought he could tell when he could see that flash of guilt. He could not be sure, but he had to trust someone. Duffy had no idea who the Tailor was. He didn't know Judas was a betrayer.

"Chief Inspector, you are probably the only person I can rely on in London at the moment."

"There are times when I don't understand a word you're saying. Shall we have a pint?"

For the next half hour Grant explained all he had learnt from Deboussey and from Trattorini.

"What is the Scorpion's Sting?" Chief Inspector Duffy finally asked.

"That's the billion dollar question."

"Look Grant, I've had a hideous month. My wife wants to divorce me. My children don't know me. The Chief Commissioner has roasted my backside more times than I have had hot dinners. I know I should take you in, but I also figure that you would not be here after all that you have been through if you were only interested in saving your own neck or breaking mine. I'm going to go along with you. Anyway, at the moment you appear to be the only person who has the faintest idea what, or who the IFFC are."

"Daniel Judas is the in house expert on anti-terrorist procedure at MI6. He is involved with them up to his neck. We did not know how, but Trattorini certainly does. She also said that Solomon Goldstein had betrayed the IFFC to the Russians. It looks like there is a power struggle going on within the IFFC."

"Can you not give this information to the SEC?"

"No, Chief Inspector, someone in the Special Executive Committee for National Security is a traitor."

"How do you know that?" The scorn in Duffy's voice was what Grant expected.

"Trattorini has a list of names obtained from Goldstein. She says she knows who it is, but wasn't ready to tell me. Looking at it logically if you are going to wage a campaign as big as this, you need someone in the enemy camp to see if your actions are having the intended result. On top of that the leaked information of my little trip to Egypt was at SEC level."

"So what can I do?" Duffy asked.

"Keep an eye on Judas. Put surveillance on Goldstein. Find Trattorini. Stay available for me to call at all times. OK?"

"Shit. Can I buy you a satellite too?"

"Maybe, if it will help me get a meeting with the Tailor."

"Now you are talking nonsense again."

When they parted, the Chief Inspector went off to his wife and children and Grant headed for Soho to see a man about a gun.

*

At 2.30 pm Grant pulled the Avis hire car to a halt outside Goldstein's house in Park Lane. He knocked on the door. It was answered by a withered Irish maid.

"Yes, what is it?"

"Excuse me. Is Miss Goldstein in?"

"Who is calling?"

"Tell her George Grant is here."

As the maid opened the lounge door, Grant could see Carmine was lying naked on the floor, clearly in the throes of a momentous sexual experience with a young man who looked like he spent his whole life doing just what he was doing. The maid grunted and retreated to shut the door. She looked quizzically at Grant.

"Does she spend all day in that position?"

"Oh no, Sir," the maid said quietly as she passed Grant and trundled towards the kitchen, "sometimes she is on top." She disappeared.

Grant sat at the foot of the stairs for five minutes. The young man came out looking rather flustered and without catching

Grant's eye scooted for the front door. Carmine slithered out of the lounge in a kimono.

"Georgey! You always turn up at the most inopportune moments. I've had to restrict myself to only three orgasms this morning. I hope you have a good reason for depriving me of my fun?"

"I don't know where you get the energy." He got up and went into the sitting room.

"I'm an Aries, we are full of energy. What sign are you?"

"Aries too. Does that mean I'm going to become your next victim?"

"No. Aries doesn't mix with Aries. Too many sparks. Mars rules your head and it would cause too much grief for me to make it with another person ruled by the same planet!"

"Fascinating," Grant replied. "When was the last time you saw your Dad?"

"Two weeks or so. Why?" She sat down and let the hem of her Kimono dressing gown ride unnecessarily high up her thigh.

"Because I want you to invite him over here tonight."

"Get stuffed George. I'm busy tonight." She flipped the dressing gown down over her previously exposed thigh petulantly.

"I want you to tell him that a woman called Trattorini is holding a gun to your head and that she says she'll kill you unless he comes alone."

"that sounds more fun but why should I?" She got up and started for the door, suddenly a little apprehensive.

"Stop there Pussy cat..." Grant pointed the lip of his modified Remington M1911 pistol at her bottom, "...or I'll shoot your favourite organ." She stopped and turned round.

"You wouldn't dare. Daddy would kill you."

"He has already tried sweetheart. Now I'm going to find out why. Make that call Carmine please."

"You wouldn't dare. The police would be here in ten seconds. The maid would call them."

Grant stood up slowly. "This is a silencer Carmine," he pointed at a cushion. "This is a cushion." He picked it up.

"When I put the cushion over the silencer and fire, the sound is imperceptible. Listen!" He fired once into the couch. A plume of stuffing appeared at the entrance site. The sound was no louder than a man's cough. He took her now trembling arm and sat her by the gold plated phone. Then he put the gun against the cushion and aimed at her leg. She picked up the phone and dialled. It look four calls to find her father. He was in Paris. He promised he would fly back that evening.

Next, Grant phoned Daniel Judas at MI6. Judas was just returning from a long lunch.

"Hello Daniel."

"Good God, Grant! Where are you?"

"Clumsy Daniel," Grant replied.

"We'll catch you. Give yourself up. At least that way you'll stay alive."

"You're threatening me?"

"Barbados was not my fault you know."

"Like hell."

"Listen. There is a D notice out on you." Grant was stunned for a moment. Section D had been instructed to eliminate him. That decision was potentially soul destroying. But Grant was beyond soul now.

"What have I done to you people?"

"You know too much. Come in and debrief. You would at least have a chance if you gave yourself up."

Judas tapped his watch. Ten more seconds and the call would be traced.

"Meet me in Covent Garden Piazza at 5 o'clock. Trattorini has told me what the Tailor intends to do with the Scorpion's Sting. I'll tell the SEC or I'll keep quiet for two million pounds in cash. Used notes only in a brown leather bag with no backup Daniel. Be there or I will take all of the poison out of the Sting." He slammed down the phone.

Grant made arrangements with Carmine. He tied Carmine's hands and legs to a chair.

"Sorry charming, but I promise you'll be fine." Then he lodged the chair into a cupboard. When he left he paid the maid £50 and gave her the day off.

It had to be a place with a lot of exits. A lot of people. Grant needed high points from which he could watch the set up start. Tube, bus and bike access were vital. If Judas was in the IFFC he would be in a state of panic. If his phone was bugged by MI5 he would be under suspicion from that call alone. Duffy should have had a tail on him for some hours. Perhaps the reason Trattorini wanted to kill Judas was because he was a KGB agent. He was part of the Tailor's great plan. Grant could feel the climax beginning to build up. The terrorist wave, the deaths, Joanne, Deboussey, Admiral James, countless others. What did the KGB want? Clearly destabilising the English State and the Government caused grave economic loss to the UK. But at such a huge cost: US$1,000 million. What prize made that sum worth spending? If Grant was wrong and Daniel Judas was not a traitor, he'd come without any money and he'd bring D Section. It was a hell of a risk either way.

*

By 4pm he had walked round Covent Garden Piazza twice. There were five main exits, two subsidiary ones and a lot of people. He waited until the street south of the market was clear then climbed onto the roof of the market using a rope and hook. At five to five he was sprawled spread eagle on the concrete roof of the market with a pair of binoculars. Two men with suits stood still at the southern corner. They had been there five minutes pretending to buy some antique jewellery. They had slight bulges in their jackets under the left arm. Had Judas used Section D or the IFFC? If they were Section D, Grant wondered what explanation Judas had given for the money in the bag. Where would he have got it? Only the Tailor, Solomon J Goldstein, could provide such large sums at such short notice without question.

At the western entrance Grant spotted two men on motor bikes, dressed in black leathers and pretending to be couriers. Couriers didn't idly sit and wait for ten minutes unless they were eating. They made profit out of delivering a vast amount of mail in one day. These two men were sitting smoking at 5pm. Prime delivery time in London. They were not couriers.

At three minutes past five Judas walked into the Piazza from the Floral Street end. He was wearing a green Macintosh over a grey suit, carrying an umbrella and a brown bag. His tall thin figure looked strangely out of place in the gay cosmopolitan scene. Grant felt a twinge of fear at the sight of this product of Eton, who may have turned against the system that had spawned him. Why? Was it a result of the murder of his parents by the Baader-Meinhof? Was the leading UK expert on anti terrorist methods working for the KGB? Paying terrorists? It seemed crazy. Trattorini could be wrong. Perhaps she was herself mad. Perhaps she had slaughtered so many human beings for her crusade that she no longer knew right from wrong

Grant climbed down off the roof and pulled on his torn overcoat. He then slipped on the filthy wig he had purchased at a cabaret stall earlier and headed towards Judas. Just another dirty tramp in London.

He passed the two D Section men in suits without mishap. Their eyes both fixed on a shapely pair of long fair legs which were strutting past them.

Judas didn't see Grant until he was right behind him. Grant handed him a small piece of paper which read:

"Don't speak at all. Follow me."

Grant shuffled off towards the covered market, just ahead of Judas. Judas was worried. He wanted to speak, but Grant's note held him spellbound. As soon as they reached the crowds around the market stalls Grant reached up, grabbed Judas' hat and threw it on top of the canvas cover of a jumper stall. Next he wrenched Judas' raincoat off his shoulders and threw it under the stall. A thin wire trailed out of the arm.

"Now let's go, Daniel," Grant grunted as he pushed Judas through the crowd to the other side of the market.

The bikers arrived at the stall twenty seconds later. They had seen Judas walk that way. They had not heard any orders from the transmitter radio in his lapel. They had followed their instructions to keep their distance until ordered to move in. They had not worried until they saw the raincoat lying under the stall.

Grant slipped off his wig and Macintosh and threw a leather jacket to Judas. "Put it on Daniel."

"You idiot Grant. Just because I've lost radio contact with D Section doesn't mean I'm going to come with you voluntarily."

"Daniel, if I leave now, you will have lost your job by Monday. Lord Carver will know by tonight that you and Goldstein planned the Scorpion's Sting and then I'll tell the IFFC how you intend to double cross them."

That really got Judas thinking and the thought clearly terrified him. Grant could now see why Judas had never been allowed out into the field. Fear made him seize up. He was not a strong man in the first place, but he lacked the practiced confidence and courage that an operative in the field requires.

"It's too late Grant. You'll never stop us now," Judas' first admission had been made.

Judas accepted the jacket and put it on. Grant climbed onto the bike and Judas got on behind. The brief case was still on the pavement. "Don't forget the cash Daniel." He picked it up.

Thirty minutes later Marianne entered the master file and records room at MI6 headquarters. Grant had passed Judas' security pass to her in the Strand. Judas had talked her through the security system with the certain knowledge that £2 million would be lost if he made a wrong move and the fear of a silenced hand gun in his ribs. Once she was in the file room she opened the security locks on the category 1 Personnel and withdrew the files for all eight members of the SEC. Marianne put them in her briefcase and the two left the building without mishap.

Marianne handed Judas back to Grant in Parliament Square and set off for her flat. Within ten minutes they were in St. James' Park. Grant pulled over to where they could talk. He turned off the engine. Judas got off the bike and took off his helmet.

"What will you do with the money George?" He looked shaken. His right hand circled nervously around the curve of his umbrella handle.

"I just want to get away Daniel. I don't owe this country anything. I've been jailed, shot at and hunted like a common thief. I just want peace."

"I can give you power George. More than you can ever imagine. If you join us now you could be in at the start of the whole new system."

Grant looked at Judas for a second. The glowing eyes full of excitement, the tension in his flimsy frame firing it up with enthusiasm.

"What sort of power?" Grant asked.

"Moscow rewards those who help her at crucial times. I know. When I turned, they offered me reward beyond my wildest dreams."

"What was that?"

"A position in the new order," Judas whispered.

The words shook Grant to the core. Moscow was offering sovereignty over British territory.

"It's not theirs to give Daniel," he said unconvincingly.

"Not yet, but it will be." Judas replied quite certain that he was correct in his prediction.

Grant turned away from Judas. He pretended to be thinking about a prize. In fact, he was trying to take in the awesome magnitude of the offer. Moscow were so sure that they would win sovereignty, that they had offered a part of it in return for a man ratting on his country. Judas had sold out. But Judas was not stupid. He wouldn't accept an offer like that unless he was more than sure that Moscow would win.

"How do you know they can deliver?" Grant asked.

Suddenly Judas pulled out a gun. It seemed to materialise in his hand. It must have been there for some time. Perhaps Grant just hadn't seen it. He didn't expect the desk man to carry one. He shuddered as the realisation of his terrible mistake overwhelmed him.

"You were bluffing, weren't you George." Judas smiled. "You really are a smart chap Delta. I'm glad we chose you." He started tightening the silencer onto the barrel of the pistol. "You see in the beginning we thought the IFFC were going to turn our way when the Sting came. We didn't realise how altruistic they really are. They are a bunch of semi-intellectual green welly urban terrorists. They want to destroy what you stand for George." He waved with the gun at the thickets down by the lake in the centre of the park and Grant started walking slowly through the damp grass.

"If you had told them what we intend to do, they would probably withdraw the Scorpion and bugger up the whole Sting. All ten months of the campaign would go."

"But the Scorpion already knows, Judas. Trattorini told him everything when we left Barbados."

"How? He wasn't there."

"Reagan was Farhad Fee, Daniel."

Judas stopped walking for a second then shouted "that's not possible. I saw him in court three days running. He looked nothing like Farhad Fee."

"He was the same height, at 6ft 2. Weighed about 13 stone. Age about 35. Only the hair and the face and the posture were different Daniel. And you yourself know he is the master of disguise."

Judas began to look concerned.

"So what if he knows?" he said without thinking.

'Trattorini told him about you Daniel. You and Goldstein and showed him the list of names: Butcher, Baker, Candlestick, Tailor and Security."

"Oh, no, you are wrong Grant - if she told him everything, then he would have pulled out. He is the IFFC. The Chairman. They all follow his lead. He was trained by Osama. He hasn't pulled out. He killed goddam Admiral James yesterday. Trattorini couldn't have told him. Perhaps that proves why you don't know it all. That's why you called me, isn't it? You wanted me to trip up, didn't you?" He chuckled. "You've had a fruitless trip, haven't you George. God, you've been blind. You thought you could run back to your beloved country and its stinking old boy system and spill the beans. God knows whether they would have believed you. They are so arrogant. Anyway, you've failed George."

Judas pointed for Grant to back into the shrubbery. Grant looked desperately round for some help. There was nothing. He should not have given the gun to Marianne.

Traffic was running by, up the Mall. Rush hour was in full flood. It was dark where they were standing. It had started to rain. He felt suddenly cold, helpless, tired and scared. At the edge of the cliff. He clutched at straws, desperate for a chance.

"Trattorini does know, Daniel and she told Fee, but not me. She doesn't trust me yet."

"That's possible." Judas stopped for a second. "But then Fee would have stopped the campaign."

"Perhaps he's going to go on with the Sting and deal with Moscow when the time comes!"

Judas nodded. Grant had hit the nerve.

"Thank you, George. I'll check up on that. Make sure all the appropriate double checks are in place. If he turns bad, someone can step into the Scorpion's shoes. He's not the only man who can sting."

"So he's not essential to the Sting?"

"Not the last phase, only the build up. That doesn't help you one bit. You really don't know anything, do you George? But you're a troublesome, naive little patriot and I'm going to kill you."

Suddenly a small trickle of blood appeared at Judas' temple. The metal of the arrow protruded about two inches out of his head in front of the right ear. His eyes, swollen and distorted, glared at Grant. His body juddered involuntarily and fell to the ground.

Grant ducked. He searched the park for the assassin with quick movements of the eyes. He saw traffic and commuters walking home. Then he spotted someone running over the bridge to his left. Grant sprinted out of the shrubbery and raced towards the direction of the receding figure. He saw a car door open. The figure got in. He had no chance of reaching the vehicle before it drove away. He stopped, noted the make and colour, then raced back to Judas. He searched through Judas' pockets.

"No position in the new order for you now, Daniel."

There was a small black pocket diary with various scribblings and a wallet. Grant took them and the brown bag containing £2 million and went back to the motorbike. Judas the betrayer had finally finished his trail of vengeance. Terrorism had destroyed not only his family but himself - what had made him give up his ideals? His country? Grant didn't feel that money was the answer. There had to be something more. Perhaps it was the imperfection of the present system. As Judas' old schoolmaster had said:

'He had an uncanny ability to criticise the masters for unnecessary authoritarianism or unfair preference.'

Perhaps the whole English system had just eaten Judas away until he was driven to criticise it at the most basic level. By destroying it.

*

"Are you coming, or are you attending to Judas' State funeral?" It was Trattorini's voice. He looked round. She was standing behind him in the rain smiling like an innocent child. He followed her back to the car and got in. The driver pulled away towards Parliament Square. Grant wiped the rain off his face and looked at Dianne Trattorini.

'That's the second time you've helped me out of a spot of trouble."

"Ha." She slapped her hands onto her thighs.

"You were a dead man, George. I saved your life. You owe me your life!" The words were said staccato and slow.

"Judas was a double agent. He worked for Moscow." Grant stated quietly and waited to see how Trattorini would react.

"I know. He was a traitor to the cause. His codename was Candlestick." Trattorini spat the sentence towards the side window. Her curry brown hair glistened with the fine drizzle caught in it. Grant had the feeling that something extraordinary was about to happen. It took no more than ten seconds before it did. The car pulled up outside the Houses of Parliament.

"Get out George," she said as she climbed out of her door. Grant stepped onto the kerb. She came round the rear of the car and waved for the driver to move on in front of them. The rain was heavier now. The sky was a mass of black and grey. Carbon monoxide and sulphur filled the rain as it fell onto the old buildings of London town. Rush hour traffic pressed impatiently on round Parliament Square. No-one seeing or recognising the hunched bronze statue of Sir Winston Churchill facing the tower housing Big Ben. Trattorini took Grant's arm and walked away towards the West.

"They, or rather we, are going to destroy that building and all that it signifies."

Grant halted and looked back at the ornate stone spires of the Houses of Parliament. The myriad leaded windows alight and glowing against the cold wet background of the evening sky.

"You must be mad," he replied.

"No George, not mad at all. They are rich and they have the right backing and they believe in what they are doing."

"The IFFC are a bunch of lunatic terrorists who believe in anarchy, not democracy. You either realise that Diane, or you are deluding yourself." Grant wondered if he had insulted her too deeply, but Trattorini was unmoved. She kept on walking with her arm in his.

"I sat on the ruling council for three years. They are not anarchists George. They are the conscience that the capitalist world has lost."

"Conscience is moral sense. It's not blind allegiance to the teachings of South American hypocrites. Since when has murdering innocent members of the public been an act of moral fortitude?" Grant stopped walking and stood in front of her.

"I don't expect you to understand George. You were brought up in a system which has conditioned you to accept that some people should get top rate education but others should make do with crummy comprehensives here in your own land. And for those aboard you don't give a damn what education they receive. In

Lybia, in Iraq, or in Sierra Leone, the majority of the populous are lucky to be given fresh water. Education is not provided.

You should accept that fat capitalists should exploit uneducated workers who slave away all day for a fixed pay packet whilst their betters have long business lunches washed down with fine claret.

You should realise that the US and the UK have raped Iran, Iraq and other states for their black gold for generations. The profits from their own land all go to big companies whilst the people whose land provides the black gold starve and remain uneducated.

You should see that the only way to get rid of those people, the only way to change the system, is to make them puke at breakfast when they read their newspapers. We have to make headlines. To do that we had to destroy that building."

"Terrorism never changes anything Diane. It only hurts innocent people." Grant thought of Joanne at the foot of the stairs in Stringfellows and felt a tightening in his gut.

"You are ignoring history. Freedom fighters changed Cuba. They changed Israel. One mans terrorist is another's freedom fighter. It may change Nicaragua and Ireland. We all use it. God, look at the United States. They openly fund the Contras in Nicaragua. What's the difference between that and what we are doing here?"

"The Contras are fighting for their own country. That's the difference," Grant fell cold. He waved at the driver who had been following at a respectable distance behind them. They got back in.

"George. You can't let the slavery of the English working man just continue forever. We can teach the plebiscites in the UK to fight for themselves. They are so used to unemployment and low pay packets and letting Eton and Harrow run the country from that glorified old boys' club next to us. They accept pampered Royalty in their dumb patriotic little minds believing that they deserve to be poor. God, the ultimate farce is that they even pay to wave at the Queen who they keep in the lap of luxury for no better reason than that she is the ultimate symbol of oppression. The Monarchy was built on the rape of the Third World through the armed conscription of the underprivileged here in the United Kingdom sent abroad for the East India Company and their ilk."

Grant sat quietly for a minute. Then he realised why they were talking. Why Trattorini had saved his life.

"You need me, don't you Dianne. What for?"

"I had to be sure George. I couldn't be sure in Barbados. Not even after the trial. But when Judas pulled that gun out, then I was sure."

"How did you find me?"

"Judas phoned the IFFC straight after you phoned him. We at INTERFERON still have contacts in the IFFC. We were originally members of it, after all. He placed a hit squad in Covent Garden as you probably guessed."

"Jesus Christ. You used to be the bloody IFFC! What are you now?"

"Just human beings, like you." Trattorini replied.

She commanded the driver to head for Hampstead.

"I must go back to Park Lane." Grant interrupted as they rounded the roundabout by Southwark Bridge.

"To see Goldstein?' she growled.

"He and his daughter."

"Why?" She asked.

"The Scorpion's sting."

"Don't bother, it's soon! And you cannot stop it" Trattorini's revelations flowed and Grant's mind was racing to keep up.

"How do you know?"

"It's a long story George," Trattorini replied.

"Well, tell me on the way to Park Lane, because Goldstein will be there in fifteen minutes."

Trattorini looked surprised. The driver headed up the Horseferry Road. Grant persevered "How do you know Diane?"

Her rather thin lips broke into an uneasy smile. She shifted the position of her hips on the seat. She looked so troubled.

"Fiona Galliani was the Tailor's driver. She was an IFFC junior operative. She had done a few little jobs for us and we were impressed. When the Tailor came to see the IFFC's council in late

1985, he offered £1,000 million for the largest terrorist campaign ever staged. Farhad Fee thought the idea was crazy but Osama loved it."

"Was Fee the chairman of the IFFC at that time?" Grant interjected.

"Yes, he still is and Osama Bin Laden was the vice chair. The Tailor had the sort of reputation you just don't argue with. He put £10 million on deposit, provided four lorry loads of heavy armaments and equipment and a list of organisations who had already been contacted and were prepared to operate the campaign in the UK for specified sums, so long as they could carry out their own hits at the same time."

"It took fourteen days of round the clock talks to thrash it out. By Christmas 1985, the deal was struck. The Tailor said that his reasons were purely financial. He had made his money worldwide. He had lived in the UK for ten years. He couldn't bear to feel the workers suffering the way they did. He could free them from their class ridden slavery and at the same time make himself the richest man on earth. All he wanted was the concessions for North Sea oil after the Sting. He was a convincing liar."

"And we were so gullible, we wanted to believe him. The words and the paper looked so impressive. His money was even more persuasive. Finally we, at the IFFC, were going to get the opportunity to shape a nation, to practice what we had preached for so long. And what a perfect choice! The UK. The seat of worldwide democracy. If it could be done with 56 million people, then it could be done in North America."

"We could see a chance of changing the world, without war. Without holocaust. Within two years we would free the proletariat in the UK. we intended to grant them self rule. Free the capital tied up in Swiss banks and huge corporations. Let the people go back to the land. Break away from 90% of the wealth being owned by 2% of the population. God, it was so exciting."

CHAPTER 16
PARK LANE

The jet black Mercedes pulled up outside Park Lane. Trattorini told the driver to return at 8pm. Grant let himself in with Carmine's key. He showed Trattorini into the lounge and checked Carmine was still comfortable. She was still trussed up like a turkey in the cupboard in the hall. He didn't bother to untie her mouth wrap. It was probably the first time she had kept her mouth shut since puberty. Then he closed the curtains and smiled. He turned around.

"What I don't understand Diane, is why you killed Goldstein's daughter." She sat on the sofa and put her finger through the small bullet hole Grant had made earlier in the day.

"Fiona was chosen by Goldstein to be his liaison officer with the IFFC. She was, to say the least, thrilled. As you will recall from her days at Stringfellows, she was not unattractive. She had been helping Fee for six months before she got the post, so she was on the way up anyway. When the funds came through, Fee found himself working night and day to ferry arms and explosive shipments through Customs to the UK and to co-ordinate the IRA, the PLO, the Red Brigade, the Lebanese et cetera. It was an impressive task. Osama helped but he decided to start Al-Qaeda after a god almighty row with Fee last year. So Fee sacked Osama and went on alone. He mobilised the most ferocious terrorists in the world to our cause. From about last January/February he was the controller of the majority of the terrorism on this planet. He would find men for the next hit and it would be done by the most experienced and fanatical terrorist organisations in the world. All in the UK and nearly all for the IFFC aims."

"And each group's kickback was to keep the arms and a huge payoff for the job, I suppose?" Grant replied.

"You have that part right George. Between 100 and 500 thousand pounds per hit."

"Who chose the targets?"

"We chose some. But most were chosen by the Tailor. He knew the establishment. He had the contacts. It was a regular thing, every Monday we'd receive a list of names and addresses from Itchenor."

"Christ. How many have there been?"

"About 14,000 were complete by the time that I left the IFFC."

"My God. Why did you let him decide?" Grant asked.

"He paid the money, he knew the establishment. It did not matter who we hit so long as the effect was destabilising."

Grant walked to the drinks cabinet and opened the walnut doors. He poured a stiff Scotch and a Gin & tonic for Dianne.

"Fourteen thousand dead!" he felt as if his heart was shrivelling.

"No, George. They weren't all killed. Many were just blackmailed or shaken up so that when the time came they would be ready."

*

Grant heard a creak from the door to the sitting room.

"They will be ready, Miss Trattorini," Goldstein was standing at the sitting room doorway. His portly size filling three quarters of the entrance. His shocking silver hair brushed tightly backwards over his scalp. He exuded confidence, calmness and control. Wrapped in a crisply pressed double breasted suit and swathed by a gabardine city trench coat. Goldstein thrived on confrontation.

"Don't you ever knock?" Trattorini asked.

"Not in my own house. What do you want?"

"Please sit down Solomon," Grant pointed to an armchair by the marble fire place.

Trattorini started to speak and Grant waved for her to be silent. She caught his eye and stopped.

Goldstein lit up a small Habana cigar and stood where he was.

"I don't want you to feel threatened Grant, but you are in my house, in my employ and I suggest that you would be safer answering my questions than putting you own. Or perhaps you would prefer to return, under arrest, to a Caribbean cell?"

Grant should have felt threatened, but instead he felt loathing.

"Go ahead Tailor. The police will enjoy hearing what Diane has told me about your 1,000 million dollar spending spree."

Goldstein didn't bat an eyelid. "Did you think I would be surprised that you knew? I have also been referred to as the Grim Reaper. Quaint titles aren't they? I am always prepared you know," he moved slowly towards the drinks cabinet and poured himself a brandy.

"Bertie and Sadie, two employees of mine, are waiting outside the front door. They are wonderful boys, big shoulders and no brains. They love hurting people. Can't stand it myself. Do you want to be hurt, Grant?"

"A few months ago I might have found your threats frightening. But oddly I don't now. Anyway if you had wanted us captured we would be by now. Sit down with us for ten minutes Goldstein. We have some talking to do. About Daniel Judas and about Moscow."

"Daniel Judas?" Goldstein asked innocently.

"A corpse," interrupted Trattorini.

Goldstein merely looked puzzled.

"Why does a dead man matter?" He raised his silver grey eyebrows in an arrogant way and looked questioningly at Grant.

"Your daughter is in a safe place Solomon, but she has a gun at her head and I have given orders that she be shot unless I call in at 20 minute intervals and say the appropriate words. That allows us to wile a few minutes away together, sorting out a few details about the Scorpion's Sting."

"You are wasting your time," Goldstein delivered the words in a dead pan way which made Grant feel exasperated.

"Diane. You were about to explain why Fiona Galliani killed Goldstein's daughter, Carole."

Goldstein shot a vicious sideways glance at Trattorini. Trattorini played with the left strap of her denim dungarees like an innocent child. Her brown eyes didn't seem to want to look at

Goldstein at all. At that moment it was hard to believe that she was who she was.

"Fiona acted as courier for the IFFC, running between Farhad and Goldstein for six months. The general objective of our actions was to filter industry and trade unions and to sieve the army so that the people sympathetic to the IFFC's cause floated naturally to the top, or as near as could be achieved in the time scale. You would be surprised how it only really takes twenty determined people to change the fate of a nation."

"Look at the Russian Revolution, my dear. How true!" Goldstein interrupted. She glared at him momentarily, then continued.

"It was not until May this year that Goldstein made his move on Fiona. He got her drunk, then seduced her at his private mansion in Itchenor. Then he and that beast Judas subjected her to the most degrading sexual perversions that I have ever had the misfortune to hear about." She turned her eyes slowly upwards and gave Goldstein a look of bare jagged hatred, then she got up.

"He stripped her naked," she walked over towards Goldstein's seat. "Then he tied her to the bed." She was standing in front of him.

"And he forced her to have anal sex with three different men." She spat into his face, then turned and walked away, shaking.

"One of the men was Daniel Judas. And of course, Goldstein took photos of the whole sordid session. Judas was trapped by his own perversion."

Grant lit a Galoise. Goldstein fumbled with a hanky and wiped his forehead.

"You can't set yourself up as a judge on sexual preferences you parsimonious bitch. You are not exactly heterosexual are you?"

Trattorini struck him hard across his face. He was momentarily dazed.

"Diane!" Grant interrupted. She stopped and in a moment Goldstein recovered his self-control. Trattorini continued.

"When he had finished, he untied her and fell asleep satiated. She cleaned herself up and made to leave. On the way out she passed his study. She was frightened but brave. She decided to steal from him. She took everything she could find on his desk and his briefcase too. The next day we found a writing pad in the case. The top sheet was clear, but by rubbing a pencil over it we could bring out the indentation of some writing from the previous top sheet. I can't remember the exact words but it read something like:

"*1. Moscow prepared for Scorpion's Sting in November.*
2. Guiding committee to determine detail. Judas becomes Candlestick.
3. Further £50 million available if required.
4. V.Z. to be in London to view Sting"

"It didn't take too much intelligence for us to realise that the Tailor was not working for the IFFC's goals. Instead he was working for the USSR. The old Soviet Union, not the new. All those instructions which we had followed to the letter were to allow Communists, Leninists and Trotskyites further up the ladder into positions of power ready for the Sting. Then of course there was the list of names. Butcher, Baker, Candlestick, who we now know was Judas, and Security.

"That's when I made the worst decision of my life. Instead of contacting Farhad Fee, I decided to try to put pressure on this unfeeling monster to change his mind. Farhad was out of touch on a hit in the Far East anyway. I couldn't tell Junior IFFC staff, they would have panicked, and perhaps some were double agents. I didn't know what to do. We are not Communists, Grant. We were independent. I was mad at Goldstein for raping Fiona. I decided to punish him. To get back at him. I decided to kill his daughter, Carole."

Goldstein shook his head and glared at Trattorini.

"We set up a trusted group to cut the KGB out of the sting. To sever the cancer. INTERFERON seemed the appropriate name for the new force."

Grant stood up and turned away from them both. He felt the rush of anger that comes with psychological stress beyond normal bounds. He thought: Joanne died because of Goldstein's perversity.

Because of Trattorini's perverted love for Galliani. Because she had hated Goldstein.

He desperately desired to quench his blood lust. To avenge Joanne's murder by these monstrous murderers. It took some two minutes before he came out of his psychological constipation and once again listened to the conversation. They had hardly noticed his distraction.

"You know about the Stringfellows' bombs. I wrote to Goldstein and tried to put pressure on him. It was naive."

"You were out of your depth. You have been for years," Goldstein crooned arrogantly and stubbed his cigar out into a silver ashtray.

Grant spoke to Goldstein next.

"Then you hired me to find Fiona Galliani."

"Yes," Goldstein responded, "and as a favour to MI6, who were looking for a suitable Delta for their operations."

"Why me, of all people?"

Goldstein chuckled. "MI6 had run a check on various suitable Deltas. You were the fourth choice. The other three were unavailable. And of course you were the only man alive who passed the critical test in the SAS. Also, you possessed the powerful motivation of the desire for revenge. You were the perfect choice." Goldstein smiled with self satisfaction and scratched his cheek.

"How did you know about my SAS history?" Grant asked.

"I have helped the SAS on many occasions. Sir John Epcot and I are old buddies."

Grant began to piece together a mental picture of Sir John, Daniel Judas and Goldstein weaving the whole vile tapestry.

"Wait a minute. When I found Galliani and she drove herself into a taxi in Oxford Street, her last words were

'INTERFERON are good. Don't trust the Tailor.'

"I wonder why she didn't say, don't trust Goldstein." Grant said. He was beginning to feel the threads come together.

*

The rain pelted down outside the bay window overlooking Hyde Park and Grant went to take a look outside. He parted the curtains and saw the two massive body guards were standing stock still, under the semicircular awning at the front door.

Diane continued:

"Then I got scared and ran. Farhad hadn't been in touch. I knew that the Tailor was closing in on me after Fiona died. I put the note through your door, George, to frighten him and skipped the country."

"To Barbados?" Grant lit another Galoise.

"Yes. But I had savings in Egypt and I needed to talk to an old friend, who would help me sort things out first."

"Francoise Deboussey?" Grant asked.

"He has always been a kind of surrogate father to me, ever since I trained at Baalbeck. He was a prisoner there for three and a half years. I was assigned to be his jailer for six months. Those were the most traumatic months of my life. I was torn between the cause I loved and a brain so clear and precise that he could dissect my innermost feelings and provide me with reasons why I felt them.

Francoise helped me realise that terrorism for its own sake is incredibly dangerous. It is such a powerful force. A form of devil worship in a way. If taught the wrong way it eats you up with hate and blood. He taught me to believe in a good cause. The causes of freedom. He taught me all he knew about religion. Oh... God..." She broke down and wept.

The room was silent for a while. Goldstein lit up another Habana and huffed and puffed for a while.

"How much more of this pathetic drivel am I to be subjected to?"

Trattorini's body shook with the thoughts of her past. Perhaps just the recollection of Baalbeck and then, eventually, it subsided.

By this time Grant had pieced it together. He walked from the window to sit beside Trattorini on the sofa.

"MI6 always wondered how the hell he escaped from Baalbeck. He never let on, you know." Grant took her hand. "He must have loved you very much to have let you continue in something which was so terribly contrary to everything he believed in."

"Francoise Deboussey doesn't have a hateful bone in his body." She was quieter now.

"He's dead, Diane," Grant let the words slip out as kindly as they could, but any which way they electrified her heart.

Her sharp Italian face turned slowly up to his. Fear and loss cutting out from her soul.

"Did you kill him, George?" she spat the words out poisonously.

"No. But I was with him when he died."

"How did he die?" she was snivelling now.

"On a ship, on the Nile. He was murdered. They nearly killed me at the same time."

Goldstein had had enough. He stood up.

"Look. Your heartaches are of no concern to me. What the hell do you want?"

"I want to know when and how the Scorpion will carry out the Sting," Grant demanded.

"Only Fee knows that." Goldstein replied.

"We're not stupid, Solomon" Trattorini said. "Before I left the IFFC, I knew damn well what the grand finale was. Farhad had been planning it for months."

"So, why don't you tell our inquisitive little private investigator then?" Goldstein smiled and blew smoke into Diane's face. She turned and looked Grant straight in the eye.

"They are going to blow up the Houses of Parliament at the State Opening on 6th November."

*

"Oh, Jesus," Grant thought. "All Members of Parliament of all parties, the Queen, the Duke of Edinburgh, countless civil servants, the House of Lords, the whole of British democracy wiped out in one sweep. Guy Fawkes all over again!" He was silent as he mulled over this revelation.

"Do you know how he plans to do it?"

"I don't know George," Trattorini replied.

"And that *would* be telling, wouldn't it Grant." Goldstein's flashing smile showed a glint of gold teeth and then disappeared into menace.

Grant needed time to let the terror of the thought filter through, so he pressed Dianne to continue.

"After I had talked to Francoise, he suggested I hide in Barbados for a while. He said he would talk to his contacts to see what he could do. I was confused."

"My heart said: *stop the whole plan.* Stop the Sting. But my head said no! Just kill Goldstein and the Sting can continue. Russia would never admit to losing £1,000 million on this operation. Who'd know it was them. And when the Sting was done, then the IFFC, free of Russia, could help the workers build their own country in justice, in light.

"Then, as I lay and thought in the warm evenings in Barbados, I realised that it was all impossible. All of the people who had been on those lists each Monday. The lists which Fiona had faithfully handed to Farhad each week were the staunch right. What the Tailor had done was alter the balance, shift the power base, so that when the Sting occurred, the left, the hard left, would surge into power. The army would mobilise first with communists at it's head!"

"Very good, my dear," Goldstein clapped. "I never thought you had enough brains to work that out."

"They have murdered or bribed the top ranks. All have been reached. Those who wouldn't turn, are dead. They are ready to impose martial law as soon as the Houses of Parliament go up in flames."

"I don't believe it," Grant replied. "You can't change the balance of power in this country just by killings a few people, or even by blowing up Parliament. Democracy is too engrained."

"The IFFC were not trying to ruin democracy, George. We were going to reshuffle it so that the poor got a better hand. But this bastard decided to switch packs and the Russians have all the aces."

Grant could feel an unpleasant sweat breaking out on his back. It was the realisation that the core of a conspiracy which was so widespread that he could barely have conceived it but an hour before might just work.

"Diane. He'd need more. The money is not enough. Even the IFFC are not enough. He'd need inside information. He'd need to stop the services, MI5, MI6 and Subsec from operating. The Sting won't have a realistic hope of succeeding without someone inside the operation feeding Fee information and stirring up trouble. Keeping the Scorpion informed. Russia have always had leads into MI6. Burgess, Maclean, Philby, even Blunt. But never this close. Never so near to Government. Goldstein must have someone in Subsec." He turned to Goldstein and pointed.

"Is it Sir John?" he asked.

"I do not know whether he has or not." Trattorini replied. It was only after I had told Farhad in the Caribbean about "the Sting" that I felt I had a chance of preventing the Russians succeeding. But it seems from what Goldstein says that Farhad is going to go through with it. I don't understand it! Why would he of all people, betray his own cause?" She implored.

"Ah, now there you have it. Money, my naive little sparrow." Goldstein crooned.

"Money!" She cried. "Farhad Fee wouldn't give up his values for money"

"Oh but he would, and he has." Goldstein revelled in seeing her collapse inwards on herself. All her ideals crumbling.

"Then I can no longer be a part of it," she said, and got up. She walked briskly behind the sofa and in a flash produced the crossbow, with which she had murdered Daniel Judas. Grant gasped and before either man could stop her she pointed it at Goldstein, shaking.

"You have ruined our dreams, you bastard," tears were streaming down her cheeks.

"It's time for me to go, children," Goldstein said quietly standing up.

"You'll never see your daughter again if you do," Grant said.

"Oh, I think I will," Goldstein said and pointed at the doorway. Ever the loving daughter, Carmine was standing in the gloom of the unlit hallway, Sadie and Bertie were beside her pointing two submachine guns inwards at Trattorini.

"Say goodbye to Mr. Grant and his friend Carmine we are about to leave." Carmine pointed at Grant.

"He locked me in the cupboard and told me he'd shoot me."

She ran towards Solomon and flung her arms around his neck, sobbing dramatically. Goldstein pushed her away as one would a lap poodle and walked out through the large sitting room door.

Goldstein said: "Kill Trattorini and bring the man with you back to Guildford. Come on Carmine."

*

The two huge bodyguards closed the double swing doors and one pointed an Uzzi sub machine gun at Trattorini.

"Put that pathetic toy down," he said. Trattorini obeyed with a wild look in her eyes,

The other man slowly pulled out a hunting knife from his ankle sheath. He sliced his finger on the upper end and it bled. "Oh good, it's nice and sharp," he giggled.

Diane Trattorini drew her breath and backed slowly away from the two thugs. She glanced at Grant.

"This was well thought out, George! How did you expect Goldstein to treat us? Did you expect him to tell you all he knew and give himself up?"

"No. But I wanted to plant a tracer on his car and if possible his body too. I planned to have him followed." Grant replied.

"Shut up, pretty boy," Bertie shouted, waving the Uzzi at him, so Grant stood up.

"How long have we got, Sadie?" Bertie asked with odd femininity.

"Bout an hour, dear," Sadie giggled again.

"You going to start on the bloke first, Sadie. He has more bits to cut off, don't he?" He laughed.

"Yer, I think so," the smaller thug crossed the room and slithered behind Grant. His finger tips touched Grant's shoulders lightly.

"You are well built, aren't you sweety?"

"Does this really get you excited?" Grant asked, shivering slightly.

"Always, darling. Now let's see what you have down below handsome." He said moving the hand towards Grant's trousers and eventually putting the left hand on the zip. Trattorini lurched forward, but Bertie raised the sub-machine gun.

"No no, bitch," was all he said. She halted. "Don't ruin our fun now."

Sadie slowly lowered Grant's fly. His hand pushed the blue cotton aside and he gripped hard at Grant's privates and started to squeeze.

*

A rough Scottish voice said:

"Stop."

Bertie turned with real speed but a sudden flash of light broke from behind the long velvet curtains and a lump of molten lead smashed into his chest. He fell hard to the floor. Sadie ripped his hand out of Grants trousers and lifted the knife to Grant's neck.

"Freeze you shit or I'll cut his throat," he shouted. He was staring at the curtain.

Grant took his chance, he swivelled, ducked, grasped the wrist behind the knife, kicked up with his right leg and connected with Sadie's stomach. The huge man tumbled sideways.

Jack MacDougal stepped out from behind the curtain and shot Sadie in the leg.

"You took your time, Jack."

"Well, I thought you were enjoying it."

Jack stayed behind in the house to clear up the mess and rewind the tape of the conversation, as Grant and Trattorini left the building on their way to contact Chief Inspector Duffy.

"I'll tell him everything." She said to Grant, as they walked down the steps. "I would rather things stayed as they are than have our revolution castrated by that inhumane devil and the bloody Russians."

"OK Diane," Grant responded.

As Grant and Trattorini left No.30, Park Lane at 8.13pm, two men walked slowly out from behind a laundry van parked in the bus lane outside the house. A third opened the back doors of the laundry van. As Diane raised her left arm as a sign to the driver of her Mercedes across the street one of the laundry men walked behind them to pick up a large bag off the pavement. Suddenly he brought the butt of his steel cosh down with a sickening force onto Grant's neck.

The blow rendered Grant unconscious.

The INTERFERON driver spotted the attack and swerved the Mercedes across two lanes of traffic, mounting the pavement. Trattorini swung her right elbow into the second laundry man's stomach, winding him and raced for the back passenger door of the Merc, which was half open. As she did so the third laundry man drew a gun and fired three shots. One hit the near tyre, one hit the near wing and one went through Trattorini's spine above the pelvis. Her legs gave way and she collapsed three feet from the rear of the car. The driver yelled at her to get in, then seeing her fall, accelerated away, struggling to keep the crippled car under control. Diane Trattorini breathed uneasily, face down on the pavement. Her blood seeping out of her wounds and pooling around her stomach and chest. A small trickle progressed down the pavement to the kerb. She could vaguely hear the laundry van drive away. Then there was someone over her. Speaking to her. Prodding her. Then darkness.

Jack MacDougal heard the shots and ran out of the house. He saw Diane on the pavement with a crowd gathering around her.

The emergency services were beginning to arrive outside 30 Park Lane, as Jack MacDougal entered the foyer of the Hilton Hotel at Hyde Park Corner and staggered down to the basement cocktail bar. He was swirling under a hurricane of shock, fear, and confusion. Grant was gone.

CHAPTER 17
OPERATION NOVEMBER

*B*ritish Nuclear Fuels' Sellafield Reprocessing Plant was destroyed by fourteen carefully placed explosive devices this morning. The devices were placed in the sea tanks and the acid baths in C Block and in the ponds where the waste radioactive water is stored. This is the tenth nuclear installation which has been attacked since Easter.'

The headline on the News at Ten made the Rt. Honourable Phillip McNaughton sweat. He had been phoning frantically all day. They had dropped concrete onto the storage ponds to prevent undue leakage in Building B205. Hundreds of millions of pounds worth of Plant had been destroyed. Countless jobs would be lost. The toll was enormous on the North East and on the whole country. The curfew had to be imposed. Phillip McNaughton phoned the Metropolitan Police Commissioner.

"Henry? Sorry to call on a Saturday night."

"Mr. Defence Secretary. What can I do for you?"

"Are you and Field Marshall Carshalton ready for Curfew?"

"Should we be?" Henry Blyth Stafford asked in his infamously bland voice.

"You will get the order on Monday morning if I have my way, so be ready."

"Ok, Phillip, whatever you say. By the way, did you hear about the Stock Exchange?"

"Oh, Christ. No!"

"Yes, 10.05 this evening. Four bombs. It is completely wrecked. I'm sorry Phillip. I know this will hit Government hard."

"That's an understatement, Henry." The Defence Secretary buried his head in his hands "When will it stop?" he whispered.

*

The long shadows of the Lubyanka Prison's walls stretched across the frozen dual carriageway to the front door of the headquarters of the KGB in Moscow. Five and a half million Russians were killed during Stalin's reign of terror in the early 20th century and many ended their days here. Nearly every KGB head since the first world war has been executed here, as the crown passed on from head to head. Lubyanka, the graveyard of Russian democracy and free speech.

Vladimyr Zachristov's eyes fell briefly on the statue of Derzensky, the first head of the KGB which stood in the courtyard. The organisation had come a long way since his time. In those days the major problem they faced was keeping internal order in the country. How he had struggled to free the people from the restrictive bonds of capitalist avarice and to educate them about the altruism of Socialism. And how many innocent intellectuals had he murdered? It never ceased to amaze Zachristov that Russian history was so poorly reported in the Soviet press. No country ever found its freedom through peace marches and flower power. Struggle, enterprise, fierce fights, courage and moral fibre. These were the building blocks of the great empires of history. These were the mothers of the Greek empire, the Roman conquests, the British empire and the Russian empire.

What he hadn't realised, until two years before, was that times had changed. War was no longer the most effective method of conquering states. There was a new and more cost effective method. Some might say even humanitarian. Fewer lives were lost, fewer cities burnt, less carnage wrought, Terrorism was the new *wage of fear*. The fire of change. The wind that blew the sails of tomorrow's ships of the empire.

Zachristov's internal intercom buzzed.

"Vladimyr, is that report on Iraqi naval bases complete yet?"
"Yes comrade."
"Good, then bring it up. We have one or two things to tidy up before you leave for Europe."

Zachristov was sick to death of Iraqi naval bases. They had been with him since 1968 when he first joined the KGB Middle Eastern section. Now he was the acknowledged Russian Guru on the region. He had spent every working hour for the last two years on Operation November, except when he was advising on the Middle Eastern naval bases. Frankly, he wouldn't give a damn if he never saw one again.

He made haste to General Uri Krasilova's office.

"Good evening, General. How are you tonight?" The General liked to have a few pleasant words before business. He would as a matter of course always offer a Vodka before a meeting. Vladimyr would, as a matter of course, refuse. This was a comforting ritual.

"Vodka, my friend?" Krasilova asked.

"No, thank you General."

"Now sit down, sit down. You are going to London tonight, yes?"

"Operation November is nearly at fruition General."

"It has gone well, no?"

"It was well planned General."

"Ah, you flatter me Vladimyr. But then I'm an old man. I'm very susceptible to flattery." He grinned broadly and looked at the small picture of number 10 Downing Street on his wall above the marble fire place at the far end of the oak panelled room.

"Do you think the rooms in Downing Street will have oak panelling, Vladimyr?"

"They do, General. I have carried out a full check. We will need to change the decor, but the house will do well for your first home in the Union of Democratic British Republics."

"It has a nice ring to it Vladimyr don't you think, UDBR?"

"It will be born soon, General. It is right that a name be chosen tonight." Vladimyr replied.

"Let's drink to that. Come on." The General poured two glasses. Zachristov couldn't refuse. He knew that his destiny awaited him in London and he needed the courage.

They lifted the tumblers, swallowed the vodka, gulped and threw the glasses into the fire. The General then assumed his normal cold, grey face.

"So! What is your agenda Colonel Zachristov?"

"I arrive in London at 11am, Greenwich mean time. Tonight I will go straight to the Embassy and brief the Ambassador, who, as you know, has no knowledge of Operation November. I then have a meeting with our Operation controller at 1am. From there, I will travel to see our contacts in the armed forces and the rest of the operation's ruling council. By 3am we should be fully briefed and ready for the operation to commence."

"Good, Colonel. Where will you be when the Operation commences?" the General asked gently.

"I have arranged to have breakfast with the American Ambassador at his Embassy to view the State Opening on television from there. This will also provide a perfect opportunity to assess their reaction to the terrorist outrage which we will view."

"Good, Colonel. Very thoughtful." The General tapped his fingers slowly on the marble top of the coffee table in front of his chair. "Are the communications jamming devices in position?"

"Yes, General. All radio, satellite and television will be blacked out for the whole day, from the time of the detonation."

"And telephones?" The General asked with a twinge of worry in his voice.

"Who's to phone? The MPs? The Queen? The army will be mobilised. The element of surprise will be total when the news blackout starts. All we need is between three and twelve hours to secure London, Manchester, Birmingham, Edinburgh, Liverpool, Cardiff and Belfast. The rest will follow soon after. Don't worry General. It has been taken care of."

The General rose carefully from his chair. He walked with pride over to his fireplace and picked up a silver photo frame surrounding a black and white photograph which had faded to yellow over the years.

"Colonel, in 1942 my son died fighting with the British for our freedom. In those days war was simple. There were the Nazi invaders and there were the Russian freedom fighters. Good and evil was a clear cut thing. Nowadays that has all changed. We never struggle against an overt aggressor. The semblance of peace has blanketed Europe. But the same forces still rule." He put down the picture 'IN OUR HEARTS'.

Colonel Vladimyr Zachristov nodded quietly. The General continued.

"It is the destiny of man that he should struggle to dominate, not only his environment, but also his neighbours. It has been so since time began. If we do not fight to conquer ourselves, how can we ever be ready for the testing times we have ahead of us? The time, which all too soon, will test us to the full."

Colonel Zachristov shuffled uneasily in his chair. The General had rarely opened his heart in his presence. He felt honoured and petrified at the same time. General Uri Krasilova pointed out of the thick glass window up to the clear Moskva sky.

"Out there, Colonel. Out there, is man's destiny. In space! In that universe are civilisations which you and I will never see. We can only dream of them. And unless we, the human race, sharpen our swords in practice. Unless we joust, unless we strive to conquer each other, we will never conquer space. We will become the Afghanistan of the Star System. Constantly invaded and trodden under heel."

The General suddenly stopped. He felt he had driven Zachristov too far. Opened up too much. He straightened his back.

"Comrade General," Vladimyr responded quietly, "only the unrelenting spread of Soviet Communism can hope to achieve your admirable goals. Civilisation will lapse into capitalist debauchery if we fail in our mission. The Roman Empire died the same death when efficient power subsided into sexually ambiguous hedonism. Our crusade alone, can prevent that. We will not fail you tomorrow General."

For a second the General's face was quite expressionless. Then a warm grin sprang into life. "You are a good friend of man, Vladimyr. Beware the transient pleasures in London. They are sent to try us, but we must resist!"

They embraced and Vladimyr left the room and later the building.

Vladimyr Zachristov bitterly regretted that he was not married. He had often taken girls to bed. Yet he had never quite been able to build the bond with them that he needed to feel safe, to open his heart to them.

By the time that he had reached his early twenties he had come to hate them. The more they enjoyed his touch, the more he despised them. The more they orgasmed, the more he envied them and the more they wanted to kill them. Whores had provided him with some release over the years but none had yet been able to give him the sexual release that he craved.

He played out a perverse dream world as he left the flat. He pretended to kiss his imaginary four year old son goodnight as he slept. Taking one last look at his imaginary shiny blond hair then shutting the bedroom door. He held his imaginary wife and she cried when he picked up his grey raincoat.

"Hellena, don't. I'll send for you soon. I love you."

"Be careful Vladimyr. Come back to us, to Victor and I. We love you so much."

In his mind they embraced then he left. He hated long goodbyes he thought to himself as he left his bachelor flat.

The KGB driver took him through the streets to the Airport. Aeroflot flight B447 to London left on time.

*

LONDON, NOVEMBER 1988

Celia Jones had been a closet communist for ten years. Her father was a senior trade unionist in Port Talbot. He had told wonderful stories around the fireside in the cottage in

Llandudnodd, a village outside Port Talbot, about his great victories against the capitalist employers. She had grown up starry eyed and romantic about equality, communism and workers' revolution to achieve fairness, justice and the one party state.

At fifteen she had booked a special trip to Russia and had seen the Kremlin and Leningrad with her own eyes. She had fallen in love with the Russian Tour guide.

To her eternal chagrin he later admitted he was married and she had come home empty handed. But her politics blossomed all the same. She moved to London and joined the underground wing of the Communist Party. Never letting on her political ambitions to her fellow employees, she did all she could, when she could, for the Party.

She was now a cleaner in the Houses of Parliament. Not a great position of power many would think. But it gave her access to so many documents, so many rooms, so much gossip. And she used her position to further her beliefs. Yes, she photocopied documents. Yes she sent pictures back to the Embassy staff. What she didn't know was that the staff at the Russian Embassy treated her as a monumental joke. Not one of the documents she had ever copied was of the slightest use. But they humoured her because some day her position would become useful.

On 1st November 1988 she received the call she had waited for all of her life. A junior clerk from the Russian Embassy asked her to come to the tea rooms of the Ritz at 4 pm. He knew that was the most ridiculous place for an embassy official to meet a cleaner from the House of Commons. Especially when they intended to keep their collusion incognito, but it had been decided by the Tailor that double bluff was the best form of cover. Who would suspect anything untoward from such an open meeting in such an obvious place?

Celia Jones, 45, and greying at the temples put on her slinkiest stockings to hide her varicose veins, her high heeled black shoes, her black suspenders and lace panties. She chose a flouncy white blouse and a dull black coat. She thought that she knew that spies liked kinky sex. She wanted to flirt as well as to serve the cause.

When she arrived at the Ritz she sat as directed next to the second window from the entrance, overlooking the park. She ordered tea.

"PG Tips please, not that Earl Grey dishwater," she said to the waiter.

"Yes, Madam," the waiter blushed and left. As he did so, Farhad Fee sat down at the table. She was startled. He was so well built with huge muscular shoulders, a dark black moustache, piercing deep brown eyes and such confidence. She bit her lip.

"You look beautiful, Miss Jones."

"Oh. Thank you Mr..."

"You are courageous to do this for the cause."

She blushed. He was so confident. So powerful.

"The First Secretary himself studied your file before choosing you, did you know that?"

"Oh, my goodness," her head was spinning. He put his large hand on her knee. She glanced down. No rings. But such dark matted black hairs on those fingers. Like tree trunks. Her juices started to flow.

"I'm going to give you something very important to do for us. And you must carry out my instructions to the word. Do you understand?" She nodded transfixed.

"I will leave you a small present in a box before I go. Unwrap it and put it into your bag. When you get back to work, take one out and place it in the toilets on the first floor above the Chamber of the House of Commons, then place the other in the pile of spare supplies which you usually keep in the under sink cupboard on the first floor behind the main entrance to the House of Lords. Do you understand?"

"One in the toilet and one under the sink, yes. But why put more soaps in the toilets?"

"These soaps contain tiny bugs. With them, we can tape the conversations which go on in the toilets and gain vital information for the cause."

She never bothered to examine the story, it was perfect for her. Mystery and intrigue. She felt a streak of electrifying excitement run through her belly. Then he was gone. He laughed as he left the hotel. 'What an ugly, despicable little toadstool,' he thought as he descended the stairway into Green Park tube station.

FRIDAY 3RD NOVEMBER 1988

At 9pm, after she had carried out her duties, Celia got into her Volkswagen Beetle and drove out of the NCP car park beside St Thomas's Hospital towards Vauxhall Bridge. She felt satisfied with the day. Her cleaning done in the House of Commons, she was ready to settle down in front of the telly with David, her cat and a bowl of hot soup.

She slightly regretted not having had more time with the rather attractive Embassy official, but that was life. As she braked and turned the steering wheel sharp left, she heard a small piece of glass crack. It sounded a bit like a perfume bottle being broken and sure enough when she looked down under the brake pedal she saw the remains of a broken glass ampoule. She smelt the rather sickly odour and decided to pull over. Before she could turn on the indicator the cyanide vapour paralysed her. Pain racked her every muscle. Her back arched and her eyes bulged in a terrifyingly distorted spasm. She collapsed onto the wheel. The beetle smashed into the rear of a parked Volvo.

The ambulance arrived ten minutes later. She was dead on arrival at St Thomas's Hospital. The Pathology Lab would carry out the Post Mortem sometime on Wednesday, after the backlog had cleared.

*

At 2.30am, on Sunday, 5th November 1988, George Grant was sitting on the side of a small wooden bunk in the basement of a large house in Fawkes Lane, just outside Guildford, in Surrey. The cool November night air drifted in through the bars of the open window which was ten feet off the ground in the far wall. It looked out over the lawn which led down the garden to a tremendous forest which enveloped the grounds.

Claustrophobia creeps into the soul of a man consuming his courage and mulching his independence. The cell door was constructed of six inch steel plates and was secured by two Chubb locks and one bolt. The walls were made of two feet thick granite blocks. The bars on the window were four inches thick and appeared to run at least three feet into the walls, either side of the sills. A layer of thick concrete covered the floor. Grant had thrown coins up at the ceiling, but it was also made of solid concrete.

Grant rubbed the swollen skin on the back of his neck. He looked at his watch. The State Opening of Parliament was set for 11.30am on Monday, 6th November. The Queen and the Duke of Edinburgh would leave Buckingham Palace at 11 am and be driven along the Mall and Horse Guards Parade, arriving at the House of Lords at 11.15am. The time for the return journey would depend on the length of the Queen's Speech, but it might never happen. The 21 Gun Salute was to be at 11.15 in Hyde Park and another was to take place at 12 noon at the Tower of London.

Only Jack and Marianne could save them all now. But Grant knew they were playing Russian Roulette. Someone in the SEC was a traitor. It seemed inconceivable that a man or woman could rise so high in British Society and still harbour the sort of hatred, fear and insecurity which would allow the betrayal of his or her whole country. Grant went through the members in his mind. Jack and he had spent twelve hours in the Daily Telegraph library collating information on all of the members of the SEC

The Prime Minister? If she was the one there was no hope for Britain, whether the terrorists were in charge or not. He dismissed the possibility from his thoughts.

The Defence Secretary? The Right Honourable Phillip McNaughton? A distinguished and highly profitable career at the commercial Bar behind him. An all round sportsman. He lived in Surrey with his wife and two children. Why would he possibly betray his peers? He had nothing to gain.

Grant had not yet been able to lay his hands on their personal files. But he hoped that after the events of the recent days, they would be in Marianne's flat. Perhaps she would find something.

The worst that could be said of Phillip McNaughton was contained in an editorial of the Sun on the day before he was appointed Defence Secretary. He was arrogant and had barely survived a scandalous affair with his parliamentary secretary. She was twenty years his junior and had spilt the beans to the 'News of the World'. Fortunately, for him, he had not made her pregnant so he just denied the whole story and weathered the storm.

The Directors General of MI5 and MI6, Lord Carver and Sir John Epcot? In many ways chalk and cheese. Lord Carver, the most respected man in British Intelligence for forty years. He had helped to clear up the pieces after the disastrous Burgess-Maclean scandal rocked the Services. It was he who replaced Sir Roger Hollis, the supposed fifth man of the Gay Cambridge traitors. Lord 'Barrow Boy' Carver was the Services answer to the Cambridge traitors. He came from Hackney in East London and had worked his way up through the Service. Not a single question mark over his credentials existed. He had almost single handedly rebuilt the trans-atlantic special relationship which had been so severely shaken by the treachery of Kim Philby and his camp friends.

In contrast Sir John Epcot was born into the aristocracy. He was a most genteel and courteous man. An Old Etonian who a graduated with a first from Balliol College, Oxford. He had became a master of international strategy. During his career in the Scots Guards he had served in Angola, West Africa, Rhodesia and Suez. He had been the British Ambassador in two different European countries and had sat on countless NATO committees. He was the backbone of the British International defence service. He had served so long in so many important capacities, it was hard to imagine anyone else being the DG. 'Disney,' to his friends and close colleagues, he was a giant amongst men. Mere mortals, even the DG of the CIA, turned to him for advice from time to time. They mistrusted the British Secret Services generally - but not him.

That left Wing Commander Harris, Field Marshall Carshalton and the replacement for Admiral James, who had been murdered so very recently.

Wing Commander Harris was an ex World War 2 spitfire pilot. He had quite wrongly been nicknamed 'Bomber Harris' by the men he commanded in later years. He served in 1944 at the age of eighteen. His record since that time was one of boozing, womanising and the most spectacular flying that even the RAF had ever seen. He tested jets between 67 and 72. He was the first pilot to fly the Concorde prototype. He was and remained the most revered, hardworking, but scurrilous commander in the armed forces. His school boy looks and infectious good humour had endeared him to three generations of WRAF ladies. He was on his third marriage and his appetite for women was only just surpassed by his love of flying. How could he be the sort of man to throw the liberty of the British Isles to the great brown bear? It just was not in character.

Field Marshall Jack Carshalton was also an old school tie man. He attended Ambleside and entered the army at eighteen. He rose faster than any young officer for the previous seventy years. By the time he was thirty he was a Colonel. At thirty-nine he was the youngest General ever in the history of the armed forces. He was an expert chess player and a quiet family man when off duty. He lived in Islington and sat on a local school council. He had been a member of the Conservative Party for twenty years. He had travelled widely and not surprisingly the army had taken him to most parts of the world. He was appointed Field Marshall after his predecessor had a heart attack on the second day of the Falkland's War with Argentina. The whole world knew what a splendid campaign he had run from the Army Ops room in HMS 'Hermes' the Flagship in the South Atlantic. He orchestrated the retaking of the Falklands in a matter of weeks, with resources at breaking point and under constant attack from Argentinean Exocets and of course, the elements.

Without him the whole structure of the English army over the last thirty years would have been different.

Admiral James replacement was an unknown quantity for Grant and as such was utterly suspect.

*

Chief Inspector Duffy picked up the telephone on the hall wall at his home in Clapham.

"Bruce, it's Pain." The female voice threw him for a second. He juggled with the possibilities. Was Grant dead or captured? Since Judas' death, MI5 and MI6 had closed ranks. All their information had stopped flowing into the Anti-Terrorist Squad. The word was out that the DGs were furious and suspected a gross breach of procedure. The SEC was talking of leaks. Henry Blyth-Stafford had himself explained to MI5 that the Anti-Terrorist Squad were only following Judas because of a confidential tip off from an unnamed source. He had then come to see Duffy for an explanation.

Chief Inspector Duffy had known that his job was on the line when he ordered two of his men to follow Judas at Grant's request but he had taken tough decisions before and the possibility of an MI6 man being a double agent was not entirely beyond the bounds of possibility. At that meeting earlier the Metropolitan Chief Commissioner had asked his first question with some subtlety.

"What the hell were you doing, Chief Inspector?"

"It was a lead I couldn't ignore Sir." Duffy had had a knot the size of a melon in his stomach.

"Where did it come from?"

"I can't say Sir."

"You what?" he had exploded into a tirade of abuse. Blyth-Stafford never exploded. Duffy was flabbergasted. Blyth-Stafford had gone on.

"I've been in this job thirty-four years, Duffy. I've walked the bloody streets and taken the shit they hand out. I've worked my way up through the ranks rung by rung. No favours. No father to put in a good word. No 'old school tie'. When I ask my men to level with me they do it because they know that I know what their jobs are like. I've been there. Now don't give me that 'my source is confidential' bull shit, who told you?"

"Delta." Duffy had looked down to the floor, feeling as nervous as a gazelle in the presence of a hungry lion.

The Metropolitan Chief Commissioner had sat down with a start. The room had fallen silent. He had looked away from Duffy for a second, then back.

"Oh shit. Look Chief Inspector we have worked together off and on for more than ten years. I trust your judgement more than these cloak and dagger boys at MI5. Have done so on many occasions. You've rarely let me down. But what on earth made you do this?"

"I trust him Sir," Duffy had felt the blood drain from his face.

"And how do I tell that to the Director General of MI6 that his most respected in-house expert on terrorism, one of the most vital people we have to combat the terrorist wave, is dead? He would tell me Daniel Judas was in all likelihood killed by Delta himself."

"I just don't know Sir. He came to me yesterday. He told me he had found out that the Russians had pumped £1,000 million into the terrorist wave through a man called Solomon J. Goldstein. He said there was a catastrophe coming soon. He called it *the Scorpion's Sting*. He guessed Judas was involved. A woman called Trattorini had told him so. He said a Francoise Deboussey in Egypt fitted in somewhere."

"I had a choice to make. Either I arrested him there and then, or played along. All he asked was for me to keep an eye on Judas, Goldstein and the girl called Trattorini. She is one of the two who carried out the Stringfellows' bombing. She was the one who gave evidence against Grant in the murder trial out in the Caribbean."

"What does it all mean, Chief Inspector?"

"Well, I don't know. But, I put a tail on Judas and we lost him in Covent Garden. He had goons with him by the way. The next we knew he turned up dead in St James Park with Grant's prints all over his body. Grant probably didn't kill him. Someone fired a crossbow arrow through Judas' neck. We found him with his own service pistol still in his hand," the Chief Inspector had said.

"So, what was the reason for Grant's meeting with Daniel Judas?"

"He believed that Judas was involved in controlling the terrorist activities."

"Controlling it! He is our own bloody expert on *fighting* terrorism for god's sake. That is ridiculous. What is your appraisal, Chief Inspector?"

Duffy had girded his loins and decided to throw his weight behind Grant.

"I have little to support this view but my belief is that Grant is right. He has no reason to come back to the UK and risk his life unless he really is trying to solve the murder of his fiancée, Henry."

The two men agreed to differ on the topic and parted, after planning further investigation.

The Metropolitan Chief Commissioner had left the meeting to go on to a SEC meeting, and Chief Inspector Duffy had gone home.

He now held the telephone tensely in his left hand.

"Pain, it's not you."

"He's caught. I'm acting for him," Marianne replied.

"How do I know?"

"The second meeting point is the George in Fleet Street," Duffy knew that meant the Cheshire Cheese.

"When?" He asked. He had decided to arrest her whatever happened. No favours this time.

"In forty minutes. Can you make it?" Marianne asked.

"I'll be there." Duffy slammed the phone into its wall holster. His wife came out of the bedroom. Sleep in her eyes.

"What's up, darling?"

"I'm going out on a wild goose chase, dear." He phoned the Night Desk at Scotland Yard and then phoned Henry Blythe-Stafford at home.

*

At 5.30am on Sunday 5th of November at a small airport just West of Watford Ivan Bulovitch blew warm air into his ungloved hands and swore for the hundredth time. The light aircraft needed more than four hundred alterations to its undercarriage to allow the equipment to be properly attached. It was important that it did not show from below and that it would fire effectively from the correct range. His tools and machinery had been flown over from Poland especially the night before. The other equipment had arrived late on that Sunday evening. He would have to strip a lot of ballast out of the plane to make up for the weight of the equipment. But then it didn't have to go too far.

*

At 5.45am on Monday, 6th November, the gates of the mansion on Fawkes Drive, Guildford opened slowly and the smooth low lines of a Jaguar slipped quietly past the guard who bowed subserviently.

Butcher was late. He had decided to say that he had spent the last four hours stuck in a lay-by waiting for his chauffeur to mend a fault on the carburettor. This was eventually done by blowing backwards through the carburettor.

Butcher stepped out of the nearside passenger door onto the gravel drive way and hopped in a sprightly manner up the stairs.

"Good evening, Sir," said the door guard. Butcher handed the man his coat and took a folder from the hall table. He opened the ten foot tall oak doors and the warmth of the room gushed out to meet him.

"Good evening Butcher. Glad you could make it, eventually!"

"I do apologise gentlemen. Believe it or not my Jaguar broke down."

"Before you sit down, let me introduce you to Colonel Vladimyr Zachristov of the KGB."

"NATUS is now in session."

*

Chief Inspector Duffy met Marianne outside the Cheshire Cheese at 1.00 am on Monday the 6th of November. It was a dark and chilly night and the streets were empty. Except for two detective Constables who were positioned nearby ready to arrest Marianne at the Chief Inspector's signal.

"Who are you?" Duffy asked bad temperedly.

"A friend of George's. Look I've got no time to explain now. The Scorpion's Sting is disclosed on this tape. I've listened to it three times. It's a conversation between George, a man called Goldstein and a terrorist called Trattorini. George taped it whilst they talked."

Duffy was visibly utterly shocked. Then he grinned broadly.

"Did he really? Crafty bugger." Inspector Duffy said. He was genuinely impressed. "Where is he now?"

"Goldstein has him I think. Grant is probably dead. Look, he knew what he was doing," she said coldly. He takes horrid risks.

"Sure does," the Chief Inspector saw the veneer of her courage crack as she mentioned Grant's name. At once he suspected more than mere indifference to Grant's survival.

"How did he get the tape to you?"

"George's colleague, a man named Jack MacDougal, managed to get this to me after they kidnapped Grant outside Goldstein's house in Park Lane."

Suddenly Duffy was not looking so nice.

"He was not there. You're lying."

"What do you mean?"

"We were following Goldstein after Grant's tip off. We saw him go into No.30, Park Lane and we saw Grant and Trattorini come out. My men witnessed Trattorini getting shot and Grant being kidnapped. I didn't get a report about MacDougal or any tape."

"Your men must have been careless. MacDougal went out of the rear." Marianne held onto Gruff Stuff's coat sleeve. Look, Inspector, go home, play the tape. Phone the SEC. Get someone onto this tonight. It's going to happen tomorrow. They are going to blow up the State Opening of Parliament today!"

A chilly wind flew around the rather pink ears. Reddish hair turning grey due to the passing of time and the demands of the job swirled in the rushing of the cold wind. The Inspector stood stock still, speechless for a minute, taking in the magnitude of what Marianne had just said. But when she handed him a brown case, with £2 million inside, he began to believe her.

He went straight to Scotland Yard, whilst Marianne walked back to her flat.

Chief Inspector Duffy locked himself in his office and listened to the tape. Thirty minutes later he phoned the Metropolitan Chief Commissioner at home.

Henry Blyth-Stafford dressed and drove to New Scotland Yard in twenty minutes flat. By 2.30am on Monday the 6th he was at the front door of the London residence of one of the Director's General of the British Secret Services.

The DG's teenage daughter answered the door in her nightie.

"Oh, hello officer," she blushed. "Dad's in the study. Go right in."

"I'm very grateful. Sorry to bother you."

"That's OK." She smiled sleepily and closed the door behind him. Henry walked briskly to the study.

"You look flustered Henry, what is it?" The DG's voice boomed out over the table.

"I would very much appreciate it if you would listen to this tape." The DG opened a side drawer of his desk. Then he stopped.

"Not safe in here, old chum. Come on, let's take a walk in the garden. Even my home could be bugged you know." He smiled comfortingly for a split second then passed a small cassette player to the Metropolitan Police Commissioner. Henry was relieved that the DG was taking it seriously.

They both put on Wellingtons. The Chief Commissioner had large feet but he squeezed them in and went out of the kitchen door, down the path to the bottom and into the unlit garden. Over the back wall lay Hampstead Heath. They sat down on an old bench in the cold sharp moonlight.

The DG, who was wearing an old overcoat, shivered and slipped the C45 into the radio cassette player. He looked terribly tired. They sat and listened. Twenty minutes later he turned it off.

Henry sat sweating. He was pleased to have unloaded his problem onto broader shoulders.

"Who else knows about this Commissioner?"

"Delta. He recorded it. A woman in the services called Marianne Merchant and Chief Inspector Duffy of the Anti-Terrorist Squad."

Suddenly Henry understood with even greater horror the situation that the country and he himself were in. The DG had viciously jabbed a long sharp blade under Henry's rib cage and straight into his heart. Henry felt the knife enter his heart and the pain was an explosion. He fell forwards onto the damp grass, spluttered twice and died.

"Treason takes many forms my dear Chief Inspector."

CHAPTER 18
THE UDBR

The reason why the Butcher was late for the NATUS meeting was that he had a minor practical difficulty to arrange at the last minute. Namely the disposal of the Metropolitan Chief Commissioner's body, before he could set out for Guildford. He didn't want to let on that he knew that the Tailor had slipped up. Not yet anyway.

*

Solomon Goldstein opened the meeting of NATUS.
"The first item on the Agenda is the demise of Candlestick. Butcher that is your territory. Please explain the background to Colonel Zachristov."
The DG shuffled uneasily in the high backed chair.
"Candlestick had served NATUS faithfully and well for more than a year. He had, if any, only two problems or failings, if you like. He was a pervert and therefore open to the perennial possibility of explosive blackmail and now of course, disease. Secondly he was a desk man. He could not handle physical situations. I must repeat my warning given when the committee took the decision to send him out to the Caribbean, that field work was never his forte."
"Unfortunately, he was the only NATUS operative then available in MI6 who could carry out the operation. His job, of course, was to ensure that if Grant got in touch with Trattorini, then to ensure that both would go down. They were the main risk Operation November.
"Fee went out at the request of Trattorini. She had information for him. He killed one of Tailor's agents and took his place.

However, after Fee and Grant were arrested, Candlestick used the unexpected situation to our advantage. He actually did an admirable job ensuring that Delta was convicted. However, he failed to ensure that the courier, Trattorini, was killed. She cut a deal with the authorities. Worse he totally mucked it up when she escaped with Fee and Grant."

"We had planned to spring Farhad Fee straight after the verdict anyway but he took the opportunity to run with Delta and the courier. That was a decision only he could take being there in the field. At least he would be able to keep an eye on them."

"So Fee slipped through the authorities' fingers and escaped to Mustique. Whilst on the trip, the courier told the Scorpion that she knew about the Sting. Being a former member of the IFFC ruling council, she of course, already knew of the climax to Operation November in the UK. But she thought that it was an IFFC operation. As we wished her to think."

"The difficulty with the courier was that her girlfriend, a woman called Galliani, had discovered the connection between the IFFC's work and Operation November, the glorious brainchild of Comrade Colonel Vladimyr Zachristov and our comrades at the KGB. She had discovered the sting within *the Sting*. She also stole a list naming the members of this NATUS committee by our pseudonyms, Butcher, Baker, Tailor, Candlestick, Security."

Butcher halted for a moment and took a sip of Perrier water from the Edinburgh Crystal glass on the boardroom table in front of him.

"Once Fee had been told that the IFFC wave was not a freedom fight but was actually *Operation November* a KGB funded coup, he decided not to fulfil his part. He left the courier and Grant alive and came back to the UK immediately, which was contrary to our instruction."

"This was the most crucial and difficult time for Operation November. If Fee had simply told the council of the IFFC what Trattorini had discovered then the operation together with about £1,500 million would have been lost. Fortunately, Farhad Fee is as we had predicted a man well motivated by greed and well trained by Osama Bin Laden.

"So he contacted Chairman Tailor and renegotiated the personal terms for his silence. Operation November would survive if another £20 million were deposited in Fee's Swiss account. That transfer is to occur this afternoon at 12pm, London time, after the Scorpion himself has carried out the final phase. The main Sting."

"As a result of the Trattorini disclosures, Delta has also become a walking time bomb. We of course had assumed that Francoise Deboussey, being a confidant of Trattorini, had already worked out, or been informed of Operation November. We had also assumed that he had informed Delta of the Sting because we had to assume the worst. We worked on the assumption that Trattorini had told all to Deboussey, whom she regarded as her tutor and emotional mentor and that he had then passed it on to Grant."

"As it happens that appears not to have been the case. In fact when Chairman Tailor sent Reagan in to investigate, we were in effect fulfilling a double function. To test Fee and to eliminate Trattorini and Grant. We figured that if Fee did find out about the Sting within *the Sting* and decided to withdraw after hearing what Trattorini knew, the operation could have been saved by the incarceration of all three in a Bajan jail. As it turned out Fee killed Reagan, took his place and they all escaped. As we know these things happen in battle"

Butcher turned over the page of his file and shuffled a note pad out of his pocket. He then continued in a more level monotone.

"I have already said that this was a worrying period for the operation. We effectively lost control. However Fee has struck a revised financial deal with NATUS and the operation has continued."

"Two problems still remained: Trattorini and Grant. Both unfortunately but predictably came back to London. By now Grant probably believed that Candlestick was part of NATUS although he may not have known the name or the details. So he arranged to ambush Judas in Covent Garden and he then killed him. At the same time taking his personal belongings, including a diary and his wallet. It is thought that little was discovered from these. It is not known how much Grant extracted from Candlestick before he murdered him."

What is clear now is that Grant and INTERFERON in the guise of the courier Trattorini, have joined forces. As evidence of this liaison, they both kidnapped Mr. Chairman Tailor's daughter in his town house at Park Lane last night. That forced a meeting with the Chairman."

"Thank you, Butcher," Solomon Goldstein cut in swiftly. "That will be sufficient. Despite your failures, I dealt with both of these two cancers quickly and terminally, Comrade Zachristov. Trattorini is dead and Grant is captured." Tailor seemed almost terse when he finished the sentence.

There was silence for a good 10 seconds. The Colonel put both of his large hands on to the arms of the high-backed chair and lifted his body out slowly. He walked round to the head of the table where Solomon J. Goldstein sat quietly puffing a short Habana stub. His demeanour reeked of his years in authority. But the straightness of his back and the width of his shoulders, betrayed a none too distant spell of intense physical training. He was a fighting machine, in mind and body. Older and wiser than a mere soldier. Stronger and more finely tuned than an armchair general. He stopped behind Goldstein's chair.

"Tailor," he murmured in pigeon English. "I am surprised at how close to calamity we have come."

He stopped and looked around the table. He did not see frightened men. He knew that he was addressing accomplished and confident leaders. He also knew that no operation ever went smoothly. Not if it was worth the price of a country. Then his eyes settled on the Director General.

"I must say, as a KGB officer, that I am especially surprised at the unfortunate mishap which our man in the British Secret Intelligence services has encountered, Comrade Butcher."

The DG felt the dagger at his back. He had known it was coming. He stood up quietly and calmly and pointed at Goldstein.

"If I am to be criticised and I do not claim to be perfect, I will not be criticised unfairly. The problems which I have encountered have been due, almost exclusively, to the unprofessional conduct of Mr. Chairman Tailor."

The council sat in stunned silence. This vicious verbal attack was tantamount to suicide.

"Unprofessional conduct! You impertinent imbecile!" Solomon J. Goldstein stated menacingly.

Colonel Zachristov interrupted immediately.

"Silence!" His tone was enough to silence them.

"Comrade Butcher. If you cannot substantiate your allegations, I may have to report you for insubordination and perhaps a court marshal."

Butcher threw the C45 cassette onto the boardroom table. It clattered plastically and came to rest by Chairman Tailor's right arm.

"Play it Comrade Colonel Zachristov." Butcher stated venomously. The tape was slipped into a small secretarial playback machine. The conversation from 30 Park Lane was played back for twenty minutes. When it was over, Solomon Goldstein had turned pale and was silent and withdrawn. The Colonel turned off the tape recorder. He thought for a full two minutes and then addressed Goldstein.

"How did you let yourself get drawn into a sexual mistake such as that?"

Goldstein sat transfixed. His eyes frozen in their sockets. His wiry grey hair, as if set in stone. He struggled with the embarrassment for a long time. Finally he surfaced and his spirit drove him back into the battle. Eventually he looked at Butcher and whispered.

"It was not a mistake. We needed to create an instrument with which to blackmail Candlestick. He was beginning to become disillusioned at the carnage the operation was creating."

"Using his perversions and filming them worked well. When I showed the video tape to him he gained a new incentive to continue. But I admit I was careless with the girl. I should have silenced her."

"I am not yet used to the brutal methods to which we must have recourse, in order to annex the proletariat of this Country. I am sorry Butcher. I have let you down and I have let NATUS down. I will of course resign, if you so desire."

"Bullshit, Solomon, resign my ass, you have always only been in this for the money," Butcher bellowed.

"Enough!" Colonel Zachristov said. "That is why we hired him to Chair the operation Butcher. We all have our own reasons for wanting the outcome of Operation November to be a success. And you yourself must admit that he has done very well in the main."

"I don't deny it." Butcher admitted.

"Good, then let it rest."

The Colonel accepted the Chairman's apology. The DG nodded graciously. The atmosphere changed. The Colonel took the tape and threw it into the fire. He walked back to the boardroom table.

"How many people know of that tape, Butcher?" The Colonel demanded.

"Grant and three others I think. The Chief Inspector of the Anti-Terrorist Squad, an MI5 operative called Marianne Merchant and the third was the Metropolitan Chief Commissioner. I killed him this evening."

"Of the other two people involved in the conversation, the courier Trattorini was shot. She is at St Thomas' Hospital, unconscious. She will probably die. She is certainly crippled for life. And Delta is the other. He is being detained by NATUS at present."

"Where?" The Colonel asked disinterestedly,

"In the basement of this building Sir."

*

The chairman concluded the first part of the meeting with a call to Farhad Fee to arrange to visit the Chief Inspector personally and to send a male nurse to St. Thomas's Hospital with some flowers for Marianne Merchant.

The meeting adjourned for breakfast and resumed at 6.30am.

The Tailor reopened the meeting.

"The second item of the Agenda is constitutional rearrangement under the new regime," Chairman Tailor continued. "Comrade Zachristov will be dealing with the outline. You will each have to get your departments to draw up the appropriate legislation in the next few days. No frills. Just get it done. For the present, the basic skeleton is what is needed. We can thrash it out later in the year. Comrade Colonel, if you would outline it for us?"

The Colonel opened the front page of a large folder marked:

Operation November
Proposed legislative amendments
New order for the United Democratic British
Republic, UDBR.

"Comrades, so to build a new Communist Socialist Society we are not intending to copy the Russian model to the letter. As you all know economically the lack of competition in the USSR has limited the country's growth potential when compared with Western European states. However, after very careful thought the policy advisory group have identified thirteen key areas where changes must be made from the outset to the British constitution. These are as follows:

    1. Education. All private fee paying schools are to be abolished. The state education system is to be run from central government. Political indoctrination by regular teaching of UDBR constitutional virtues is to be compulsory from the age of five. There is to be no class streaming. Brighter pupils are to be moved from their present schools to special State schools set aside for the serious contenders for top positions in the new Communist Republic.
    2. Welfare. All private medicine will be abolished or absorbed into the NHS which is to be controlled by central

government. Special clinics will be set up to service senior government officials, party members, army staff, like personnel in senior industrial and trade union jobs.

3. Industry. The top 500 companies will be nationalised and run on a competitive basis by boards appointed by central government. Success is to be gauged not only by profit, but also by the number of employees. Variable wage rises will be determined by the government, according to trade and employment success. The government, being the sole share holder, will be the sole beneficiary of profits that will be distributed amongst the whole of the country by reducing taxes for the low paid and subsidising education and health.

4. Trade Unions. These are to be extended to become part of government and membership is to be compulsory for all employees. Their functions will include education of the workers as to the benefits of the new UDBR constitution. They will arrange welfare for the sick and pensions for workers.

Their present functions as politically active units will be terminated because all workers will be working for the state, and being part of the state, they will in effect be working for themselves. By definition, the trade union will cease to be of any political use. Industrial unrest to gain higher pay will cease to be a struggle because of the workers' desire to help themselves and others, by working for the state.

5. Religion. All religions will be conglomerated into one state religion. All churches, synagogues, mosques and chapels are to be registered as government approved or destroyed. The state religion is to be determined at a later date, with higher emphasis on social cohesion and greater conformity. Bishops and Archbishops are to be appointed by central government. Church funds will be sequestrated as from the date of the Sting and used to finance community projects. It will probably be a monotheistic religion.

6. Finance. The five major clearing banks and fifteen other large banks are to be nationalised. All accountancy firms with over twenty partners are to be nationalised. Central government will employ them all, thereby ensuring efficient inspection and control of all company data.

The Stock market is to be kept open since all stock broking is to be done through a central government agency. Complete exchange control will be introduced. Limited foreign investment will be allowed.

7. Law and Order. Criminal and civil law will continue on a similar basis to the present, but Judicial Review of administrative action will be abolished. Central government will have the final say over and above the House of Lords on cases crucial to public or national interest. All the top city law firms will be nationalised and employees will become State lawyers. The Judiciary will be appointed and dismissed by the State. The Police force will become a state controlled organisation. All senior appointments will be from party ranks. An internal security service is to be set upon similar lines to the KGB. All barristers will be employed by the state.

8. Property. All estates over one acre will be registered at the central land registry. Sizeable estates will be nationalised and redistributed to smallholders as tenants of the state. All ex-council property sold in the last ten years will be purchased at half cost price.

9. Art. All valuable art treasures are to be nationalised and displayed as state art treasures rather than being hoarded in private collections. Compensation will be paid at 1960 values.

10. Media and Journalism. The BBC and ITV Television and all Radio stations will be state controlled. Strict censoring of all news to ensure quality control and consistency of approach will be introduced. All national newspapers will be nationalised in present form. Editorial boards are to be appointed by central government with complete editorial control.

A more productive and optimistic line is to be taken on leaders and front pages.

11. Defence. We will immediately withdraw from NATO. The present nuclear capability will be retained in its present form. We will reject the Trident system from the USA. Expulsion of all US forces and bases and cruise missiles from Molesworth and Greenham Common and all other sites will occur immediately. A bilateral treaty of non aggression and mutual defence will be signed with the USSR and a massive defence rearming programme using Russian equipment will be undertaken. Present UK suppliers will be nationalised and full exchange of information under the defence treaty between the USSR and the UDBR will take place immediately.

12. Trade. Trade with the EEC and Commonwealth will continue, save that free movement of persons cannot continue. If the EEC is not prepared to tolerate such dissention, we will immediately withdraw and withhold budget contributions.

13. Transport. Nationalisation of road, air and rail transport is of course vital.

That is the bare skeleton gentlemen."

The Colonel sat down. It was 7.30am on Monday 6th November. The fire at the end of the room crackled quietly as the old logs settled down into its base.

*

At five points, carefully chosen on the outskirts of London, army convoys rolled quietly into position. Under the auspices of the expected curfew, Field Marshall Jack Carshalton, Commander in Chief of the armed forces had positioned the troops on advice from his steering committee. The SEC had sent the order down the line to the army that morning. When the huge convoys of mud covered green trucks and armoured vehicles lumbered through Surbiton, it caused the few inhabitants who saw them from their bedroom windows, little fear. They had all been conditioned for weeks to expect it. The newspapers and the radio stations had cried out for curfew.

*

In the Queen Victoria ward at St Thomas' Hospital, Nurse Jane Phillips was on duty for the night rota. It had been a quiet evening. She had rung her boyfriend, Dr Knocker twice. He had been so amorous the previous day that he had suffered colic and couldn't move from her bed for the pain. She, slightly more flustered than usual had arrived at work five minutes late.

At 7am she was reading the latest Jeffrey Archer novel when the fire alarm sounded. She dropped her book on the linoleum floor and put her head round the cubicle door to view the corridor. No smoke. No noise, except the bell. She turned on the lights in the ward. Twenty sleeping patients began to awaken, moaning and groaning about the intrusion into their troubled dreams.

The guards at the door of room 115 conversed for a second, then one walked up the corridor towards her wolf whistling. His steel toecaps making the floor vibrate as they clattered on the bare lino.

"What's up nurse?" he asked with the eloquence of a rhinoceros.

"That is a fire bell, private."

"You don't like me much, do you Nurse?"

"If I bothered to waste my time thinking about you, I would be worried about my mental stability I suppose."

"Eh?"

"Oh, forget it. That noise is a fire alarm. It means that the building is on fire. Do you know what fire is? It's hot and red!"

"Shit!" he twisted his hulking frame and raced down the hall.

"Sergeant, it's a fire alarm. What the hell do we do now?" the private said.

"Stay here, soldier." Sergeant Verdant stood steady at the door to room 115 as the corridor began to fill with human beings in various states of undress. The nurses tried to create an orderly queue to the stairs but the patients who could walk, ignored them.

As the corridor filled up, the guards found themselves being battered about in the commotion. Sergeant Verdant felt slightly queasy. He scratched his calf, then lost his equilibrium and fell to the floor unconscious. Private Dawkins was flabbergasted. He bent down over the Sergeant and tried to resuscitate him.

"Sarge! What's up?" He cried. A doctor arrived twenty seconds later.

"Is he all right?" the doctor asked.

"I don't know," Dawkins replied, "he just keeled over."

"Probably the heat and the confusion. Let's get him inside, out of the corridor."

Private Dawkins unlocked and opened the door. He dragged the Sergeant inside by his shoulders. Dawkins closed the door then turned round and tensed. The doctor finished screwing the silencer onto his gun aimed it at Dawkins' head and shot him four times.

*

Farhad Fee turned round and looked at Dianne Trattorini. She was conscious and staring at him. A drip feed ran out of a vein in her left elbow. She moved her right hand a wiped her mouth. Her brown wavy hair was bunched up under a blue theatre beanie. She raised an eyebrow.

"You won't find it easy to move me Farhad, I'm paralysed from the waist down."

He did not respond.

"Then you're here to kill me." She looked down at her body and sobbed. "I thought you shared my vision Farhad. You swore the same oaths as me. We were going to change the world, free the oppressed, tear down the establishment and start a new fairer way. What happened to you? Have you lost your faith?"

A tear rolled down her face from her right eye and she wiped it away with the back of her right hand.

"Faith has nothing to do with it. I am Muslim, you are Christian. What we shared was a common upbringing in utter poverty and the same deep desire to change things, nothing more."

The alarm was still clanging in the hall and he looked uncomfortable standing there, stock still in the centre of the hospital room.

"But when we talked on the boat in Barbados I thought we had reached an agreement!"

"The fact that the Russians were behind the whole movement was a shock, I'll admit. But you were always more committed than I am to the idea of creating a fair world. I never really thought we would create one. Just destroying the old one was enough for me."

"What would the point of that have been?" Dianne pleaded.

"A first step ..." his voice trailed off a little.

"But not backwards to communism! Surely you see that?"

"I was going to kill Goldstein after we spoke, but he is persuasive."

Trattorini pushed her feeble frame upwards on the bed and felt a rage growing inside her.

"What are you? A feeble minded child? He lied to us, the money was Russian, it was never him funding us to free the workers. It was Moscow. It is a fucking communist coup Farhad! What are you doing?"

"I'm going ahead with it anyway." And then she saw it. The dead look had returned to his eyes. The world weary, cynical, hopeless, selfish killer had once again stamped on the part of his psyche which had once made him the man she had known as a fellow freedom fighter.

"He offered you more money didn't he," she said.

"Enough for Osama and I to fund Al-Qaeda for the next 20 years, to grow it into an international organisation and to free my own people, Muslims. I don't care about Christina British peasants Dianne, never have, it was always for the money, always for my people."

He shot her three times, spat at her dead body and then put the gun onto the bed and left the room. The fire alarm then stopped, as suddenly as it had started. A loud speaker announcement explained that it was a false alarm.

Farhad Fee walked to the stairs and went calmly down to the basement. He threw the white coat into a large metal bin. He put on some blue overalls with the inscription, 'Maintenance' on the back, and picked up a battered tool box and a hat. He then put on a wig and glasses. He walked slowly to the lift and took it up to the ground floor.

The Police cordon at the front door of the hospital had created a queue of people waiting to get out. Chief Inspector Duffy arrived at that moment. Fee knew his face. He had studied photos of it the night before.

Fee reached out and grabbed a passing nurse
"Nurse, where is the Admin block?"
"What?" she replied blankly.
"Who knows where the alarm was activated?"
"Oh, I don't know. Ask Admin. They are over there, near Reception."

Fee walked briskly in the direction she pointed to. A young lady from the Administration department took Fee to a point on the first floor where, as he already knew, the alarm had been set off.

"Good of you boys from maintenance to turn up so soon. I didn't expect you till morning to be honest," she said.

"Well, it's all overtime, isn't it dear?" Fee replied, clearing the glass from the red box.

"In fact, I didn't even know that you had been called," the administrator looked a little puzzled.

"I was actually on another job on the fourth floor when the alarm went off so I came to help. The air conditioning up there has been on the blink." The administrator raised her eyebrows as if to say, who cares.

"I see. Well, I'll get back to the office."

"Wait for a minute or two would you?" Fee replied. "This will only take a bit, then you can sign my sheet and I'll be off and out of your hair. Otherwise, I'll have to wait until the new admin shift come on." Fee offered her a cigarette.

"OK, just a minute or two." The fair haired administrator sat down on an orange and lime green velvet chair and smoked, whilst Fee mended the switch and replaced the glass.

Chief Inspector Duffy arrived at great speed two minutes later. He was accompanied by six officers and the senior Hospital Administrator.

"What the hell is going on?" Duffy blurted at Fee and the Junior Administrator.

"We were mending the switch, Sir," the Administrator responded.

"You idiot," the senior Administrator's eyebrows reached the ceiling. Duffy, in a blind rage, shoved Fee out of the way and looked for a second at the broken alarm.

"Well, we won't get any prints from this, will we boys? Let's get back to room 115. Don't let anyone out of this building unless he or she is checked and passed."

Five feet five of Scottish anger stomped off up the corridor leaving Fee and the Administrator apparently dumbfounded. As Duffy went, Fee shouted out. "Shall I finish the repair, Sir?" In his most subservient voice.

"Christ, yes. No point checking the blasted thing now."

Five minutes later the Junior Administrator personally showed Fee out of the building. After she went inside, he took off his overalls and hat and threw them into the nearest waste bin. He hailed a taxi and instructed it to go to Waterloo. Having picked up his Adidas bag from the left luggage office at exactly 8.30am, he phoned Guildford.

"Butcher speaking," the voice on the other end said.

"The courier won't be talking anymore."

"Good. And the other two?"

"They are being worked on. I don't have time to take either myself. I've got to get to Watford. See you at the embassy for lunch?"

"Well done, Scorpion."

"No problem. The Sting draws ever nearer."

*

The Butcher returned to the council chamber.

"Trattorini is not a problem anymore. We are still working on the Chief Inspector and the girl from MI6."

"Good," Colonel Vladimyr Zachristov nodded approvingly. "Don't kill Grant until the Marchant girl has been found. We may need him to find her. That's all for now, Gentlemen."

The meeting dispersed and the Colonel walked down to the cells in the basement.

The clanks of the bolts being unlocked woke George Grant from a light slumber.

"Don't get up." Zachristov said.

Grant stayed on the bed, but sat up. Colonel Zachristov sat on a wooden chair opposite him.

"My name is Colonel Vladimyr Zachristov. You have come very close to destroying a two year operation and losing the Soviet Union 1,500 million US$."

"I though it was sterling not dollars."

Grant said and sat still, trying to adjust to the light. The Colonel had something to say.

"Don't be humorous. I don't care about humour."

"No surprise there then."

"The strong will always control the weak, Grant. It is the way of things."

"How long have I been here?"

"A few hours."

"You have some reason for keeping me alive?" Grant asked.

"We do not waste food on worthless captives. When we have found Marchant and silenced her, you will be of no further use."

The Colonel smiled briefly, "bus t let's not talk of such things. Tell me, what has motivated you to cause so much trouble?"

"Would the word 'patriotism' mean anything to you?" Grant replied.

"Of course. Everything I do is for my Country. Your country used you for a purpose, then threw you into a Caribbean jail to rot. Patriotism didn't bring you back to England. I was wondering what did?"

"Do you have a wife?" Grant asked. The Colonel looked suddenly disturbed, his face took on a slightly fantastic glaze and then he answered in a rather unconvincing way.

"Yes. She is in Moscow. I have a son too. But you are unmarried, I believe?" Grant though that Zachristov was lying but he had no idea why. Grant thought of how he would have been, had he not taken Joanne to Stringfellows that night.

"There was a woman whom I loved. The operation you funded murdered her as it swept through London."

"I am sorry. It was not meant to be so. But this is a far less expensive way to bring about change in terms of loss of life than war you know."

"Maybe but you knew when you started this that innocent people would be murdered! She just happened to be in the wrong place at the wrong time and you made her pay for your vision with her life." Grant got up and walked over to the Colonel.

"Do you have a cigarette?" he asked.

"Yes," the Colonel lit it for him. He drew the smoke deep into his lungs.

"So where is the profit for you Colonel? 1,500 million US$ and countless lives. How will Russia profit from all this?" Grant asked.

The Colonel laughed, "we don't measure success in terms money. Your country will change today. The whole of your Parliament and its Royalty will be swept away. The military will impose martial law and the working man will breathe a sigh of relief."

"You sound like a press agent for the IFFC."

"That's what *they* wanted to hear. But our cause is more far reaching. They wanted to release the Proletariat. A noble desire perhaps but they haven't thought what would happen once the old system is destroyed. A country cannot be ruled by a vacuum. The strong always step in to take over. In the middle east war lords step in. Here it would have been the pillars of the establishment. The IFFC are dreamers with no practical follow up plan. Or just money grabber with their own agenda. We of course have had a plan all along. Whatever you may think of communism, we always have a plan."

"Now we have a chance to set up a real success. A communist Revolution in a capitalist free market. It is terrifically exciting." The Colonel said.

"Do you really expect the British people to stand by and let Moscow take over?" Grant asked.

"Moscow would not be taking over. We will merely provide the protection the new society will need. Your old ties with the United States will be severed. Fresh new equality will sweep through the land. You would have be surprised how fair the new system will be, if you could have survived to have seen it."

"And yet you are prepared to let a tarantula like Goldstein run the new system?"

Again the Colonel laughed. "No. He will merely be paid for his services. The military will start the ball rolling. Then in a few years time when the situation has calmed down, a new communist system will be created. Free of privilege and royalty. Based on merit and strength."

"Like Czechoslovakia?"

"Like no other country on earth," the Colonel rose to his feet. "I don't think you will ever understand. I am sorry for you, but you are a thing of the past."

"I don't suppose Mr. Gorbachev will lose any sleep over my death?"

"Oh, but you're wrong again. He will most probably die soon after you. We in the Soviet Union who have brought this operation to fruition are not part of Gorbachev's Perestroika. Far from it. This will be the turning point for the USSR too. Gorbachev's spineless familiarity with the USA and his cowardly reforms will die with the nationalistic fervour rekindled in Russia by this new communist revolution. The Russian empire is just now beginning. This is a new dawn. Be sorry that you will not be alive to see it." He turned to leave and the guard at the door stepped inside.

"We will not meet again," Colonel Zachristov said as he marched out of the cell.

THE SCORPION'S STING

*

Three hours later, George Grant was perched nine feet off the ground with both feet wedged against the far wall and his back against the near wall, in the small area overhanging the entrance door to the cell. As the key turned in the door he lifted his shoe in his left hand up to shoulder height.

The guard walked briskly into the cell with his gun in his right hand. The heel of the shoe swung down fast and hit the guard's right temple. The guard staggered and Grant kicked the door with the sole of his foot so that it slammed into the guard's shoulder. Again he staggered and Grant dropped clumsily on top of him, smashing his own shoulder against the door as he fell. He thrust his fist into the guard's nose and then he pulled the guard upwards for a split second and viciously smashed his torso down onto the stone floor of the cell. The head followed a split second later. The guard was knocked unconscious.

Grant disentangled himself and took the guard's hand gun. He stuck his head round the door. He saw a long stone walled corridor with low lighting and a heavy door at the far end. Another guard stood beside it just raising his weapon. Grant fired one shot into the guard's chest. He kept low and ran bare foot to the end of the corridor.

The door was unlocked. He opened it and stepped into a small hall with a wooden staircase at the far end. When he had reached halfway up the stairs, the door at the top started to open.

"Shit," he whispered and slipped under the banister. He landed barefoot on the carpet six feet below then backed under the stairs. As the guard came down Grant slipped his hand through the gap under one stair and caught his left foot. The body lost balance and fell head first. Looking up, Grant saw that there was no-one else coming, so he ducked out from under the stairs and caught the slightly dazed guard from behind as he was raising himself from the floor. He swung the handle of the pistol down hard onto the man's left cheek and he fell again. Grant kicked twice at the neck and the man stopped moving.

At the top of the stairs was a large hall with a marble floor. The tall wooden front door of the mansion stood at the far end. Two men in a grey uniforms stood motionless beside a large dark set of doors twenty feet to Grant's left and past them lay a set of tall windows. To Grant's right was a large antique Maplewood table with a Georgian grandfather clock placed in the centre. Behind that lay a large window and beside it a corridor.

Grant took a pound coin from his pocket. He threw the coin over the heads of the two uniformed men and it landed with an audible tinkle near the far windows. Both men looked at the windows, then paused for a brief conversation. One went towards the windows whilst the other stood at the doors watching the first. In the next ten seconds Grant crept round into the corridor behind the table and out of sight. It led to a rear door and from there, out into the garden.

Grant slipped out through the door and down the steps to the soil below. As he moved along the wall of the building he came up against a window with its blind drawn down. He heard voices inside. He pressed his ear against the glass.

"Colonel Zachristov will return tomorrow. It is thought wise to keep the Russian presence at a low level for the first few months until the IFFC have cooled off and the populous get used to the new system. There will be resistance, of course. There will also be dissention from the upper classes. We expect that. It happened in Afghanistan and Cuba and it will happen here but the first broadcast from Bush House will be terribly important. Comrade Butcher will make it himself on the radio, followed by a statement by Comrade Baker in a television broadcast on BBC TV. No-one will occupy Buckingham Palace. The Psychological effect of a new face there would disturb the people."

Suddenly Grant heard a noise from behind him. He turned round and focused on the noise through the moonlight.

"Hey, you. Don't move!"

Crouch, turn, aim, fire! The shot missed. He rolled twice to his right and steadied, aimed and fired again. Two rounds. The guard was running towards him. The first shot missed, the second hit his stomach. He seized his abdomen and fell. A Doberman appeared from nowhere and then a second.

Grant thrust himself from his crouch, and sprinted towards the woods. It was over sixty yards. The dogs were running at twice his speed. He soon realised he had no chance.

He stopped and turned. Thirty yards, twenty-five yards. They raced towards him, barking, their legs pounding the lawn, their teeth bared behind gnarled lips. He could handle one, but two would be difficult. Their eyes shone like four fireflies in the darkness. Grant whipped his belt away from his trousers and he began to swing it. The dog to the right jumped first. His hunting companion was only a split second behind.

Grant side stepped and swung the buckle at the end of the belt through its third arc, upwards into the dog's loins. The buckle disappeared between the hind quarters, the dog squealed and landed awkwardly breaking its leg. Its companion landed freely and turned quickly to its left. It growled and sprang at Grant from a distance of three feet. The belt was not moving fast, it was on its first arc. The dog bit into Grant's left forearm as the belt slapped harmlessly onto the dog's chest. Pain shot up the arm and he fell backwards and dropped the gun. The dog's eyes shone wildly with fear and anger and its saliva sprayed about interspersed with the dark red splatters of Grant's blood. The dog yanked its head from side to side ripping the pale flesh of his arm. Grant knew he had to stand up. If he stayed down on his back the dog would release and go for his throat. For a second he was dazed. The pain chilling his mind, then he resurfaced.

He raised his right knee and swung it into the dogs ribs, pushing it over onto the ground. He rolled on top and grabbed the dog's hind feet with his right hand. In a swift movement, he sprang to his feet. The dog's jaws were still clenched, albeit more lightly, into his arm but the rear quarters were hanging upside down. He raised the dog above his head and swung it down violently. Just as it reached the ground, it realised the danger and released its grip on Grant's arm but it was too late. The dog's spine was broken.

Grant heard three shots coming from the mansion. He had no choice now but to run like the wind. He picked up the gun and shot the second dog that lay heaving on the lawn then he dodged to his left and right as he ran the thirty yards to the woods.

As he crashed through the undergrowth he stumbled and swore and disentangled his foot

"Trip wires," he rasped as sirens started to wail like a pack of hungry wolves. He knew that a hoard of guards would be out with more dogs within seconds. The adrenalin was pumping round his body, his eyes concentrated on the path and his mind on examining any tiny piece of assistance to evade capture. This was his one chance of survival. If he failed he would surely die.

The dogs were the most immediate problem. He reached a clearing, and stripped off his shirt. For thirty seconds he ran round the clearing, swaying in and out of trees. Then he ran to the North for twenty paces and dropped his shirt. He retraced his steps and ran West for twenty paces and took off his T-Shirt. Then he ran back and rolled in the mud in the centre of the clearing. He could hear men approaching now so he ran as fast as he could to the Southern end of the clearing and long jumped onto a stump of a tree and then swung from a low branch, the pain in his left arm stabbing like a red hot poker. He landed well and ran cowering to the South.

The first Doberman reached the clearing and followed the smell round and then raced off towards the South. All of a sudden it stopped at the tree stump. Sniffed around the stump then retraced its steps and circled the clearing. Now it was joined by another dog. This one went quickly to the North. It stopped and started to dig. It found the shirt and tore it apart. The first dog now caught the scent to the West and ran off into the undergrowth. The guards arrived and waited in the clearing.

Eventually Grant reached a fourteen foot stone wall. A barbed wire coil had been placed along its top. It was too high to jump. He looked back and he could hear the dogs barking. They were still confused. He looked down at the ground. He desperately needed some foot holds.

He found a thick branch and broke it in half, then went back to the wall with a hand size rock. He worked at hip height and gouged a lump of pointing out from between two bricks. He jammed the branch in and hit it with the stone. It looked loose but it would have to do.

He reached up and did the same again. He jammed the second part of the branch into a gap and whacked it in with the rock. Then he stepped up onto the first branch. By climbing up onto the second piece of wood he was within a few feet of the top of the wall. He reached up desperately and could just feel the top of the wall with his fingers.

Letting out a low groan as he pulled himself up, the blood from his forearm dripping onto his forehead, suddenly nausea overwhelmed him. He swivelled his head away to the right and saw two figures emerging from the woods. His heart thrashed three times in that second and he heaved himself up onto the lines of barbed wire.

The terrifying swish of a bullet shot flew past his shoulder. He had no time to negotiate the barbed wire. He rolled over it, felt his stomach skin tear open and fell fourteen feet to the ground. The landing winded him. He lay flat on his back for seconds breathing in short, frantic gasps. His left forearm was aflame and damp with blood and his stomach and chest riddled with tears from the wine. A wave of nausea swept around his consciousness. He was losing his focus. He could no longer reason where he should run, what he should do. The only ability he had left was flight. It was the basic instinct that needed no cerebral function to trigger it.

Struggling to his feet, he ran an unquantifiable distance and the whole world lit up. It seemed like an explosion of light. He fell. He didn't know if he was hurt but he couldn't hear or see any longer. His eyes closed as he was no longer even capable of the basic instinct to hide. He just fell to the ground.

CHAPTER 19
MADAM PETRA'S PART II

General Uri Krasilova had no intention of sleeping that night. He looked out of his office window on the fourteenth floor of the KGB headquarters in Dzerzhinsky Square. The statue of the first head of the KGB, unveiled in 1961 by Nikita Krushchev stood hunched in darkness, in the square below.

"Comrade! You didn't know how far we could go when you created us," he whispered to the statue. He smiled and thought of the KGB in its infancy. So ruthless, so naive. So much less effective than the clean, clever, well oiled machine which he now ran.

Lubyanka Prison, situated behind the headquarters, had been the symbol of the KGB's ultimate power since the Polish nobleman, Feliks Dzerzhinsky first crushed counter revolutionaries in 1917 and became the first head and founder of the Vechieka.

How the power had grown through the years. The NKUD, the GPU, the OGPU and the Opravlenie Gosudarstvenoe Beco Pasnost. They said that Nikolai Yezhov was the most terrible head of the KGB back in 1936. The bloody dwarf he was called. He didn't last long. But during his reign he exterminated 2,500 of his own countrymen. That was the tip of the iceberg. He eventually died in Lubyanka. Lavrenti Beria was the next head.

Krasilova knew that the KGB had started life as the Extraordinary Commission for combating counter-revolution, speculation, sabotage and misconduct in office. But it had grown by the time Lavrenti Beria had come to be the head. The terror instilled in the Russian people had never been so fierce.

Lenin had written in the early 1920s that, *'the law should never abolish terror'*. During the Stalin years the Obedinennoe Gosvchastuennoe Politicheskoe Upravlenge (OGPU), chaired by Dzerzhinsky, turned the agriculture of Russia into a collective, by force. Twelve million personal farms were collectivised. Krasilova estimated that five million peasants had died during the change. The OGPU themselves conceded that three million had died.

When Beria took over, the service was a huge spider controlling every aspect of life inside the State. He had poor eyesight and wore a pinz-nez, yet he controlled daring espionage activities throughout the first world war and created the precursor to the KGB in the 1940s - the Narodnyi Komissariat Gosudarstenoe Bezopasnost (NKGB). Back then, it controlled internal security, counter espionage, the secret services and labour camps.

After the war, the ministries had developed. The KGB, controlling state security and the MVW, controlling internal security.

Beria survived a fierce battle with General Vicktor Seridrovich Abakumov, the head of SMERSH, the anti-spy arm of the Services. Eventually Abakumov was shot in Lubyanka Prison in the early 1950s.

When Stalin died in 1953, Beria had schemed to take over power but he was out manoeuvred by Georgi Matenkov who made arrangements with the army to have Beria tried and shot at Lubyanka. So the thread of death at Russia's most feared prison ran through the historical corridors of power at the KGB all the way to General Yuri Krasilova.

At that time the Soviet Politburo decided to bring the KGB to heel. The right of imprisonment without trial and power to sentence to death was taken away. The KGB proper was born. The Komitet Gosudarstvenoe Bezopasnost.

It grew in maturity over the next twenty years and learned about espionage and foreign affairs. Like a huge and bloody twenty year old farm labourer, it washed itself, clothed itself, educated itself and travelled the world.

THE SCORPION'S STING

In 1967 Yuri Andropov became the KGB chairman. When the Czechs attempted revolt in 1968, Andropov struck hard and fast. He murdered one thousand dissidents in one week to quell the rebellion. He was more worldly wise than his predecessors but just as ruthless.

He was the first man to work out how to gain control of the State, despite having been the head of the KGB. He had to separate himself from it. So in April 1972 he moved sideways to the Communist Party Central Committee ready to succeed Leonid Brezhnev. His timing was brilliant. In November 1982, Brezhnev died and Andropov succeeded. The ex KGB head had finally made the dinosaur, created by Feliks Dzerzhinsky, politically respectable. He was the First Secretary of the Soviet Union.

For Krasilova the 1980s has been hard. Thatcher and her damned capitalist success. Regan and his warmongering. But worst of all, the famine in the USSR and the economic failures of the old communism were destroying the ideal.

Then most ironically Andropov had been succeeded by the great reformer, Michaelle Gorbachev and perestroika was destroying Krasilova's beloved Russia.

Now General Uri Krasilova stood on the threshold. He was to become the first head of the KGB to succeed, where all others had failed. The KGB had come of age inside Russia. It was time for it to start flexing its muscles abroad. Yes, in the past, Poland, Czechoslovakia and Afghanistan had fallen to the bear's roar, but the west had maintained a puritanical aloofness to Soviet Democracy, which had been a psychological dagger in Uri's back. This was so, even in his early childhood, when he had been perverted by the BBC world service broadcasts.

Now the pomposity and arrogance of the British upper classes were going to be destroyed.

Uri Krasilova was horn outside Rybindk, on a small farm. He had worked on the farm collective for his first sixteen years, then left to go into the army. After a short training, he transferred to a technical college and after two years became an engineer at a local factory. At that time he joined the Party and became chairman of his local youth movement. During the war he fought in Hungary and took part in the liberation of Budapest. He was then twenty-two.

At sixty-five, he was now standing on the edge of international greatness and he felt like he had been waiting all his life for that day, the 6th of November, 1988.

He smiled as he recalled the evening two years ago when he had sat with the young Colonel Vladimyr Zachristov in the lounge of Madam Petra's Whore House in Krasnovodsk, beside the Caspian Sea.

"They were full breasted little things, your two, Vladimyr."

"With mouths like vacuum cleaners, I can tell you." The Colonel had said.

They had spent the whole evening at Madam Petra's. In Moscow, she catered for the Central Party conferences and other important events but down at her villa in Krasnovodsk she allowed only selected guests to visit. The privileged could taste the finest flowers of Soviet youth.

Her speciality was twin sixteen year old sisters. She scoured the State for them. Her pass allowed her to travel more freely than many highly placed party members but then she was in effect one herself. She had heard and kept more secrets than any Soviet woman in history. She fulfilled the natural position of a bawdy madam in Soviet society with the expected degree of raucous debauchery and polite sophistication. You could talk at Madam Petra's and no-one would ever repeat a word.

One girl back in the early 70s had done so. She was sent to Lubyanka within three hours of her breach of trust.

Uri recalled the conversation.

"Vladimyr, I am worried about the future. The KGB, my own bloody organisation, spend more than four billion US dollars a year. We have networks in every city around the globe. We have 35,000 agents."

"We run internal Soviet security and we used to control the workings of our eastern block allies."

"But this wave of disguised power grabbing called 'Democracy,' sweeping through our satellites is poisoning us. You and I know that the Czechoslovakians and the Polaks cannot run their own countries. They cannot even wipe their own arses without help from us. They are a bunch of lazy, uneducated peasants. Their so called *new democracy* is simply allowing the old capitalists to take over the reins of power. They will sell their souls to the IMF and the American Banks."

"Lord help us, even the Royalty are talking of returning to *"save their people"*. The ultimate sponges may be let back in through the side door.

"This domino effect must be halted. We have the onerous task of reversing it for the good of those poor urchins, and for our own security.

"Imagine the consequences, if Lithuania and our other border states, turn independent Vladimyr! Put a corrupt Government into a small farming community like that and we all step back to our feudal past. Then sprinkle a little CIA destabilisation similar to the sort used in El-Salvador and each state becomes a tinderbox."

"Vladimyr, we have a duty to our families and our country, to stop this irresponsibility. Gorbachev must be exposed for the arrogant, simpleminded, capitalist lap dog, that he really is."

The General had downed a tall glass of vodka and wiped his mouth with the back of his left hand and then continued:

"You see, to stage a conventional war now will never work. The nuclear bomb has effectively terminated war as a useful method of annexing people because it destroys the very people one is trying to annex. And as you and I know a country without people is like a whore house without girls. It's no fucking good."

Vladimyr had nodded and replied.

"So, perhaps this is where the Soviet Union stops expanding? It's happened to all great empires, Uri. The Greeks, the Romans, the British. At some time they all reached critical capacity and then plateaued. After a while they declined. All the more so now that Perestroika has arrived."

Krasilova condemned these words and spat them out.

"Never!"

He supported a short crop of silver hair, crowning a brow so furrowed that it resembled a used bed sheet at Madam Petra's. His nose was short and upturned, so that in conversation one could see more than a pleasant distance into his nasal cavity. He was a dapper dresser always sporting a red paisley neckerchief. He continued:

"There must be a better way. Do you know that we are spending over five billion US dollars this year on nuclear arms? God you could finance a whole country on that. You could employ 100,000 American agents for one year at US$50,000 salary for that. Think of the information we could collect with that budget. It's crippling."

After a short silence the General's friend had spoken.

"There is always another way, Uri," Vladimyr said, "but we have to hit their weak spots. For instance take Britain. Their weakness is the fact that their security is so haphazard. We've penetrated their services since before the war.

We have contacts with 50 MPs in their Parliament. We have agents in industry, finance and the Civil Service, even the Royal family. Do you remember the announcement of the wedding of Charles and Diana. We knew two days before their Prime Minister did! We have had Burgess at the Foreign Office. Remember Philby in Turkey and Washington. Donald Maclean in Washington and Cairo. We tried to recruit Edward Heath in the early 70s, do you recall?"

"Oh God yes. That despicable little organ player, Jiri Reihberger." the General had replied.

"Heath wasn't queer, so it didn't work, but it was brilliant. Heath conducting and our plant eyeing him up lecherously from the orchestra. What stage management! That was one of our funniest, Uri!"

"What about the Georgi Makev assassination?" Uri had roared with laughter. The old stories were always the best.

"The planning we put into that! Bulgaria will never be the same. Did you think of the umbrella trick or did I?" The Colonel had asked.

"Neither of us did it. Don't you recall. After he defected, he married Annabel Dilke. When they were living in Clapham in South London and his broadcasts on the BBC World Service were driving the population of Bulgaria to distraction. We commissioned a wonderful assassin named *Farhad Fee* to carry out the hit. What a madman. Brilliant, was he not? He wanted half a million pounds. We nearly killed him on the spot but then he came up with that idea. The metal ball with a 0.35 millimetre hole sealed with wax. As the wax melted the poison, Ricin, I think it was killed the target. What was that stuff?"

"It was Botulinus, tetanus and diphtheria all mixed up. Deadly. Bloody efficient tough." Vladimyr replied.

"And the British never quite understood how it worked. God, he was inventive."

General Uri Krasilova had stopped still for a second.

"You see, one of the weakest points of the western system is terrorism. They have an awful problem dealing with it. On the other hand we have no problem at all."

Vladimyr drew a deep draw on his American Marlboro cigarette, one of the perks of an evening at Madam Petra's and threw an offhand comment into the night air.

"Perhaps we should fund more terrorism in the UK."

He didn't expect the volcanic reaction that the comment produced from the chairman of the KGB.

"That's it! Oh my God, Vladimyr, don't you see?" His eyes bulged rabidly. He suddenly looked twenty years younger.

"That's the way. The lack of security at the top. The achilles heel to terrorism. The availability of quality terror in the middle east and the finance raised from here or through our friends in Romania, Poland, Czechoslovakia and East Germany. We could succeed in destabilising the whole economy and slowing down the arms race. It would save us millions."

"That's not enough. The aim isn't just to save money. We must go for the throat, Uri." Vladimyr had prompted.

The General resembled a puppy seeing snow for the first time. A wonderland of thought and light shone out of his face.

"You're right. The very idea of Democracy itself should be tarnished. Revolution! All we need to do is destroy the Parliament and the Royal Family and what do they have? Nothing." He had shouted.

"Then we would need the army to step in." Vladimyr Zachristov was beginning to feel the excitement.

"We have contacts there and in industry. We'd need to hone the field down a lot. Narrow the odds. We'd need to go through the normal period of readjustment of public understanding."

"You mean, *Terror*, Uri?" Vladimyr had said.

"Exactly," the General got out of his chair with a light spring and walked out to the balustrade of the balcony. From there the Caspian Sea sparkled like a huge diamond tiara.

"We need that man from the Makev job." His change from the future tense to the present suddenly frightened the Colonel.

"Farhad Fee you mean?"

The General Uri Krasilova turned round and gave the first of a hundred thousand orders for the plan which became *Operation November*.

"Find me that man Colonel Zachristov. And also find me a money broker to set the deal up. Someone multinational. Someone ruthless, but trustworthy." Vladimyr put his fingertips to his lips and thought for a second... The Grim Reaper?"

"Perfect, Vladimyr. Solomon Joshua Goldstein will do perfectly."

"What about the finance? Gorbachev must never know."

"Don't worry about that, Vladimyr. I know where to find the money," the General said with certainty. "If this works, it will send reverberations throughout the Eastern world Vladimyr. The effect on the budding capitalist democracies in Poland, Czechoslovakia, East Germany and Romania would be enormous. They are only supported at present by the childish belief that democracy is clean, peaceful and fair. Once we can expose that sordid lie, we can reverse the tide.

They would begin to question their destination. They would turn back to communism. They would question their own security.

"Democracy has always been vulnerable to terrorism. A well thought out campaign to destabilise the country. Widespread terror. Proper publicity worldwide about the troubles.

Then a revolution and a careful campaign thereafter to discredit the Royals. We would not run a pathetic circus similar to the Romanian drivel to discredit Ceausescu after his execution but some really powerful disinformation. We will show the world that the oldest democracy was a sham. It hides enormous perversion and gross injustice. Hordes of jewels and piles of riches owned by Royalty will be displayed for the world press, next to the impoverished unemployed workers and single parent families. We can show that Parliament was a corrupt sham, supporting a hierarchy of upper class sycophants and paedophiles."

"If we can do this, we will halt the tide of democratic revolution in Eastern Europe and in our beloved country." Krasilova stopped to draw breath. He was having an epiphany.

For a while Vladimyr sat fearing to breathe. But eventually he could no longer restrain himself.

"Then, General, we can choose the time to destroy Gorbachev. As the climate of opinion starts to turn against his 'perestroika' and back to the safe refuge of communism we will finish him off too."

CHAPTER 20
UNINVITED GUESTS

WATFORD, MONDAY 6TH NOVEMBER, 1988

At 5.30am, at a small airfield just west of Watford, Ivan Bullovitch closed the metal shutters over the new undercarriage to the Piper Cherokee. The noise of a Diesel car engine was barely audible as he walked slowly out of the aircraft hangar. The taxi pulled up a hundred yards away. A large, well built man got out, and paid the fare. He walked towards Ivan as the cab pulled away. Bullovitch had not slept all night. His work was all but finished. Expert though he was, there were always little hitches in any job. In this one, there had been a lack of the correct type of wire. He had been forced to send out a last minute message to pick up some more. The Tailor had arranged it. The wire was obviously just coming. The messenger walked briskly up to Bullovitch and handed him a coil of 3mm copper wire. He nodded, and smiled briefly.

"Thanks. I'll just be a minute, then I'll be off. Call me another taxi would you?" He spoke with a crisp Polish accent. Five minutes later he came back out of the hangar.

"It is done. Complete. Now I need some sleep and a ticket back to Poland. Do you have them?" He asked.

"Yes. Come with me." The messenger walked with Bullovitch to the small hut beside the hangar. They went in together through the wooden door partially covered with peeling green paint. Twenty seconds later, Farhad Fee walked out with his gun safely back in its leather chest holder. Ivan Bullovitch was dead.

SLOANE SQUARE, MONDAY 6TH NOVEMBER

By 7am, George Grant had reached Sloane Square. The car that had nearly run him over outside Guildford, had stopped and taken him to town. From there, he had taken a taxi. He had a tourniquet, dressed his arm and taken some pain killers, bought at an all night chemist. He felt marginally better.

Five minutes later, he reached Marianne's street. As he turned the corner, he stopped and stepped back two paces. There was a brown Austin Princess parked outside her front door. He waited for a second. There was no movement in the car. It was empty. Suddenly an overwhelming sense of foreboding hit him in the stomach, and he ran like a mad man towards the door. It was open. He ran upstairs. There was a terrifying silence. Then a loud scream. A woman! His stomach contracted. He could feel the nausea coming. Not another Joanne.

The door at the top of the stairs was closed. He didn't have time to check if it was unlocked. He jumped at it with one foot raised to chest level. Through a thunderous crash, the door latch gave way, and he landed, surrounded by splinters, in Marianne's hallway. He crouched with the berretta in his right hand. Not a sound. Then a footstep. He swivelled. His forefinger pressing tightly on the trigger. The bathroom door opened slowly. A hand curled around the door, carrying pink nail varnish.

"George!"

He breathed out sharply. "Marianne. Are you OK?"

"Of course. So was my door until you sat on it."

"Oh! I'm sorry, I thought you were in trouble."

"Why?"

"That scream, the car outside."

"Neighbours having a fight I think. Is it a service car?"

"I think so." Grant replied.

"Come and have some coffee, George. I didn't think we'd ever see you again!" She said, taking him by the arm. He flinched. "I've got a lot to tell you, Marianne."

When he moved into the light in the lounge she gasped. "You are hurt. God you look awful. What happened?"

"Too much to tell. I cannot put it all together at the moment. Just tell me what has happened to you, whilst I get into the shower." He said.

She retraced her movements since Jack had handed the tape of the Park Lane meeting to her at Trader Vics, in the Hilton Hotel. He threw his clothes onto the floor, and climbed under the stinging needles of the shower. He stood quietly there for ten minutes, just feeling the cold water wash the past few hours out of his bruised body. When he had finished showering, Marianne carefully dressed the wounds on his chest and the nasty tears in his arm.

"Didn't Duffy get back to you?" Grant asked.

"No." Marianne replied.

"Do you know who he took the tape to?"

"No."

"Well his boss is that stiff neck Blythe-Stafford so we'd better find out." Grant phoned Chief Inspector Duffy at home.

The Chief Inspector hadn't been able to sleep that night. He had drunk two pints of milk, but still, his ulcer was biting like a hungry dog. When the phone rang, he walked towards it with relief.

"Chief Commissioner?"

"No Bruce, it's Pain."

"Pain! Oh Fuck!" There was silence at Duffy's end for a few seconds. "Old Church Street, Bruce." Grant hung up.

Marianne was standing in front of Grant, tying a new dressing around his forearm.

"Do you think he'll come, George?"

"If he listened to the tape, he must. If not, then he's either stupid, or he's been turned by NATUS, or the IFFC. What I can't believe is that he's still at home. The goddamn Houses of Parliament are going to be blown sky high in five hours. He knows it, and he's at home. What the fuck's going on?" Grant sat down on a sofa in Marianne's lounge.

"Tell me about last night." She demanded.

"They took me to Guildford. That's where NATUS hold their council meetings. There is a Russian colonel over for the Sting, called Vladimyr Zachristov. He confirmed what Trattorini was saying all along. A group in the Soviet Union has been funding the whole, nasty episode."

*

They both met Gruff Stuff outside the Falcon, in Wardour Street. Grant was apprehensive as the Chief Inspector approached the pub. Since their last meeting Dianne Trattorini had been shot in Park Lane. As soon as the Chief Inspector spotted Grant, he ran over the road.

"George. I am so glad to see you." Grant was stunned.

"You are?" He replied.

"What's up, Chief Inspector?" Marianne interjected as the three of them huddled into a doorway.

"I gave that tape to the MFC at 3.30am and I haven't heard a peep from him since." The Chief Inspector carried sacks of potatoes under his eyes. He'd been awake for forty-two hours.

"What's more worrying, is that someone got into St Thomas' and finished off Dianne Trattorini."

"Oh, God! She survived Park Lane?" Grant said.

"Yes, but not for long. We don't know how they knew she was there. It must be an inside job."

"Like Egypt." Grant responded, in a daze.

They ignored him and continued their conversation.

"Who did the Chief Commissioner take the tape to?" Marianne asked.

"I don't know. It could have been any member of the SEC. Lord Carver, Sir John Epcot or the Defence Secretary are the most likely. But if he couldn't reach them, then Field Marshal Carshalton, Rear Admiral Perkins, Commander Harris, the Foreign Secretary or even the PM."

They all stood close together. A group of frightened pigeons on a wet London street corner.

"Who's the most likely?" Grant finally asked.

"Head of MI5, I suppose. He, after all, is the man responsible for internal security."

"It's possible that the wheels are in motion now, is it not? Could they be heading down to Goldstein's place at this very moment?" Marianne asked hopefully.

"Unlikely?" The Chief Inspector said blankly. "I would have been contacted. Nothing has been done. It's inconceivable. What's worse is that there are reports coming in from all over the suburbs that the army are assuming position for the curfew."

"Then it has really begun. Just as the Tailor said," Grant shivered. It was still raining and the last dregs of Soho night life were walking forlornly past the pubs, fresh out of the live sex shows. They didn't realise that this would be their last night of such freedom.

"What can we do George? I don't know who I can trust anymore." The Chief Inspector whispered.

"We'll have to cut through the layers and go to the top. We need to see the Prime Minister. Can you get us inside No.10?"

Inspector Duffy froze. It took him a while to understand the magnitude of the request. Finally he replied.

"Probably. So long as I've still got a job I can, but will she believe us?"

"It's our only hope. If we raid the Guildford address at which I was held we won't find anything. That is where the Group controlling the Terrorist wave were meeting in the early hours of this morning. They will have fled now because they know that I know where they were."

"I see," Duffy replied. "Is there anything else?"

Marianne handed him the files she had stolen from MI5 headquarters.

"Copy these Inspector and read them. Then we'll talk and see if we can spot something that will point the finger at the traitor in the Special Executive Committee for National Security."

*

The SEC convened at 8.30am, on 6th November, at No.10 Downing Street, London, W1.

"Good morning, Gentlemen. I'm glad you could all come so soon. I apologise for the short notice," the Prime Minister stated in a weary manner.

There was an air of disillusionment in the room that damp November morning and a strange smell of uneasiness. The Prime Minister went over to the fire at the end of the Conference Room and put two further half logs into the orange flames.

"Bring us up to date Mr. Defence Secretary," she demanded.

Phillip McNaughton opened his note pad. He read in a depressed and gloomy way the list of catastrophes which had happened over the weekend.

The Sellafield bombs; the Stock Exchange bomb; the killings in Park Lane; a further run of investment abroad; horrific new unemployment figures; the national press haranguing the government for its failure to curb the carnage and the clarion call, from all sides, for a curfew. The rate of inflation had increased by 15%. Industrial production had fallen drastically. Absenteeism at work had increased 20% since January. The armed forces were baying for blood and the Police were demanding further funds and manpower to fight the onslaught.

"What does the Metropolitan Chief Commissioner have to say Phillip?"

Phillip McNaughton felt like a hangman. He buried his head in his hands and spoke through them.

"He's dead Prime Minister. Murdered last night. We found his body at 7 o'clock on the steps of New Scotland Yard. You can imagine what that has done for morale. It won't hit the newspapers till 12 o'clock."

"Oh my Lord." The colour was draining from the Prime Minister's face. Wing Commander Harris slipped out of his chair and guided her to her seat. She took a glass of water to her and tried to steady her nerves.

"Not even my closest advisers are safe! Only last week Phillip's children were kidnapped. Why are we so vulnerable to this horrific urban terrorism?"

Phillip McNaughton shook his head slowly.

"It is a terribly effective force in today's society Prime Minister. The simple volume of people in London makes it very difficult for the police and armed forces to protect all possible targets."

He stopped and cleared his throat. The Prime Minister finished her glass of water and noticing the Defence Secretary's apparent verbal distress asked, "what is it Phillip, is there more?"

"Yes, Prime Minister. Our internal best expert on terrorism, Daniel Judas, was murdered in St James' Park, a few days ago."

"I find this soul destroying. Lord Carver, what is the latest intelligence on this?" She was struggling to maintain her usually iron self control.

"From the fifteen terrorists captured to date we know that there is central co-ordination of the terrorist wave by the IFFC. It appears that this man Farhad Fee is the leader. Someone chooses the targets and the various factions carry them out after receiving instructions from couriers. A Palestinian we captured last week admitted to being given a list of targets to hit on Monday evening each week."

"Who sets the targets?" Thatcher asked.

"We just do not know," he answered.

"What about the funding, Sir John, what have you got?"

Sir John Epcot replied: "we've been able to open some of Fee's Swiss accounts under our secret bi-lateral co-operation agreement with the Swiss Government. It is clear that Fee has received substantial sums in the last six months for his work in Britain."

"From whom? Goddamn it!" she barked and Sir John lurched back in his chair at the force of the demand.

"The cheques are traced to various diplomatic accounts in the Swiss banking system."

"Whose?" she demanded.

"We can't tell without breaking the secret information exchange agreement. That would mean the loss of ten years of careful negotiation to get where we are today. Prime Minister, you know the deal. They only agreed to provide the info if we promised not to use the source in evidence. You know the Swiss."

"Disney the country is being raped and you are worrying about a bloody bilateral agreement?"

"Well, it is important..." he whimpered.

"Sorry," she said, with her palms upwards to calm herself and those in the room. "I am sorry. I should not have sworn. But tell me, what do they hope to gain by trying to destabilise us?"

"Financially, nothing," the Foreign Secretary interjected, "but in terms of world prestige, if they can cripple us then they have developed the most devastating non-nuclear force the world has yet to experience. Urban warfare as an economic weapon. It's a frightening new idea."

At that moment there was a knock on the door and the Chief Inspector of the Anti-Terrorist Squad walked in, followed by George Grant.

The Cabinet Secretary scuttled after them and in a disturbed voice grumbled, "they barged right through me Prime Minister. I'm sorry. The officers at the door let them straight in."

Wing Commander Harris stood up quickly his chair tumbling behind him onto the floor. He strutted towards the Chief Inspector with his right arm raised. "What the hell is the meaning of this intrusion, Chief Inspector?"

"Sit down please Wing Commander," Duffy replied.

"I'll be damned if I'll do what you order," the Wing Commander shouted and lurched forward to grasp the Chief Inspector.

"Stop where you are," Grant said lifting his berretta out of his pocket and pointing it at the man's knees.

"You'll be crippled, if you don't. just sit down and be quiet please Wing Commander."

The Wing Commander halted and sized up his adversary. Then he wisely sat down.

Chief Inspector Duffy walked to the head of the oval table and put a file down in front of the Prime Minister. He bowed slightly and spoke.

"I apologise for barging in Prime Minister but I have always maintained that security in this building is not tight enough. Now, I'm sure of it."

The Prime Minister appeared suddenly calm.

"Thank you Chief Inspector. Is this file all?" she said.

"No, Ma'am. I have put my job and my life on the line to come here to tell you what I believe is the truth. I couldn't pass it through the ranks because my gaffer, the Metropolitan Chief Commissioner, disappeared last night."

"Because he was murdered," Phillip McNaughton interjected sombrely.

"Oh, my dear Lord," the Chief Inspector said. Then he turned slowly to face the table at large. He shook his head slowly from side to side, and then announced: "I believe that in this room sits a traitor. A man who has sold this country to the Soviet Union!"

The room erupted. Lord Carver got up and shouted abuse at the Chief Inspector. Wing Commander Harris was making a desperate lunge for Grant and Rear Admiral Perkins was shouting directions to the officers who were on duty outside the door.

Grant fired a single shot into the ceiling.

"Don't move, Wing Commander."

Grant stepped forward and waved the gun at the assembled crowd.

"Don't act like fools. If I had wanted to kill any of you I would have done so and left already. Sit and listen. This will take ten minutes, then we will leave."

The Prime Minister smiled.

"He's right. Sit down. It is Grant it is not? or should I call you Delta? Tell me, do you support the Chief Inspector's allegation?"

"Yes Prime Minister. As you know I was employed by the firm to act as Delta in their operation to counteract the terrorist insurgence. During that time we discovered that there were several different groups operating in the UK, not just one. And that they were being funded from a large private source.

"I chose to follow a particular track which concerned me personally. A bomb at Stringfellows killed my fiancée. It also killed the daughter of a millionaire called Solomon J Goldstein, the chairman of Goldstein International Enterprises Ltd. You may know that he hired me, coincidentally perhaps, to find who killed his daughter. I later found out from Daniel Judas that Her Majesty's Services had asked Solomon Goldstein to hire me as a sort of tester."

"We already knew this, go on."

"That led me into the middle of the terrorist hurricane. Then the heads of your Security Services together offered me the job of becoming Delta. They offered to provide the back up so that I could be a sweeper. A double check, if you like. I would remain outside the Beta Cells, set up by the SEC"

"We around this table set that up" the Prime Minister replied.

"After investigating the terrorists for some time, I was asked by Sir John to meet a Frenchman called Francoise Deboussey in Egypt. I understood that he was a close friend of Sir John's and had information to report to us which he had learnt from his contacts in the Middle East."

"So what did he tell you?"

"He told me the KGB was funding the terrorist wave."

The room was utterly silent.

The Prime Minister started making notes on a piece of paper in front of her.

"Go on," she said.

"He led me to a woman called Diane Trattorini. I had previously discovered that she was one of the bombers who destroyed Stringfellows and killed Solomon Goldstein's daughter.

"I followed her to the Caribbean and there found out that she and another woman called Galliani had both been members of the IFFC. She told me that initially Solomon J Goldstein was funding the terrorist wave in the UK. The IFFC were trying, as they have stated in the national Press, to free the workers in this country from what they saw as the oppression of the masses by the capitalist establishment and the property owning aristocracy. Her words, not mine."

Grant took a glass of water from the polished mahogany table and swallowed it down then continued.

"But Prime Minister the Sting in the tail was that Solomon J. Goldstein was not what he had appeared to be when setting up the deal with the IFFC. He was in fact a front man working for a group in the Soviet Union."

The room sat stunned in silence. After some time, the Prime Minister spoke.

"Let's assume that I believe this, what evidence do you have that there is a traitor in *this* room?"

"Various sources. Firstly Francoise Deboussey. Secondly what happened when I was out to Egypt. Sir John sent me out to talk to Deboussey. When I got there someone was waiting, so someone knew I had gone. Only Sir John and a few MI6 operatives knew I was there. Deboussey was killed, but before he died he told me that one of the two IFFC girls: Trattorini, had confided in him. He also told me that the Libyan Government had "lost" a large sum of money and the KGB had "replenished" the lost funds. They invested £1,000 million in this operation. I believe that the USSR has channelled the funds through Libya into the UK.

"Deboussey also said that 'the Tailor,' or the 'Grim Reaper', as he called the man, was a the lynchpin. So I followed Trattorini to Barbados and to cut the story short eventually discovered that Solomon Goldstein himself is the Tailor."

The Prime Minister nodded and finished noting down what Grant had said. Sir John Epcot threw his pencil onto the mahogany table.

"Is that all you have Grant? Speculation? and the word of a terrorist? Do you really expect Her Majesty's Government to act on that rubbish? To accuse another State of plotting a terrorist wave in Great Britain?"

"There is more Sir John, but what interests me is why you tried to have me locked up in a stinking Caribbean prison for a murder I didn't commit. You sent me to see Deboussey. You were in charge of the operation and yet someone knew I was in Egypt. Did you tell Goldstein I was there?"

"I don't have to justify the actions of H.M. Government to a convicted killer like you, Grant," Sir John barked defensively. The Prime Minister smiled for the second time that morning.

"Why not Sir John? He has the gun! Go ahead, tell us all." The Prime Minister was beginning to enjoy the drift of the meeting again.

Sir John's face drained of colour. He sat rigid for a few seconds with the whole group looking quizzically at him.

"All right, Prime Minister. As you obviously knew, Francoise and I had been closer than old friends for years. He and I were..." he couldn't bring himself to say the words, but the meaning was clear.

"Deboussey was ... one of my oldest friends. Why would I send Mr Grant out to Egypt if only to have him killed? Look Grant, the decision to imprison you in Barbados was taken so as to avoid any possible security breach. You had become a liability. You had seen Deboussey and we had grounds to believe you had killed him. And you wouldn't come in to debrief. In those circumstances the only alternatives we had were to kill you or silence you for the short term. We chose the most humane route."

"He's right. National Security was more important than your freedom," Phillip McNaughton added forcefully. "But I must say Sir John, at the time I was worried about your own personal involvement in that decision."

"I must say, at present, I couldn't go to the UN or NATO and present this with any conviction. What real evidence do you have of Russian involvement?" The Prime Minister pressed.

"This girl, Trattorini was one of only two IFFC council members who discovered the Russian connection," Grant replied.

"I was about to interview her," Inspector Duffy interrupted suddenly.

"But she was murdered last night Prime Minister. In St Thomas' Hospital. Only the security services and a few selected policemen knew she was there. We leaked again."

"So that's another dead end. We need something positive." The Prime Minister was becoming impatient.

"Last night I was kidnapped by Goldstein and taken to the headquarters of NATUS in Guildford."

The Prime Minister sat up straighter.

"Who are NATUS?"

"Please let me explain. When I was there I met a man called Colonel Zachristov. I think he is here to view the Scorpion's Sting. According to Trattorini, it is set for today."

"What exactly is the meaning of the phrase the Scorpion's Sting?" The Prime Minister asked as she made a further note.

"Farhad Fee is called "the Scorpion". He, or they, are going to destroy the Houses of Parliament today whilst Government and Royalty are present for the Queen's Speech."

"Good grief!" the Prime Minister sat back flabbergasted. "I suppose that what you warn us of is the logical conclusion to the terrorist activities we have suffered this last year."

"Yes. And that was confirmed early last night by the murder of the Metropolitan Chief Commissioner to whom Chief Inspector Duffy had given a tape. He took it to the head of one of the Services. And it was also confirmed by the words of a senior officer in your Security Services just before his death."

"Who?" Lord Carver interjected almost shaking.

"Daniel Judas was his name. He was a traitor and he admitted it to me before he died."

Now Lord Epcot shook his head in disbelief.

"Never. He worked for me for ten years. He hated terrorism more than any man alive, look, have you been down to this so called 'headquarters,' Chief Inspector?" He demanded.

"No, Sir," the Chief Inspector replied.

"So once again we have nothing firm to prove Mr. Grant's wild assertions," Lord Carver butted in.

"Nothing?" Grant asked. He reached under the table and lifted the suitcase containing £2 million into view. He had carried it in with him.

"Daniel Judas gave me this before he was killed. I had threatened to expose him unless he paid me off. Tell me where an MI6 operative could obtain this sum?"

"Perhaps your master Goldstein supplied it," Sir John sneered. "It proves nothing."

"Perhaps," Grant responded. "Yesterday I taped a conversation I held with Goldstein. It was enough to convince me and the Inspector here that he was involved. The Inspector gave the tape to the MPC. He took it higher up, to one of the people sitting around this table and he was murdered. Whoever he took that tape to is the traitor amongst us."

The room fell silent again.

The Prime Minister stood up slowly.

"Is this true, Inspector?" She asked.

"You have my word on it, Prime Minister."

"The normal chain of command would be for him to take it to the Defence Secretary or the Internal Security Services, Phillip?"

McNaughton looked decidedly ill at ease. Suddenly the finger was pointed at him.

"I was at home all night. Look, this is crazy. This convicted murderer comes in here waving a gun around and accusing us of being traitors, and we are being asked to explain our actions to him! I won't do it Prime Minister. After all, my own goddamn children were kidnapped last week. Bloody fool terrorist I would be kidnapping my own kids."

"You could have arranged that yourself Defence Secretary. I understand they were released unharmed?" Grant conjectured.

"Well, yes, but …" the Defence Secretary replied.

"It's been done before." Field Marshal Carshalton said, looking at the Defence Secretary suspiciously.

"Look! This is preposterous. Anyway, the MPC may have been killed before he got to me, or Lord Carver."

"Calm down Phillip. What do you think, Lord Carver?" The Prime Minister said.

"I think we have little to gain by accusing each other and everything to lose. There can be little doubt that the Chief Inspector and Mr. Grant do truly and genuinely believe that the Soviet Union are at the bottom of the nation's present problems. And for my part I must say that is an attractive proposition. It would explain a lot of the unanswered funding questions. But we have no hard evidence to prove anything of the sort.

"I consider that we must now impose a military 24 hour curfew, primarily for the State Opening but we should extend it indefinitely thereafter until the crisis is over. We must fight this terrorism and if we find evidence of this so called Russian conspiracy then we will act fast and without mercy to crush the perpetrators. Also no doubt you Prime Minister will make the normal objections to the UN and close the Russian Embassy in London."

The Foreign Secretary nodded his approval. Grant put the gun back into his pocket. He could feel the consensus turn against him.

"I'll show the Chief out," the Prime Minister said and stood up.

Thatcher walked them out of the meeting room and winked at Grant as she passed him. He followed her and when Grant reached the front door of Number 10 Downing Street she touched his elbow gently. He turned round to face her despondently.

"Cheer up. I want you to take this number. It is my "portable" private line. Although looking at the size of this thing it is like carrying around a brick. If you can discover anything else I want you to phone me directly. Use a codename. What do you suggest?"

"*Pain*, Prime Minister. Would you do one thing for me?"

"Perhaps," she replied smiling.

"Ask MI6 to cancel the D Notice on me please?" he asked.

"Of course, good morning to you both and thank you for coming Chief Inspector. For the next twenty-four hours Grant I will ensure that you are not hampered by my Security Services. Do what you must. Good morning."

*

Once the accusatory atmosphere had cleared Lord Carver made a suggestion.

"It would seem wise, in view of what our uninvited guests have said, for the curfew forces to make themselves useful today. I suggest that the convoy is brought into the city to tighten security at the State Opening."

Field Marshal Carshalton nodded and spoke. "We are ready to do so Prime Minister. We have fifty-six units on the outskirts of London."

"How efficient of you Field Marshal. What do you think Phillip?"

"I think we cannot be too careful. I'll have the police and anti-terrorist squad double check the Parliament building this morning. After all, we don't want another Guy Fawkes."

"We'll take a vote now gentlemen. Do we postpone the State Opening for 24 hours or more to investigate the Chief Inspector's claims? Or shall we press on?"

Six to two, the SEC voted for tighter security at the State Opening and that it should continue.

"And Sir John," the P.M added, "I want you to find out all you can about this Colonel Zachristov. Bring me your report within the hour please."

"Yes Ma'am." Sir John replied.

The meeting adjourned and the Prime Minister went upstairs to change for the State Opening. Her hand was shaking as she brushed her hair and she was unable to put Dennis Thatcher's cufflinks into his shirtsleeves due to her nerves.

*

As Grant and the Chief Inspector walked away from Downing Street, in a cloud of despondency the Chief Inspector patted Grant on the shoulder.

"We did our best, George. You can't blame yourself for not being able to persuade any Government to see the truth. I've been warning bloody politicians for years about State funded terrorism.

This Urban Terrorism is not new as you know but when they listen they hear only what they want to hear."

They got into the Chief Inspector's car and drove round the road block at the end of Horseguards Parade, which was in place for the Queen's short journey down to Parliament. The journey was scheduled to occur at 11am.

"Where can I drop you?"

"I don't know. I just don't know where to turn. Without knowing how they are going to do it there is not much I can do but sit and wait for the Scorpion to sting. If only we could find Colonel Zachristov."

"Surely. But what would we do if we did?" Duffy asked.

"I'd break his neck."

"Very constructive, George. Before or after he told us how the Sting will go down?" He chuckled. "Do you, MacDougal and Marianne want to come and see the security set up at Parliament? You are the only one who has recently seen Fee. You may be able to identify him. It's a long shot but that's as good as I can do, George."

"OK, thank you. Drop me off at Sloane Square, I'll grab a bite at Marianne's flat and meet you back at Parliament by say 10?"

*

As Grant walked slowly West along the Kings Road a short convoy of army trucks approached from the East. The soldiers looked relaxed and at ease. The pedestrians stopped and stared aghast. It was the first time since 1945 that the streets of London had seen soldiers on active duty in large numbers.

He met Marianne at her front door. She saw his despondency and she herself looked terribly nervous.

"I don't like it, George. It feels so threatening to be swamped by the Army."

"Neither do I, Marianne. But there is nothing we can do. We can't stop the Sting by killing Goldstein. The Scorpion will be in place by now. Nothing short of death will stop him."

They headed into her flat and she started to prepare a late breakfast.

"Let's call Jack and see what his investigations produced."

*

The Piper Cherokee flew low over the Talgarth roundabout. No one seemed to notice it. It was just a part of London's daily routine. Farhad Fee held his Russian made hand gun so close to the Disc Jockey weather man's temple that the silencer made a half centimetre dimple in the skin. Sweat dropped slowly off the man's chin as he spoke excitedly into the microphone in his hand.

"The Westway is choked up more than usual because a military convoy is heading into town. The A40 is at a standstill. Stay calm commuters, the State Opening of Parliament will be over by midday."

*

Some guests for the State Opening of Parliament were arriving at 8.30am. The MPs had nearly all arrived by 9. The car park was full. The 1069 hall into the Houses of Commons and the Lords was laid with red carpets and the restaurants were brimming with hungry MPs wolfing huge plates of breakfast.

Inspector Duffy had one hundred and twenty-nine men working flat out searching every corner of the building.

*

Grant sat, reading the files that Marianne had obtained for him from MI5 headquarters. The information was too much to take in at one reading. He needed time to put the facts into perspective.

When he had finished he threw unanswerable questions at her.

"What's the best way to blow up the Houses of Parliament, Marianne?"

"With a bomb in the cellar George. We all know that from primary school. Guy Fawkes: *"remember, remember the 5th of November, Gunpowder, Treason and Plot.""*

"And if you can't get into the cellar, or if the cellar has been checked and found to be secure, then what?"

"The car park or the bars, I'd guess." Marianne responded opening the curtains of the sitting room and lifting off her shirt to expose her naked top half.

"A car bomb. Surely the police would check for one of those?"

"They do George. They have sniffer dogs and electronic surveillance staff. Mirrors on sticks to view the underside of vehicles. It's very unlikely anything would get through."

"So that leaves the river. What about a rocket launched from a boat on the river?"

"They close it off from both directions during the State Opening, you can't get within five hundred yards by boat."

"What about a submarine?"

Marianne returned from the bedroom now wearing only her briefest briefs: "That's a possibility. But it's not feasible unless you're a kamikaze captain. If you fired into the walls beneath the house, you'd do nothing, unless the charge was so big that the whole area would be destroyed. That would knock out the sub without a doubt. If they fired at surface level, or just below, they'd be in with a chance. It might work, but it's very clumsy. It would be more accurate and effective to fire an air to ground missile from an aeroplane. Then at least you'd have a good chance to escape."

"Believe me, Marianne. Farhad Fee will want to escape. He's no martyr."

"So, it's a plane then."

"Must be! What else is there?" Grant replied.

"A short or medium distance cruising missile might do it. You could launch it anywhere in London and programme it to land on Parliament. It's a bit risky for the landing site and you'd have a problem with radar and with tall buildings. If it was a bit inaccurate you could miss by miles. That's unless they had a homing device at the target," she said.

"A homing device in the Houses of Parliament? They'd be crazy not to have it. If they can infiltrate MI5 and MI6; if they can get a convoy of military to enter London ready to grab power; why couldn't they put homing devices into the House. How big would it need to be?"

"If the missile was fired from within half a mile it could be as small as a golf ball. Maybe even smaller." She turned back into the bedroom. He sat at her coffee table and stared unseeingly at its surface.

"But could they get a plane near to the houses?" he asked.

"That is the point. No they could not. There are RAF bases all round London. If an unidentified plane entered London civilian airspace, a jet would be up and on to it in about four and a half minutes."

The doorbell rang. Grant went to open it and was pleased to see the lined, weather beaten, ruby face of Jack MacDougal.

"George!" Jack grabbed Grant by the arms and hugged him hard. Grant winced at the pain in his forearm. "I thought that you were planning to be a daisy pusher! What happened?"

"Jack. It's good to see you too." Grant responded. When the hug finished Grant led him inside and explained the events since the kidnapping in Park Lane. Twenty minutes later Jack had a stiff scotch in his hand and was sitting down on the sofa.

"I've been through the diary you lifted from Judas. There are a few entries you might be able to interpret." MacDougal said.

George Grant picked up the diary and leafed through it stopping at the flagged pages. On the inside cover it said 'D. Judas'.

He turned to the 6th November and froze. In it was written:

"6th November, 1988, 10 am LWT."

There were no entries for 7th November and after. None at all. Grant broke out in to a cold sweat. He leafed back through the book. One other entry caught his eye. He shouted at Marianne. "Oh, God!"

'1st November 1988,

*Cleaner Ms Celia Jones
to meet FF 0207-242-1214.'*

He skipped forward a few pages and then closed the book and smiled.

"Marianne. I think we have a chance!" Marianne walked through to the lounge wearing a light blue pinstripe skirt and white cotton blouse, half undone.

"Show me."

He showed her the entry.

"*FF* means Farhad Fee, doesn't it?" she said.

"It could be."

"And the cleaner?"

"The method of getting a transmitter into the Houses of Parliament!"

"Phone up the number then," she replied.

Grant dialled the number. It rang twice.

"Human resources. Hello?"

"Good morning, this is Hubert James from Reed Employment." Grant said.

"We don't need temporary staff at the moment thanks." The man replied.

"It is a call about a tax refund. Is Celia Jones at work today?" Grant asked.

"No, I am sorry, she died last week. I'll can put you through to payroll if you want?"

"Thank you." Grant replied. A few seconds later another voice came on the line.

"Hello?" Grant opened.

"I believe you are asking for Celia Jones?"

"Yes." Grant replied.

"Why?"

"We are from Reed Employment. We have a cheque for her."

"Well, she died last week."

"We'd like to offer our condolences to her family. I have a cheque for £1,000 for Celia's outstanding pay. Can you tell me who was her immediate employer so I can contact him to sort out the tax details?"

"Yes. Hold on." Silence descended for a few seconds and Grant held his breath.

"It was Percy Smith in Personnel." The woman said.

"What is the address?"

"The Houses of Parliament, Parliament Square ..."

Grant replaced the receiver without listening to the end.

"You crafty bugger, George." Jack said.

"Marianne. Call Duffy. Get him to contact the Staff Manager at Parliament and to find out what she did on her last day at work. His name is Percy Smith."

Duffy phoned back in fifteen minutes. She had been a full time employee at the Houses of Parliament since May 1988. She had left work on Friday 3rd November as usual but not returned on Saturday for her weekend overtime. She had a good work record. It was out of character. She did her usual shift on her last day. Which involved various cleaning jobs around the House.

CHAPTER 21
THE SCORPION'S STING

By 9.35am on Monday the 6th of November 1988 the elected members of Parliament of England and Wales were gathered to rehearse the ceremonial arrival of Her Majesty Queen Elizabeth II at the Houses of Parliament in Westminster.

The House of Lords was in its usual quiet turmoil.

George Grant changed his clothes and returned to the lounge of Marianne's flat.

"We have two major problems Marianne. The most immediate one is how to get that homing device out of the House. The second is how to nail Goldstein and uncover the traitors in the SEC. So I've developed some ideas about the second from the files you stole. What do you think about the first?"

"If we had the frequency of the homing device's signal we could transmit a stronger one from a place nearby and the missile would probably follow the stronger signal," she replied.

"Can you arrange that?"

"If you find me the wave length, I can find the hardware."

"It's a hope." Grant sighed.

Jack looked uneasy about the idea. "You have no chance of finding a transmitter in two hours in a place that big, George. Just clear the damn building and bugger the bricks and mortar."

"I would if I could Jack but the PM would not agree to postpone the ceremony. This is our only way of avoiding the catastrophe." Jack poured himself another Scotch and downed it in one gulp. "God damn bloody politicians. I never thought I'd see the day when I was sweating to save their bloody hides."

"You won't be Jack. I want you to find out where Colonel Zachristov is and then to tell me. If this little plan doesn't work the best we can do is nail that bastard. Ok for you?" Jack MacDougal grinned broadly.

"My pleasure George. He'll be at the US Embassy this morning won't he. There is an official function there."

"How do you know that?" Grant asked astonished.

"I called the Russian Embassy last night," he replied.

"And I overheard him saying that he would be when I was in Guildford," Grant said.

"So we are not completely useless are we?"

MacDougal slapped Grant on the shoulder and Grant winced with the pain of the wound to his left forearm.

"Jack, I'll get you an invite via Gruff Stuff, but don't get pickled."

The words hit Jack hard. He put down his glass straight faced and breathed deeply twice.

"All right."

Grant made two calls. Inspector Duffy arranged an invitation for Jack to the US Embassy via the Foreign Office and told Grant where he could meet Percy Smith. He also arranged for Professor Sam Jacobs to bring his technical hoys into the House to search for the transmitter. Later, he told Grant about the results of his investigations into the persons named in the files that Marianne had stolen from MI6.

Grant was shocked but not as much as he had expected to be.

"Bring them to the House, Gruff Stuff, and you and I will indulge in a little rat catching."

Next, Grant called the Prime Minister. It took some three minutes for her to pick up the phone.

"Yes?"

"Prime Minister. *Pain* here. We think the attack will come from the air. Probably a guided missile. We have found out that a cleaner who worked in the Houses of Parliament, named Celia Jones, died last week. She was mentioned in Daniel Judas' diary as having a meeting with the Scorpion on 1st November. She had ample opportunity to put a homing device in the House last week."

"You never cease to amaze me. So we will need to know her duty roster and then search the House for a transmitter, is that right?"

Grant was astonished by her speed of thought.

"Yes, Prime Minister. But we don't have the time to do it. You must call off the State Opening."

"I would need to talk to the SEC before I could do that."

"Please don't do that. If you do, you'll tell the traitor. That will either make them change the plan, or it will mean we'll never find out who he is."

"If they call the Sting off have we not won?"

"If you had paid £1,500 million US dollars for this moment, would you call it off?"

"No I don't think I would." The Prime Minister replied.

Grant hung on, desperately hoping that she would call the State Opening off. That decision would save a thousand lives.

The Prime Minister, who was standing in her office in Parliament, turned to the Right Honourable Phillip McNaughton and covered the phone with her hand.

"Delta is demanding that the ceremony be cancelled. He has guessed that the attack will be made by guided missile from the air. He has found a cleaner who was contacted by the IFFC last week and is now dead. Can we call the ceremony off, Phillip? It is a bomb threat after all."

"Yes Ma'am. But politically it would destroy the Conservative Party. You know damn well that our majority hangs on a thread. The Press are baying for our blood. The people elected us on a platform of strong defence and the terrorist wave has proven us to be helpless. If we can't open Parliament on time because of these bloody terrorists how can we say that we have control of the country? We can't give in Prime Minister. We have to go on. Democracy has to go on. I say no." Phillip McNaughton shook his head and placed it into his hands. "Even if it means we have to take the chance of dying today. *We must go on.*"

The Prime Minister took her hand off the mouthpiece and said the words: "We will not give in to terrorism, Mr. Grant. The

Ceremony will go ahead. Do what you can. I pray that you are wrong, but if you are right, God give you strength and success. For all our sakes."

She replaced the receiver and collapsed into a chair.

"Oh my God Phillip. What have we done? Our very democracy is threatened and we are sticking out our damn stupid stiff upper lips and ignoring it. Are we mad?"

"No not mad, just stubborn. I believe that the course which we are taking is the only right one, but whether or not we are right, I won't bow to these bastards."

"OK Phillip. But today we may die for our beliefs."

"We have to stick by our decisions. If you and I were not prepared to die protecting our system of democracy what would we be worth? Nothing."

"Let us trust in God that you're right, Phillip."

*

The doorbell rang twice. Marianne walked towards it and Jack pushed her roughly to one side.

"Get behind the sofa and stay there," he ordered.

"George, watch the windows." Grant walked over to the lounge windows and peered out from behind the curtains. The Kings Road was jammed with traffic and pedestrians. There was a light rain falling. He couldn't see any cars which looked unusual. Then he saw a flashing reflection and heard a tinkling of glass. A rush of air and a thud. Grant withdrew his head with a jerk.

"Jack !" He cried. They are on the roof top across the road. Keep down, they have optics."

"'Jesus be damned. We need weapons. We'll not stand a chance without them." MacDougal shouted.

"That depends upon what THEY want." There was a second ringing of the doorbell. No-one moved.

"Is there a rear exit, Marianne?" She shook her head. "Only the bathroom window."

The front door juddered thunderously as a body collided with it.

"How long will it hold Marianne?"

"It's the new metal one the Service put in last night after you destroyed the old one. It has a metal frame with a Chubb, a Yale and a chain and two straight across security bolts. It will give us a minute or two at the most."

Jack appeared from the hallway as a volley of shots came through the window. He flattened himself onto the floor with a thump and lay stretched out. Grant stood with his back to the exterior wall and closed his eyes.

"If this is D Section, Jack, there is little we can do but pray."

"I thought you'd asked the Prime Minister to call this off."

"I did Jack. But the order may have been delayed between her and D Section."

"It must be that bastard John Epcot, George. Who else would it be?"

"It could be anyone of them, Jack," Grant replied.

A further volley of shots shattered the lounge window and sent glass tumbling onto the carpet. A small line of holes appeared in the far wall.

"Ok, Jack, let's go." Grant dropped to his knees and crawled to Marianne. Together they scampered towards the hallway and into the bathroom, as the first hole appeared in the front door.

Marianne opened the window, Grant squeezed through it and onto a flat roof at the rear of the building. Marianne followed and as Jack climbed through and pushed the window shut they heard a thunderous crash. The front door had finally given way.

Grant looked over the edge of the flat roof. Three storeys up. No chance of jumping. There was a drain pipe which given time and strong fixing screws, they might all get down, but they had no time.

"We're trapped, George!" Marianne stated, croaking due to the fear.

Grant looked back at the bathroom window. He and Jack saw the chance together.

"It might work, George. You do it, you're lighter." There was a small flat ledge above the bathroom window.

When the door locks finally gave way D3 swivelled his machine pistol round into the hall and sprayed twenty cartridges. The hall furniture smashed into a cascade of splinters. D4 waited for the volley to end, then ran through the carnage. D3 slapped his back when they slammed against the wall by the lounge door. He nodded to D4 and the latter fired a volley into the lounge which spattered the china and glass on Marianne's breakfast bar into a thousand pieces of junk. D3 swivelled round the open door and fired in a circular pattern across the lounge. He knelt down and waited for movement. There was none. Within thirty seconds he had checked the study and the bedroom.

Now at ease, he walked to the lounge window and gave the all clear to D2, who was positioned on the roof across the street. D2 indicated, by raising two fingers, that he had seen two occupants inside. D3 nodded and returned to D4.

"They must be in the bathroom. Use a grenade," D3 said.

D4 pulled a small grenade out of his breast belt and fired a round through the plywood door which created a fist sized hole. He pulled the pin with his teeth and dropped it through the hole into the bathroom. Both men stepped back. The explosion occurred two seconds later.

D3 waited a further twenty seconds then kicked away what was left of the door. The bathroom was empty and wrecked. The window glass was shattered. D3 stepped over the rubble and pointed his machine pistol out through the jagged glass.

"Don't move lady," he shouted to Marianne. She turned shocked and her bare breasts jiggled enticingly as she did so. She looked as though she had climbed out of the window having escaped from the shower.

"Hey 4! Come and look at what I've found!" D4 poked his machine pistol out through the jagged glass and whistled when he saw Marianne naked save for a towel over her hips.

"Hey come here, sweetheart."

A hand from above grabbed D4's gun and yanked it upwards. At the same moment, two hands from below pulled D3's pistol downwards. The glass from the window thrust deeply into D3's forearm and he yelled out.

"Shit!"

One more yank and Jack had the pistol in his possession. As Grant struggled with the other machine pistol, Jack stood up from beneath the window and fired shots into the bathroom. D3 and D4 fell. Jack leant inside and put another two shots into the squirming hell on the bathroom floor.

"It's amazing what a nice pair of breasts will do to a soldier's brain." Marianne said as she retrieved her top.

"Well done, Marianne. Now, let's go, see you later Jack." Grant started down the drain pipe.

Grant and Marianne caught a cab to the Houses of Parliament. Jack headed off to the American Embassy in Grosvenor Square.

*

George Grant met Percy Smith in the lobby of the House at 10.50am. "Good morning, Mr Smith."

"I don't know what you want, but this is the most inconvenient time ever! Follow me, I have work to do, we'll talk as we walk." He was a portly man dressed smartly in a grey pin stripe suit with a balding head and a yellow spotty tie. In his late 50s he seemed efficient yet at the same time annoyingly bureaucratic.

"Some information, that's all." Grant said as they walked quickly out of the Great Hall.

"Couldn't it wait?" he said scurrying across the hall to a curved wooden and stone stairway which led upwards to the first floor.

"No. Look, would you please stop running!" Smith stopped.

"I need to see Celia Jones' work sheet for the day she died."

"Why?" Percy wrinkled his face up with strained incredulity.

"Security."

"What? Are you kidding? Celia? Is this really a personal matter?"

"No, Percy, it's not personal."

"Well, I was told it was a matter of national security. That's why I broke off from my *very* important duties."

" 'National security,' the Chief Administrator said, ha ha!"

"Celia Jones may have planted a tiny transmitter in this building sending..." Grant hesitated for a minute, then the thought, what the hell? We only have less than an hour, "a homing signal for a missile which will blow this place to smithereens."

"Oh my God!" Percy Smith's face went white. Then he gathered his wits, hunched his shoulders and turned around to make for his room. "Quick," he said, "we must hurry ...." he confirmed as he raced away up the stairs.

"I always thought she was a bit of a quiet one. Never really got to know anyone. Always kept herself to herself. Then, last week on Tuesday or Wednesday, she just said to me as I was telling her off for some little error, 'don't speak to me like that, I have connections'. I didn't take it seriously at the time. I just laughed and went on. 'Connections'? I wonder what she meant?"

They walked into Percy Smith's office. It was a small room containing all the cosy personal trappings of a lifetime spent in one job.

*

The security guard from the main gate approached Marianne as she sat in the great hall of the Houses of Parliament reading the sign which said that it was built in 1069 by William the Conqueror.

"Excuse me, ma'am. Are you Miss Marchant?"

"Yes," she replied.

"There is a Mr MacDougal at the entrance who insists on speaking to you."

Jack should have been at the American Embassy. They had parted company at least thirty minutes beforehand. Marianne thanked the guard and walked out of the Hall and over to the swing doors. Jack wouldn't have come to the Houses of Parliament if it was not important. She felt her muscles tense for the hundredth time since she had started down the crazy path that George Grant had found. As she exited through the oak swing doors the sunlight temporarily blinded her. She saw Jack standing by a black Mercedes at the far end of the car park. He spotted her and waved her over.

The Mercedes was probably an American Embassy car. That meant something had happened at the Embassy and he had come to tell George about it. She quickened her step. As she approached the car Jack looked into the car then nodded and looked back at her. She was only a few feet away and his face said it all. Danger!

She ducked and turned away but the passenger door was already open. She moved her right leg to run but the dart had already been fired. It entered her thigh and the chemical coursed up towards her heart. She had but a few seconds to escape before the poison would steal her consciousness. She tried to scream but the words stuck in her lungs. Her throat became parched and her tongue seemed to take up the whole of her mouth. Then as her left leg landed on the ground it just gave way.

"God help me. This can't be happening," she whispered helplessly.

Strong hands came and picked her up. Soothing words failed to ease her alarm as she was packed into the rear of the Mercedes. It was not an embassy car.

"Get back in you Scottish bastard," the driver said waving the business end of a hand gun at Jack, who looked longingly at the Houses of Parliament then slid into the back seats beside Marianne.

"Don't even think about shouting out or you'll get a pellet too. And let me tell you sonny, they give you one hell of a hangover."

Jack MacDougall looked around the House of Lords car park and saw to his astonishment that no one had noticed the kidnapping. The door guards were tied up with the entrance. Others were walking into the great hall. No one even raised an eyebrow.

The Mercedes glided out of the car park onto the Embankment and headed West.

"Where are we going?" MacDougal asked as they passed a convoy of army troop vehicles heading towards Parliament Square.

"A place where your old chum the private investigator won't be able to find you, that's for sure. And you can kiss goodbye to London, because you won't be seeing it again."

Jack MacDougal shivered. He was stone cold sober and he was scared to death.

CHAPTER 22
THE FLYING EYE

The Piper Cherokee flew low over the M25 as the Flying Eye DJ told the commuters where the traffic was heavy and what the weather was doing. The roads remained particularly busy that November morning in 1988. His chatter was as amusing and inane as usual, interspersed with trivial insults from the studio based Disc Jockey who hosted the morning show on Capital Radio, London's premier independent station.

"So, what's the weather like up there Biggles?" the DJ asked, from the safety of his seat in the Euston Tower.

"It's stopped raining but we have had to fly pretty low today to avoid the clouds. We're just over the M25 at Junction 11 now and it's jammed solid for three miles heading South and North. There is another convoy of military vehicles going in towards the City slowing it all down."

The banter continued for thirty seconds then the DJ from Euston Tower said, "OK. Thanks Ric. Hear from you in a minute or two."

Ric Florentino removed the headset from his ears to rub his neck and wiped his brow.

"OK, Ric. Not so bad. And if you want to keep your little manhood intact, stay happy."

Ric dared not look down at his groin but his eyes were drawn there as if by a mystical force.

His trousers were lying in a pile on the floor. A small shiny metal box about six inches tall and half an inch wide, lay between his legs. At the centre of the box was a round hole about one inch in diameter. At the top of the hole was a Wilkinson Sword razor blade, at the bottom a wooden block. In between lay his most sensitive organ. It had taken him no more than a few seconds to get over the embarrassment of being asked to drop his trousers. Then the fear had taken over. The swarthy man in the front seat had held a stiletto blade to his throat, as he had sat in the rear seat of the plane.

"Put it on or I'll slice off a little bit of your ear." He had leered as Ric had strapped the leather belt around his waist and stuffed his penis into the hole in the guillotine. Then the man had stepped into the front co-pilot's seat and picked up the button on the end of the tube which ran out of the guillotine. One slight press, or a jolt, or perhaps a sudden fall in altitude of the aircraft and the razor would fall and he would feel the pain and see the blood and he would never make love again. His pulse raced and he was sweating profusely. Ric Florentino was a terrified man clinging desperately to his self control.

Farhad Fee looked at his Rolex chronometer. It was 10.42am. "Ok," he said to the pilot, "let's head into town."

The Piper Cherokee banked to the East and headed towards the Houses of Parliament along the line of the Thames. Strapped onto the undercarriage of the plane was the missile which would lay waste to one hundred square yards of central London; four hundred and sixty duly elected members of Parliament, countless top ranking civil servants, the unelected members of the House of Lords, the Queen and the Duke of Edinburgh. For in 20 minutes they would all be gathering there in the great hall for the state opening of Parliament. British Royalty and democracy was to meet, as it always did, at the start of the new term in office. The venue was the birthplace of democracy in Great Britain and the mother of countless democracies around the globe.

10.47AM, MONDAY 6TH NOVEMBER, 1988

"Mornin' Colonel Zachristov. A pleasure to welcome you to the American Embassy. The Ambassador is in the lounge with his other guests. Please come this way," the doorman said.

"Thank you." Colonel Zachristov replied. He wore his full military uniform. Walking crisply into the lounge of the Embassy he was floating on a wave of expectation. Everything was going to plan. The end was in sight.

About sixty heads turned as the Colonel approached the new Ambassador who had replaced Henry Klein Jnr. He held out his hand.

"Colonel Zachristov. We meet at last."

"Mr Ambassador. I bring the greetings of the Soviet Ambassador with me. I apologise for his absence but he has been rearranging his security since the terrible attack on your own predecessor."

"Very wise Colonel. We are honoured that he should ask the future DG of the KGB to come in his place."

"Oh. You flatter me, Mr Ambassador," the Colonel replied.

"I mean it Colonel. What can I get you to drink?" The formalities over, the two men headed for the bar.

As the other guests returned to their conversations the Colonel and the new Ambassador stopped a few feet from the bar and out of earshot of the barman the Ambassador said:

"It's good to see you again Vladimyr."

"You too Simon. Are you prepared for this morning's entertainment?"

"We have been ready for weeks."

"Good. This is an historic day, Simon. Your part in the future of this operation will be vital." Suddenly the Colonel's face lost its smile and took on the steely tone of a commander addressing a subordinate.

"Don't let us down."

Simon Collyer Jnr. smiled a little nervously. Then he straightened his back and responded. "You can rely on me, Colonel," and turned towards the bar.

"Champagne barman," he said a little loudly. The Colonel shot a salutary glance at the Ambassador then retorted politely.

"Soda water with ice please barman."

"Well, perhaps later barman. Give me one of those soda's too!" said Collyer.

*

"She cleaned the toilets on the first floor, also rooms 20 to 44 and she polished the floor too. It's all here on the work sheet." Percy Smith smiled triumphantly. His hero Samuel Pepys had been meticulous in the mid 1600s at keeping records and organising the victualling and financing of the Navy. Percy Smith was no less of an organiser, but had one read his diary one would soon have realised that he was far less of a womaniser than Pepys.

"OK. Percy. I'll take that, many thanks," Grant commanded. He returned to the lobby and ran into the police room where Chief Inspector Duffy was seated.

"Start the search, here is her rota." Grant said, "And what have you found out?" he asked.

"More than you would expect," Duffy replied, "read this resume." He handed Grant a wad of handwritten notes and Grant read it for the next ten minutes. When he finished he ran out of the small police office. He was beginning to sweat. He slipped slightly and turned the corner to climb to the second floor.

Time was getting very short indeed. The Queen would arrive at 11.45. From then onwards, for the next thirty to forty minutes, the Houses of Parliament faced the greatest threat in the history of the English speaking people. This time it was not a threat they could face head on. Not even a threat that a great leader such as Churchill, a leader who in times of trouble the English people seemed always to produce, could defeat. For this new danger was insipid and unseen. It was urban terrorism. An animal that lives and thrives on fear and brainwashing and breeds on foreign money and fights with the weapons of war. An animal which destroys the fabric of society from within. A truly pernicious cancer.

At 10.55am as Grant sat in a conference room on the second floor waiting for the Prime Minister to arrive. He was thinking about why Fiona Galliani and Diane Trattorini had grouped together and called themselves INTERFERON. The naïve, street urchin Italian girls who had given their lives for their cause. Who had believed so fervently that they were liberating the underprivileged that they would kill for it. Who had desired to give freedom to the plebeians and to destroy the aristocracy. Who wanted to destroy privilege and to create a society based solely on merit yet without free competition.

Those two girls had spotted a cancer in the body of the IFFC. The cancer was Solomon J. Goldstein. The Jewish kid from Hamburg who escaped from the Nazis and built an enormously powerful empire. The man to whom insider dealing was merely a means to raise means. God knows how many terrorist organisations Goldstein had funded in the United Kingdom. How many innocents he had sent to their graves for money. The man whose father was killed by the Nazis, whose race was hunted and murdered so viciously in the 1930s and 1940s had himself become as bad as his parents persecutors. He had in effect become a progeny of his persecutors. He was a power junkie. But he was also just a well paid puppet. The men pulling the strings sat in Moscow.

So INTERFERON was formed to destroy the IFFC cancer. But like the drug itself, the side effects were uncertain and unfortunately it failed to cure the disease,

"Morning, Mr Grant," the Prime Minister walked into the Conference Room.

"Good morning Prime Minister," Grant stood up.

"It's not really at all good," the Prime Minister answered. She was followed by four men into the room. The Right Honourable Phillip McNaughton, Professor Sam Jacobs, Sir John Epcot and Lord Carver. The Defence Secretary nodded to Grant and sat down. Samuel Jacobs shook Grant's hand and sat beside him. Sir John Epcot couldn't bring himself to acknowledge Grant's presence. Lord Carver caught Grant's eye then looked away and sat down. He looked shattered. For a few seconds, an uneasy silence hung in the air. The Prime Minister arranged three files on the conference table in front of her and then looked up.

"Time is very short this morning gentlemen. I have asked you here because one man amongst you has achieved what the rest of us failed to do. He has given us the chance to avoid a catastrophe of such monumental proportions that I tremble to think of it." She looked at Grant then continued.

"This morning at 9.45, I received a phone call from the General Secretary of the Communist Party of the Union of Soviet Socialist Republics, Mr Gorbachev. He was responding to an urgent message that I had sent to him in the early hours of this morning. What he told me has been of the utmost importance."

George Grant could not wait any longer. He interrupted. "Prime Minister, there is no time for this. By 11.40am the building we sit in will face the greatest threat it has ever known. We have to get out now whilst they search for the transmitter... " he was cut short.

"It is being done. Have patience, let me finish please."

"But... " he tried to continue but she held up her hand and motioned to Samuel Jacobs to speak.

The Professor lifted a small parcel onto the table. He pulled out a black metal box with a row of coloured lights positioned along its face.

"This is a frequency analyser," he stated calmly. It detects waves transmitted into the air by radios, microwaves, radar, ultrasound and all other electronic equipment. It is quite simple. It does not decipher, it merely pinpoints what is transmitting and from where the transmission comes. Using three of these positioned around a transmitter, the vector of the transmissions can be coordinated. Then a search can be effected and the offending transmitter traced. It is accurate in a confined space to about thirty feet."

"That is a useful box of tricks." Grant was reaching for the box.

"Be calm," the Prime Minister cut in. There are three of the Professor's colleagues searching the building at this moment."

"Where did they start?" Grant asked.

Sam took a large folded piece of paper out of his bag and carefully unfolded it at the table.

"This is a floor plan of the Houses of Parliament. After I was contacted early this morning I worked out a search pattern to cover the building from top to bottom in the shortest possible time."

"How long will it take?" Grant asked. The Professor shook his head slightly. "Ah, and there is the problem, between one and two hours."

"That's too long!" Grant mumbled, "once the Queen has arrived we are all in the danger zone. They may strike at any time after 11.40am. We only have thirty minutes. It's 11.10 now!"

"Well unless we can narrow down the field of our search we have to follow the Professor's system," the Defence Secretary stated.

"We can!" Grant replied. "I told you that Celia Jones was in Judas' note book. I have found out that she worked only on the first floor last Friday."

"Who?" The Professor asked.

"The cleaning lady," the Prime Minister responded.

"I take it that you have found out what her roster was last week?"

"Yes. She worked here for six months. On the 1st November she met Farhad Fee, the Chairman of the IFFC. She died, I assume she was murdered, on the 3rd November. We can therefore assume that between the 1st and the 3rd she had the opportunity of placing the homing device in this building."

"I see," Sam Jacobs replied. "Then we shall start at her rota for the 3rd and work back."

"Percy Smith is in his office on the 3rd floor Sam. He has already informed me that Celia Jones cleaned the first floor of the West Wing rooms 20-44 on the 3rd. Why don't you start there?"

"OK," the Professor rose to leave. "God help us Prime Minister!"

"Keep us informed, Professor." The Prime Minister said as he left.

*

At that moment Chief Inspector Duffy brushed past the Professor and entered the room.

"Oh, excuse me Prime Minister," he gasped.

"Don't worry, Chief Inspector. What is it?"

"The autopsy on Mrs Jones has been completed. She was found dead after a car crash on Friday 3rd at about 9.30pm. But she died before the crash."

"What does that mean?" Grant asked.

"She was poisoned. Cyanide gas capsule under the pedals. Bloody nasty way to go, I can assure you."

For a few seconds the conference room fell silent. Then the Prime Minister spoke. She started slowly but her voice climbed gradually as her sentence formed.

"So the pattern emerges as Grant predicted. I think that this only goes to confirm our fears gentlemen. I have to go to the ceremony in a few minutes. In the meantime I can tell you that I have received confirmation that the funding of the terrible carnage that we have suffered since early this year came from within the Soviet Union.

"It did not, however, come from the sources one might have expected." The Prime Minister opened the first folder in front of her.

"We have been aware for a considerable time that Perestroika has had its opponents. None have been more vehemently opposed than the Russian equivalent of the Mafia. But worse than that and far more powerful are various high ranking officials from the communist parties of Czechoslovakia, Poland, East Germany and Romania. Men, recently deposed by their own people as a result of Perestroika. They are all smarting from the losses they have suffered."

She paused whilst the effect of her words sunk in.

"We around this table have known for a long time that Russia had its own Mafiosi similar to the Italian capos. The Godfathers of which have made millions upon millions of Roubles from activities such as prostitution, the supply of drugs to citizens and latterly the army in Afghanistan and of course trading in arms. They operate right across the Soviet Union from the Ukraine to Uzbekistan. They, together with the deposed party officials, have plotted to overthrow President Gorbachev.

"At present Leonid Brezhnev's son in law, Uri Churbanov, is on trial on charges of corruption relating to the Soviet Mafia. This fact and many others including the present leader's desire to stamp out corruption has led to a strong opposition to President Gorbachev. He informs me that Soviet bureaucracy was the fertile soil in which the mobsters bred. They work best within the cumbersome one party system created by Krushev and sustained by Brezhnev. If it is dismantled then the Godfathers will lose their power base and of course immense amounts of income.

"The first secretary told me this morning that there was a breakthrough recently. A few days before my recent message he had himself been made aware of the tip of the subversive movement which was plotting to overthrow his new reforms. He has arranged for his loyal intelligence officers to investigate the group. He himself told me this morning that at their last conference on a Black Sea coastal resort the Officials and the Mafiosi took a crucial decision. At that time it appears that the head of the KGB, General Uri Krasilova, was looking for a way to recapture the power which Perestroika had begun to remove from the KGB."

She stopped for a minute as a commotion outside reached a crescendo. The Conference Room door opened and the Chief Whip for the Conservative Party walked in.

"The Queen has just left Buckingham Palace, Prime Minister. The television cameras are ready to start filming. You really must come now, or it will look odd!"

"OK, Frank. I'll be down in a minute." The Chief Whip left and the Prime Minister rose.

"Phillip will finish this for me. Before I go, I will say one more thing. If we survive this day gentlemen, one of you will be indicted for high treason, so don't any of you leave this building until I return."

With those words chilling the room, she left.

The Defence Secretary picked up the file and read on...

11.30AM MONDAY, 6TH NOVEMBER, 1988

The Piper Cherokee swooped into a low turn over Putney Bridge and started following its final course up the river Thames towards the Houses of Parliament. Ric Florentino began to realise what they were going to do and he was choked up.

Earlier that morning when Ricardo Edwardo Florentino had reached the small airfield outside Watford at 5.30am he had been surprised to see that Johnny, his pilot, was not checking the plane over. As a matter of habit he always did so. He'd done so for two years every week day morning before they set off in 'the Flying Eye' to report to the whole of London on the traffic in the capital.

Ric had parked the car and walked over to the changing rooms. As he had stepped inside he had understood the reason. Johnny was dead. He was lying face down in a pool of his own blood on the floor of the mess room.

The rest of the morning had been a blur. The terrorists had roughed him up a little and then one of them had piloted the aircraft and the other had fitted the guillotine onto his body.

Ricardo Florentino had often wondered what it would be like to die in a plane crash. He had always lived with that constant niggling fear. On any normal day he could take it. But this day his fear was greater because it was so immediate and it was so personal. Now he had the most terrifying choice to make. Either he could announce to the world that terrorists were in his plane because he was "on air" and if he did he had no doubt that he would lose his love life and probably his life. Or he could stay silent and be part of a terrible crime against the whole country.

For a second he shut his eyes and prayed, but he couldn't avoid the terrible choice. When he opened them again there was the face of the terrorist, cool, calm and frighteningly serious. This man intended to do what he set out to do and Ricardo was paralysed with fear. He did not regard himself as a brave man. But he had never before realised how sacred to him all life was. Not just his. And how integrally bound up with his life, was the freedom that he had always taken for granted.

11.32AM MONDAY, 6TH NOVEMBER 1988

"From the information which President Gorbachev passed to the Prime Minister this morning it appears that the Russian "Godfathers" put up the money to pay for a terrifying scheme devised by the KGB in 1985. They planned to use international terrorists to destabilise a western democracy and to persuade the civilians and pressure groups to call for martial law to restore peace and tranquillity. We have seen the results here. They are terrifying."

"I would never have allowed it had I known!" Sir John Epcot.

"Neither would I, call it off!" Lord Carver stated.

"I don't think either of you would have been allowed to survive today, if you had objected" Grant said. Both men sat shocked. Phillip McNaughton continued.

"Gentlemen, we have been hit in our achilles heel. The soft under belly of democracy. Urban terrorism has destroyed our citizens' trust in their authorities and turned back the clock to a time when they believed that the armed forces were the only bodies capable of restoring order. In the last month we have seen the results. Massive street marches demanding martial law in Manchester, Birmingham and London. The National Press, together for once, urging the Government to act. And so we did. The Cabinet decided to impose a night time curfew as from last night. At the time, we didn't realise that we were playing right into their hands. We thought that they wanted to prevent a curfew. Their kidnapping of my children must have been a double bluff. Today, now, we know the truth.

"President Gorbachev is taking steps to catch the perpetrators in the Soviet Union. At our end, we have but a few minutes to save ourselves and our democracy."

George Grant lit a Galoise cigarette. He was shaking slightly. Then the tension in the room was broken by a clanging. The telephone at the far end rung twice and Phillip McNaughton walked over and picked it up.

"A call for you, ... er Mr. Grant." The Defence Secretary's face was drawn and colourless.

Grant took the phone.

"Grant?" the question came from an unknown voice.

"Speaking."

"We have Marchant and MacDougal." Grant lost his breath and seized up. He couldn't breathe. For a second his legs felt weak, then he steadied himself and tried to regain control.

"Marianne and Jack? Why?"

"Never mind. Do as I say now or they will be killed. Do you understand?"

He turned to the men in the conference room and gasped. So little time. So little time! What steps could he take? If he complied, he lost. If he refused, he lost. It was the critical test all over again, only this time he couldn't reprogramme the computer because there was no computer. Only human beings. Blasted, deceptive human beings. He indicated to McNaughton to pick up the other phone by the drinks cabinet. McNaughton looked quizzical but did so.

"What is it you want me to do?"

McNaughton was looking puzzled. He mimed the words "Who is it?" Grant took a piece of paper and wrote the words. 'Them'. The voice on the other end continued.

"You met a man a few days ago from abroad whilst you were in Guildford, remember?"

"Yes, how could I forget?"

"If you mention his name or continue in any way to pursue him, your friends will be killed. Do you understand?"

"Yes," Grant whispered.

"We will contact you again later today, to tell you how you can recover your friends."

'Click,' the line was cut off.

Grant replaced the phone in its cradle and steadied himself on the sideboard. "Oh my God." He whispered.

"Who was he talking about, George?" Phillip McNaughton asked softly. Grant rehearsed the threat in his head. The traitor was sitting in that very room. Listening to their conversation. If he answered the question, he was sending Jack and Marianne to almost certain death. If he did not he was as good as letting the KGB architect of the terrorist wave escape. For an eternity, he stood sweating and frozen.

Suddenly he realised that he might not be in a catch 22 at all. They were getting desperate. If they succeeded in blowing up the Houses of Parliament, no one would ever know he had broken the command. If they failed then they had nothing to gain by killing their hostages.

"Colonel Vladimyr Zachristov of the KGB and Solomon J. Goldstein."

Phillip McNaughton nodded. "They *are* getting nervous." He said smiling.

*

Lord Epcot glanced at his watch.

"It's 11.41, where the hell are those homing devices!" Phillip McNaughton crossed the room and closed the first file.

"I wish we knew, Disney." He opened the second file and started to read;

"From the information that we have received, it is clear now that Mr Grant was right when he warned us that the KGB were controlling the terrorist wave. Francoise Deboussey, the wise old man of Middle Eastern politics had smelt a rat and guessed correctly. That means that we owe you an apology, George."

"Thanks Phillip, but it's no bloody use now! What are we going to do?"

"We are doing all that we can. There are two choppers presently circling the building to intercept any aircraft that might fly by, but Wing Commander Harris sees no possibility of that happening. All airspace within five miles of the Houses of Parliament is closed. Nothing could get through. If a jet tried, by the time it approached within forty miles we would have four rapid attack aircraft airborne and within striking distance of it in forty-eight seconds. The procedures are set. The defences are well thought out. There is practically no chance of an airborne attack succeeding."

"I do not like the word 'practically,' Phillip." Grant replied.

At that moment there was a knock on the door. It opened and the joint chiefs of the armed forces, Wing Commander Harris and Admiral Perkins, entered and sat down. After brief hellos, Phillip McNaughton continued. His voice raised a little. His pulse rate quickening. He looked at his watch. It was 11.54am.

In the House of Lords, the Queen would have risen to start her speech. The television cameras of the world would be watching.

"Before I recommence gentlemen, I'll ask Wing Commander Harris to update us on the situation in the air."

The Wing Commander stood up.

"Well, Phillip, I have nothing to report at all. No air traffic over the coast that is out of the ordinary. The flights in and out of Heathrow, Gatwick, Stansted and the City airport are as normal and no other light aircraft is within the area without licence."

"Good." Phillip McNaughton was relieved. There was a scuffle outside the door and it suddenly flew open. Grant couldn't put his finger on it but something the Wing Commander said had not sounded right.

Sam Jacobs was not a fit man but he ran quickly into the Conference Room and threw an object onto the table.

"That's it!" He screamed. A bar of soap shot along the polished leather and came to rest beside George Grant.

"What is it Sam?" the Defence Secretary asked.

"It's a fucking transmitter. Smash it open. We found it beneath the sink in a cloakroom on the first floor."

Grant picked it up.

"Quick man, we don't have any time!"

Grant placed the soap on the rim at the edge of the table and broke it open. A small metal object clattered onto the floor. He picked it up. Sam Jacobs ran to him and ripped it out of his hand.

"Crafty bloody bastards," he shouted and put the object onto the floor. He stamped his foot down hard onto it and it smashed into fragments of wire and silicone.

"It's a Russian homing device. Works on a high frequency, at the top of our scale. Range about a quarter of a mile. They are going to fire a goddamn guided missile at us. No-one should be in this building, it's suicide!"

"We have to stay, Professor." Phillip McNaughton responded. "That decision has been taken and it is irreversible. If we run, then they have won, without needing to destroy Parliament. That is final."

Grant looked at the shattered metal and held his breath. The thoughts which ran through his mind were going through the minds of the other men at the same time. He said the words the others only thought.

"There will be more of these you know."

"Oh my God!" the Professor yelled. "There is no time. The Queen is on her feet." He ran out of the room and shouted a command to the man outside. Then it hit Grant. The Wing Commanders words *'without licence.'*

12.05AM 6TH NOVEMBER, 1988

The Piper Cherokee came within sight of the tall ornate spires of the Houses of Parliament. The radio crackled.

"Hi Rick. How's the traffic from up there in the sky?" the DJ called into the microphone.

Ric's trembling hand hit the speak button. His mouth was dry, he couldn't form the words. The violent brown eyes of the terrorist Farhad Fee burnt into his. He spoke.

"Hi, Chris. Vauxhall Bridge is clearing and the Embankment is looking OK. Not the same for the convoy of trucks outside the Tate, which is slowing the traffic." Then he swallowed. He had to do it now. The terrorist was leaning forwards, looking towards the newly installed instrument panel with the firing instructions. He was pressing one of the switches. He had to say it. He couldn't let them do it!

"Oh God, Chris, they are going to blow up the Houses of Parliament. Tell everyone - arrh." Pain flooded into his brain, blood spurted out of his penis as the razor blade struck brutally downwards through the soft flesh. He dropped the mike and struggled to release the guillotine but it was too firmly attached. He daren't look down. He was on fire with agony.

"No! You bastards! You can't." He lunged forwards and Farhad Fee cursed and shot three bullets into his chest. Ric Florentine's lifeless body slumped backwards into the passenger seat.

Farhad Fee opened the firing switch lock and flicked the primary ignition button. The panel lit up. Twenty more seconds and he would fire. He smiled knowingly at the pilot who nodded.

*

Grant leant forwards and pointed at the Wing Commander.

"What do you mean by *without licence*, Wing Commander?"

"Answer me!" the tone shocked Commander Harris and he glanced briefly at McNaughton, who said: "Answer him!"

"No planes are allowed into the security zone except those with a licence."

"Who has a licence?" Grant asked.

"The weather men for their balloons, two private helicopters for guests of the Royal family, the Goodyear Zeppelin for TV coverage and Capital Radio's Flying Eye." Then he realised the terrible error. "Oh my God," he said, "the plane."

"Get a radio!" yelled the Defence Secretary.

Field Marshal Carshalton entered the room and then turned and reflected the order down the line. A soldier returned with a portable radio. Grant tuned it to the Capital Radio frequency and heard the voice of the London based DJ. "Hi Ric, how's the traffic then up there in the sky?"

"Hi, Chris. Vauxhall Bridge is clearing and the Embankment looks OK. Not the same for the convoy of trucks outside the Tate which is slowing the traffic!"

There was a pause and Grant breathed more steadily. It was OK. They were not on the plane. Thank God for that. He walked over to the window and ushered McNaughton to do the same. The small red and white plane was just coming into view. The radio crackled then he heard the DJ continue.

"Oh God, Chris, they are going to blow up the Houses of Parliament, Tell everyone! - Arrh..." The scream ran through the room like a sabre through each man's heart. The blood curdling gasp of a man in eternal agony.

Wing Commander Harris ran out of the room and grabbed a walkie talkie from his orderly in the hallway.

"Intercept squadron! Harris here. Red alert. Get Choppers 12 and 13 to shoot down the bloody radio plane, now!"

He paused and Grant heard a crackling voice on the other end question the command.

"No, it's not. Blow it out of the bloody sky!" the Wing Commander restated. The sound and down draft of a helicopter passing the window of the Conference Room rattled the glass as Grant reached for the phone and dialled security. He passed the phone to McNaughton.

"Yes sir?" Security responded.

"This is the Defence Secretary. Clear the House immediately."

"Are you joking?"

"Don't argue ......do it now!"

Farhad Fee flicked up the cover and put his forefinger over the button. He watched in the strap-on external mirror as the missile lowered out of the box, suspended from the undercarriage of the Piper. Ten seconds to go. He could hear the mechanism lowering the missile into a firing position.

Suddenly he saw the helicopter appear from behind Big Ben. It was eight hundred yards away and heading straight towards them.

"Come on," he shouted to the inanimate box in front of him. A puff of smoke appeared from the rocket launchers on the helicopter and a red flame burst out exposing a deadly heat seeking missile.

"Dive left, now!" Farhad shouted to the pilot.

The Cherokee banked sharply to the left and the missile flew past the tip of the right wing and carried straight on. The missile was designed to seek and follow jets with hot trails not a light plane with a propeller. The RAF pilot had made an error over his choice of weapon. The heat seeking device wouldn't detect the Piper.

"Stupid fuckers," Farhad shouted and pressed the big red firing button.

CHAPTER 23
ON THE WING OF A PRAYER

An earth shattering explosion spewed out from the undercarriage of the Cherokee and for a split second the plane seemed to stand still as the reverse thrust of the missile counteracted the forward momentum. Then it appeared. A gleaming metal tube with a tail of fire rushing forward toward the towers of the Houses of Parliament

"Yes," cried Farhad Fee and smashed his hand onto the control panel.

"Now get me the hell out of here," he shouted at the pilot as the Piper banked hard left and flew away over Westminster Abbey, hotly pursued by the two helicopters.

*

George Grant stood transfixed as the smoke and flame of the missile firing mechanism appeared from the underbelly of the plane.

"Oh, my lord," said the Defence Secretary. Lord Carver bolted for the door of the Conference Room and shoved the Defence Secretary to the ground as he passed.

For an eternity, time froze. The murky waters of the River Thames sparkled unknowingly and the pleasant background sounds of London town continued their daily routines unawares. Democracy was about to collapse. A plan conceived six thousand miles away and executed by men with a terrible dream was about to come to fruition. Four hundred years of struggle and torment for the English speaking people would end. Their desire for democracy which had preceded the hopes of all other nations and had come to be symbolised by the strong brick towers of the Houses of Parliament, stood like a feeble willow tree, bowed before the might of a ferocious tornado.

Grant fell to his knees and he prayed. There was nothing left to be done. Beside him the Defence Secretary lay flat on his belly with his hands over his head mouthing the Lord's Prayer. The joint Chiefs of staff stood stiffly to attention, acting out some unreal ceremony. Each man reacting in his own way to his last moments of life.

And so they waited. Five men of power and one civilian, naked before their ends, expecting death. And yet the time passed and death did not come. Perhaps seconds, perhaps a lifetime later, Grant raised his head slowly not quite believing that he was still there. Still alive.

The sunlight caught the crest of a wave on the Thames and the glowing water frothed. He smiled and breathed out for the first time since he had made his peace with his God.

A curved smoky trail lay in the morning sky around the west wing of the Houses of Parliament. He leant out of the window and watched the red tail of the missile drop down over the Embankment and then heard the terrifying explosion. A mushroom of smoke erupted over Dolphin Square and yellow flames jumped two hundred feet into the air. The thunderous roar of the explosion took but a split second to reach his ears. It shook him to the bone.

*

"And so I am delighted once again to open this new term of Parliament." Queen Elizabeth the II closed her notes and returned slowly to her chair. The Duke of Edinburgh clapped quietly and spoke to her as she sat down.

"Well done dear. Another fine speech."

"Thank you, Phillip," she replied.

"We seem to have survived the morning. No doubt only our Lord knows how."

"The Prime Minister will tell us when she's ready."

"Perhaps she just got her wires crossed?" the Duke replied.

"I don't think so, Phillip. Thatcher does not do crossed wires."

The Prime Minister re-entered the conference room on the second floor of the Houses of Parliament with a broad grin on her face.

"Well gentlemen, we seem to have survived. I take it that no attack materialised." The room held an uneasy silence for a few seconds. George Grant watched the Defence Secretary as he struggled to find the words.

"We were bloody lucky, Prime Minister." Words were not so difficult to find after all.

"They launched an air to ground missile from the Capital Radio Flying Eye. It looked for a few seconds as if we would all be blown sky high."

"So what happened?" The Prime Minister responded after a moment, her voice trembling.

"The missile turned around the west tower and headed away. It appears to have destroyed Dolphin Square, Prime Minister."

"What a relief!" She whispered. "I mean, what a tragedy." She said louder.

"We came within a hairs breath of total annihilation. I do not mind admitting that I was terribly scared." Phillip said, his voice wavering.

"So was I, but we have not been annihilated have we Phillip?" The Prime Minister sat down slowly. The pain and tension of the last few months finally catching up with her.

"There must have been only one homing device. The one Professor Jacobs destroyed before our very eyes." She said, exhausted by the strain.

The phone rang and the Prime Minister went to answer it. Two minutes later she replaced the receiver.

"That was the Foreign Secretary. Our embassy in Moscow has reported that the head of the KGB, Uri Krasilova, has been arrested and imprisoned at Lubyenka for treason. President Gorbachev was as good as his word. I knew he would be. Do you think they will find the Godfathers, Disney?"

Sir John Epcot shook his head twice.

"Extremely unlikely, Prime Minister. They will have covered their tracks so deeply it would take a lifetime to uncover them. It appears that they risked only their money, not their lives. In any event they are beyond out jurisdiction."

"That is always the way isn't it, Disney. The soldiers perish but the Generals and the Field Marshalls survive to fight again." The Prime Minister stated. "Where is Lord Carver?"

"He ran out," Phillip McNaughton replied. "Just before the missile was fired."

"I am sorry to hear that Phillip. He had done so much for the service, especially after the Hollis affair. I find it hard to believe he was involved."

"Believe it?" Grant asked. "Maybe he was not involved! Perhaps he wanted to live to fight another day. We should all have been away from here at 11.10 am this morning. His leaving proves nothing other than his desire to save his own life."

"You don't mince your words do you, George?" It was the first time she had used his first name. He was grateful. "I hope you don't mind me being convivial, but you seem to have become part of our lives these last few days. Would you mind explaining?" The Prime Minister asked.

Grant picked up a pen and wrote down the following words:-

"1. The Godfathers.
2. General Uri Krasilova.
3. Colonel Vladimyr Zachristov.
4. Farhad Fee - The Scorpion.
5. Solomon J. Goldstein – Tailor.
6. Daniel Judas – Candlestick.
7.　　　- Butcher
8.　　　- Baker
9.　　　– Security"

He handed the list to Mrs Thatcher.

"This is the shortlist of men responsible for today's events. Three are still unnamed. Moscow has cut the ties between the organisers and the operators. Now we must clear up the rest."

"Do you mean that one of them could still be standing in this room after what happened a few minutes ago?" The Defence Secretary asked with strained incredulity.

"Quite possibly," Grant responded. "Prime Minister, with your leave?" he continued.

"Go ahead George," she nodded her approval as well and sat down at the head of the table.

Grant walked over to the telephone and called the Chief Inspector. Duffy arrived shortly and Grant turned to face Rear Admiral Perkins, the man who had replaced Admiral James after his assassination. Chief Inspector Duffy opened his brief case and pulled out a file of papers three inches thick and passed it to Grant.

"On 23rd of August, 1968 you and General Uri Krasilova were the coordinators of the East-West peace talks meeting in Geneva. The meeting was declared a success in the Press, but in reality it was a sham, wasn't it Admiral?"

"What do you mean?" the Rear Admiral expelled.

"After that meeting you and the present head of the KGB kept in contact over the years. First through MacLean at MI5 and later, through Daniel Judas."

"This is preposterous," the Admiral spluttered.

"Do you deny your trip to East Berlin in February 1985?"

"No of course not. It is all on my record. I was there as a representative of Her Majesty's Government and of the Navy for the exchange of information about further NATO manoeuvres in the North Sea. What does that prove?"

"Nothing, unless one adds the presence of Solomon J. Goldstein and Daniel Judas staying at the Royal Hotel, not fifty yards from your own. And the private calls which you made, twenty-two in all, from your rooms to theirs. Add to that the meeting at the cafe on Ledenstrasse on the 15th and the fact that Admiral James was killed by the IFFC conveniently close to today's date so that you would become his successor!"

"Prime Minister," the Admiral cried, "you cannot believe this? Surely?"

"It doesn't sound good does it? Can you explain it Rear Admiral?" The Prime Minister said coldly.

He shifted uneasily in his chair. A man caught between self deception and fear.

"The sting has failed. What was there left to cover up Admiral?" Grant prompted.

When it came, it broke out in a flood of self pity and emotion. Admiral Perkins crumpled into himself in a way. He started to sob.

"Krasilova is a strong man. An honest man. He believes that Perestroika will lead to the third world war. It cannot continue. Country after country falling into anarchy. The Iron Curtain being pulled aside. Intellectuals and poets taking the reins of power. Do not think that it will stop with communism. That is only the start. It will come here soon enough.

"The old values will be usurped by Greenpeace and anti nuclear wimps. Uri contacted me. He asked if I believed that a reduced Navy and a castrated Air Force could truly defend the United Kingdom. I have seen what cutbacks do to the men. To our ability to defend ourselves. They chew up morale and destroy discipline. It couldn't be allowed to continue.

"He promised that under his plan it was not communism which was to come, but a safer and more secure democracy. And the worst part is that I still believe him."

Grant responded: "So they offered you a place in the new order? The military order? One where the decline of the forces would stop and there would be no corruption and no cutbacks? You would be able to rebuild the Navy to its former strength?"

"Yes, to defend out great country not to attack it! I believed in it. I suppose I was a fool. I really knew nothing of what they planned to do," the Admiral cried.

"But later came the nightmare." Grant added. "Where is your wife, Admiral? Where are your children?"

His face went white. "You bastard, Grant."

"Not me, Admiral. You gave in to the blackmail. You gave them the opening and they capitalised on it."

"Oh my humble God! I tried to stop them after the killings. They took her. They told me I'd never see my children again. My daughters! I had no choice after that."

"What was your codename, Admiral?" An old man buried his head in his hands.

"Baker," he mumbled. "Oh my humble God, forgive me. I had no choice."

Grant took the handwritten paper from the Prime Minister and he wrote "Admiral Perkins" beside "Baker". He nodded at Gruff Stuff and Duffy handed Grant the next file.

"Then there is *the Butcher*," he said looking at Sir John Epcot.

"Not me!" Sir John replied.

'Tell me about Francoise Deboussey?" The words hit John Epcot like a slap in the teeth. At first he couldn't bring himself to answer. Eventually he straightened his back and looked at the Prime Minister.

"We had been lovers for many years. The Services knew about my proclivities. There was no shame in it. I was proud of my chosen way. By being open with the High rank in the Services I prevented any possible blackmail.

"Francoise contacted me covertly. He told me he had vital information which might help solve the riddle of who was financing the terrorist atrocities. You may recall our conversation about it, Prime Minister?"

"Yes, Disney, I do." She replied, clearly disturbed by his own emotional fragility.

"I wouldn't have sent Grant out to him if I had thought it would have caused his death. When Grant told me Francoise was dead I couldn't help but blame him. Francoise was too wise and too experienced to have been found by the IFFC. I concluded it had to have been be Grant's mistake."

"Perhaps reasonable," the Prime Minister agreed.

"But not quite the truth," Phillip McNaughton interrupted.

"You called the meeting of Sub-Sec which decided to cold store Grant because you said he was *a liability*. He had probably *'turned'*. Those were grave words, Sir John. You said that he had failed to debrief after a fiasco. We accepted your conclusions. We agreed to cold store Grant. Why did you push that avenue so hard?" The accusation was all too clear. Grant put the finishing touch to it.

"Because he knew I had found the trail to Trattorini, the IFFC courier who had uncovered the Sting. He intended to have me followed and then when I had led him to her I was expendable."

"Yes," Sir John responded. His resistance rising. "And what was wrong with that? We needed her knowledge. I believed that she was a link to the IFFC. Others told me I was wrong, but I did believe that. You were emotionally involved Grant because she killed Joanne Schaeffer. You were unreliable. Egypt showed that. This chance could not be left in your hands."

"So you sent out Daniel Judas?" Grant threw the words over the conference table.

"He was the right man for the job. Our best expert in interrogation and terrorism and he knew the operation and the full extent of the terrorist onslaught. Furthermore, he was the man who tutored you when we signed you up. If anyone could control you, it would be him. Who better?"

"He was Candlestick, he was an IFFC agent, Sir John."

"I didn't know that!" he shouted, slamming his fist onto the table futilely. Grant sat looking calmly at Sir John for a moment.

"Daniel Judas' file was marked *"field controlled"*, Sir John. He was known to be unable to handle field work. You knew of his limitations. Any senior beta cell operator could have carried out that operation. There was another reason wasn't there?" Grant threw Judas' file onto the table. The words stamped in red on the front were clear *'field controlled'*.

"How did you get those files?" Sir John shrieked. "What are you?"

"Just a man trying to understand why? What was your reason, Sir John? Was it because 'Candlestick' would ensure that Trattorini would never leave Barbados alive. Never be able to blow the

Scorpion's Sting apart? She knew about the Moscow connection. She killed Solomon Goldstein's daughter to try to persuade him to cut the link, so that the IFFC could continue their operation uncontrolled by the KGB."

"What do you mean?" The Prime Minister interjected.

"The IFFC always meant to liberate what they call the working classes in Great Britain, Prime Minister. They truly believed that Solomon Goldstein was the sole financier. Goldstein led them to believe that he would finance the disruptions and the havoc. In fact he was the KGB's conduit. Their front man. The deal was that his payment was to be the grant of exclusive rights to UK North Sea Oil Production after the new order took over.

The IFFC believed or were led to believe that after the destruction of both our Royalty and our Parliament today, democracy would wither and after a period of enlightenment and calming martial law, with the right military officers in command, a new, more fair communist style democracy would emerge. An English version of the French revolution. With the old values destroyed. No more privilege. No more Royalty. Just a fair system based on merit and hard work."

"Perhaps their aims were more admirable than we believed, even if their methods were so despicable," the Prime Minister responded to the astonishment of the room.

"But the sting was that Goldstein was a mere front man for the KGB, and through that organisation, as you Prime Minister have recently discovered, for the Russian and Eastern European Godfathers. Once the battle was won, the KGB and their funders intended to take over. In fact the people that Goldstein instructed the IFFC to target, hit or blackmail, were carefully drawn up players in a plan to put certain people with certain political persuasions in key positions. They reached senior industrialists, trade unionists and military personnel.

"The new order would march to old Moscow's old beat. At the same time, I think that Zachristov and Krasilova planned for the KGB to use their victory to throw Perestroika back on its heels. The ultimate aim was to overthrow Gorbachev and his hated reforms. To allow certain ex-leaders of various ex-communist states to return to power. Gorbachev has made a hell of a lot of enemies in the last few years as you know."

"It was an audacious plan," The Defence Secretary was beginning to recover his composure. "And this Trattorini girl found that out?" he asked.

"No. A friend of hers called Fiona Galliani was raped by Goldstein and Judas and when she escaped from Goldstein's house she found a list of names. The master list and other information which exposed the basic Sting. The KGB connection." Grant once again turned to Sir John.

"Sp why did you send Judas out?"

"I didn't, in fact." Sir John responded. "I was too involved personally after Francoise died. I passed the decision over. Lord Carver suggested that he should deal with it. But I do not seek to pass the buck. The principle was correct, Prime Minister."

"But the day to day control of the operation was under the control of the DG of MI6. You, Sir John." The Prime Minister responded.

Then suddenly the clouds lifted and Grant saw the solution.

"Oh, my, Goodness," whispered the Prime Minister at that moment. She had seen it too.

"It was Lord Carver. And that tape which you made, Mr Grant, of the conversation with Goldstein and this Trattorini girl at Park Lane. The one Chief Inspector Duffy handed to the Metropolitan Chief Commissioner. The right person for the Commissioner to take that to was the DG of internal Security: Lord Carver!"

"There's one more point, Prime Minister." Grant continued. It was a guess, but it might work.

"Who reactivated D Section, Sir John?"

"I did, with the Prime Minister's consent, of course."

"Yes." The Prime Minister added.

The next question would seal Sir John's fate.

"Prime Minister. After the Chief Inspector and I broke in on the SEC meeting at Downing Street a few days ago, who did you instruct to lift the D Notice on me?"

"Lord Carver of course," she replied.

"There are two dead men in Marianne Marchant's flat Prime Minister. No identification on them. Weapons with the serial numbers erased. Military experts in murder. They tried to murder me this morning. Hired killers carry ID. If they are caught, it's sometimes the only thing that saves their lives. They usually try to show that they did it for money. Hired guns don't carry unmarked weapons either. Those men were D Section operatives."

The commercial lawyer interjected. "There could be a hundred reasons why someone wanted to kill you George. The two that occur to me are: first: the men were IFFC operatives. Or second: Lord Carver failed to cancel the D Notice."

"If we find the third D Section operative involved in the hit, then maybe we will have our answer. Can you do that, Sir John?"

"There are only eighteen D Section operatives. Sixteen, after what you have told me. I will have the answer in half an hour. May I go, Prime Minister?" He stood up shakily. His hands trembling.

"Yes, Disney. I'm sorry but this was... necessary."

The words that the Director General used to Grant all those months ago now returned home to roost.

"I understand, Prime Minister."

An old and honest man left the conference room with his head held high. He knew he would retire before the week was out. He had played the game for long enough, let the young men take over.

The Prime Minister rose and went to the window overlooking the Thames. "So *the Butcher* is Lord Carver."

"Yes, Prime Minister." Grant replied. "After Galliani and Trattorini bombed Stringfellows to get at Solomon Goldstein, the police interviewed Goldstein. He mentioned a call from INTERFERON. That was the name Galliani and Trattorini had given themselves. That interview was removed from the records by Lord Carver when he visited Scotland Yard. He must have leant on the officer to keep quiet about it."

"Then we only have one to find. A man called Security!"

"My guess is that he and Colonel Zachristov are one and the same man." Grant said.

She looked out at the Thames and then turned back to the men inside.

"I want this stopped today gentlemen. Phillip, you find Colonel Zachristov and quickly. Do you know what his official functions were today?"

"Yes, Prime Minister. He was at the American Embassy for the morning." The Defence Secretary replied.

"Good. Phone them and ensure he stays there. He is the key to ensnaring the others. He is caught anyway. If he returns home tomorrow he faces arrest and imprisonment along with his superior, General Uri Krasilova.

"If we persuade him to reveal the identities of the key personnel in this organisation and to provide us with full documentation and evidence of their involvement we may be able to strike a deal with him."

"Do you mean immunity, Prime Minister?" The Defence Secretary asked astonished.

"It is a possibility Phillip. He has no other route to follow."

Grant saw the logic in the solution. Without the evidence of one of the organisers the whole group would probably escape.

"What about Goldstein, Prime Minister?' Grant asked.

"Do we have enough evidence to arrest him?"

"He has probably left the country already."

"I don't think so George. He will have loose ends to tie up and from what you've told me I imagine he considers himself safe unless either you or the State can convince a Court of law that he was involved. He will not know that we suspect Lord Carver. He also will also not know that we have plans for Colonel Zachristov."

Grant liked the way she thought.

"If you are right there may be a way, Prime Minister. But we must move fast." Grant replied. "First of all, I suggest that Field Marshal Carlshalton and Wing Commander Harris both take a very close look at their officers and seconds in command."

"General Randolf is above reproach." Field Marshall Carshalton stated feebly.

"Are you sure?" The Prime Minister said, "we'll check, shall we?"

CHAPTER 24
THE POISON EXTRACTED

The terrifying flames of an air borne missile burst past the glass window to the right of Farhad Fee's seat.

"Dive you fool," he shouted to the pilot and then released the belt around his waist.

"I am going to see if I can find a parachute," he shouted as he crawled into the rear of the light aircraft. Five seconds later the pilot felt a blast of cold air as the emergency exit was opened. He screwed his neck round to see Farhad Fee pointing a hand gun at him.

"No! Why?" The bullet entered his skull and a myriad spots of blood landed onto the windscreen of the plane.

"Why not?" Fee replied as he jumped from a thousand feet. The shoot opened quickly and he was momentarily winded as the uplift caught him.

The two Air Force helicopters raced after the light aircraft which had begun spiralling into a nose dive. One radioed back to base.

"One passenger ejected over Kilburn. What shall we do? Kill the man or follow the plane?"

The radio operator put the line through to Wing Commander Harris in the conference room at the Houses of Parliament.

"It is the pilot of Helicopter 13 Sir. A passenger of the plane has ejected over North London. He wants to know what to do."

The Wing Commander put the phone on speaker function. He turned round and looked at the Prime Minister.

"If we don't kill him now we may lose him. I say shoot the bastard." The Wing commander said firmly.

"We don't know who he is." The Prime Minister retorted.

"Yes we do Prime Minister. It is Farhad Fee. I would stake my life on it. He would not have left this hit to anyone else. It would have crowned his ungodly career." Grant said.

"Then he must be killed for the safety of all of us," the Prime Minister said.

Farhad Fee was a mere 100 feet above the rooftops of the Odeon cinema on the Edgware Road when the helicopters opened fire on him. His last sight was the hoarding in large red letters on the front of the Cinema which carried the words: *'Hellraiser.'* He smiled as the bullets rattled the buildings around him and he dropped below the roofline.

*

When George Grant returned to his flat in Old Church Street he collapsed into an armchair in the lounge. A lifetime had passed since he had received that first call from Solomon J. Goldstein. The start of the trail that had eventually led to that terrifying moment, when he had fallen to his knees and prayed in the Houses of Parliament. The logic of the moment had escaped him. One homing device! Why only one? It was too risky. Too much rested on it. One mistake, a technical fault and more than $1,500 million were thrown away. Goldstein was too smart to make that mistake. There must have been two. Perhaps one malfunctioned, or perhaps there was a God.

Also Grant sat with a heavy heart and on the verge of tears, thinking of Marianne and Jack. But his thoughts were shattered by the clanging of the phone. He slowly walked to the cabinet and picked it up.

"George, is that you?" A woman asked.
"Who is it?"
"Marianne."
"Oh, thank Christ."
"Help me!"
Her words came in short spurts. Her voice a million miles away.

"I escaped. I don't know where I am. I prayed you'd be at home. Thank God you are. They are after me. Help me!" Her panic shook him to the core.

"Look around you. What do you see?" He asked.

"A village. A pub. Some cars. I'm in a pay phone."

"Good. Now breathe deeply and look again. I want names."

"The Old Ship. I'm by an estuary. There is a street sign. 'Bosham Lane'. Oh, God, George. Help me."

"Bosham is near Itchenor Marianne. Goldstein's villa is near there. He must have held you there."

"I don't know. I killed a man. I swam. I don't know how far. I'm so tired, George."

"Marianne, stay there. Go to the pub. It's lunchtime, it will be open. Stay in a crowd. Don't leave for anyone. Strike up a conversation with the barman. Don't move. I'll be there in three quarters of an hour." He slammed the phone down and ran to the door. He jumped into the Alfa Spider 2000 and the tyres burnt the tarmac as he headed for the A3. Jack MacDougal was surely still there in Itchenor. Grant shook himself, trying not to think what they would do to him. Tired old Jack.

"Oh shit." He shouted as he crossed Chelsea Bridge. "Why Jack? Why Marianne? What's the point now?" But in his heart, he knew the point.

To Goldstein there was only one threat left. One more string to tie him into the failed terror that had swept the country. The conversation with Grant at Park Lane.

George Grant could not be left alive to give evidence if Goldstein wanted to stay safe. Grant made two calls from the car. One to Chief Inspector Duffy and one to the Defence Secretary. The first got through, the second created a message on a desk, somewhere in Whitehall.

The Chief Inspector knew what to do.

At 1.20pm on 6th November, Grant entered the Old Ship pub in Bosham. It reeked of smoke. The throng of jostling people couldn't hide the timid figure of Marianne Marchant sitting at the far end of the bar. When she saw him her face lit up. She pushed through the crowd and flung her arms around him.

"Thank you. Thank you for being there for me George."

It took fifteen minutes to calm her down and to find out how she had escaped from an old hut near the villa in Itchenor. She had killed a man, run for the water and swum for her life. A passing dinghy from the Bosham Yacht Club had picked her up. They took her back to Bosham. She had been too scared to talk to them.

He held her for a time and they waited for the Chief Inspector. At 1.45 the stout frame of Chief Inspector Duffy entered the pub. His greasy orange hair in a mop of tangles. Two men walked in with him.

*

The tall young man pulled a packet of cigarettes out of his jacket and flipped open a Zippo lighter. His Uzzi sub machine gun slung nonchalantly over his shoulder. As he took the first drag he heard a twig snap behind him. It was the last sound he ever heard. George Grant reached for his head and pulled the hair backwards with his right hand covering the guard's mouth. Grant's knee jerked violently up into the small of the guard's neck. The sickening sound of the broken spine made no impression on Grant. The body falling to the beautifully mowed lawn was forgotten as he raced to the clump of bushes near his objective.

A career of pain and fear was clicking into place. This was what he was trained for. Emotion had no place in this world. The regrets would come later as they always did. He might cry later, but now was the time for action.

Inspector Duffy turned away when he saw the body fall. The two Anti-Terrorist squad officers signalled by hand to Grant that the sailing dinghy in which they had arrived had been stored out of sight and took up flanking positions in the shrubbery around the Gardens.

Grant removed the cool weight of the hand gun from his shoulder holster and surveyed the lawn which ran up to the villa.

Two guards were standing talking on the sunny pool veranda. A third stood stock still beside the double doors at the rear entrance to the villa.

They were all disturbingly calm. Neither appeared in the slightest bit worried. That meant only one thing. Dogs! Grant shivered and felt his wounded forearm instinctively. The barking came only seconds later. One, then two more appeared from behind the oval library, underneath the East wing of the villa.

The guards stiffened and the two by the pool began to jog towards the harbour after the dogs. Grant flattened himself in the dirt and turned to look at the ATS man to his right called Joe. He signalled twice. Joe nodded. He then looked to his left and the other ATS man, Frank. He was the youngster with the fire in his eyes. He nodded. Grant nodded back. The kid was trigger happy. The trouble would come from the left and the dogs were on them.

The first Rottweiler jumped when it was six feet away from Joe. A shot broke the cool tranquillity of the afternoon and the dog yelped, fell, and kicked in its last throes of life. The guards split apart. One ran to the left and the other to the right but Grant and Joe fired simultaneously. Grant winged one and he faltered. Joe's bullet entered the other man's chest and he fell immediately.

"Three men!" the wounded guard shouted towards the villa and fired two shots at Grant. The soil erupted at Grant's shoulder and he rolled away once, then fired twice. The wounded guard's neck was ripped open as he fell to the ground. Within seconds Grant expected the rest of the villa to be awash with guards. He raised himself from the dirt and sprinted for the double doors at the rear. Joe was already sprinting to the pool.

"Shit!"

Grant heard the words and turned to see Frank desperately beating a Rottweiler over the head with his hand. His gun lay on the lawn by his feet. The third dog was about to jump and Grant loosed three shots spread widely to increase the chances of a hit. The dog yelped in mid air, turned head over heels and fell juddering to the soil.

The second dog hung tenaciously onto Frank's arm but he was too close for Grant to use the gun. The Chief Inspector and Marianne ran to help. Joe and Grant turned and sprinted once more to the villa.

Grant flattened himself beside the double doors and raised a flat palm in Joe's direction. Joe nodded and dropped to a crouch. For four seconds they waited. The footsteps came from inside the villa. Suddenly the double doors crashed open and three men fired a lethal spread of bullets into the garden beyond. The Chief Inspector and Frank threw themselves onto the turf as two further men burst onto the veranda.

Grant tripped one up with his boot and fired repeatedly into the group. He hit all three. The gunfire from Joe finished the job. The devastating carnage they had caused briefly disgusted Grant. He breathed in sharply and repeated in his mind, 'Objective.'

He gritted his teeth and put a new cartridge into the hand gun.

Joe jogged over and pointed to the chest pocket of one of the men, which was bulging. Grant nodded and removed some of the grenades. Then Joe raced back to the pool. Ten seconds later Frank and Joe threw grenades through four windows on the first floor. The juddering explosions scattered a billion tiny fragments of glass down onto the lawn.

Grant stepped gingerly into the hall. The large marble floored hallway led straight through to the front doors. Four doors lay to his right. The staircase and two doors lay to the left. A magnificent gold and crystal chandelier wobbled dangerously above his head. He dropped to his knees on reaching the stairs and waited, listening. Whispered voices came from below the library door.

The Chief Inspector appeared behind him at the charred hole where the two back doors into the villa used to be. He was panting heavily. Grant signalled for him to bring Marianne in and slipped silently over to the other side of the library door.

A click and a crack! He frowned and slid silently over to the third door opposite the stairway. He caught his breath and held it. A hand appeared. Two fingers up to the sky. It was Joe.

"All clear." He said as he emerged grinning.

Frank slithered into the hall from behind Marianne and the Chief Inspector.

Joe sprinted for the bottom of the stairs and waited.

"If there was anyone up there the grenades would have flushed them out." He whispered to Grant. No one descended.

"Get Down!" Grant shouted suddenly. His sixth sense told him that the whole operation so far had been too easy.

They all crouched silently for a minute, then Frank crawled over to the Library door. Grant blocked his path. Frank glared at him.

"Hold on Frank. There is something missing. It's far too easy."

"What?" Frank raised his voice and Grant clapped his hand over the young man's mouth.

The Library door opened at that second and Solomon Joshua Goldstein stepped gingerly out with his head straining forwards to see around the door.

"Stop all this!" he shouted when he saw them. "This behaviour has gone quite far enough. Put away your weapons and come into the library. I do not want to see any further killing here today."

The Chief Inspector was still trying to catch his breath. He looked at Grant with the words, 'I do not trust him an inch,' pasted all over his face. But Grant could see little reason in waving his gun at Goldstein, when both Joe and Frank were paid to do so. He put it in his pocket and walked into the library. As he did so, he pointed to Joe and Frank to wait either end of the hallway. Marianne followed him in, clutching his arm.

Goldstein's mother in law was standing by the log fire against the west wall and Carmine was seated at her side in a deep armchair. She was shaking and couldn't hold Grant's eye for more than a split second, before looking at the carpet.

"How are you, George?" Goldstein's mother in law welcomed him in as if there had been no killing. Just the courtesy visit of an old friend.

"No too bad, thank you, Mrs Bertelson." Grant replied adding, "hello, Carmine."

"Humph." She replied, not lifting her head.

Grant introduced Marianne and the Chief Inspector who were shown to seats beside the fire as well. Goldstein then shut the doors and walked over to the drinks cabinet. He poured himself one and looked inquisitively at the guests. They all shook their heads. So he went ahead and poured himself a large whisky. When he turned around he looked at Grant.

"So you have come," he said.

"Where is Jack MacDougal?" Grant replied.

"He is here, safe."

Grant breathed an audible sigh. Goldstein shouted loudly at the fireplace and from a wall that appeared to be without a door, a crack appeared and then an opening and two men stepped out with Jack between them. Jack MacDougal smiled at Grant and then walked towards Marianne and hugged her as he leant over her chair.

"I told you that I would come back for you Jack," she said crying.

"I never doubted it Marianne." Jack replied and turned around. "Tell me, George, what happened at Parliament?"

"They failed Jack. The Queen's speech finished without interruption and Parliament is now in session," Grant replied.

"What is this all about?" Goldstein asked with feigned innocence.

"The missile skimmed the roof tops and eventually fell in Dolphin Square. Not exactly storming the Bastille this time, I am pleased to say Solomon. You murdered 53 innocent members of the public though."

"The best laid plans of mice and men," Goldstein said and downed his scotch appearing wholly unmoved by the lives he had destroyed.

Carmine looked up for the first time and shook her head.

"What the fuck is going on Papa? These men just killed your private body guards. They have trespassed on your house. Why don't you call the police?"

"Oh, my dear daughter. You are so young. So innocent." Goldstein said.

"I'm bloody well not innocent," she retorted indignantly.

"I will vouch for that," Grant added.

"Enough," Goldstein said beginning to look all of his fifty-nine years. "I have something to tell you." He continued dramatically looking at his mother in law. "I have made a terrible mistake my dear. And now, for the first time, perhaps in my life, I am going to have to face up to the consequences of my mistakes."

"I don't understand, Papa," Carmine interrupted.

"Neither do I, Solomon. What does this have to do with us?" His mother in law demanded.

Solomon Goldstein smoothed his chubby fingers through his wiry grey hair and went to the drinks cabinet to pour himself another drink.

"We will have to leave this country. I am no longer welcome here. In time I will try to explain to both of you what has happened. It all started with your daughter Carole's death. When the terrorists took her, I lost the only woman I had ever loved, as you know. Without a wife a man is only half a man. But now is not the time. Not here. Not in front of all of these people."

"Why not, Solomon?" Grant asked. "Don't your family deserve an explanation for all of the pain that you have caused them? Goddamn it, don't we all?"

Goldstein threw his glass into the wall and took two paces towards Grant. He was a bull of a man albeit past his prime. For a second Grant thought that he would strike out but he stopped as suddenly as he had started.

"You are not the only one who has suffered pain Grant. Do you truly believe you hold a monopoly on righteousness? Do you presume to be possessed of some divine quality to judge others because you have suffered one loss? Are you so perfect?"

Grant stepped back a pace in surprise.

"No of course not. But I have not tried to destroy the whole system. You have. I am not a traitor."

"I have done no more than any other active reformer in history. No more than any man would wish to do if he had the courage. Does the struggling miner not sell some coal on the side to help feed his children? Does the professional middle class man not fiddle his expenses to help pay for his children to go to an expensive private school? Does the member of Parliament not take directorships in companies and take cash for questions, to bolster his pathetic parliamentary salary.

"We all break the rules from time to time. We all have conflicts of interest and propagate dishonesties. Featherbedding goes on in all walks of life. Each and every man and woman milks the system to his or her own advantage.

"The only difference between them and I is that my horizons are a thousands times broader. My capabilities a thousand times more developed. My influence a million times greater. My decisions affect the lives of hundreds of thousands, rather than just a hand full."

"You financed the most murderous terrorist orgy in this country's recent history Goldstein. How do you seek to justify that?" Duffy demanded.

"I financed nothing. And I admit to nothing. Perhaps I merely did a job in return for compensation. The job would have been done by someone else if I had rejected it. They might have done it better than I."

"The job should never have been conceived in the first place Goldstein," Grant replied. "It was evil."

"Ha. Now you set yourself up as the arbiter of good and evil?" Goldstein scorned.

"We all have to draw the lines. Each of us has to decide from day to day whether to resist the temptations that life offers. But your whole life is a testimony to your inability to resist. Insider dealing in New York, breaking trade embargoes behind the iron curtain, trading with South Africa during the Aparthied years. At every turn you have taken the money and ignored the consequences in human suffering. How do you sleep at night?" Grant found himself shaking with fury, so he stopped abruptly.

Goldstein was also shaking slightly. But he was fuming with resentment. He turned away from the occupants of the room and slumped his shoulders. Then he turned round again.

"Go to your room Carmine, my dear. On the way please ask Matilda to pack your things. We will be leaving soon." Carmine looked at Grant and awe showed in her naïve young face.

"Is it true? I have never heard anyone speak to dad like that before," she whispered.

"Go upstairs Carmine, and Francesca!" Goldstein demanded of Mrs Bertelson, "pack your things and tell the chauffeur to bring the car round to the front," he commanded.

Chief Inspector Duffy made slowly to stand, but Grant caught his eye and he sat down again. They were both wondering what next to do.

"I admit nothing. But you of all people should understand what happens to a man when his wife is murdered by terrorists. For my part I simply plotted my revenge on the bastards. The International Freedom Fighters were the guiding force behind the death of my wife Carole. To get to them I might have needed to become involved in their trade and then double cross them. Work it out for yourself if you're so damn smart. I'm not admitting to anything."

"You are all free to leave now." Goldstein continued tersely.

Marianne stood up.

"Are you mad? You kidnapped me! I had to fight for my life to get away." She then turned to the Chief Inspector. "Surely you are going to arrest him?"

"It was not he that kidnapped you, Marianne. It was two men. You were held some few miles from here in a hut, no doubt owned by someone else. Did anyone mention that they were working for Goldstein?"

Marianne sat down with a bump. She did not answer the question. "What about Jack?" She said?

Jack answered, "the men turned up about half an hour after you escaped Marianne. They just let me go. As I was walking down the road, a car drove up and offered me a lift. I asked for the nearest phone and they brought me here. I phoned the office but there was no one there. So I phoned the police. They will probably arrive at any minute, but I am afraid that I have nothing to prove that Goldstein held me captive. I didn't even know it was his house till the two men brought me in. They hid me in there when all the shooting started." Jack replied

"There, you see my dear, you have quite the wrong impression of me!" Goldstein said, smiling forcedly.

"On the other hand I'd like to break you stinking neck," Jack said under his breath.

"Right." Goldstein stated, taking charge again. "Please leave now, or I will call the police and have you all arrested for murdering my security men and trespassing on my land. I note that you have not shown me a search warrant, Chief Inspector."

"No, I have not," the Chief inspector looked distinctly uneasy at the situation Grant had rushed him into. Grant took Marianne's hand and walked her into the hall.

"Is that it then, George? Do we just walk away? I cannot believe it. What about all the evidence?"

"What evidence, M?"

"The Park Lane tape for a start?"

"They destroyed it," Grant replied.

"Well, you and Jack were there. Can't you testify against him?"

"It wouldn't be enough, M. He made no admissions there. It only meant something to us because we had the whole picture. He has been very clever indeed. Believe me if Chief Inspector Duffy could arrest him he would," Grant replied.

"I don't believe this. What about Joanne!"

Grant stopped dead. He let go of Marianne's hand and walked away. He had realised in the last few months that he would probably never get over Joanne's death. But he had come to terms with the fact by submerging himself in the pursuit of Goldstein. Now, with that objective gone, he was deflated. He stood at the rear hall window looking out over Chichester Harbour for a few minutes then he turned back to face Marianne.

"It is not over yet, Marianne. Believe me. Anyway, the real reason why Joanne died was not Goldstein. There are men in the

Soviet Union who are involved in a bitter power struggle. They are the cause of her death. Goldstein was just their on the spot organiser. A very wise old man told me a story about a Colonel who ruined his career for revenge a few months ago. I do not want to ruin what is left of my life for the same reason.

"Goldstein knows has failed to help the Russians, and he has his revenge on the IFFC terrorists. They also know that. I do not think that our conventional methods of punishment have the ability to cope with his type of crime. But I am sure that somewhere out there, at some time in the not too distant future, in an alleyway in Paris, or New York, Solomon J. Goldstein will see a shadow of the man who has come to settle the debt run up by this little fiasco.

"Then and there he will have no escape. Justice will be done."

"Does that satisfy you, George?" Marianne asked, as they walked away from the villa.

"Frankly, I am not sure that I give a damn anymore."

Jack MacDougal appeared beside them and patted Grant on the back. "I would not want to be in his shoes for the next few weeks George. I can almost see the noose hanging over his head," he said.

"So can I, Jack. Come on, let's get out of here."

Solomon Joshua Goldstein's Bentley turbo glided quietly out of the driveway towards the road. Grant only caught a glimpse of the boot as it turned into the thickly covered lane leading up to the gates. Then it halted abruptly. Through the gloom created by the trees overhanging the lane, Grant could just distinguish three figures advancing slowly towards the car. The Bentley reversed violently.

Field Marshal Carshalton emerged into the sunlight a few feet away from the bonnet of the car surrounded by a score of troops. He caught Grant's eye and smiled. Grant nodded and walked forwards, as Solomon Goldstein emerged from the passenger door of the Bentley.

"What's the meaning of this intrusion?" he demanded.

Field Marshal Carshalton stood in front of Goldstein and shook his head, "It's over Mr Goldstein."

"Like hell it is," Goldstein replied.

Grant looked up to see the tall majestic figure of the commercial lawyer push through the troops towards Goldstein. Phillip McNaughton stopped beside Carshalton.

"You are under arrest for treason."

McNaughton read Solomon J. Goldstein his rights and Chief Inspector Duffy, beaming all over his face, took his arm.

Goldstein pleaded: "you have no proof. No evidence. You'll be a laughing stock." He yanked his arm out of Inspector Duffy's grip.

Phillip McNaughton pulled a sheaf of papers out of his jacket pocket.

This is an Affidavit sworn by Colonel Vladimyr Zachristov of the Russian Secret Service attesting to the atrocities you have organised in this country Goldstein. You can either come quietly or the Field Marshal will have his men take you forcibly."

Goldstein grabbed the papers and read the first four lines aloud:

'I, Vladimyr Zachristov, Colonel in the KGB, HEREBY MAKE OATH AND SAY AS FOLLOWS:
1. In the summer of 1985, Uri Krasilova and I were at a Bordello in Krasnovodsk. We conceived of a plan to overthrow the Government in the United Kingdom... "

Goldstein shook violently. He stared in disbelief at the Defence Secretary. "I don't believe it? Why?" He whispered.

"Asylum and Immunity I suppose," the Defence Secretary replied.

The Tailor turned slowly towards George Grant and brought his eyes up to his face.

"Perhaps this is a safer way for me in any event?" he said. "Will you accompany Francesca and Carmine to Heathrow?"

Grant did not move.

"Please?"

Mrs Bertelson nodded slightly as she looked at Grant who nodded in return.

Shrugging his shoulders Goldstein walked into the troops around Field Marshal Carshalton and was enveloped.

EPILOGUE
THE KLEPTOMANIAC

WEDNESDAY, 8TH NOVEMBER 1988

The Right Honourable Phillip McNaughton finished his Gin and Tonic and walked quietly out of his office on the second floor of the Home Office building in Marsham Street, Westminster. He had read five witness statements that night. Those of George Grant, Sir John Epcot, Solomon J. Goldstein, Colonel Zachristov and Chief Inspector Duffy. He had done so with quiet astonishment.

He now knew that a junior anti-terrorist squad officer called Michael Douglas had started an affair with one Fiona Galliani. When Douglas had overheard a conversation she had held on her home telephone line with Solomon J. Goldstein, she had heard the extension line click, before she had replaced the receiver. She then had killed him. If only he had been able to reach Grant that evening the whole ugly build up might have been stopped.

Lord Carver had committed suicide on the evening of the 7th November 1988. He had left a full statement admitting his treason together with a note for his family. It was he who had set up the hit in Egypt. He who had left D Section to attack Marianne's flat in the Kings Road. And of course, he who had repeated each of the SEC's decisions to NATUS and hence to Uri Krasilova in Russia. He did not explain why he had forsaken the system which had spawned him. But he admitted in the note that he had been offered the very highest office in the new order.

Solomon Joshua Goldstein had been charged with treason and was in Pentonville prison awaiting trial.

Phillip McNaughton had tried to persuade Grant to agree to make a public statement and accept an honour from the Queen. He was not surprised when Grant refused.

"All I ever wanted was to find out why Joanne was murdered. Now I understand," he had said.

As the Defence Secretary got into his car and started up the engine, he nodded quietly to himself. "If the old system can produce men like that, it can't be all bad," he said to his driving mirror.

Phillip McNaughton couldn't go back to his flat in Dolphin Square. It had been destroyed by the rocket.

He glanced briefly at his back seat and winced, three bars of soap and two ashtrays from various official functions lay on the seat.

"I really must stop doing this." He said and drove away towards his country house in Epsom.

During the afternoon of that Wednesday, George Grant was lying prostrate under the bonnet of his old 2000 litre Alfa Spider, which had been returned to him "renovated" on the 7th November. As he struggled with the monkey wrench on a particularly stubborn nut he heard the telephone ringing. He slithered out from under the car and went to the phone on the garage wall.

"Grant speaking," he said.

"It's Mrs Dilworthy here. No one has answered my calls at the Agency for a week. What's going on?"

"Well, Mrs Dilworthy, Jack and I have been a bit tied up lately. Now, what can we do for you?"

THE END

Made in the USA
Charleston, SC
19 January 2016